THREE BY CAIN

OTHER BOOKS
BY JAMES M. CAIN AVAILABLE IN VINTAGE

The Postman Always Rings Twice

Double Indemnity

Mildred Pierce

JAMES M. CAIN

THREE BY CAIN

SERENADE

LOVE'S LOVELY COUNTERFEIT

THE BUTTERFLY

VINTAGE CRIME

Vintage Books
A DIVISION OF RANDOM HOUSE, INC.
NEW YORK

First Vintage Books Edition, may 1989

Copyright © 1989 by Alice Marie Piper
Serenade copyright 1937 by James M. Cain
Copyright renewed 1964 by James M. Cain
The Butterfly copyright 1946 and renewed 1974
by James M. Cain
Love's Lovely Counterfeit copyright 1942 and renewed 1970 by
James M. Cain

Library of Congress Cataloging-in-Publication Data
Cain, James M. (James Mallahan), 1892–1977.
    Three by Cain.—1st Vintage Books ed.
        p.   cm.—(Vintage crime)
    Contents: Serenade—The butterfly—Love's lovely counterfeit.
    ISBN 0-679-72323-4: $9.95
    I. Title.
PS3505.A3113A6   1989   88-40551
813'.52—dc19   CIP

Designed by Ann Gold

Manufactured in the United States of America

10 9 8 7 6 5 4 3 2

CONTENTS

SERENADE

I was in the Tupinamba, having a *bizcocho* and coffee, when this girl came in. Everything about her said Indian, from the maroon *rebozo* to the black dress with purple flowers on it, to the swaying way she walked, that no woman ever got without carrying pots, bundles, and baskets on her head from the time she could crawl. But she wasn't any of the colors that Indians come in. She was almost white, with just the least dip of *café con leche*. Her shape was Indian, but not ugly. Most Indian women have a rope of muscle over their hips that give them a high-waisted, mis-shapen look, thin, bunchy legs, and too much breast-works. She had plenty in that line, but her hips were round, and her legs had a soft line to them. She was slim, but there was something voluptuous about her, like in three or four years she would get fat. All that, though, I only half saw. What I noticed was her face. It was flat, like an Indian's but the nose broke high, so it kind of went with the way she held her head, and the eyes weren't dumb, with that shiny, shoe-button look. They were pretty big, and black, but they leveled out straight, and had kind of a sleepy, impudent look to them. Her lips were thick, but pretty, and of course had plenty of lipstick on them.

It was about nine o'clock at night, and the place was pretty full, with bullfight managers, agents, newspaper men, pimps, cops and almost everybody you can think of, except somebody you would trust with your watch. She went to the bar and ordered a drink, then went to a table and sat down, and I had a stifled feeling I had had before, from the thin air up there, but that wasn't it this time. There hadn't been any woman in my life for quite some while, and I knew what this meant. Her drink came, and it was Coca-Cola and Scotch, and I thought that over. It might mean that she was just starting the evening, and it might mean she was just working up an appetite, and if it meant that I was sunk. The Tupinamba is more of a café than a restaurant, but plenty of people eat there, and if that was what she expected to do, my last three pesos wouldn't go very far.

I had about decided to take a chance and go over there when she moved. She slipped over to a place about two tables away, and then she moved again, and I saw what she was up to. She was closing in on a bullfighter named Triesca, a kid I had seen a couple of times in the ring, once when he was on the card with Solorzano, that seemed to be their main ace at the time, and once after the main season was over, when he killed two bulls in a novillada they had one Sunday in the rain. He was a wow with the cape, and just moving up into the money. He had on the striped suit a Mexican thinks is pretty nifty, and a cream-colored hat. He was alone, but the managers, agents, and writers kept dropping by his table. She didn't have much of a chance, but every time three or four or five of them would shove off she would slip nearer. Pretty soon she dropped down beside him. He didn't take off his hat. That ought to have told me something, but it didn't. All I saw was a cluck too stuck on himself to know how to act. She spoke, and he nodded, and they talked a little bit, and it didn't look like she had ever seen him before. She drank out, and he let it ride for a minute, then he ordered another.

When I got it, what she was in there for, I tried to lose interest in her, but my eyes kept coming back to her. After a few minutes, I knew she felt me there, and I knew some of the other tables had tumbled to what was going on. She kept pulling her *rebozo* around her, like it was cold, and hunching one shoulder up, so she half had her back to me. All that did was throw her head up still higher, and I couldn't take my eyes off her at all. So of course a bullfighter is like any other ham, he's watching every table but his own, and he had no more sense than to see these looks that were going round. You understand, it's a dead-pan place, a big café with a lot of mugs sitting around with their hats on the back of their heads, eating, drinking, smoking, reading, and jabbering Spanish, and there wasn't any nudging, pointing, or hey-get-a-load-of-this. They strictly minded their business. Just the same, there would be a pair of eyes behind a newspaper that weren't on the newspaper, or maybe a waitress would stop by somebody, and say something, and there'd be a laugh just a little louder than a waitress's gag is generally worth. He sat there, with a kind of a foolish look on his face, snapping his fingernail against his glass, and then I felt a prickle go up my spine. He was getting up, he was coming over.

A guy with three pesos in his pocket doesn't want any trouble, and when the room froze like a stop-camera shot, I tried to tell myself to play it friendly, to get out of it without starting something I couldn't stop. But when he stood there in front of me he still had on that hat.

"My table, he interest you, ha?"

"Your—what?"

"My table. You look, you seem interest, Señor."

"Oh, now I understand."

I wasn't playing it friendly, I was playing it mean. I got up, with the best smile I could paste on my face, and waved at a chair. "Of course. I shall explain. I shall gladly explain." Down there you make it simple, because spig reception isn't any too good. "Please sit down."

He looked at me and he looked at the chair, but it looked like he had me on the run, so he sat down. I sat down. Then I did something I wanted to do for fifteen minutes. I lifted that cream hat off his head, like it was the nicest thing I knew to do for him, slipped a menu card under it, and put it on a chair.

If he had moved I was going to let him have it, if they shot me for it. He didn't. It caught him by surprise. A buzz went over the room. The first round was mine.

"May I order you something, Señor?"

He blinked, and I don't think he even heard me. Then he began looking around for help. He was used to having a gallery yell *Olé* every time he wiped his nose, but it had walked out on him this time. It was all deadpan, what he saw, and so far as they were concerned, we weren't even there. There wasn't anything he could do but face me, and try to remember what he had come for.

"The explain. Begin, please."

I had caught him with one he wasn't looking for, and I decided to let him have another, right between the eyes. "Certainly. I did look, that is true. But not at you. Believe me, Señor, not at you. And not at the table. At the lady."

". . . You—tell me this? You tell me this thing?"

"Sure. Why not?"

Well, what was he going to do? He could challenge me to a duel, but they never heard of a duel in Mexico. He could take a poke at me, but I outweighed him by about fifty pounds. He could shoot me, but he didn't have any gun. I had broken all the rules. You're not supposed to talk like that in Mexico, and once you hand a Mexican something he never heard of, it takes him about a year to figure out the answer. He sat there blinking at me, and the red kept creeping over his ears and cheeks, and I gave him plenty of time to think of something, if he could, before I went on. "I tell you what, Señor. I have examined this lady with care, and I find her very lovely. I admire your taste. I envy your fortune. So let us put her in a lottery, and the lucky man wins. We'll each buy her a ticket, and the one holding the highest number buys her next drink. Yes?"

Another buzz went around, a long one this time. Not over half of them in there could speak any English, and it had to be translated around before they could get it. He took about four beats to think it through, and then he began to feel better.

"Why I do this, please? The lady, she is with me, no? I put lady in *lotería*, what you put in, Señor? You tell me that?"

"I hope you're not afraid, Señor?"

He didn't like that so well. The red began to creep up again, but then I felt something behind me, and I didn't like that so well either. In the U.S., you feel something behind you, it's probably a waiter with a plate of soup, but in Mexico it could be anything, and the last thing you want is exactly the best bet. About half the population of the country go around with pearl-handled automatics on their hips, and the bad part about those guns is that they shoot, and after they shoot nothing is ever done about it. This guy had a lot of friends. He was a popular idol, but I didn't know of anybody that would miss me. I sat looking straight at him, afraid even to turn around.

He felt it too, and a funny look came over his face. I leaned over to brush cigarette ashes off my coat, and out of the tail of my eye I peeped. There had been a couple of lottery peddlers in there, and when he came over they must have stopped in their tracks like everybody else. They were back there now, wig-wagging him to say yes, that it was in the bag. I didn't let on. I acted impatient, and sharpened up a bit when I jogged him. "Well, Señor? Yes?"

"*Sí, sí.* We make *lotería!*"

They broke pan then, and crowded around us, forty or fifty of them. So long as we meant business, it had to be hands off, but now that it was a kind of a game, anybody could get in it, and most of them did. But even before the crowd, the two lottery peddlers were in, one shoving pink tickets at me, the other green tickets at him. You understand; there's hundreds of lotteries in Mexico, some pink, some green, some yellow, and some blue, and not many of them pay anything. Both of them went through a hocus-pocus of holding napkins over the sheets of tickets, so we couldn't see the numbers, but my man kept whispering to me, and winking, meaning that his numbers were awful high. He was an Indian, with gray hair and a face like a chocolate saint, and you would have thought he couldn't possibly tell a lie. I thought of Cortés, and how easy he had seen through their tricks, and how lousy the tricks probably were.

But I was different from Cortés, because I wanted to be taken. Through the crowd I could see the girl, sitting there as though she had no idea what was going on, and it was still her I was after, not getting the best of a dumb bullfighter. And something told me the last thing I ought to do was to win her in a lottery. So I made up my mind I was going to lose, and see what happened then.

I waved at him, meaning pick whatever one he wanted, and there wasn't much he could do but wave back. I picked the pink, and it was a peso, and I laid it down. When they tore off the ticket, they went through some more hocus-pocus of laying it down on the table, and covering it with my hat. He took the green, and it was half a peso. That was a big laugh, for some reason. They put his hat over it, and then we lifted the hats. I had No. 7. He had No. 100,000 and something. That was an *Olé*. I still don't get the chemistry of a Mexican. Out in the ring, when the bull comes in, they know that in exactly fifteen minutes that bull is going to be dead. Yet when the sword goes in, they yell like hell. And mind you, there's nothing as much like one dead bull as another dead bull. In that café that night there wasn't one man there that didn't know I was framed, and yet when the hats were lifted they gave him a hand, and clapped him on the shoulder, and laughed, just like Lady Luck had handed him a big victory.

"So. And now. You still look, ha?"

"Absolutely not. You've won, and I congratulate you, *de todo corazón.* Please give the lady her ticket, with my compliments, and tell her I hope she wins the Bank of Mexico."

"*Sí, sí, sí.* And so, Señor, *adiós.*"

He went back with the tickets, and I put a little more hot *leche* into my coffee, and waited. I didn't look. But there was a mirror back of the bar, so I could see if I wanted to, and just once, after he had handed her the tickets, and they had a long jibber-jabber, she looked.

■　■

It was quite a while before they started out. I was between them and the door, but I never turned my head. Then I felt them stop, and she whispered to him, and he whispered back, and laughed. What the hell? He had licked me, hadn't he? He could afford to be generous. A whiff of her smell hit me in the face, and I knew she was standing right beside me, but I didn't move till she spoke.

"Señor."

I got up and bowed. I was looking down at her, almost touching her. She was smaller than I had thought. The voluptuous lines, or maybe it was the way she held her head, fooled you.

"Señorita."

"*Gracias,* thanks, for the *billete.*"

"It was nothing, Señorita. I hope it wins for you as much as it lost for me. You'll be rich—*muy rico.*"

She liked that one. She laughed a little, and looked down, and looked up. "So. *Muchas gracias.*"

"*De nada.*"

But she laughed again before she turned away, and when I sat down my head was pounding, because that laugh, it sounded as though she had started to say something and then didn't, and I had this feeling there would be more. When I could trust myself to look around, he was still standing there near the door, looking a little sore. From the way he kept looking at the *damas,* I knew she must have gone in there, and he wasn't any too pleased about it.

In a minute, my waitress came and laid down my check. It was for sixty centavos. She had waited on me before, and she was a pretty little *mestiza,* about forty, with a wedding ring she kept flashing every time she got the chance. A wedding ring is big news in Mexico, but it still doesn't mean there's been a wedding. She pressed her belly against the table, and then I heard her voice, though her lips didn't move and she was looking off to one side: "The lady, you like her *dirección,* yes? Where she live?"

"You sure you know this *dirección?*"

"A *paraquito* have told me—just now."

"In that case, yes."

I laid a peso on the check. Her little black eyes crinkled up into a nice friendly smile, but she didn't move. I put the other peso on top of it. She took out her pencil, pulled the menu over, and started to write. She hadn't got three letters on paper before the pencil was jerked out of her hand, and he was standing there, purple with fury. He had tumbled, and all the things he had wanted to say to me, and never got the chance, he spit at her, and she spit back. I couldn't get all of it, but you couldn't miss the main points. He said she was delivering a message to me, she said she was only writing the address of a hotel I had asked for, a hotel for *Americanos*. They must like to see a guy framed in Mexico. About six of them chimed in and swore they had heard me ask her the address of a hotel, and that that was all she was giving me. They didn't fool him for a second. He was up his own alley now, and speaking his own language. He told them all where to get off, and in the middle of it, here she came, out of the *damas*. He let her have the last of it, and then he crumpled the menu card up and threw it in her face, and walked out. She hardly bothered to watch him go. She smiled at me, as though it was a pretty good joke, and I got up, "Señorita. Permit me to see you home."

That got a buzz, a laugh, and an *Olé*.

I don't think there's ever been a man so moony that a little bit of chill didn't come over him as soon as a woman said yes, and plenty of things were going through my head when she took my arm and we headed for the door of that café. One thing that was going through was that my last peso was gone at last, that I was flat broke in Mexico City with no idea what I was going to do or how I was going to do it. Another thing was that I didn't thank them for their *Olé*, that I hated Mexicans and their tricks, and hated them all the more because the tricks were all so bad you could always see through them. A Frenchman's tricks cost you three francs, but a Mexican is just dumb. But the main thing was a queer echo in that *Olé*, like they were laughing at me all the time, and I wondered, all of a sudden,

which way we were going to turn when we got out that door. A
girl on the make for a bullfighter, you don't exactly expect that
she came out of a convent. Just the same, it hadn't occurred to
me up to that second that she could be a downright piece of
trade goods. I was hoping, when we reached the main street,
that we would turn right. To the right lay the main part of
town, and if we headed that way, she could be taking me almost
anywhere. But to our left lay the Guauhtemolzin, and that's
nothing but trade.

We turned left.

We turned left, but she walked so nice and talked so sweet
I started hoping again. Nothing about an Indian makes any
sense. He can live in a hut made of sticks and mud, and sticks
and mud are sticks and mud, aren't they? You can't make
anything else out of them. But he'll take you in there with the
nicest manners in the world, more dignity than you'd ever get
from a dozen dentists in the U.S., with stucco bungalows that
cost ten thousand dollars apiece, kids in a private school, and
stock in the building and loan. She went along, her hand on
my arm, and if she had been a duchess she couldn't have
stepped cleaner. She made a little gag out of falling in step,
looked up once or twice and smiled, and then asked me if I
had been long in Mexico.

"Only three or four months."

"Oh. You like?"

"Very much." I didn't, but I wanted anyway to be as polite
as she was. "It's very pretty."

"Yes." She had a funny way of saying yes, like the rest of
them have. She drew it out, so it was "yayse." "Many flowers."

"And birds."

"And señoritas."

"I wouldn't know about them."

"No? Just a little bit?"

"No."

An American girl would have mauled it to death, but when
she saw I didn't want to go on with it, she smiled and began
talking about Xochimilco, where the best flowers grew. She

asked me if I had been there. I said no, but maybe some day she would take me. She looked away at that, and I wondered why. I figured I had been a little previous. Tonight was tonight, and after that it would be time to talk about Xochimilco. We got to the Guauhtemolzin. I was hoping she would cross. She turned, and we hadn't gone twenty yards before she stopped at a crib.

I don't know if you know how it works in Mexico. There's no houses, with a madame, a parlor, and an electric piano, anyway not in that part of town. There's a row of adobe huts, one story high, and washed blue, or pink, or green, or whatever it happens to be. Each hut is one room deep, and jammed up against each other in the way they are, they look like a barracks. In each hut is a door, with a half window in it, like a hat-check booth. Under the law they've got to keep that door shut, and drum up trade by leaning out the window, but if they know the cop they can get away with an open door. This door was wide open, with three girls in there, two of them around fourteen, and looking like children, the other big and fat, maybe twenty-five. She brought me right in, but then I was alone, because she and the other three went out in the street to have a palaver, and I could partly catch what it was. They all four rented the room together, so three of them had to wait outside when one of them had a customer, but I seemed to be a special case, and if I was going to spend the night, her friends had to flop somewhere else. Most of the street got in it before long, the cop, the café woman on the corner, and a flock of girls from the other cribs. Nobody sounded sore, or surprised, or made dirty cracks. A street like that is supposed to be tough, but from the way they talked, you would have thought it was the junior section of the Ladies' Aid figuring out where to bunk the minister's brother-in-law that had blown in town kind of sudden. They acted like it was the most natural thing in the world.

After a while they got it straightened out to suit them, who was to go where, and she came back and closed the door and closed the window. There was a bed in there, and a chest of drawers in the early Grand Rapids style, and a washstand with a mirror over it, and some grass mats rolled up in a corner, for sleeping purposes. Then there were a couple of chairs. I was tilted back on one, and as soon as she had given me a cigarette, she took the other. There we were. There was no use kidding myself any longer why Triesca hadn't taken off his hat. My lady love was a three-peso whore.

She lit my cigarette for me, and then her own, and inhaled, and let the smoke blow out the match. We smoked, and it was about as electric as a stalled car. Across the street in front of the café, a *mariachi* was playing, and she nodded her head once or twice, in time with the music. "Flowers, and birds—and *mariachis.*"

"Yes, plenty of them."

"You like *mariachi?* We have them. We have them here."

"Señorita."

"Yes?"

"... I haven't got the fifty centavos. To pay the *mariachi.* I'm—"

I pulled my pockets inside out, to show her. I thought I might as well get it over with. No use having her think she'd hooked a nice American sugar papa, and then letting her be disappointed. "Oh. How sweet."

"I'm trying to tell you I'm broke. *Todo* flat. I haven't got a centavo. I think I'd better be going."

"No money, but buy me *billete.*"

"And that was the last of it."

"*I* have money. Little bit. Fifty centavos for *mariachi.* Now— you look so."

She turned around, lifted the black skirt, and fished in her stocking. Listen, I didn't want any *mariachi* outside the window, serenading us. Of all things I hated in Mexico, I think I hated the *mariachis* the worst, and they had come to make a kind of picture for me of the whole country and what was wrong with it. They're a bunch of bums, generally five of them, that would be a lot better off if they went to work, but instead of that they don't do a thing their whole life, from the time they're kids to the time they're old men, but go around plunking out music

for anybody that'll pay them. The rate is fifty centavos a selection, which breaks down to ten centavos, or about three cents
a man. Three play the violin, one the guitar, and one a kind of
bass guitar they've got down there. As if that wasn't bad enough,
they sing. Well, never mind how they sing. They gargle a bass
falsetto that's enough to set your teeth on edge, but all music
gets sung the way it deserves, and it was what they sang that
got me down. You hear Mexico is musical. It's not. They do
nothing but screech from morning till night, but their music is
the dullest, feeblest stuff that ever went down on paper, and
not one decent bar was ever written there. Yeah, I know all
about Chavez. Their music is Spanish music that went through
the head of an Indian and came out again, and if you think it
sounds the same after that, you made a mistake. An Indian,
he's about eight thousand years behind the rest of us in the
race towards whatever we're headed for, and it turns out that
primitive man is not any fine, noble brute at all. He's just a
poor fish. Modern man, in spite of all this talk about his being
effete, can run faster, shoot straighter, eat more, live longer,
and have a better time than all the primitive men that ever
lived. And that difference, how it comes out in music. An Indian, even when he plays a regular tune, sounds like a seal
playing My-Country-'Tis-of-Thee at a circus, but when he makes
up a tune of his own, it just makes you sick.

Well, maybe you think I'm getting all steamed up over something that didn't amount to anything, but Mexico had done
plenty to me, and all I'm trying to say is that if I had to listen
to those five simple-looking mopes outside the window, there
was going to be trouble. But I wanted to please her. I don't
know if it was the way she took the news of my being broke, or
the way her eyes lit up at the idea of hearing some music, or
the flash I got of that pretty leg, when I was supposed to be
looking the other way, or what. Whatever it was, her trade
didn't seem to make much difference any more. I felt about her
the way I had in the café, and wanted her to smile at me some
more and lean toward me when I spoke.

"Señorita."

"Yes?'

"I don't like the *mariachi*. They play very bad."

"Oh, yes. But they only poor boy. No estoddy, no take lessons. But play—very pretty."

"Well—never mind about that. You want some music that's the main thing. Let me be your *mariachi*."

"Oh—you sing?"

"Just a little bit."

"Yes, yes. I like—very much."

I went out, slipped across the street, and took the guitar from No. 4. He put up a squawk, but she was right after me, and he didn't squawk long. Then we went back. There's not many instruments I can't play, some kind of way, but I can really knock hell out of a guitar. He had it tuned cockeyed, but I brought it to E, A, D, G, B, and E without snapping any of his strings, and then I began to go to town on it. The first thing I played her was the prelude to the last act of Carmen. For my money, it's one of the greatest pieces of music ever written, and I had once made an arrangement of it. You may think that's impossible, but if you play that woodwind stuff up near the bridge, and the rest over the hole, the guitar will give you almost as much of what the music is trying to say as the whole orchestra will.

She was like a child while I was tuning, leaning over and watching everything I did, but when I started to play, she sat up and began to study me. She knew she had never heard anything like that, and I thought I saw the least bit of suspicion of me, as to who I was and what the hell I was doing there. So when I went down on the low E string, on the phrase the bassoon has in the orchestra, I looked at her and smiled. "The voice of the bull."

"Yes, yes!"

"Am I a good *mariachi*?"

"Oh, fine *mariachi*. What is the *música*?"

"Carmen."

"Oh. Oh yes, of course. The voice of the bull."

She laughed, and clapped her hands, and that seemed to do

it. I went into the bullring music of the last act and kept step-
ping the key up, so I could make kind of a number out of it
without slowing down for the vocal stuff. There came a knock
on the door. She opened, and the *mariachi* was out there, and
most of the ladies of the street. "They ask door open. So they
hear too."

"All right, so they don't sing."

So we left the door open, and I got a hand after the bullring
selection, and played the intermezzo, then the prelude to the
opera. My fingers were a little sore, as I had no calluses, but I
went into the introduction to the Habanera, and started to sing.
I don't know how far I got. What stopped me was the look on
her face. Everything I had seen there was gone, it was the face
at the window of every whorehouse in the world, and it was
looking right through me.

"... What's the matter?"

I tried to make it sound comical, but she didn't laugh. She
kept looking at me, and she came over, took the guitar from
me, went out and handed it to the *mariachi* player. The crowd
began to jabber and drift off. She came back, and the other
three girls were with her. "Well, Señorita—you don't seem to
like my singing."

"*Muchas gracias,* Señor. Thanks."

"Well—I'm sorry. Good evening, Señorita."

"*Buenos noches,* Señor."

Next thing I knew I was stumbling down the Bolivar, trying to
wash her out of my mind, trying to wash everything out of my
mind. A block away, somebody was coming toward me. I saw it
was Triesca. She must have gone out and phoned him when I
left. I ducked around a corner, so I wouldn't have to pass him.
I kept on, crossed a plaza, and found myself looking at the
Palacio de Bellas Artes, their opera house. I hadn't been near
it since I flopped there three months before. I stood staring at
it, and thought how far I had slid. Flopping in Rigoletto, in
probably the lousiest opera company in the world, before an
audience that didn't know Rigoletto from Yankee Doodle, with

a chorus of Indians behind me trying to look like lords and ladies, a Mexican tenor on one side of me that couldn't even get a hand on *Questa o Quella,* and a coffee cake on the other side that scratched fleas while she was singing the *Caro Nome*— that seemed about as low as I could get. But I had wiped those footprints out, with my can. I had tried to serenade a lady that was easy serenaded, and I couldn't even get away with that.

I walked back to my one-peso hotel, where I was paid up to the end of the week, went to my room, and undressed without turning on the light, so I wouldn't see the concrete floor, the wash basin with rings in it, and the lizard that would come out from behind the bureau. I got in bed, pulled the lousy cotton blanket up over me, and lay there watching the fog creep in. When I closed my eyes I'd see her looking at me, seeing something in me, I didn't know what, and then I'd open them again and look at the fog. After a while it came to me that I was afraid of what she saw in me. There would be something horrible mixed up in it, and I didn't want to know what it was.

2

As well as I can remember, that was in June, and I didn't see
her for a couple of months. Never mind what I did in that time,
to eat. Sometimes I didn't eat. For a while I had a job in a
jazzband, playing a guitar. It was in a nightclub out on the
Reforma, and they needed me bad. I mean, the place was for
Americans, and the music they handed out was supposed to be
the McCoy, but it wasn't. I went to work, and got them so they
could play the hot stuff hot and the blue stuff blue, anyway a
little bit, and polished up a couple of them so they could take
a solo strain now and then, just for variety. Understand, you
couldn't do much. A Mexican's got a defective sense of rhythm.
He sounds rhythmic on the *cucaracha* stuff, but when you slow
him down to foxtrot time, he can't feel it. He just plays it
mechanically, so when people get out on the floor they can't
dance to it. Still, I did what I could, and figured a few combos
that made them sound better than they really were, and business picked up. But then a guy with a pistol on his hip showed
up one night and wanted to see my papers, and I got thrown
out. They got Socialism down there now, and one of the rules
is that Mexico belongs to the Mexicans. They're out of luck, no
matter how they play it. Under Diaz, they turned the country

over to the foreigners, and they had prosperity, but the local boys didn't get much of it. Then they had the Revolution, and fixed it up so that whatever was going on, the local boys had to run it. The only trouble is, the local boys don't seem to be very good at it. They threw me out, and then they had Socialism, but they didn't have any jazzband. Business fell off, and later I heard the place closed.

After that, I even had to beg to stay on at the hotel until I got the money from New York, which wasn't ever coming, as they knew as well as I did. They let me use the room, but wouldn't give me any bedclothes or service. I had to sleep on the mattress, under my clothes, and haul my own water. Up to then, I had managed to keep some kind of press in my pants, so I could anyway bum a meal off some American in Butch's café, but I couldn't even do that any more, and I began to look like what I was, a beachcomber in a spig town. I wouldn't even have eaten if it hadn't been for shagging my own water. I started going after it in the morning, and because the tin pitcher wouldn't fit under the tap in the washroom at the end of the hall, I had to go down to the kitchen. Nobody paid any attention to me, and then an idea hit me, and next time I went down at night. There was nobody there, and I ducked over to the icebox. They've got electric iceboxes all over Mexico, and some of them have combinations on them, like safes, but this one hadn't. I opened it up, and a light went on, and sure enough, there was a lot of cold stuff in there. I scooped some frijoles into a glass ashtray I had brought down, and held them under the pitcher when I went up. When I got back to my room I dug into them with my knife. After that, for two weeks, that was what I lived on. I found ten centavos in the street one day and bought a tin spoon, a clay soapdish, and a cake of soap, The soapdish and the soap I put on the washstand, like they were some improvements of my own I was putting in, since they wouldn't give me any. The spoon I kept in my pocket. Every night when I'd go down, I'd scoop beans, rice, or whatever they had, and sometimes a little meat into the soapdish, but only when there was enough that it wouldn't be missed. I never touched anything that might have counted, and only took off the top of dishes where there was quite a lot of it, and then smoothed them up to look right. Once there was half a Mexican ham in there. I cut myself off a little piece, under the butt.

And then one morning I got this letter, all neatly typewritten, even down to the signature, on a sheet of white business paper.

> Calle Guauhtemolzin 44b,
> Mexico, D. F.
> A 14 de agosto.

Sr. John Howard Sharp,
Hotel Dominguez,
Calle Violeta,
Ciudad.
Mi Querido Jonny:

En vista de que no fue posible verte ayer en el mercado al ir a las compras que ordinariamente hago para la casa en donde trabajo, me veo precidada para dirigirte la presente y manifestarte que dormí inquieta con motivo de tus palabras me son vida y no pudiendo permanecer sin contacto contigo te digo que hoy por la noche te espero a las ocho de la noche para que platiquemos, por lo que así espero estaras presente y formal.

Se despide quien te ama de todo corazón y no te olivida,
JUANA MONTES

How she got my name and address didn't bother me. The waitress at the Tupinamba would have been good for that. But the rest of it, the date I was supposed to have with her yesterday, and how she couldn't sleep for thinking about me, didn't make any sense at all. Still, she wanted to see me, that seemed to be the main point, and it was a long time before sundown. I was down past the point where I cared how she had looked at me, or what it meant, or anything like that. She could look at me like I was a rattlesnake, for all I cared, so she had a couple of buns under the bed. I went back upstairs, shaved, and started up there, hoping something about it might lead to a meal.

When I rapped on the door the window opened, and the fat one poked her head out. The four of them were just getting up. The window closed, and Juana called something out to me. I waited, and pretty soon she came out. She had on a white dress this time, that must have cost all of two pesos, and white socklets, and shoes. She looked like some high school girl in a border town. I said hello and how had she been, she said very well, *gracias,* and how had I been? I said I couldn't complain, and edged toward the door to see if I could smell coffee. There didn't seem to be any. Then I took out the letter and asked her what it meant.

"Yes. I ask you to come. Yes."

"I caught that. But what's all this other stuff about? I didn't have any date with you—that I know of."

She kept studying me, and studying the letter, and hungry as I was, and bad as she had walloped me that night, and dumb as it had been up to now, I couldn't help having this same feeling about her I had had before, that was mainly what any man feels toward a woman, but partly what he feels toward a child. There was something about the way she talked, the way she held her head, the way she did everything, that got me in the throat, so I couldn't breathe right. It wasn't child, of course. It was Indian. But it did things to me just the same, maybe worse on account of it being Indian, because that meant she was always going to be like that. The trouble was, you see, that she didn't know what the letter said. She couldn't read.

She called the fat one out, and had her read it, and then there was the most indignant jabbering you ever heard. The other two came out and got in it, and then she grabbed me by the arm. "The auto. You make go, yes?"

"Well I could once."

"Come, then. Come quick."

We went down the street, and she turned in at a shack that seemed to be a kind of a garage. It was full of wrecks with stickers pasted on the windshield, that seemed to be held for the sheriff or something, but halfway down the line was the newest, reddest Ford in the world. It shone like a boil on a sailor's neck. She went up to it, and began waving the letter in one hand and the key in the other. "So. Now we go. Calle Venezuela."

I got in, and she got in, and it was a little stiff, but it started, and I rolled it through the murk to the street. I didn't know where the Calle Venezuela was, and she tried to show me, but she didn't have the hang of the one-way streets, so we got tangled up so bad it took us a half hour to get there. As soon as I backed up to park she jumped out and ran over to a colonnade, where about fifty guys were camped out on the sidewalk, back of tables with typewriters on them. They all wore black suits. In Mexico, the black suit means you got plenty of education, and the black fingernails mean you got plenty of work. When I got there, she was having an argument with one guy, and after a while he sat down to his machine, stuck a piece of paper in it, wrote something, and handed it to her. She came over to me waving it, and I took it. It was just two lines, that started off "Querido Sr. Sharp" instead of "Querido Jonny," and said she wanted to see me on a matter of business.

"This letter, big mistake."

She tore it up.

Well, never mind the fine points. The result of the big Socialist educational program is that half the population of the city have to come to these mugs to get their letters written, and that was what she had done. But the guy had been a little busy, and didn't get it quite straight what she had said, and fixed her up with a love letter. So of course, she had to go down there and get what she had paid for. I didn't blame her, but I still didn't know what she wanted, and I was still hungry.

"The auto—you like, yes?"

"It's a knockout." We were coming up the Bolivar again, and I had to keep tooting the horn, according to law. The main thing they put on cars for Mexican export is the biggest, loudest horn they can find in Detroit, and this one had a double note to it that sounded like a couple of ferryboats passing in an East River fog. "Your business must be good."

I didn't mean to make any crack, but it slipped out on me. If it meant anything to her at all, she passed it up.

"Oh no. I win."

"How?"

"The *billete*. You remember?"

"Oh. My *billette?*"

"Yes. I win, in *lotería*. The auto, and five honnerd pesos. The auto, is very pretty. I can no make go."

"Well, I can make it go, if that's all that's bothering you. About those five hundred pesos. You got some of them with you?"

"Oh yes. Of course."

"That's great. What you're going to do is buy me a breakfast. For my belly—*muy* empty. You get it?"

"Oh, why you no say? Yes, of course, now we eat."

I pulled in at the Tupinamba. The restaurants don't open until one o'clock, but the cafés will take care of you. We took a table up near the corner, where it was dark and cool. Hardly anybody was in there. My same old waitress came around grinning, and I didn't waste any time. "Orange juice, the biggest you got. Fried eggs, three of them, and fried ham. Tortillas. Glass of milk, *frío*, and *café con crema.*"

"*Bueno.*"

She took iced coffee, a nifty down there, and gave me a cigarette. It was the first I had had in three days, and I inhaled and leaned back, and smiled at her. "So."

"So."

But she didn't smile back, and looked away as soon as she said it. It was the first time we had really looked at each other all morning, and it brought us back to that night. She smoked, and looked up once or twice to say something, and didn't, and I saw there was something on her mind besides the *billete*. "So—you still have no pesos?"

"That's more or less correct."

"You work, no?"

"I did work, but I got kicked out. Just at present, I'm not doing anything at all."

"You like to work, yes? For me?"

". . . Doing what?"

"Play a guitar, little bit, maybe. Write a letter, count money, speak *Inglés,* help me, no work very hard. In Mexico, nobody work very hard. Yes? You like?"

"Wait a minute. I don't get this."

"Now I have money, I open house."

"Here?"

"No, no, no. In Acapulco. In Acapulco, I have very nice friend, big *político.* Open nice house, with nice music, nice food, nice drink, nice girls—for American."

"Oh, for Americans."

"Yes. Many Americans come now to Acapulco. Big steamboat stop there. Nice man, much money."

"And me, I'm to be a combination professor, bartender, bouncer, glad-hander, secretary, and general bookkeeper for the joint, is that it?"

"Yes, yes."

"Well."

The food came along, and I stayed with it a while, but the more I thought about her proposition the funnier it got to me. "This place, it's supposed to have class, is that the idea?"

"Oh yes, very much. My *político* friend, he say American pay as much as five pesos, gladly."

"Pay five—what?"

"Pesos."

"Listen, tell your *político* friend to shut his trap and let an expert talk. If an American paid less than five dollars, he'd think there was something wrong with it."

"I think you little bit crazy."

"I said five bucks—eighteen pesos."

"No, no. You kid me."

"All right, go broke your own way. Hire your *político* for manager."

"You really mean?"

"I raise my right hand and swear by the holy mother of God.

But—you got to get some system in it. You got to give him something for his money."

"Yes, yes. Of course."

"Listen, I'm not talking about this world's goods. I'm talking about things of the spirit, romance, adventure, beauty. Say, I'm beginning to see possibilities in this. All right, you want that American dough, and I'll tell you what you've got to do to get it. In the first place, the dump has got to be in a nice location, in among the hotels, not back of the coconut palms, up on the hill. That's up to your *político*. In the second place, you don't do anything but run a little dance hall, and rent rooms. The girls came in, just for a drink. Not mescal, not tequila. Chocolate ice-cream soda, because they're nice girls, that just dropped in to take a load off their feet. They wear hats. They come in two at a time, because they're so well brought up they wouldn't dream of going in any place alone. They work in the steamboat office, up the street, or maybe they go to school and just came home for vacation. And they've never met any Americans, see, and they're giggling about it, in their simple girlish way, and of course, we fix it up, you and I, so there's a little introducing around. And they dance. And one thing leads to another. And next thing you know, the American has a room from you, to take the girl up. You don't really run that kind of place, but just because it's him, you'll make an exception—for five dollars. The girl doesn't take anything. She does it for love, see?"

"For *what?*"

"Do I know the *Americano,* or don't I?"

"I think you just talk, so sound fonny."

"It sounds fonny, but it's not just talk. The *Americano,* he doesn't mind paying for a room, but when it comes to a girl, he likes to feel it's a tribute to his personality. He likes to think it's a big night for her, too, and all the more because she's just a poor little thing in a steamboat office, and never had such a night in her life until he came along and showed her what life could be like with a real guy. He wants an adventure—with him the hero. He wants to have something to tell his friends. But don't have any bums sliding up to take their *foto*. He doesn't like that."

"Why not? The *fotógrafo*, he pay me little bit."

"Well, I tell you. Maybe the *fotógrafo* has a heart of gold, and so has the *muchacha*, but the *Americano* figures the *foto* might get back to his wife, or threaten to, specially if she's staying up at the hotel. He wants an adventure, but he doesn't want any headache. Besides, the *fotos* have got a Coney Island look to them, and might give him the idea it was a cheap joint. Remember, this place has class. And that reminds me, the *mariachi* is going to be hand-picked by me, and hand-trained as well, so maybe somebody could dance to the stuff when they play it. Of course, I don't render any selections on the guitar. That's out. Or the piano, or the violin, or any other instrument in my practically unlimited repertoire. And that *mariachi,* they wear suits that we give them, with gold braid down the pants, and turn those suits in every night when they quit. It's our own private *mariachi,* and as fast as we get money to buy more suits we put on more men, so it's a feature. The main thing is that we have class, first, last, and all the time. No *Americano,* from the time he goes in to the time he goes out, is going to get the idea that he can get out of spending money. Once they get that through their heads, we'll be all right."

"The *Americanos,* are they all crazy?"

"All crazy as loons."

It seemed to be settled, but after the gags wore off I had this sick feeling, like life had turned the gray-white color of their sunlight. I tried to tell myself it was the air, that'll do it to you at least three times a day. Then I tried to tell myself it was what I had done, that I had no more pride left than to take a job as pimp in a coast-town whorehouse, but what the hell? That was just making myself look noble. It was, anyway, some kind of work, and if I really made a go of it, it wouldn't make me squirm. It would make me laugh. And then I knew it was this thing that was drilling in the back of my head, about her. There hadn't been a word about that night, and when she looked at me her eyes were just as blank as though I'd been some guy she was talking to about the rent. But I knew what those eyes could say. Whatever it was she had seen in me that night, she still saw it, and it was between us like some glass door that we could see through but couldn't talk.

She was sitting there, looking at her coffee glass and not saying anything. She had a way of dozing off like that, between the talk, like some kitten that falls asleep as soon as you stop playing with it. I told you she looked like some high school girl in that little white dress. I kept looking at her, trying to figure out how old she was, when all of a sudden I forgot about that and my heart began to pound. If she was to be the madame of the joint, she couldn't very well take care of any customers herself, could she? Then who was going to take care of her? By her looks, she needed plenty of care. Maybe that was supposed to be my job. My voice didn't quite sound like it generally does when I spoke to her.

"... Señorita, what do I get out of this?"

"Oh—you live, have nice cloth, maybe big hat with silver, yes? Some pecos. Is enough, yes?"

"—And entertain the señoritas?"

I don't know why I said that. It was the second mean slice I had taken since we started out. Maybe I was hoping she'd flash jealous, and that would give me the cue I wanted. She didn't. She smiled, and studied me for a minute, and I felt myself getting cold when I saw there was the least bit of pity in it. "If you like to entertain señoritas, yes. Maybe not. Maybe that's why I ask you. No have any trouble."

Early next morning I shaved, washed, and packed. My earthly possessions seemed to be a razor, brush, and cake of soap, two extra shirts, a pair of extra drawers I had washed out the night before, a pile of old magazines, and the black-snake whip I had used when I sang Alfio. They give you a whip, but it never cracks, and I got this mule-skinner's number with about two pounds of lead in the butt. One night on the double bill a stagehand laid it out for Pagliacci, and the Nedda hit me in the face with it. I still carry the scar. I had sold off all the costumes and scores, but couldn't get rid of the whip. I dropped it in the suitcase. The magazines and my new soap-dish I put on top of it, and stood the suitcase in the corner. Some day, maybe, I would come back for it. The two extra shirts I put on, and tied the necktie over the top one. The extra drawers I folded and put in one pocket, the shaving stuff in another. I didn't mention I was leaving, to the clerk, on my way out. I just waved at him, like I was on my way up to the postoffice to see if the money had come, but I had to slap my hand against my leg, quick. She had dropped a handful of pesos in my pocket, and I was afraid he'd hear them clink.

The Ford was an open roadster, and I lost a half hour getting the boot off and the top up. It was an all-day run to Acapulco, and I didn't mean to have that sun beating down on me. Then I rolled it out and pulled down to 44b. She was on the doorstep, waiting for me, her stuff piled up around her. The other girls weren't up yet. She was all dressed up in the black dress with purple flowers that she had had on when I first saw her, though I thought the white would have been better. The main baggage seemed to be a round hatbox, of the kind women traveled with fifteen years ago, only made of straw and stuffed full of clothes. I peeled off the extra shirts and put them and the hatbox in the rumble seat. Then there was the grass mat that she slept on, rolled up and tied. I stuck that in, but it meant I couldn't close the rumble. Those mats, they sell for sixty centavos, or maybe twenty cents, and it didn't hardly look like it was worth the space, but it was a personal matter, and I didn't want to argue. Then there was a pile of *rebozos,* about every color there was, but mainly black. I put them in, but she ran out and took one, a dark purple, and threw it over her head. Then there was the cape, the *espada,* and the ear. It was the first time I ever saw a bullfighter's cape, the dress cape, I mean, not the fighting cape, up close so I could really look at it. I hated it because I knew where she had got it, but you couldn't laugh off the beauty of it. I think it's the only decently made thing you'll ever see in Mexico, and maybe it's not even made there. It's heavy silk, each side a different color, and embroidered so thick it feels crusty in your hands. This one was yellow outside, crimson in, and against that yellow the needlework just glittered. It was all flowers and leaves, but not in the dumb patterns you see on most of their stuff. They were oil-painting flowers, not postcard flowers, and the colors had a real tone to them. I folded it, put a *rebozo* around it, to protect it from dust, and laid it beside the hatbox. The *espada,* to me, was just one more grand-opera prop. It's what they use to stick the bull with, and I didn't even take it out of the scabbard to look at it. I threw it down in the bottom.

While I was loading the stuff in, she was standing there stroking the ear. I wouldn't have handled it with tongs. Some-

times, when a bullfighter puts on a good show, they give him
an ear. The crowd begins to yell about it, and then one of the
assistants goes over and cuts an ear off the bull, where he's
lying in the dirt with the mules hooking on to his horns. The
bullfighter takes it, holds it up so you can see all the blood and
slime, and goes around with it, bowing every ten steps. Then
he saves it, like a coloratura saves her decoration from the King
of Belgium. After about three months it's good and rank. This
one she had, there were pieces of gristle hanging out of it, and
it stunk so you could smell it five feet away. I told her if it went
on the front seat with us the deal was off, and she could throw
it back there with the *espada.* She did, but she was plenty
puzzled.

The window popped open then, and the fat one showed, with
some kind of a nightgown on, and her hair all frazzled and
ropy, and then the other ones beside her, and there was a lot
of whispering and kissing, and then we got in and got started.
We lost about ten minutes, out on the edge of town, when we
stopped to gas up, and another five when we came to a church
and she had to go in and bless herself, but finally, around eight
o'clock we leveled off. We passed some wooden crosses, another
little feature they've got. Under Socialism, it seems that there's
only one guy that really knows how it works, and if some other
guy thinks he does, it's a counter-revolutionary act, or, in un-
socialist lingo, treason. So back in 1927, a guy named Serrano
thought he did, and they arrested him and his friends down in
Cuernavaca, and started up to Mexico with them in a truck.
But then up in Mexico somebody decided it would be a good
idea if they never got there at all, and some of the boys started
out in a fast car to meet them. They fastened their hands with
baling wire, lined them up beside the road, and mowed them
down with a machine gun. Then they said the revolution was
over, and the American papers handed it to them that they had
a stable government at last, and that a strong man could turn
the trick, just give him the chance. So wooden crosses mark the
spot, an inspiring sight to see.

We had some coffee in Cuernavaca, then pushed on to Taxco

for lunch. That was the end of the good road. From there on it was just dust, curves, and hills. She began to get sleepy. A Mexican is going to sleep at one o'clock, no matter where he is, and she was no exception. She leaned her head against the side, and her eyes drooped. She wriggled, trying to get set. She slipped off her shoes. She wiggled some more. She took off a string of beads around her neck, and unfastened two buttons. She was open to her brassiere. Her dress slipped up, above her knees. I tried not to look. It was getting hotter by the minute. I didn't look, but I could smell her.

I gassed in Chilpancingo, around four o'clock, and bathed the tires with water. That was what I was afraid of, mostly, that in that heat and sliding all over that rough road, we would have a blow-out. I peeled down to my undershirt, knotted a handkerchief around my head to catch sweat, and we went on. She was awake now. She didn't have much to say. She slipped off her stockings, held her bare legs in the air stream from the hood vent, and unbuttoned another button.

We were down in what they call the *tierra caliente,* now, and it turned cloudy and so muggy the sweat stood out on my arms in drops. After Chilpancingo I had been looking for some relief, but this was the worst yet. We had been running maybe an hour when she began to lean forward and look out, and then she told me to stop. "Yes. This way."

I rubbed the sweat out of my eyes and looked, and saw something that maybe was intended to be a road. It was three inches deep in dust, and cactuses were growing in the middle of it, but if you concentrated we could see two tracks. "That way, hell. Acapulco is the way we're going. I looked it up."

"We go for Mamma."

". . . What was that you said?"

"Yes. Mamma will cook. She cook for us. For the house in Acapulco."

"Oh, I see."

"Mamma cook very nice."

"Listen. I haven't had the honor of meeting Mamma, but

I've just got a hunch she's not the type. Not for the high-class joint we're going to run. I tell you what. Let's get down there. If worse comes to worst, *I'll* cook. I cook very nice, too. I studied in Paris, where all the good cooks go when they die."

"But Mamma, she have the *viveres.*"

"The what?"

"The food, what we need. I send Mamma the money, I sent last week. She buy much things, we take. We take Mamma, Papa. All the *viveres.*"

"Oh, Papa too."

"Yes, Papa help Mamma cook."

"Well, will you tell me where you, me, Mamma, Papa, and the *viveres* are going to ride? By the way, do we take the goat?"

"Yes, this way, please."

It was her car, and I turned into the road. I had gone about a hundred yards when the wheel jerked out of my hands and I had to stamp on the brake to keep from going down a gully that must have been two hundred feet deep. I mean, it was that rough, and it didn't get any better. It was uphill and down, around rocks the size of a truck, through gullies that would have bent the axles of anything but a Ford, over cactuses so high I was afraid they would foul the transmission when we went over them. I don't know how far we went. We drove about an hour, and the rate we were moving, it might have been five miles or twenty, but it seemed more like fifty. We passed a church and then a long while after that, we began to pass Mexicans with burros, hurrying along with them. That's a little point about driving in Mexico they don't tell you about. You meet these herds of burros, going along loaded up with wood, fodder, Mexicans, or whatever it is. The burro alone doesn't give you much trouble. He knows the rules of the road as well as you do, and gets out of the way in time, even if he's a little grouchy about it. But if he's got a Mexican herding him along, you can bet on it that that Mexican will shove him right in line with your fender and you do nothing but stand on your brake and curse and sweat and cake up with their dust.

It was the way they were hurrying along, though, that woke

me up to what it looked like outside. The heat and dust were enough to strangle you, but the clouds were hanging lower all the time, and over the tops of the ridges smoky scuds were slipping past, and it didn't look good. After a long time we passed some huts, by twos and threes, huddled together. We kept on, and then we came to a couple more huts, but only one of them seemed to have anybody in it. She reached over and banged on the horn and jumped out, and ran up to the door, and all of a sudden there was Mamma, and right behind her, Papa. Mamma was about the color of a copper pot, all dressed up in a pink cotton dress and no shoes, to go to Acapulco. Papa was a little darker. He was a nice, rich mahogany after it's had about fifteen coats of dark polish. He came out in his white pajama suit, with the pants rolled up to his bare knees, and took off his big straw hat and shook hands. I shook hands. I wondered if there had been a white iceman in the family. Then I pulled up the brake and got out.

Well, I said she ran up to the door, but that wasn't quite right. There wasn't any door. Maybe you never saw an Indian hut, so I better tell you what it looks like. You can start with the colored shanties down near the railroad track in New Orleans, and then, when you've got them clearly in mind, you can imagine they're the Waldorf-Astoria Hotel, and that the Mexican hut is a shanty standing beside it. There's no walls, or roofs, or anything like you're used to seeing. There's four sides made of sticks, stuck down in the ground and wattled together with twigs, about as high as a man's head. In the middle of the front side is a break, and that's the door. The chinks between the twigs are filled up a little bit with mud. Just plain mud, smeared on there and most of it falling off. And on top is a thatch of grass, or palmetto, or whatever grows up on the hill, and that's all. There's no windows, no floor, no furniture, no pictures of the Grand Canyon hanging on the walls, no hay-grain-and-feed calendars back of the clock, with a portrait of a cowgirl on top of a horse. They've got no need for calendars, because in the first place they couldn't figure out what the writing was for, and in the second place they don't care what day it is. And they've got no need for a clock, because they don't care what time it is. All I'm trying to say is, there's nothing in there but a dirt floor, and the mats they sleep on, and down near the door, the fire where they do their cooking.

So that was where she came from, and she ran in there, barefooted like they were, and began to laugh and talk, and pat a dog that showed up in a minute, and act like any other girl that's come home after a trip to the city. It went on quite a while, but the clouds weren't hanging any higher, and I began to get nervous. "Listen, this is all very well, but how about the *viveres?*"

"Yes, yes. Mamma have buy very good estoff."

"Fine, but let's get it aboard."

It seemed to be stored in the other hut, the one that nobody was living in. Papa ducked in there and began to carry out iron plates for cooking tortillas, machetes, pots, and jars and such stuff. One or two of them were copper, but most of them were pottery, and Mexican pottery means the worst pottery in the world. Then Mamma showed up with baskets of black beans, rice, ground corn, and eggs. I stowed the stuff in the rumble seat, shoving the pots in first. But pretty soon it was chock up to the top, and, when I came to the baskets I had to lash them to the side with some twine that they had so they rode the running board. Some of the stuff, like the charcoal, wasn't even in baskets. It was done up in bundles. I lashed that too. The eggs I finally found a place for in back, on top of her hatbox. Each egg was wrapped in cornhusk, and I figured they would ride all right there and not break.

Then Papa came grinning out with a bundle, bigger than he was, of brand-new mats, all rolled up and tied. I couldn't figure out why they were so nuts about mats, but later I found out. He mussed up my whole rumble seat by dragging out the mat she had brought, unrolling his pile, rolling out her mat with the others and tying them up again. Then he lashed them to the side on top of the charcoal. I stood on the fender, grabbed the top and rocked the car. The twine broke and the mats fell out in the dirt. He laughed over that. They got a funny sense of humor. Then he got a wise look on his face, like he knew how to fix it, and went out back of the hut. When he showed again he was leading a burro, all saddled up with a rack. He opened the mats again, split them into two piles and rolled them separate. Then he lashed them to the burro, one pile on each side. Then he led the burro to the car and tied him to the rear bumper.

I untied the burro, took the mats off him, and rolled them into one pile again. I lifted them. They weren't so heavy. I hoisted them on to the top so one end was on the top, the other on the rumble seat, where it was open, and lashed them on to the top brace. I went in the hut. Juan was tying up one more basket, the old lady squatting on the stove bricks, smoking a cigar. She jumped up, ran out the door and around back, and came back with a bone. Juana had to untie the basket again, and in it was the dog. The old lady dropped the bone in, Juana put the top on and tied it up.

I went out, took the key out of my pocket, got in, and started the car. I had to back up to turn around, and all three of them started to scream and yell. It wasn't Spanish. I think it was pure Aztec. But you could get the drift. I was stealing the car, the *viveres*, everything they had. Up to then I was nothing but a guy going nuts, and trying to get started in time to get there if we ever were going to get there. But the way they acted gave me an idea. I put her in first, hauled out of there, and kept on going.

Juana was right after me, screaming at the top of her voice, and jumped on the running board. "You estop! You steal auto! You steal *viveres*. You estop! You estop now!"

I did like hell stop. I stayed in first, so she wouldn't get shaken off, but I kept on over the hill, sounding like a load of tin cans with all that stuff back there, until Mamma and Papa were *todo* out of sight. Then I threw out and pulled up the brake.

"Listen, Juana. I'm not stealing your car. I'm not stealing anything—though why the hell you couldn't have bought all this stuff in Acapulco where you could get it cheap, instead of loading up here with it, that's something I don't quite understand. But get this: Mamma, and Papa and the burro, and that dog—they're not coming."

"Mamma, she cook, she—"

"Not tonight she doesn't. Tomorrow maybe we'll come back and get her, though I doubt it. Tonight I'm off, right now. I'm on my way. Now if you want to come—"

"So, you steal my car, yes."

"Let's say borrow it. Now make up your mind."

I opened the door. She got in. I switched on the lights and we started.

By that time I would say it was about seven o'clock. It was dark from the clouds, but it still wasn't night. There was a place down the line called Tierra Colorado that we might make before the storm broke, if I could ever get back to the main road. I had never been there, but it looked like there would be some kind of a hotel, or anyway cover for the car, with all that stuff in it. I began to force. I had to go up the hills in first, but coming down I'd let her go, with just the motor holding her. It was rough, but the clock said 20, which was pretty good. Well, you take a chance on a road like that, you're headed for a fall. All of a sudden there was a crash and a jerk, and we stopped. I pedaled the throttle. The motor was dead. I pulled the starter, and she went. We had just hit a rock, and stalled. But after that I had to go slower.

Up to then I was still sweating from the air and the work. So was she. Then we topped a rise and it was like we had driven into an icebox. She shivered and buttoned her dress. I had just about decided I would have to stop and put on my coat when we drove into it. No sheet of water, nothing like that. It just started to rain, but it was driving in on her side, and I pulled up. I put on my coat, then made her get out and lifted up the seat to get the side curtains. I felt around in there with my hand. There wasn't a wrench, a jack, or tool of any kind, and not a piece of a side curtain.

"Nice garage you picked."

In Mexico you even have to have a lock on your gasoline tank. It was a wonder they hadn't even stripped her of the lights.

We got in and started off. By now it was raining hard, and most of it coming in on her. While I was hunting for curtains she had dug out a couple of *rebozos* and wrapped them around her, but even that woven stuff stuck to her like she had just come out of a swimming pool. "Here. You better take my coat."

"No, *gracias.*"

It seemed funny, in the middle of all that, to hear that soft voice, those Indian manners.

The dust had turned to grease, and off to the right, down near the sea, you could hear the rumble of thunder, how far off you couldn't tell, with the car making all that noise. I wrestled her along. Every tilt down was a skid, every tilt up was a battle, and every level piece was a wrench, where you were lifting her out of holes she went in, up to her axles. We were sliding around a knob with the hill hanging over us on one side, and dropping under us on the other, so deep you couldn't see the bottom. The drop was on my side, and I had my eyes glued to the road, crawling three feet at a time, because if we took a skid there it was the end. There was a *chock* overhead, all the top braces strained, and something went bouncing down the gully the size of a five-gallon jug. I was on the brake before it hit the ground, and after a long time I heard her breathe. The engine was still running and I went on. It must have been a minute before I figured out what that was. The rain had loosened a rock above us, and it came down. But instead of coming through and killing us, it had hit the end of the mat roll and glanced off.

It cut the fabric, though, and as soon as we rounded the knob that was the end of the top. The wind got under it, and it ripped and the rain poured down on me. It was coming from my side now. Then the mats began to roll, and there came another rip, and it poured down on her.

"Very bad."

"Not so good."

We passed the church, and started down the hill. I had to use brake *and* motor to hold her, but down at the bottom it looked a little better ahead, so I lifted my foot to give her the gun. Then I stamped on the brake so hard we stalled cold. What lay ahead, in the rain, looked like a wet sand flat where I could make pretty good time. What it was was yellow water, boiling down the arroyo so fast that it hardly made a ripple. Two more feet and we would have been in, up to the radiator. I got out, went around the car and found I had a few feet clear behind. I got in, started, and backed. When I could turn around I did, and went sliding up the hill again, the way we had come. Where we were going I didn't know. We couldn't get to Tierra Colorado, or Acapulco, or any place we wanted to go, that was a cinch. We were cut off. And whether we could make Mamma's hut, or any hut, was plenty doubtful. With the top flapping in ribbons, and all that water beating in, that motor was due to short any minute, and where that would leave us I hated to think.

We got to the top of the hill and started down the other side, past the church. Then I woke up. "All right, get in the church there, out of the wet. I'll be right after you."

"Yes, yes."

She jumped out and ran down there. I pulled off to one side, set the brake, and fished out my knife. I was going to cut those mats loose and use some of them to blanket the motor, and some of them to protect the seat and stuff in back until I could carry it in there. But the main thing I thought about was the car. If that didn't go, we were sunk. While I was still trying to get the knife open with my wet fingernail she was back. "Is close."

"What was that?"

"The church, is close. Is lock. Now we go on, yes. We go back to Mamma."

"We will like hell."

I ran over to the doors, shook them and kicked them. They were big double doors and they were locked all right. I tried to think of some way I could get them open. If I had a jack handle I could have shoved it in the crack and pried, but there wasn't any jack handle. I beat on the doors and cursed them, and then I went back to the car. The engine was still running and she was sitting in it. I jumped in, turned, and pointed it straight at the church. The steps didn't bother me. The church was below the road and they went down, instead of up, and anyway they were just low tile risers, about three inches high, and pretty wide. When she saw what I was going to do, she began to whimper, and beg me not to, and grabbed the wheel to make me stop. "No, no! Not the *Casa de Dios*, please, no! We go back! We go back to Mamma."

I pushed her away and eased the front wheels down the first step. I bumped them down the next two steps, and then the back wheels came down with a slam. But I was still rolling. I kept on until the front bumper was against the doors. I stayed in first, spun the motor, and little by little let in the clutch. For three or four seconds nothing happened, but I knew something had to crack. It did. There came a *snap*, and I was on the brake. If those doors opened outward I didn't want to tear out their hinges.

I backed up the width of the last step, pegged her there with the brake and got out. The bolt socket had torn out. I pulled the doors open, shoved Juana in, went back and started to work on the mats again. Then I thought, what's the matter with you? Don't be a fool. I ran back and pulled the doors as wide open as they would go. Then I ran in and began to drag pews around, working by the car lights, until there was an open space right up the center aisle. Then I went back and drove the car right in there. I went back and pulled the doors shut. The headlights were blazing right at the Blessed Sacrament, and she was on her knees at the altar rail, begging forgiveness for the *sacrilegio*.

I sat down in one of the pews where it was turned sidewise, just to sit. I began to worry about the car lights. At the time it seemed I was thinking about the battery, but it may have been the Blessed Sacrament, boring into the side of my head, I don't know. I got up and cut them. Right away the roar of the rain was five times as loud. In with it you could hear the rumble of thunder, but you couldn't see any lightning. It was pitch dark in there, except for one red spot. The sacristy light was burning. From up near it came a moan. I had to have light. I cut the switch on again.

Off to one side of the altar was what looked like a vestry room. I went back there. The water squirted out of my shoes when I walked. I took them off. Then I took off my pants. I looked around. There was a cassock hanging there, and some surplices. I took off everything, wet undershirt, wet drawers, wet socks, and put on the cassock. Then I took a lighter that was standing in a corner and started out to the sacristy lamp. I knew my matches wouldn't work. Walking on a tile floor barefoot you don't make much noise, and when she saw me with the lighter, in the cassock, I don't know what she thought, or if she thought. She fell on her face in front of me and began to gibber, calling me *padre* and begging for *absolución*. "I'm not the *padre*, Juana. Look at me. It's me."

"Ah, *Dios!*"

"I'm lighting the candles so we can see."

But I mumbled it low. I pulled down the lamp, lit the lighter and slipped it up again. Then I went around through the vestry room and up on the altar and lit three candles on one side, crossed over and lit three on the other. I cut the lighter, went back to the vestry room, put it in its place again. Then I went back and cut the car lights.

One funny thing about that that I didn't realize until I snapped that switch. Each time I crossed that altar I went down on one knee. I stood there, looking at the six candles I had lit, and thought that over. It had been twenty years, ever since I had been a boy soprano around Chicago, since I had thought of myself as a Catholic. But they knock it into you. Some of it's there to stay.

I lifted eggs and about fifteen other things from the rumble, until I could get out her hatbox. It was pretty wet but not as wet as the rest of the stuff. I took it back to the vestry room, set it down, then went out and touched her on the shoulder. "Your things are back there. You better get out of that wet dress."

She didn't move.

By that time it must have been about half past eight, and it dawned on me that why I felt so lousy was that I was hungry. I got a candle off the altar, lit it, went back and stuck it to the rear fender of the car, and took stock. I lifted out most of that stuff from the rumble seat, and unlashed what was riding the running board, and all I could see that was doing us any good was the eggs. I unwrapped one and took out my knife to puncture the end so I could suck it, and then I noticed the charcoal. That gave me an idea. There were some loose tiles in the floor and I clawed up a couple of them and carried them to the vestry room and stood them on their sides. Then I got one of the iron plates for cooking tortillas, and laid it across them and carried in the charcoal.

Next thing was how I was going to cook the eggs. There were no skillets or anything like that. And I went through every basket there was and there wasn't any butter, grease, or anything you could use for grease. But there was a copper pot, bigger than I wanted but anyway a pot, so that meant that anyway I could boil the eggs. While I was rooting through those beans and rice and stuff that would take all night to cook, I smelled coffee and started looking for it. Finally I hit it, buried in with the rice in a paper bag, and then I found a little coffee pot. The coffee wasn't ground, but there was a metate there for grinding corn, and I mashed up a couple of handfuls with that, and put it in a bowl.

I went in the vestry room with what I had and the next thing was what I was going to use for water. It was dripping through every seam in the room and running down the windows in streams, but it looked kind of tough to get enough of it to cook. Still, I had to get some. Out back I could hear a stream pouring off the roof, so I took the biggest of the bowls and pulled the bolt on the rear door, right back of the altar. But when I opened it I could see a well, just a few steps down the hill. I took off the cassock. It was the only dry thing there was, and I wasn't letting it get wet. I went down to the well stark naked. The rain came down on me like a needle shower and at first it was terrible, but then it felt good. I threw out my chest against it and let it beat me. Then I pulled up the bucket and poured the water in the bowl. When I got back in the church with it I was running water even from my eyeballs. I felt around back of the altar for a closet. Oh, it was coming back to me, fast. I knew where they kept everything. Sure enough, I found a door and opened it, and there they were, the altar cloths, all in a neat pile. I took one, rubbed myself dry with it and put on the cassock. It was warm. I began to feel better.

The choir loft was off to one side and I started there to get a hymn book, so I could tear it up to start the fire. Then I changed my mind. Except for the window, there was no vent in the vestry room, and I didn't want to be smoked out, right at the start. I took four or five pieces of charcoal, laid them in a little pile between my tiles, went back to the altar and got another candle. I held the flame under the charcoal, turning all the time to keep the melting even, and pretty soon I got a little glow. I fed a couple more pieces on, and it glowed still redder. In a minute it was off, and I blew out the candle. There was hardly any smoke. Charcoal doesn't make much.

I laid the plate over the tiles, put the pot on it, and dipped some water in the pot. Then I dropped in some eggs. I started with six, but then I kept thinking how hungry I was, and I wound up with a dozen. I filled the coffee pot, scooped in some coffee, and put that on. Then I sat there, feeding the fire and waiting for the eggs to boil. They never did. The pot was too big or the fire too small, or something. The most I got was smoke coming off the top, but they were cooking all the time, so I didn't worry much. Anyway, they'd be hot. But the coffee boiled. The old smell hit me in the nose, and when I lifted the lid the grounds were simmering around. I took an egg, went to the back door, broke it, and let the egg spill out on the ground. The shell I took back and dropped in the coffee. That was what it needed. It began to clear.

I watched the eggs some more, and then I thought about my cigarettes and matches. They were in my coat, and I went to the car to get it. Then I thought about her things. I put the cigarettes and matches on the end of the tortilla plate to dry. Her stuff I took out of the hatbox and draped them near the fire on a bench that was back there. What she had I could only half see. It was all damp, but it smelled like her. One dress was wool, and I put that nearest the heat, and a pair of shoes, on the floor near it. Then I got to wondering how we were going to eat the eggs, even if they ever got cooked. There were no spoons or anything like that, and I always hated eggs out of the shell. I went out to the car again and half filled a little bowl with corn meal. I came back, dipped a little water into it. I worked it with my fingers, and when it got pasty I patted some of it into a tortilla, or anyway into some kind of a flapjack that was big enough to hold an egg. I put it on the plate to cook, and when it began to turn color I turned it over. When it was done on both sides I tasted it. It didn't taste right. I went out and got some salt I had found and forgotten to take. I mixed a little salt in, tried another one, and anyway you could eat it. Pretty soon I had twelve. That was one for each egg, and I thought that was enough.

All that took a long time, and there wasn't one peep out of her the whole time I was at work. She had moved from the altar rail to a pew, but she was still out there, a *rebozo* over her head and her bare feet sticking out behind, where she was kneeling with her face in her hands. I slid in the pew, took her by the arm and led her into the vestry room. "I told you once to take off that wet dress. Here's one that's fairly dry, and you go back there and change it. If your underwear's wet, you better take it off."

I picked up the woolen dress and shoved her behind the altar with it. When she came back she had it on. "Sit on the bench so your feet will be on the warm tiles near the fire. When those shoes are dry you can put them on."

She didn't. She sat on the bench, but with her back to the fire, so her feet were on cold tiles. That was so she could face the altar. She dropped her head in her hands and began to mutter. I got out my knife, broke an egg tortilla, and shoved it at her. The egg was half hard and half soft, but it rode the tortilla all right.

She shook her head. I put the tortilla down, went to the altar, got three or four candles, lit them, came back and stuck them around. Then I closed the door, the one that led to the altar and that I had kept open, to have more light. That kind of blocked her off on the muttering and she half turned around. When she saw the tortillas she laughed. That seemed to help. "Look very fonny."

"Well, maybe they look fonny but I didn't notice you doing much about them. Anyway, you can eat them."

She picked up the tortilla, half wrapped it around the egg and bit into it. "Taste very fonny."

"The hell it does."

I had bit into my first one by then, and it hit the spot. We wolfed them down. She ate five and I ate seven. We were talking in a natural tone of voice for the first time since we got in out of the storm, and it came to me it was because that door that led to the altar was shut. I got up and closed the other door, the one leading into the church, and that made it still better. We got to the coffee and there was nothing we could drink it out of but one little bowl, so we took turns. She would take a guzzle and then I would. In a minute I reached for the cigarettes. They were dry, and so were the matches. We lit up and inhaled. They tasted good.

"You feel better now?"

"Yes, *gracias.* Was very cold, very hongry."

"You still worried about the *sacrilegio?*"

"No, not now."

"There wasn't any *sacrilegio,* you know."

"Yes, very bad."

"No, not a bit. It's the *Casa de Dios,* you know. Everybody's welcome in here. You've seen the burros in here, haven't you? And the goats? On the way to market? The car is just the same. If we had to break the door in, that was only because we didn't have any key. I showed plenty of respect, didn't I? You saw me genuflect every time I crossed, didn't you?"

"Genu—"

"Bow—in front of the Host?"

"Yes, of course."

"No *sacrilegio* there, was there? You're all upset about nothing. Don't worry, I know. I know as much about it as you do. More probably."

"Very bad *sacrilegio.* But I pray. Soon, I confess. I confess to the *padre.* Then, *absolución.* No bad any more."

By that time it must have been somewhere around eleven o'clock at night. The rain hadn't let up, but sometimes it would be heavy, sometimes not so bad. The thunder and lightning would come up and go. There must have been three or four storms rolling up those canyons from the sea, and we'd get it, and it would die away and then we'd get it again. One was coming up now. She began to do what I'd noticed her doing once in the car, hold her breath and then speak, after a second or two when you could almost hear her heart beat. I tumbled that the *sacrilegio* was only part of what was eating on her. Most of it was the storm. "The lightning bother you?"

"No. The *trueno,* very bad."

It didn't look like it would pay to try to explain to her that the lightning was the works, the thunder nothing but noise, so

I didn't try. "Try to sing a little. That generally helps. You know *La Sandunga?*"

"Yes, very pretty."

"You sing and I'll be *mariachi.*"

I began to drum on the bench and do a double shuffle with my feet. She opened her mouth to sing, but there came a big clap of thunder just then, and she didn't quite make it. "Outside, I no feel afraid. I like. Is very pretty."

"A lot of people are like that."

"Home, with Mamma, I no feel afraid."

"Well—that's practically outside, at that."

"Here, afraid, very much. I think about the *sacrilegio,* think about many things. I feel very bad."

You couldn't blame her much because it wasn't exactly what you'd call a gay place. I understood how she felt. I felt a little that way myself.

"Anyhow, it's dry. In spots."

The lightning came and I put my arm around her. The thunder broke and the candles guttered. She put her head on my shoulder and hid her face in my neck.

It died off after a while and she sat up. I opened the window a crack to get a little oxygen in the air, and put a couple more sticks of charcoal on the fire. "You had a good dinner?"

"Yes, *gracias.*"

"You feel like a little work?"

"... Work?"

"Suppose you be fixing us up a place to sleep while I wash up."

"Oh yes—gladly."

I went and brought the mats and then got out a pile of altar cloths. Then I took the pots, bowls, and water out back and washed them up. I couldn't see very well, but I did the best I could. I had to duck out to the well once or twice, stripped down like I was before, and rub off with the same old cloth, so it took me about a half hour. When I got done I piled the things up inside the door and went in there. She was already in bed.

She had taken three or four of the mats and some altar cloths, for herself, and bedded me down across the room.

I blew out the candles we had eaten by, and stepped out on the altar to blow out the ones I had lit there, and then I noticed the other one, the one I had stuck to the car fender, was still burning. I stepped over the rail, went back there and blew it out. Then I started up to the altar again. My legs felt queer and shaky. I slipped in a pew and sat down.

I knew what it was all right, and it came to me then why I had put her to fixing the mats and taken all that time to wash up. I had hoped she would just fix one bed, and then when she didn't, it was like a wallop in the pit of the stomach to me. I had even quit wondering why I was the only man on the face of the earth she wouldn't sleep with. What I hated was that it made any difference to me.

I don't know how long I sat there. I wanted to smoke, and I had the cigarettes and matches with me, but I just held them in my hand. I was over by the choir loft, out of line with the Blessed Sacrament, but I was right in line with the crucifix, and I couldn't make myself light up. Another storm began to come up. I enjoyed it that she was across there in the vestry room, all alone, and scared to death. It kept rolling up, the worst we had had yet. There came two flashes of lightning, and then one terrific shot of thunder right after them. The candles were just guttering up again when there came a blaze of lightning, and the thunder right with it, and every candle up there went out. For a second you couldn't see a thing but the red spot of the sacristy lamp.

Then she began to scream. From where she was, with the door to the altar open like I had left it, maybe she caught it sooner than I did. Or maybe for a split second I had my eyes closed. I don't know. Anyway, the church filled with green light, and then it seemed to settle over the crucifix, so the face looked alive, like it was going to cry out. Then you couldn't see anything but the red spot.

She was screaming her head off now, and I had to have light.

I dived for the choir loft, scratched a match, and lit the organ candles. I don't know how many there were. I lit them all, so it was a blaze of candles. Then I turned to go and light the altar candles again, but I would have to cross in front of the crucifix and I couldn't do it. All of a sudden I sat down to the organ. It was a small pedal organ, and I pumped with my bare feet and started to play. I kept jerking out stops, to make it louder. The thunder rolled, and the louder it rolled the louder I played. I didn't know what I was playing, but after a while I knew it was an *Agnus Dei.* I cut it off and started a *Gloria.* It was louder. The thunder died off and the rain came down like all Niagara was over us. I played the *Gloria* over again.

"Sing."

I couldn't see her. She was outside the circle of light, where I was sitting in the middle. But I could feel her, up at the altar rail again, and if singing was what she wanted, that suited me too. I skipped the *Qui Tollis,* the *Quoniam,* and the rest of it down to the *Credo,* and went on from there. Don't ask me what it was. Some of it was Mozart, some of it was Bach, some of it was anybody you can think of. I must have sung a hundred masses in my time, and I didn't care which one it was, so I could go on without a break. I went straight through to the *Dona Nobis,* and played off soft after I finished it, and then I stopped. The lightning and thunder had stopped again, and the rain was back to its regular drumming.

"Yes."

She just whispered it, but she drew it out like she always did, so the end of it was a long hiss. ". . . Just like the priest."

My head began to pound like it would split. That was the crown of skunk cabbage, all right, after all the years at harmony, of sight-reading, of piano, of light opera, of grand opera in Italy, Germany and France—to be told by this Indian that couldn't even read that I sounded like a priest. And it didn't help any that that was just what I sounded like. The echo of my voice was still in my ears and there was no getting around it. It had the same wooden, dull quality that a priest's voice has, without one particle of life in it, one echo that would make you like it.

My head kept pounding. I tried to think of something to say that would rip back at her, and couldn't.

I got up, blew out all the candles but one, and took that one with me. I started up past the crucifix to cross over to the vestry room. She wasn't at the crucifix. She was out in front of the altar. At the foot of the crucifix I saw something funny and held the candle to see what it was. It was three eggs, in a bowl. Beside them was a bowl of coffee and a bowl of ground corn. They hadn't been there before. Did you ever hear of a Catholic putting eggs, coffee, and corn at the foot of the cross? No, and you never will. That's how an Aztec treats a god.

I crossed over, and stood behind her, where she was crouched down, on her knees, her face touching the floor and her hands pressing down beside it. She was stark naked, except for a *rebozo* over her head and shoulders. There she was at last, stripped to what God put there. She had been sliding back to the jungle ever since she took off that first shoe, coming out of Taxco, and now she was right in it.

A white spot from the sacristy lamp kept moving back and forth, on her hip. A creepy feeling began to go up my back, and then my head began to pound again, like sledge hammers were inside of it. I blew out the candle, knelt down, and turned her over.

4

When it was over we lay there, panting. Whatever it was that she had done to me, that the rest of it had done to me, I was even. She got up and went back to the car. There was some rattling back there, and then I felt her coming back, and got up to meet her. I was getting used to the dark by then, and I saw the flash of a machete. She came in on a run, and when she was a couple of yards away she took a two-handed chop with it. I stepped back and it pulled her off balance. I stepped in, pinned her arms, and pressed my thumb against the back of her hand, right at the wrist. The knife fell on the floor. She tried to wriggle free. Mind you, neither one of us had a stitch on. I tightened with one arm, lifted her, carried her in the vestry room and closed both doors. Then I dumped her in the bed she had been in, piled in with her, and pulled up the covers. The fire still made a little glow, and I lit a cigarette and I smoked it, holding her with the other arm, then squashed it against the floor.

When she tired, I loosened up a little, to let her blow. Yes, it was rape, but only technical, brother, only technical. Above the waist, maybe she was worried about the *sacrilegio,* but from

the waist down she wanted me, bad. There couldn't be any
doubt about that.

There couldn't be any doubt about it, and it kind of put an
end to the talk. We lay there, then, and I had another cigarette.
I squashed it out, and from away off there came a rumble of
thunder, just one. She wriggled into my arms, and next thing I
knew it was daylight, and she was still there. She opened her
eyes, closed them again, and came closer. Of course there wasn't
but one thing to do about that, so I did it. Next time I woke
up I knew it must be late, because I was hungry as hell.

It rained all that day, and the next. We split up on the cooking
after the first breakfast. I did the eggs and she did the tortillas,
and that seemed to work better. I got the pot to boil at last by
setting it right on the tiles without any plate, and it not only
made it boil, but saved time. In between, though, there wasn't
much to do, so we did whatever appealed to us.

That afternoon of the second day it let up for about a half hour,
and we slid down in the mud to have a look at the arroyo. It
was a torrent. No chance of making Acapulco that night. We
went up the hill and the sun came out plenty hot. When we got
to the church the rocks back of it were alive with lizards. There
was every size lizard you could think of, from little ones that
were transparent like shrimps, to big ones three feet long. They
were a kind of a blue gray, and moved so fast you could hardly
follow them with your eyes. They leveled out with their tail,
somehow, so they went over the rocks in a straight line, and
almost seemed to fly. Looking at them you could believe it all
right, that they turned into birds just by letting their scales
grow into feathers. You could almost believe it that they were
half bird already.

We climbed down and stood looking at them, when all of a
sudden she began to scream. "Iguana! Iguana! Look, look, big
iguana!"

I looked, and couldn't see anything. Then, still as the rock it was lying on, and just about the color of it, I saw the evilest-looking thing I ever laid eyes on. It looked like some prehistoric monster you see in the encyclopedia, between two and three feet long, with a scruff of spines that started at its head and went clear down its back, and a look in its eye like something in a nightmare. She had grabbed up a little tree that had washed out by the roots, and was closing in on him. "What are you doing? Let that goddam thing alone!"

When I spoke he shot out for the next rock like something on springs, but she made a swipe and caught him in mid-air. He landed about ten feet away, with his yellow belly showing and all four legs churning him around in circles. She scrambled over, hit him again, and then she grabbed him. "Machete! Quick, bring machete!"

"Machete, hell, let him go I tell you!"

"Is iguana! We cook! We eat!"

"Eat!—that thing?"

"The machete, the machete!"

He was scratching her by that time, and if she wouldn't let him go I wasn't letting him make hash out of her. I dove in the church for the machete. But then some memory of this animal caught me. I don't know whether it was something I had read in Cortés, or Diaz, or Martyr, or somebody, about how they cooked it when the Aztecs still ran Mexico, or some instinct I had brought away from Paris, or what. All I knew was that if we ever cut his head off he was going to be dead, and maybe that wouldn't be right. I didn't grab a machete. I grabbed a basket with a top on it, and dug out there with it. "The machete! The machete, give me machete!"

He had come to by now, and was fighting all he knew, but I grabbed him. The only place to grab him was in the belly on account of those spines on his back, and that put his claws right up your arm. She was bleeding up to her elbows and now it was my turn. Never mind how he felt and how he stunk. It was enough to turn your stomach. But I gave him the squeeze, shoved him headdown in the basket, and clapped the top on. Then I held it tight with both hands.

"Get some twine."

"But the machete! Why no bring—"

"Never mind. I'm doing this. Twine—string—that the things were tied with."

I carried him in, and she got some twine, and I tied the top on tight. Then I set him down and tried to think. She didn't make any sense out of it, but she let me alone. In a minute I fed up the fire, took the pot out and filled it with water. It had started to rain again. I came in and put the pot on to heat. It took a long while. Inside the basket those claws were ripping at the wicker, and I wondered if it would hold.

At last I got a simmer, and then I took the pot off and got another basket-top ready. I picked him up, held him way above my head, and dropped him to the floor. I remembered what shock did to him the first time, and I hoped it would work again. It didn't. When I cut the string and grabbed, I got teeth, but I held on and socked him in the pot. I whipped the basket-top on and held it with my knee. For three seconds it was like I had dropped an electric fan in there, but then it stopped. I took the top off and fished him out. He was dead, or as dead as a reptile ever gets. Then I found out why it was that something had told me to put him in the pot alive, and not cook him dead, with his head cut off, like she wanted to do. When he hit that scalding water he let go. He purged, and that meant he was clean inside as a whistle.

I went out, emptied the pot, heated a little more water, and scrubbed it clean with cornhusks, from the eggs. Then I scrubbed him off. Then I filled the pot, or about two thirds filled it, with clean water, and put it on the fire. When it began to smoke I dropped him in. "But is very fonny. Mamma no cook that way."

"Is fonny, but inspiration has hit me. Never mind how Mamma does it. This is how I do it, and I think it's going to be good."

I fed up the fire, and pretty soon it boiled. I cut it down to a simmer, and this smell began to come off it. It was a stink, and yet it smelled right, like I knew it was going to smell. I let it cook along, and every now and then I'd fish him up and pull one of his claws. When a claw pulled out I figured he was done. I took him out and put him in a bowl. She reached for the pot to go out and empty it. I almost fainted. "Let that water alone. Leave it there, right where it is."

I cut off his head, opened his belly, and cleaned him. I saved his liver, and was plenty careful how I dissected off the gall bladder. Then I skinned him and took off the meat. The best of it was along the back and down the tail, but I carved the legs too, so as not to miss anything. The meat and liver I stowed in a little bowl. The guts I threw out. The bones I put back in the pot and fed up the fire again, so it began to simmer. "You better make yourself comfortable. It's a long time before dinner."

I aimed to boil about half that water away. It began to get dark and we lit the candles and watched and smelled. I washed off three eggs and dropped them in. When they were hard I fished them out, peeled them, and laid them in a bowl with the meat. She pounded up some coffee. After a long time that soup was almost done. Then something popped into my mind. "Listen, we got any paprika?"

"No, no paprika."

"Gee, we ought to have paprika."

"Pepper, salt, yes. No paprika."

"Go out there to the car and have a look. This stuff needs paprika, and it would be a shame not to have it just because we didn't look."

"I go, but is no paprika."

She took a candle and went back to the car. I didn't need any paprika. But I wanted to get rid of her so I could pull off something without any more talk about the *sacrilegio*. I took a candle and a machete and went back of the altar. There were four or five closets back there, and a couple of them were locked. I slipped the machete blade into one and snapped the lock. It was full of firecrackers for high mass and stuff for the Christmas crèche. I broke into another one. There it was, what I was looking for, six or eight bottles of sacramental wine. I grabbed a bottle, closed the closets, and came back. I dug the cork out with my knife and tasted it. It was A-1 sherry. I socked about a pint in the pot and hid the bottle. As soon as it heated up a little I lifted the pot off, dropped the meat in, sliced up the eggs, and put them in. I sprinkled in some salt and a little pepper.

She came back. "Is no paprika."

"It's all right. We don't need it. Dinner's ready."

We dug in.

Well, brother, you can have your Terrapin Maryland. It's a noble dish, but it's not Iguana John Howard Sharp. The meat is a little like chicken, a little like frog-legs, and a little like muskrat, but it's tenderer than any of them. The soup is one of the great soups of the world, and I've eaten Marseilles bouillabaisse, New Orleans crayfish bisque, clear green turtle, thick green turtle, and all kinds of other turtle there are. I think it was still better that we had to drink it out of bowls, and fish the meat out with a knife. It's gelatinous, and flooding up over your lips, it makes them sticky, so you can feel it as well as taste it. She drank hers stretched out on her belly, and after a while it occurred to me that if I got down and stuck my mouth up against hers, we would be stuck, so we experimented on that for a while. Then we drank some more soup, ate some more meat, and made the coffee. While we were drinking that she started to laugh. "Yeh? And what's so funny?"

"I feel—how you say? Dronk?"

"Probably born that way."

"I think you find wine. I think you steal wine, put in iguana."

"Well?"

"I like, very much."

"Why didn't you say so sooner?"

So I got out the bottle, and we began to swig it out of the neck. Pretty soon we were smearing her nipples with soup, to see if they would stick. Then after a while we just lay there, and laughed.

"You like the dinner?"

"It was lovely dinner, *gracias.*"
"You like the cook?"
"Yes. . . . Yes. . . . Yes. Very fonny cook."

God knows what time it was when we got up from there and went out front to wash up. She helped me this time, and when we opened the door it had stopped raining and the moon was shining. That set us off again. After we got the stuff clean we started to laugh and dance out there in the mud, barefooted. I started to hum some music for it, and then I stopped. She was standing out there in the glare of the moon with that same look on her face she had the first night I met her. But she didn't turn away from me this time. She came closer and looked at me hard. "Sing."

"Oh, the hell with it."

"No, please, sing."

I started over again, what I had been humming, but this time I sang it instead of humming it, and then I stopped again. It didn't sound like a priest any more. I walked over to the edge of the rocks and threw one down the arroyo, with a wide-open throttle. I don't know what it was. It came full and round, the way it once had, and felt free and good. I cut, and had just taken breath for another one when the echo of the first one came back to me. I caught my breath. That echo had something in it my voice had never had before, some touch of sweetness, or excitement, or whatever it was, that I had always lacked. I cut the second one loose, and she came over and stood looking at me. I kept throwing them, each one tone higher than the last. I must have got up to F above the staff. Then I did a turn in the middle of my voice and shot one as high as I dared. When the echo came it had a ring to it almost like a tenor. I turned and ran into the church and up to the organ, to check pitch. It was A flat, and church organs are always high. At orchestra pitch, it was at least an A natural.

I was trembling so bad my fingers shook on the keys. Listen, I was never a great baritone. I guess you begin to place me by now, and after the Don Giovanni revival, and especially after the Hudson-to-Horn hookup, you heard I was the greatest since Bispham, and some more stuff like that. That was all hooey. I was no Battistini, no Amato, no John Charles Thomas. On voice, I was somewhere between Bonelli and Tibbett. On acting, I was pretty good. On music, I was still better. On singing, I was as good as they come. I ought to be, seeing it was all I ever did, my whole life. But never mind all that. I had a hell of a good voice, that's all I'm trying to say, and I had worked on it, lived for it, and let it be a part of me until it was a lot more than just something to make a living with. And I want you to get it straight why it was when this thing happened in Europe, and it cracked up on me for no reason that I could see, and then when I got sold down to Mexico as a broken-down hack that couldn't be sent any place better, and then when I wasn't even good enough for that,—it wasn't only that I was a bum, and down and out. Something in me had died. And now that it had come back, just as sudden as it went, I was a lot more excited than you would be if you found a hundred-dollar bill somewhere. I was more like a man that had gone blind, and then woke up one morning to find out that he could see.

I played an introduction, and started to sing. It was *Eri Tu*, from Ballo in Maschera. But I couldn't be bothered with pedaling that old wreck. I walked out in the aisle, and walked around with it, singing without accompaniment. I finished it, sang it again, and checked pitch. It had pulled a little sharp. That was right, after that long lay-off, it ought to do that. I played a chord for pitch, and started another. I sang for an hour, and hated to quit, but at that high pitch an hour was the limit.

She sat in a pew, staring at me as I walked around. The *sacrilegio* didn't seem to bother her much any more. When I stopped, she came in the vestry room with me, and we dropped off what we had on, and lay down. There were six or seven cigarettes left. I kept smoking them. She lay beside me, up on one elbow, still staring at me. When the cigarettes were gone I closed my eyes and tried to go to sleep. She opened one eye, with her finger, and then the other eye. "That was very beautiful, *gracias.*"

"I used to be a singer."

"Yes. Maybe I made a mistake."

"I think you did."

". . . Maybe not."

She kissed me then, and went to sleep. But the fire was dead, the moon had gone down, and the window was gray before *I* went to sleep.

5

We pulled into Acapulco the next afternoon around five thirty. We couldn't start before four, on account of that busted top, that I had to stow away in the boot. I didn't mean to get sunstroke, so I let her sleep and tried to clean up a little, so I would leave the church about the way I found it, except for a few busted locks and this and that. Getting the car out was a little harder than getting it in. I had to make little dirt run-ways up the steps, soak them with water, and let them bake in the sun, so I could get a little traction for the wheels in reverse. Then I had to tote all the stuff out and load it again, but I had more time, and made a better job of it. When she came out of her siesta, we started off. The arroyo was still a stream, but it was clear water now, and not running deep, so we got across all right.

When we got to Acapulco she steered me around to the hotel where we were going to stop. I don't know if you ever saw a hotel for Mexicans. It was a honey. It was just off the road that skirts the harbor, on the edge of the town, and it was just an adobe barracks, one story high, built around a dirt patio, or court, or whatever you'd call it, and that was all. In each room was a square oil can, what they use to carry water in all over Mexico, and that was the furnishings. You used that to carry

your water in, from the well outside, and there wasn't anything
else in there at all. Your mat, that you slept on, you were supposed to have with you, and unroll it on the dirt floor yourself.
That was why she had been packing all those mats around. Your
bedclothes you were supposed to have with you too, except that
a Mexican doesn't need bedclothes. He flops as is. The plumb-
ing was al fresco exterior, just over from the well. In the patio
was a flock of burros, tied, that the guests had come on, and
we parked our car there, and she took her hatbox, the cape, the
espada, and the ear, and the *hostelero* showed us our room. It
was No. 16, and had a fine view of a Mexican with his pants
down, relieving his bowels.

"Well, how do you feel?"

"Very nice, *gracias.*"

"The heat hasn't got you?"

"No, no. Nicer than Mexico."

"Well, I tell you what. It's too early to eat yet. I think I'll
have my suit pressed, then take a walk around and kind of get
the lay of the land. Then after sundown, when it's cooler, we'll
find a nice place and eat. Yes?"

"Very nice. I look at house."

"All right, but I got ideas on the location."

"Oh, the *político* already have house."

"I see. I didn't know that. All right, then, you see the *político,* have a look at the house, and then we'll eat."

"Yes."

I found a *sastrería,* and sat there while they pressed my suit,
but I didn't waste any time on the lay of the land after that.
You think I was going to bookkeep for a whorehouse now? A
fat chance. Those high notes down the arroyo made everything
different. There was a freighter laying out there in the harbor,
and I meant to dig out of there, if there was any way in God's
world I could promote passage on her.

It was nearly dark before I found the captain. He was having
dinner at the Hotel de Mexico, out under the canopy. He was

a black Irishman, named Conners, about fifty, with brows that met over his nose, a face the color of a meerschaum pipe, and blistered sunburned hands that were thin and long like a black-jack dealer's. He gave me a fine welcome when I sat down at his table. "My friend, I don't know your uncle in New York, your brother in Sydney, or your sister-in-law back in Dublin, God bless her, nevertheless. I'm not a member of the Ancient, Free, and Accepted Order of Masons, and I don't care if you ever get the twenty pesos to take you to Mexico City. I'll not buy you a drink. Here's a peso to be off, and if you don't mind I'll be having my dinner."

I let the peso lay and didn't move. When he had to look at me again I recited it back to him just like he had handed it to me. "I have no uncle in New York, no brother in Sydney, no sister-in-law in Dublin, thanks for the benediction, nevertheless. I'm not a member of the Ancient, Free, and Accepted Order of Masons, and I'm not on my way to Mexico City. I don't want your drink, and I don't want your peso."

"By your looks, you want something. What is it?"

"I want passage north, if that's where you're headed."

"I'm headed for San Pedro, and the passage will be two hundred and fifteen pesos, cash of the Republic, payable in advance, and entitling you to a fine deck stateroom, three meals a day, and the courtesies of the ship."

"I offer five."

"Declined."

I picked up his peso. "Six."

"Declined."

"I offer sweat. I'll do any reasonable thing to work this passage out, from swabbing decks to cleaning brass. I'm a pretty fair cook."

"Declined."

"I offer a recipe for Iguana John Howard Sharp that I have just perfected, a dish that would be an experience for you, and probably improve your disposition."

" 'Tis the first sensible thing you have said, but there would

be a difficulty getting the iguana. At this season they move up
to the hills. Declined."

"I offer six pesos and a promissory note for two hundred
and nine. The note I guarantee to redeem."

"Declined."

I watched him eating his fish, and by that time I was beginning to be annoyed. "Listen, maybe you don't get this straight.
I intend to haul out of here, and I intend to haul out on your
boat. Write up your contracts any way you want. The thing to
get through your head is: I'm going."

"You're not. You've taken my peso, so be off."

I lit a cigarette and still sat there. "All right, I'll level it out,
and quit the feinting and jabbing. I was a singer, and my voice
cracked up. Now it's coming back, see? That means if I ever
get out of this hellhole of a country, and get back where the
money is, I can cash in. I'm all right. I'm as good as I ever
was, maybe better. To hell with the promissory note. I guess
that was a little tiresome. I ask you as a favor to haul me up to
San Pedro, so I can get on my feet again."

When he looked up, his eyes were smoky with hate. "So
you're a singer, then. An American singer. My answer is: It
wouldn't be safe for me to take you aboard. Before I was out
of the harbor with you I'd drop you into the water to rid the
world of you. No! And don't take up any more of my time with
it."

"What's the matter with an American singer?"

"I even hate the Pacific Ocean. On the Atlantic side, I can
get London, Berlin, and Rome on my wireless. But here what
is it? Los Angeles, San Francisco, the blue network, the red
network, a castrated eunuch urging me to buy soap—and Victor
Herbert!"

"He was an Irishman."

"He was a German."

"You're wrong. He was an Irishman."

"I met him in London when I was a young man, and I talked
German with him myself."

"He talked German, through choice, especially when he was with other Irishmen. You see, he wasn't proud of it. He didn't want them to know it. All right, look him up."

"Then he was an Irishman, though I hate to say it.—And George Gershwin! There was an Irishman for you."

"He wrote some music."

"He didn't write one bar of music. Victor Herbert, and George Gershwin, and Jerome Kern, and buy the soap for me schoolboy complexion, and Lawrence Tibbett, singing mush. At Tampico, I got Mozart's Jupiter Symphony, that I suppose you never heard of, coming from Rome. Off Panama, I picked up the Beethoven Seventh, with Beecham conducting it, in London—"

"Listen, never mind Beethoven—"

"Oh, it's never mind Beethoven, is it? You would say that, you soap-agent. He was the greatest composer that ever lived!"

"The hell he was."

"And *who* was? Walter Donaldson, I suppose."

"Well, we'll see."

There were two or three *mariachis* around, but the place wasn't full yet, so there was a lull in the screeching. I called a man over, and took his guitar. It was tuned right, for a change. My fingers still had calluses on them, from the job in Mexico City, so I could slide up to the high positions without cutting them. I went into the introduction to the serenade from Don Giovanni, and then I sang it. I didn't do any number, didn't try to get any hand, and the rest of them in there hardly noticed me. I just sang it, half-voice, rattled off the finish on the guitar, and put my hand over the strings.

He was to his tamales by now, and he kept putting them down. Then he called the guitar player over, had a long pow-wow in Spanish, and laid down some paper money. The guitar player touched his hat and went off. The waiter took his plate and he stared hard at the table. ". . . It's a delicate point. I've been a Beethoven enthusiast ever since I was a young man, but I've often wondered to myself if Mozart wasn't the greatest musical genius that ever lived. You might be right, you might be right. I bought his guitar, and I'll take it aboard with me. I'm in with a cargo of blasting powder, and I can't clear till I've signed a million of their damned papers. Be at the dock at midnight sharp. I'll lift my hook shortly after."

I left him, my heels lifting like they had grown wings. Everything said lay low until midnight, and never go back to the hotel. But I hadn't eaten yet, and I couldn't make myself go in a café and sit down alone. Along about nine o'clock I walked on up there.

I no sooner turned in the patio before I could see there was something going on. Two or three oil lamps were stuck around, on stools, and some candles. Our car was still where I had left it, but a big limousine was parked across from it, and the place was full of people. By the limousine was a stocky guy, dark taffy-colored, in an officer's uniform with a star on his shoulder and an automatic on his hip, smoking a cigarette. She was sitting on the running board of our car. In between, maybe a couple of dozen Mexicans were lined up. Some of them seemed to be guests of the hotel, some of them the hired help, and the last one was the *hostelero*. Two soldiers with rifles were searching them. When they got through with the *hostelero* they saw me, came over, they grabbed me, stood me up beside him, and searched me too. I never did like a bum's rush, especially by a couple of gorillas that didn't even have shoes.

When the searching was over, the guy with the star started up the line, jabbering at each one in Spanish. That took quite a while. When he got to me he gave me the same mouthful, but she said something and he stopped. He looked at me sharp, and jerked his thumb for me to stand aside. I don't like a thumb any better than I like a bum's rush.

He fired an order at the soldiers then, and they began going in and out of the rooms. In a minute one of them gave a yell and came running out. The guy with the star went in with them, and they came out with our beans, our eggs, our ground corn, our pots, bowls, charcoal, machetes, everything that had been packed on the car. A woman began to wail and the *hostelero* began to beg. Nothing doing. The guy with the star and the soldiers grabbed them and hustled them out of the court and up the street. Then he barked something else and waved his hand. The whole mob slunk to their rooms, and you could hear them in there mumbling and some of them moaning. He walked over to her, put his arm around her, and she laughed and they talked in Spanish. Quick work, getting the stolen stuff back, and he wanted appreciation.

She went into No. 16 and came out with the hatbox and the other stuff. He opened the door of the limousine.

"Where you going with that guy?"

I didn't know I was going to say it. My play was to stand there and let her go, but this growl came out of my mouth without my even intending it. She turned around, and her eyes opened wide like she couldn't believe what she heard. "But please, he is *politico.*"

"I asked you where you're going with him."

"But yes. You stay here. I come *mañana,* very early. Then we looked at house, yes."

She was talking in a phoney kind of way, but not to fool me. It was to fool him, so I wouldn't get in trouble. She kept staring at me, trying to get me to shut up. I was standing by our car, and he came over and snapped something. She came over and spoke to him in Spanish, and he seemed satisfied. The idea seemed to be that I was an American, and was all mixed up on what it was about. I licked my lips, tried to make myself take it easy, play it safe till I got on that boat. I tried to tell myself she was nothing but an Indian girl, that she didn't mean a thing with me, that if she was going off to spend the night with this cluck it was no more than she had done plenty of times before, that she didn't know any different and it was none of my business anyway. No dice. Maybe if she hadn't looked so pretty out there in the moonlight I might have shut up, but I don't think so. Something had happened back in that church that made me feel she belonged to me. I heard my mouth growl again. "You're not going."

"But he is *politico*—"

"And because he's *político,* and he's fixed you up with a lousy sailor's whorehouse, he thinks he's going to take part of his graft in trade. He made a mistake. You're not going."

"But—"

He stepped up, then, and shot a rattle at me in Spanish, so close I could feel the spit on my face. We hadn't been talking loud. I was too sore to yell, and Mexicans say it soft. He finished, straightened up, and jerked his thumb at me again, toward the hotel. I let him have it. He went down. I stamped my foot on his hand, grabbed the pistol out of the holster. "Get up."

He didn't move. He was out cold. I looked at the hotel. All you could hear was this mumbling and moaning. They hadn't heard anything at all. I jerked open the car door and shoved her in, hatboxes and all. Then I ran around, threw the pistol on the seat, jumped in and started. I went out of the court in second, and by the time I hit the road I was in high.

I snapped on the lights and gave her the gun. In a few seconds I was in the town, and then I knew what a mistake I had made when I came out of that court, and cut right instead of left. I had to get out of there, and get out of there quick before that guy came to, and I couldn't turn around. I mean literally I couldn't turn around. The street was so narrow, and so choked with burros, pigs, goats, *mariachis,* and people, that even when you met a car you had to saw by, and a turn was impossible. It was no through street. It went through the town, and then, at the hill, it led up to the big tourist hotel, and that was the end of it. I crawled along now, the sweat coming out on my brow, and got to the bottom of the hill. There was no traffic there, but it was still narrow. I turned right on a side road. I thought I might hit a way, after a block or two, that would lead back where I had come from. I didn't. The street just tapered off into two tracks on an open field, that as far as I could see just wandered up in the hills. I pulled into the field, to turn around. I thought I still might have time to slip back through the town, though it didn't look like even Jess Willard could stay out that long. Then back of me I heard shots, yells, and the screech of a motorcycle siren. It was too late. I was cut off. I doused the lights and bumped over to a grove of coconut palms, where anyway I would be shaded from the moonlight.

I lined up toward the town, so I could see, and tried to think. It all depended on whether I had been noticed, turning off the main street. If I hadn't, I might be able to lay low till the moon went down and they were asleep, then go through the town fast, and be on my way to Mexico City before they even knew I had got away. I tried not to think about the ship.

In a minute or so, the sirens began to screech louder, and three single lights streaked out of town around the harbor. That meant they had no idea I was still around. They thought I was on my way to Mexico, and were out after me. That meant we would be safe here for a little while, maybe the whole night. But where it put me, when I did start up to Mexico, and met those patrols coming back, I hated to think. And Mexico was the only place you could go. There wasn't any other road.

We sat there a long time, and then I knew she was crying. "Why you do this? Why you do this to me?"

"Don't you know? Why I—" I tried to make myself say "I love you," but it stuck in my throat. "*I* wanted you. I didn't want him to have you."

"That is not true. You go away."

"What makes you say that?"

"You sing now, yes? You sing better anybody in Mexico. You stay in Acapulco, in a house? Why you lie? You go away."

"I never even thought of it."

"Now for me, very bad. No house, no. Maybe he shoot me, yes. I can no work more in Mexico. He is very big *político*. I— why you do this? Why you do this?"

We sat there some more, and I wondered why I didn't feel like a heel. She had called it on me all right, and I had certainly busted up her run of luck with plenty to spare. But I didn't feel like a heel. I was in a spot, but my face wasn't red. Then it hit me between the eyes: *I wasn't going to run out on her.*

"Juana."

"Yes?"

"Listen to me now. I've got some things to say."

"Please, say nothing."

"In the first place, you were right when you said I was going away, and I did lie to you. While I was out, pretending to look the town over, I arranged passage to the *Estados Unidos del Norte,* on a boat. I was to leave at twelve o'clock."

"I know you lie, when you go out. Yes."

"All right, I lied. You want to hear the rest?"

She didn't answer for a long time. But you could always tell when something was going on inside of her, because her breath would stop for a two beat, and then go on. She turned her head to me once, and then looked away. "Yes."

"When I went up to the hotel, I intended to take you out to dinner, sit around a while, then drift out to the *caballeros,* and not come back. Then you started off with him, and I knew I wasn't going to let you go, and it wasn't only that I didn't like him. I wanted you myself, and I wasn't going to let him have you, or anybody have you."

"But why?"

"I'll get to that. I'm not done yet. Now I'm going away. I told you I used to be a singer. I used to be a very good singer, one of the best in the world, and I made a lot of money, and I will again. But I can't do anything in Mexico. I'm going back to my own country, the *Estados Unidos del Norte.* Now, here's what I'm getting at. Do you want to come with me?"

"Is that very big country?"

"Much bigger than Mexico."

"How you go?"

"We have the car, and you still have a little money. In a little while, after things quiet down, we'll slip through the town and go as far as we can before daylight. Then tomorrow night, we'll start out again, and with luck we'll make Mexico City.

We'll lay low another day, and the next night we'll be in Monterey. One more night and we're at Laredo, and I'll figure a way to get you across. Once we're in my country, we're all right."

"That is impossible."

"Why?"

"They know the auto. They catch us, sure."

I knew that was right, even before she said it. In the United States, once you're across a state line, you could go quite a while without being caught. But down there, the state line doesn't mean much. Those guys with rifles, they're federal troops, and with just a car now and then up that road, there wasn't a chance they would miss us, night time, day time, or any other time. ". . . In bus, perhaps."

"What was that, Juana?"

"Ride little way, hide auto. Then in morning, take bus. Maybe they no catch."

"All right, we'll do that."

"But why? Why you no go alone?"

"All right, now we come to the big why. You like me?"

"Yes, much."

"I like you."

I sat looking at her, wondering why I couldn't go the whole hog, tell her I loved her and be done with it. Then I remembered how many times I had sung those words, in three or four different languages, how phoney they sounded, and how much trouble I had in putting them across. Then it came to me that I hated them, not for what they said, but for what they didn't say. They told it all except what you felt in your bones, your belly, and all those other places. They said you might die for a woman, but missed how hungry you could get for her, just to be near her, just to know she was around. ". . . I could make it stronger than that, Juana. Maybe I don't have to."

"They catch us, sure. They kill us."

"You willing to take a chance?"

It was a long time before she said anything, and before she did she took my hand and pressed it. Then she looked up, and

I knew that whatever it was going to be, there was no fooling around about it. It was the works. . . . "Yes."

A little tingle went over me, but what I said was dumb enough. "Yes, what?"

"What do you mean?"

"Don't you think it's about time for us to pick out something for you to call me? I can't very well keep on being *Señor.*"

"I call you Hoaney."

I half wished she had picked out something different than what she had called every Weehawken slob that had showed up at her crib, but I didn't say anything. Then something caught my throat. It came to me that she wasn't calling me "Honey." She was calling me Johnny—her way. "Kiss me, Juana. That's exactly what I want you to call me."

The town was dark now, and quiet. I started, pulled out of the grove, and got over the road. As soon as I could I went into high, not for speed, but for quiet. With all that stuff out of the car we didn't make much noise, but I cut her back to the slowest roll that was in her, and we crept along until we got to the main street. I stopped, and listened. I didn't hear anything, so I started up again, and turned the corner, to the left. I hadn't put the lights on, and the moon was hanging low over the ocean, so the right side of the main street was in shadow. I had gone half a block when she touched my arm. I rolled in to the curb and stopped. She pointed. About three blocks down the street, on the left, where the moonlight lit him up, was a cop. He was walking away from us. He was the only one in sight. She leaned to me and whispered: "He go, so."

She motioned with her hand, meaning around the corner. That's how I went. I gave him about five seconds, then reached for the started. The car tilted. Somebody was beside me, on the running board. I still had the gun beside me. I snatched it and turned. A brown face was there, not six inches from mine. Then I saw it was Conners.

"Is that you, lad?"

"Yes. God, you gave me a start."

"Where've you been? I've been looking all over for you! I've broken out my hook, I'm ready to go, I'm out of humor with you."

"I got in some trouble."

". . . Don't tell me it was you that hit the general?"

"I did."

His eyes popped open and he began to talk in a whisper. "The penalty is death, lad, the penalty is death."

"Irregardless of that—"

"Not so loud. It's all over town. One of them could be sleeping, and if they hear the English, they'll yell and it'll be the end of you. . . . Did you mind what I said? The penalty is death. He'll take you to the jail and they'll spend an hour booking you, filling out every paper they've got. Then he'll take you out and have them shoot you—for trying to escape."

"If they catch me."

"They'll catch you. For God's sake, come on."

"I'm not coming."

"Did you hear me? The penalty—"

"Since I saw you, there are two of us. Miss Montes, Capitán Conners."

"I'm happy to know you, Miss Montes."

"*Gracias*, Capitán Conners."

He treated her like a princess, and she acted like one. But then he leaned close and put it in my ear. "You can't do it, man. You can't take up with some girl you met tonight, and you'll be putting her in terrible danger, too. She's a pretty little thing, but hark what I'm telling you. You must come on."

"I didn't just meet her tonight, and she's with me."

He looked up and down the street, and then at his watch. Then looked at me hard. "Lad—do you know the Leporello song?"

"I do."

"Then come on, the pair of you."

He slipped around the car and helped her out. She had the hatbox in her lap. He took it. She carried the other stuff. I grabbed the door, for fear he would slam it mechanically. He didn't. I slipped out on the right side, after her. He pulled us back of the car. "We'll keep the automobile between us and that policeman, down the street."

We tiptoed back to the corner I had just turned, and instead of going the way I had, he pulled us the other way, toward the beach. We came to a crooked alley, and turned into that.

Two minutes after that we trotted out on a dock, and dropped into a launch. Two minutes after that, we were on the deck of the *Port of Cobh,* with beer and sandwiches coming up. Two minutes after that we were slipping past the headland, and I was cocked back with a guitar on my knee, rolling the Leporello song out for him, and she was pouring beer.

6

It was a happy week, all right. I didn't sing much, except a little at night if he wanted it. Most of the time we sat around and fanned about music. She would be with us and then she wouldn't be. He gave us the royal suite, and the main feature was a shower bath, with sea water coming out of it. It was the first time she had been under one. Maybe it was the first time she ever had a bath, I don't know. Mexicans are the cleanest people on earth. Their face is clean, their feet are clean, their clothes are clean, and they don't stink. But when they bathe, or whether they bathe, I can't tell you. To her it was a new toy and every time I'd go looking for her I'd find her in there, stripped clean, under the water. I guess I generally hung around. She was something for a sculptor to hire, and she had just enough of the copper in her to make her look like something poured from metal, especially with the water shining on her shoulders. I didn't let her see me look, at first, but then I found out she liked it. She'd stand on her toes, and stretch her arms, and let her muscles ripple, and then laugh. So of course that led to this and that.

The second night out, he got off on a harangue against Verdi, Puccini, Mascagni, Bellini, Donizetti, and "that most unspeakable wop of all, Rossini." That was where I stopped him. "Hold on, hold on, hold on. On those others, I haven't got much to say. I sing them, but I don't talk about them, though Donizetti is a lot better than most people think. But on Rossini, you're crazy."

"The William Tell Overture is the worst piece of music ever written."

"There's music in it, but it's not his best."

"There's no music in it of any kind."

"Well, how's this?"

I picked up the guitar and gave him a little of Semiramide. You can't play a Rossini crescendo on a guitar, but I did what I could. He listened, his face set like flint. I finished and was going to start something else, when he touched my arm. "Play a little of that again."

I played it again, then gave him some Italians in Algiers, and then some Barber. It took quite a while. I know a lot of Rossini. I didn't sing, just played. On the woodwind strain in the Barber overture, I just brushed the strings with my fingers, then for the climax came in big over the hole, and it really sounded like something. I stopped, and he smoked his pipe a long time. " 'Tis fine, musicianly music, isn't it?"

"It's all of that. And it's no worse for being gay, and not taking itself too seriously."

"Aye, it has a twinkle in its eye, and a sparkle in its beat."

"Your friend Beethoven patronized him, the son-of-a-bitch. Told him to keep on writing tunes, that was what he was good for. All Rossini was doing at the time was trying to give him a lift, so he wouldn't have to live like a hog in the dump he found him in."

"If he patronized him it was his right."

"The hell it was. When a Beethoven overture is as good as a Rossini overture, then it'll be his right. Until then, let him keep his goddam mouth shut."

"Lad, lad, you're profaning a temple."

"No, I'm not. You say he's the greatest composer that ever lived, and so do I. He wrote the nine greatest symphonies ever put on paper, and that makes him the greatest composer. But listen, symphonies are not all of music. When you get to the overtures, Beethoven's name is not at the top, and Rossini's is. The idea of a man that could write a thing like the Leonora No. 3 high-hatting Rossini. Why, when those horns sound off, off-stage, it's a cheap vaudeville effect that makes the William Tell Overture sound like a Meistersinger's Prelude, by comparison."

"I confess I don't like it."

"Oh yeah, he would show the boys how to write an overture, wouldn't he? He didn't have overtures in him. You know why? To write an overture, you've got to love the theatre, and he didn't. Did you ever hear Fidelio?"

"I have, and it shames me—"

"But Rossini loved the theatre, and that's why he could write an overture. He takes you into the theatre—hell, you can even feel them getting into their seats, and smell the theatre smell, and see the lights go up on the curtain. Who the hell told Beethoven he could treat that guy as somebody with an amusing talent that he ought to cultivate?"

"Just the same he was a great man."

I played the minuet from the Eighth Symphony. You can get most of that on the guitar. ". . . That was something to hear. By the way you play him, lad, you think he's a great man yourself, I take it?"

"Yes."

"The other too. From now on I shall listen to him." We were several days out before he got around to McCormack, and he kind of brought it up offhand, as we were sitting on deck at sundown, like it was just something he happened to think of. But when he found out I thought McCormack was one of the greatest singers that ever lived, he began to talk. "So you say the singers admire the fellow?"

"Admire him? Does a ballplayer admire Ty Cobb?"

"Between ourselves, I'm no enthusiast for the art. As you've observed, I'm a symphony man myself, and I believe the great music of the world has been written for fiddlers, not singers.

But with McCormack I make an exception. Not because he's an Irishman, I give you my word on that. You were right about Herbert. If there's one thing an Irishman hates more than a landlord it's another Irishman. 'Tis because he makes me feel music I had previously been indifferent to. I don't speak of the ballads he sings, mush a man wouldn't spit into. But I have heard him sing Händel. I heard him sing a whole program of Händel at a private engagement in Boston."

"He can sing it, all right."

"Until then, I had not cared for Händel, but he revealed it to me. 'Tis something to be grateful for, the awakening to Händel. What is the reason for that? I've heard a million of your Wops, Frogs and Yankees sing Händel, aye and plenty of Englishmen, but not one of them can sing it the way that fellow can."

"Well, in the first place, he's good. That's something you can't quite cut up into pieces and measure off. And when a man's good, he's generally good all the way down the line. McCormack has music in him, so he no sooner opens his trap than there's a tingle to it, no matter what he sings. He has an instinct for style that never lets him down. He never drags an andante too slow, or hustles an allegro too fast. He never turns a dumb phrase, or forces, or misgauges a climax. When he does it, it's always right, with a big R. What he did for Händel was to bring it to life for you. Up to then, you probably thought it was pale, thin, tinkle-tankle stuff—"

"To my shame I did."

"And then he stepped into it, like a bugler at dawn—"

"That's it, that's it, like a bugler at dawn. You can't imagine what it was like, lad. He stood there, the most arrogant figure of a man I ever saw, with his chest thrown out and his head thrown back, and his thumbs in his little black book of words, like a cardinal starting the mass. And without a word, he began to sing. And the sun came up, and the sun came up."

"And in the second place—"

"Yes, lad, in the second place?"

"He had a great voice."

"He could have the Magic Flute in his throat and I'd never know it."

"Well, he goddam near *had* the Magic Flute in his throat, if somebody happened to ask you. And your ears knew it, even if your head didn't. He had a *great* voice, not just a good voice. I don't mean big. It was never big, though it was big enough. But what makes a great voice is beauty, not size, and beauty will get you, I don't care if it's in a man's throat or a woman's leg."

"You may be right. I hadn't thought of it."

"And in the third place—"

"Go on, 'tis instructive to me."

"—There's the language he was born to. John McCormack comes from Dublin."

"He does not. He comes from Athlone."

"Didn't he live in Dublin?"

"No matter. They speak a fine brogue in Athlone, almost as fine as in Belfast."

"It's a fine brogue, but it's not a brogue. It's the English language as it was spoken before all the other countries of the world forgot how to speak it. There's two things a singer can't buy, beg or steal, and that no teacher, coach or conductor can give him. One is his voice, the other is the language that was born in his mouth. When McCormack was singing Händel he was singing English, and he sings it as no American and no Englishman will ever sing English. But not like an Irishman. Not with all that warmth, color, and richness that McCormack puts into it."

"'Tis pleasant to hear you say that."

"You speak a fine brogue yourself."

"I try to say what I mean."

We were creeping past Ensenada, four or five miles out, and we smoked a while without saying anything. The sea was like glass, but you could see the hotel in the setting sun, and the white line of surf around the harbor. We smoked a while, but I'm a bit of a bug on that subject of language, and what a man brings on stage with him besides what he was taught. I started up again, and told him how all the great Italian singers have come from the city of Naples, and gave him a few examples of singers with fine voices that never made the grade because they were bums, and people won't listen to bums. About that, I knew plenty. Then I got off on Mexico, and about that, I guess you can realize I was pretty bitter. I began getting it off my chest. He listened, but pretty soon he stopped me. "Not so fast, lad, not so fast. 'Tis instructive that Caruso came from Naples, as McCormack came from Athlone, and that it was part of his gift, but when you speak so of Mexico, I take exception."

"I say they can't sing because they can't talk."

"They talk soft."

"They talk soft, but they talk on top of their throats—and *they've got nothing to say!* Listen, you can't spend a third of your life on the dirt floor of an adobe hut, and then expect people to listen to you when you stand up and try to sing Mozart. Why, sit down, you goddam Indian, and—"

"I'm losing patience with you."

"Did you ever hear them sing?"

"I don't know if they can sing, and I don't care. But they're a great people."

"At what? Is there one thing they do well?"

"Life is not all doing. It's part being. They're a great people. The little one in there—"

"She's an exception."

"She's not. She's a typical Mexican, and I should know one when I see her by now. I've been sailing these coasts for fifty years. She speaks soft, and holds herself like the little queen that she is. There's beauty in her."

"I told you, she's an exception."

"There's beauty in them."

"Sure, the whole goddam country is a musical comedy set, if that's what you mean. But when you get past the scenery and the costumes, what then? Under the surface what do you find? Nothing!"

"I don't know what I find. I'm no great hand at words, and

it would be hard for me to say what I find. But I find *something*. And I know this much: if it's beauty I feel, then it must be under the surface, because beauty is *always* under the surface."

"Under the bedrock, in that hellhole."

"I think much about beauty, sitting alone at night, listening to my wireless, and trying to get the reason of it, and understand how a man like Strauss can put the worst sounds on the surface that ever profaned the night, and yet give me something I can sink my teeth into. This much I know: True beauty has *terror* in it. Now I shall reply to your contemptuous words about Beethoven. He has *terror* in him, and your overture writers have not. Fine music they wrote, and after your remarks I shall listen to them with respect. But you can drop a stone into Beethoven, and you will never hear it strike bottom. The eternities and the infinities are in it, and they strike at the soul, like death. You mind what I'm telling you, there is terror in the little one too, and I hope you never forget it in your relations with her."

There wasn't much I could say to that. I had felt the terror in her, God knows. We lit up again, and watched Ensenada turn gray, blue and violet. My cigarettes were all gone by then, and I was smoking his tobacco, and one of his pipes, that he had cleaned out for me on a steam jet in the boiler. Not a hundred feet from the ship a black fin lifted out of the water. It was an ugly thing to see. It was at least thirty inches high, and it didn't zigzag, or cut a V in the water, or any of the things it does in books. It just came up and stayed a few seconds. Then there was the swash of a big tail and it went down.

"Did you see it, lad?"

"God, it was an awful-looking thing, wasn't it?"

"It cleared up for me what I've been trying to say to you. Sit here, now, and look. The water, the surf, the colors on the shore. You think they make the beauty of the tropical sea, aye, lad? They do not. 'Tis the knowledge of what lurks below the surface of it, that awful-looking thing, as you call it, that carries death with every move that it makes. So it is, so it is with all beauty. So it is with Mexico. I hope you never forget it."

■　■

We docked at San Pedro around three in the afternoon, and all I had to do was walk ashore. He gave me dollars for our pesos, so I wouldn't have any trouble over that part, and came down the plank with me. It took about three seconds. I was an American citizen, I had my passport, they looked at it, and that was all. I had no baggage. But she was different, and how she was going to get ashore was making me pretty nervous. He had her below decks, under cover, and so far so good, but that didn't mean she was in, by a long way. He didn't seem much upset, though. He walked through the pier with me, waving at his friends, stopping to introduce me to his broker, taking it easy. When he got to the loading platform outside, he stood there and lit a cigar his broker had given him. "Across there is a little cove they call Fish Harbor. It is reached by a ferry, and you should find out how to get there this afternoon, but don't arrive before dark, as you should not be seen hanging around. By the wharves runs a street, and on the main thoroughfare leading down to it is a little Japanese restaurant, about a stone's throw from the water. Be there at nine o'clock, sharp. Order beer, and drink it slowly till I come."

He clapped me on the shoulder, and went back to the ship. I walked down and found how the ferry ran. Then I went in a lunchroom and had something to eat. Then I went in a moving picture, so I could sit down. I don't even know what the show was. Every fifteen or twenty minutes I would go out in the lobby to look at the clock. Whatever it was, I saw it twice. Around seven I left the theatre and walked down to the ferry. It was quite a while coming, but just about dark it showed up and I went across. It took about ten minutes. I walked down to Fish Harbor, found it without having to ask anybody about it, and then spotted the restaurant. I walked past it, then found a clock and checked on the time. It was half past eight. I walked on to where the street turned into a road, and kept on going until I figured I had covered three quarters of a mile. Then I turned around and came back. When I passed the clock it said five minutes to nine.

■ ■

I went in and ordered beer. There were five or six guys in there, fishermen by their looks, and I raised my glass at them, and they raised back. I didn't want to act like some mysterious stranger, looking neither right nor left. After that they paid no attention to me. At ten after he came in. He shook hands all around in a big way, then sat down with me, and ordered beer. They seemed to know him. When his beer came, he sent the Jap out for a cab, and then began telling me, and telling them, about this trouble he had on his ship. He had his things packed, and was all ready to come ashore, when a launch showed up out of the night, and began yelling up at the pier for somebody named Charlie. "They kept it up, until I got so sick of Charlie I could have thrown a pin at them."

He was pretty funny, but I wasn't in the humor for it. They were, though. "Who was Charlie?"

"I never did find out. But wait a minute. Of course my second officer had his face out the hatch, ogling the girls, and do you know what the young upstart did? He called out: 'Forget about Charlie! Come aboard, girls. I'll give you a hand through the hatch—and let a real man take care of you!' And before I knew it he had a line down, they had made the launch fast, and they were aboard my ship!"

"What did you do?"

"I was down there in a flash and I ordered them off! 'Off and begone!' I said to them. 'Out of the hatch where you came in, and let me see no more of you!'"

"Did they go?"

"They did not! They stood laughing at me, and invited me to go with them! Then the man that was with them seconded the invitation, and my second officer had the effrontery to second him. I was so furious I could not trust myself to speak. But then with an effort, I got myself under control, and I said to him: ' 'Tis an official matter,' I reminded him, 'to be entered on your papers and reported to your owners. Get these girls out of here, and at once.' Do you know what those girls said to me?"

"What they say?"

" 'Nuts.' "

That got a laugh. "I argued with them. I pleaded with them, as I didn't want any trouble. At last I had to appeal to the guard on the pier, who was standing there, looking down into the hatch, listening to it. 'Is that right, my man?' I said to him, 'that such entry into a ship is in violation of law? That they must enter by the plank, and pass the guard, otherwise be subject to arrest?' "

" 'It is, captain,' he said, 'and they'll not pass the guard if I have anything to do with it.' "

"That seemed to frighten them, and out they went, the girls, the man and my second officer. Him I will deal with in the morning. But what I cannot understand about these American girls is the boldness of them. Not one of them could have been more than nineteen, and where were their mothers all that time? What were they doing in that launch at all? Will you tell me that?"

They all chimed in with what a tough bunch the young girls are nowadays, and then the Jap came in and said the cab was ready. He paid, and we took the valise he had brought with him, and went out and put it in the cab, and he told the driver to wait. Then he started to walk down toward the wharves. "Well, what about her?"

He didn't seem to hear me. " 'Twas a noisy ten minutes. Of course, if the guard on the pier had been observant, he would have noticed that the man in the launch was my first officer. He would also have noticed that whereas three young girls came into the hatch, four of them went out of it."

"Oh."

We got to the wharves, strolled out on one, then strolled back, and stood on the corner, smoking. Out in the basin somewhere a launch started up. In a minute or two it slipped in to the wharf, stopped a second, and she hopped ashore and came running to us. Then it shoved off and disappeared. I had wanted to go down and thank those guys for all they had done for us, but he wouldn't let me. "I'll tell them all you say. The three girls they found have no idea what they've been a party to, and the less they know, the less they have to tell. They will see a nice picture show, now, and that's enough."

It was always catching me by surprise, how glad I was to be with her, and I got this catch in my throat when she came running up to us, laughing like it had all been a big joke. We walked back to the cab, got in, and told the driver to take the ferry and go to the nearest Los Angeles bus stop. She sat in the middle and I took her hand. He looked out the window. She turned to him, but he kept staring at the buildings going by. Then she reached out and took his hand. He came out of it on that. He took her hand in both of his, and patted it, but it was a minute or two before he said anything. "... There's something I'd like to say to both of you. I've enjoyed every minute of your stay on my ship. I wish you all happiness, and as you're in love, you may have it. 'Tis a big world, and I bob around it like a cork in a tub. But should you ever need me, and should I be there, you have only to say the word. Only to say the word."

"... *Gracias,* Señor Capitán.—... This big world, I go around, too ... But, you need me—you say word, say word only."

"Me too."

"... 'Tis a pretty night."

On the ferry the driver went forward to have a smoke, and we were alone. He sat up and began to talk. "Her things are all in the valise. It holds them better than her own little box, especially that sword that she carries with her. She's wearing no hat, and it would be a good idea if you were to stow your own hat with her stuff. You're both well burned by the sun, and without hats you could well be a couple that has spent a day at the beach, and arouse no suspicion that you're just off a boat."

I opened the valise, put my hat in it, and he went on. "Inquire of the busman, and get off as near what they call the Plaza as you can. In that neighborhood are many small hotels catering to Mexicans of the town, and you will attract no attention. Register as Mr. and Mrs. Perhaps you will not believe it, but under American laws you must write it so, and so long as you do, they will not care. In the morning, get up very early, and as soon as you can, get a hat on her. I have packed all her shawls, and forbidden her to carry one, as they will betray her sooner than anything else. I doubt if she has ever had a hat on in her life, so be careful that you pick one yourself, a little hat exactly like all the other hats in the place. When you have bought the hat, buy her a little dress. I know nothing of girls' clothes myself, but her little things make me think of Mexico, and sharper eyes than mine might become suspicious. Buy her a dress like every other dress in the place. When you have bought her a hat and bought her a dress, you can breathe easier about illegal entry. Her accent will attract no attention. In America are as many accents as the countries of the world, and she could have lived here all her life and still speak as she does. But the clothes will mark her. She should meet few Mexicans. There is a belief among them that the United States government pays informers against immigrants of her kind. It does not, but one of them might turn her in for the sake of the legendary reward. As soon as you can, get work. A working man is his own answer to all questions, an idle man is a riddle they all try to guess. It would be a good idea if she learned to read and write."

We got out at the bus stop, and shook hands, and then she put her arms around him and kissed him. He was shaken up as I stepped over to help him into the cab. "And you'll mind what I've been telling you, lad?—about her, and Mexico, and all the rest of it?"

"I'll mind. For the rest of my life."

"See that you do. For the rest of your life."

We found a little hotel, a two-dollar joint on Spring Street, and didn't have any trouble. It was about what you would expect, but after Mexico it was like a palace, and they gave us a room with a shower, so she was happy. After she had splashed enough water to suit her, she came and lay in my arms, and I lay there thinking about how we were starting our life together in my own country, and wanted to say something about it, but next thing I knew she was asleep. We got up early the next morning, and as soon as the stores were open, went out to get that hat. Then we got a dress and a light coat. The hat was $1.95, the dress $3.79, and the coat $6. That left us $38 out of her 500 pesos. We stopped by a little restaurant, had a little breakfast, and then I took her back to the hotel and went out to find work.

First thing I did was wire my agent in New York, the one that had sent me down to Mexico. I told her I was all right again, and to see what she could do, as I wanted to get going. Then I bought a Variety, the Hollywood edition, and looked in there to see if any agents carried ads. Quite a few of them did, and the one that seemed to be what I wanted was named Stoessel, and had offices in Hollywood, so I got on a bus and went out there. It took me an hour to get in to see him, and he never even bothered to look at me. "Brother, out here singers are a drug on the market, and they've quit fooling with them. They've had them all, and how many come through? Eddy, MacDonald, Pons, Martini, and Moore—and even Pons and Martini ain't so hot. The rest of them, flops, nothing but flops. And it ain't only that they flop, they have a hell of a time getting stories for them. They're through with singers. When they want a singer, little production number maybe, they know where to get him. Outside of that—out. I'm sorry, but you're in the wrong place."

"I didn't mean pictures. How about theatres?"

"I could book you twelve weeks straight, right up the coast, book you in a minute, if you was a name. Without a name for the marquee, you ain't worth a dime."

"I'm fairly well known."

"I never heard of no John Howard Sharp."

"I sang mainly in Europe."

"This ain't Europe."

"How about night clubs?"

"I don't fool with that small stuff. You want to go on in a night club, there's plenty of them around. If that interests you, you might pick up quite a little time here and there, this and that. Try Fanchon and Marco. Maybe they got a spot for you."

I walked down on Sunset, to Fanchon and Marco. They were putting up a dance act, and a singer didn't seem to fit. I went in a radio station. They gave me an audition, and said they'd let me have some sustaining time in the afternoon, but they wouldn't pay for it, and I'd have to bring my own accompanist. I said I'd be back.

Around four o'clock I went in a night club on La Brea, and they let me sing for them, and then said they'd put me on, $7.50 a night, tips and meals, report in evening clothes at nine o'clock. I said I'd let them know. I found a costume place to go in and rent an evening outfit. The price was $3 a night, $10 by the week, and that would leave a little profit, but they had nothing in there that would fit. I'm six feet, and weighed nearly two hundred, and that's an out size for a costume place. I went back to Spring Street. There was a little place still open, and I went in and bought a second-hand guitar for $5. I wasn't going to pay an accompanist to get me on the air. With that guitar, I could do my own accompanying.

I kept that up three or four days. I parked the guitar in the radio station, and went in there every day at two thirty. I was to get fifteen minutes, and be announced under my name, but when I cut myself up into two pieces, John Howard Sharp, baritone, and Signor Giuseppe Bondo, the eminent Italian guitar player, they gave me a half hour. I'd sing a couple of numbers, and then I'd introduce the Signor, and the Signor would announce his selections in a high voice, in Italian. Then I'd try to translate, and get it all wrong, so if I said it was to be Hearts and Flowers, the Signor would play Liebestraum, or something like that. The station manager thought that was a pretty good gag, and made us a regular feature, and put our names in the paper. After the second day he got twenty or thirty letters about me, and two or three hundred about the Signor, and he got all excited and said he was going to find a sponsor for us. A sponsor, it turned out, was an advertiser that would pay us.

One of those days, after the broadcast, I took the guitar out with me and went to Griffith Park, where the Iowa Society was having a picnic, forty or fifty thousand of them. I thought if I went singing around, there might be some tips. I had never taken a tip, and I wondered how I was going to feel about it. I needn't have worried. The Iowa Society liked me fine, but none of them dug into their pocket. But next day I went in the Biltmore, where the Rotary Club was having lunch. I marched right in with the guitar, just like I was supposed to be there, and when I got into the dining-room I went to the center of the U table that they were all sitting around, hit a chord and started to sing. I picked the Trumpeter, because you can rip into it right from the start without any waiting around for a chorus to get started on. A captain and three waiters hustled over to throw me out, but two or three of them yelled, "Let him alone! Let him alone!"

I got a hand, and piled a couple of numbers on top of it. I

remember one of them was the Speaks Mandalay. Then some egg up in the corner began to yell, "Pollyochy! Pollyochy!" I didn't think it was a Pagliacci crowd, so I didn't pay any attention to him, but he kept it up, and then some of the others yelled "Pollyochy!" too, mostly to shut him up. So I whammed into the introduction, and began singing the Prologue. It's not my favorite piece of music, but I do it all right, and at the end of the andante I gave them plenty of A flat. By rights, you sing A flats for dough, and for nothing else, but it had been a long time since anybody wanted to hear mine. I swelled it and cut, and then on the E flat that follows it I shook the windows. When I finished I got a big hand, and gave them some Trovatore and Traviata.

When it was time for the speeches the president, or chairman, or whatever he was, called me up, and told me to wait, and they began making up a pot for me. They borrowed a tray from a waiter and passed it around and when it came back it was full of silver. He handed it to me, and I thanked him, and dumped it in my pocket. I had taken a tip, but I didn't feel anything. I went out in the washroom to count it.

It was $6.75, but we were getting low, getting low. Even with that, we were down to $22, and nobody showing the least interest in John Howard Sharp. Still, there was an outdoor performance of Carmen that night at the Hollywood Bowl, at a dollar and a half top but with some seats at seventy-five cents, so of course we had to go. If you want to know where to find an opera singer the night some opera is being given you'll find him right there, and no other place. A baseball player, for some reason, prefers a ball game.

So I told her to get dressed, so we could eat early, and try to get out there in time to get some kind of decent seat. By that time she had quit playing with the shower bath to play with the hat. She'd put it on, and take it off, and put it on again, and look at herself in the mirror, and ask if she had it on right, then take it off and start all over again. I generally said it looked swell, but it was funny how dumb she was, catching on to how it worked. Up to then, I had always thought of a woman's hat as something that she put on, and forgot about, and that was that. But the way she did it, was the funniest-looking thing you ever saw in your life. Half the time she would get it on backwards, and even when she didn't, she would pull it down on her head some way that made it look like it didn't even belong to her. I tried the best I could and it was better than her way, but it always looked like a man's necktie would if somebody else tied it for him.

It was a warm night, so she wasn't wearing the coat. She decided to wear the bullfighter's cape. It looked pretty swell, so it was all right with me. When she had laid it out, she came over for me to put the finishing touches on the hat. I fixed it so it looked almost right and then she went over to the mirror to have a look. She gave it one last pull that made it all wrong, put on the cape, and turned around to be admired. "Am I very pretty?"

"You're the prettiest thing in the world."

"Yes."

The curtain was advertised at eight thirty, and we got there at seven thirty, but I found out I didn't even know what early meant on a night when they're giving opera in the Hollywood Bowl. Most of those people, I think, had been there since breakfast. The best we could get was up on the rim, at least a quarter of a mile from the show. It was the first time I had ever seen the Hollywood Bowl, and maybe you've never been in it. It's so big you can't believe it. It was just about dark when we got there, and they were pouring into it through every ramp, and everywhere you looked there were people. I counted the house as well as I could, and by my figuring when they all got in there would be twenty thousand of them. As it turned out, that was about right. I sat there wondering whether they used amplifiers or what the hell they did. It frightened you to think of singing in such a place.

I looked on the program to see who was singing. I had heard of a couple of them. The José and the Micaela were second-line

Metropolitan people. There was a program note on the Carmen. She was a local girl. I know the Escamillo. He was a wop named Sabini that sang Silvio in Palermo one night when I was singing Tonio. I hadn't heard of him in five years. The rest of them I didn't know.

They played the introduction and the lights went up and we began to have a good time. I'm telling you, that was opera that you dream about. They didn't have any curtain. They put the lights up, and there it was, and when they finished they blacked out and came up with a baby spot for the bows. The orchestra was down front. Beyond was a low flight of wide steps, and quite a way beyond that was the stage, without the shell they use for concerts. On that they built a whole town, the guardhouse on one side, cafés on the other, the cigarette factory in back. You had to rub your eyes to believe you weren't in Spain. The way they lit it was great. They've got a light box in that Bowl that tops anything I ever saw. And that stage town was just filled with people. The performance seemed to be given with some kind of hook-up between a ballet school and some local chorus, and they must have had at least three hundred out there. When the bell rang and the girls began pouring out of the factory, they poured out. It was really lunch time. Between acts, they rolled that stuff off, and rolled on the café for the second act, and the rocks for the third act, and the bullring entrance for the fourth act. The place is so big that with the lights down nobody paid any attention to what they were doing out there. They didn't use any amplifiers. Big as it was, the acoustics were so perfect you could hear every whisper. That was the thing I couldn't get over.

The principals were just fair, maybe not as good as that, except for the two from the Met, but I didn't mind. They were giving a performance, and that's enough. So when this little thing happened, I didn't pay any attention to it. A singer can spot trouble a mile away, but I was there for a good time, so what the hell? But then I woke up.

What happened was that in the middle of the scene in the first act, where the soldiers bring Carmen out from the factory after she's cuffed another girl around, a chorister in a uniform stepped up to the Zuniga, jerked his thumb backstage, and began to sing the part. The Zuniga walked out. That was all. They did it so casually that it almost seemed like part of the opera, and I don't think twenty people out there thought anything of it. You would have had to know the opera to have spotted it. I wondered about it, because the Zuniga had a pretty good bass voice, and he had been doing all right. But I was listening to the Carmen, and she started the Seguidilla before I tumbled to what was up.

I jumped up, grabbed the bullfighter cape off her, whipped off my own coat and put it on her, and pointed down the hill. "Meet me after it's over! You understand?"

"Where you go?"

"Never mind. Meet me there. You got it?"

"Yes."

I skipped around the rim, took the ramp on the run, ducked back of the stage, and asked a stagehand for the manager. He pointed to some cars that were parked out back. I went back there, and sure enough, there was the Zuniga, still in his captain's uniform, and a fat guy, standing by a car and arguing with somebody inside. I tapped the fat guy on the shoulder. He batted at me with his hand and didn't even look. "I'm busy. See me later."

"Goddamn it, I'm singing your Escamillo for you!"

"Get the hell away!"

"What's the matter with you—are you snowed in? You called this guy off to get dressed—*and he can't sing it!*"

The Zuniga turned around. "You heard him, Morris. I can't sing F's. I can't do it."

"I've heard you do it."

"Transposed, yes."

"They'll set it down for you!"

"How? They can't rescore a whole number between acts! They got no parts to set it down *with!*"

"For Christ sake! They can read it down—"

"They can like hell. It's out!"

About that time, the man in the car put his head out, and it was Sabini. When he saw me he grabbed me and began kissing me with one side of his mouth and selling me to the manager with the other. Then he began giving me an earful of Italian, a mile a minute, explaining to me he didn't dare get out of his car, didn't even dare to be seen, or his wife's process servers would get him, and that was why he couldn't sing. Then he did get out, on the far side, lifted a trunk out of the rumble, and called me around. He began stripping me, and as fast as he got one piece off me, he'd have a piece of the Toreador costume out of the trunk for me to put on. The manager lit a cigarette and stood there watching us. Then he went off. "It's up to the conductor."

There was a big roar from the Bowl that meant the first act was over. Sabini jumped in the car and snapped on the lights. I sat down in front of them and the Zuniga took the make-up kit and began making me up. He stuck on the *coleta* and I tried the hat. It fit. When the manager came back he had a young guy with him in evening clothes, the conductor. I got up and spoke. He looked me over. "You've sung Escamilla?"

"At least a hundred times."

"Where?"

"Paris, among other places. And not at the Opera. At the Comique, if that means anything to you."

"What name did you sing under?"

"In Italy, Giovanni Sciaparelli. In France and Germany my own, John Howard Sharp."

He gave me a look that would have curdled milk, turned his back, and beckoned to the Zuniga.

"Hey, what's the matter?"

"Yes, I've heard of you. And you're washed up."

I cut one loose they must have heard in Glendale.

"Does that sound like I'm washed up? Does it?"

"You lost your voice."

"Yeah, and I got it back."

He kept looking at me, opened his mouth once or twice to say something, then shook his head and turned to the manager. "It's no use, Morris. He can't do it. I just happened to think of that last act. . . . Mr. Sharp, I wish I could use you. It would pull us out of a spot. But for the sake of the ballet school, we've interpolated Arlésienne music into Act IV, and I've scored the baritone into it, and—"

"Oh, Arlésienne, hey? Listen: Cue me in. That's all I ask. Just cue me in!"

You think that's impossible, that a man can go on and sing stuff he never even saw? All right, once there was an old Aborn baritone that's dead now, by the name of Harry Luckstone, brother of Isidore Luckstone, the singing teacher. He had a cousin named Henry Myers, that writes a little music now and then. Myers had written a song, and he was telling Luckstone about it, and Luckstone said fine, he'd sing it.

"I haven't put it on paper yet—"

"All right, I'll sing it."

"Well, it goes like this—"

"God Almighty, does a man have to know a song to sing it? Get going on your goddam piano, and I'll sing it!"

And he sang it. Nobody but another singer knows how good a singer really is. Sure, I sang his Arlésienne for him. I got a look at his score after Act III, and what he had done was put some words to the slow part, let the baritone sing them, then have baritone and chorus sing them under the fast part, in straight counterpoint. I didn't even bother to look what the words were. I bellowed *"Auprès de ma blonde, qu'il fait bon, fait bon,"* and let it go at that. One place I shot past a repeat. The dancers were all frozen on one foot, ready to do the routine again, and there was I, camped on an E that didn't even belong there. He looked up, and I caught his eye, and hung on to it, and marched all around with it, while he spoke to his men and wigwagged to his ballerina. Then he looked up again, and I cut, and yelled, "Ha, ha, ha." He brought his stick down, the show was together again, and I began flapping the cape at the dancers. In the Toreador Song, on the long "Ah" that leads into the chorus, I broke out the cape and made a couple of passes at the bull. Not too much, you understand. A prop can kill a number. But enough that I got that swirl of crimson and yellow into it. It stopped the show, and he let me repeat the second verse.

Some time during the night I had been given a dressing room, and after the last bow I went there. My clothes were there, piled on the table, and Sabini's trunk. Instead of taking off the make-up first, I started with the costume, so he could get away, if he was still around. I had just stripped down to my underwear when the manager came in, to pay me off. He counted out fifty bucks, in fives. While he was doing it the process server came in. He had a summons to appear in court and a writ to attach costumes. It took all the manager and I could do to convince him I wasn't Alessandro Sabini, but after a few minutes he went. I was scared to death he would see the "A. S." on that trunk, and serve the writ anyhow, but he didn't think of that. The conductor came in and thanked me. 'You gave a fine performance, and I'd like you to know it was a pleasure to have somebody up there that could troupe a little."

"Thanks. I'm sorry about that bobble."

"That's what I'm talking about. When you gave me the chance to pull it out of the soup, that was what I call trouping. Anybody can make a mistake, especially when they're shoved out there the way you were, without even a rehearsal. But when you use your head—well, my hat's off to you, that's all."

"They be pleasant words. Thanks again."

"I don't think they even noticed it. Did they, Morris?"

"Notice it? Christ, they give it a hand."

I sat on the trunk, and we lit up, and they began telling me what the production cost, what the hook-up was, and some more things I wanted to know. Up to then I didn't even know their names. The conductor was Albert Hudson, who you've probably heard of by now, and if you haven't you soon will. The manager

was Morris Lahr, who you've never heard of, and never will. He
runs a concert series in the winter, and manages a couple of
singers, and now and then he puts on an opera. There's one
like him in every city, and if you ask me they do more for music
than the guys that get their name in the papers.

We were fanning along, me in my underwear with my make-up
still on, when the door opens and in pops Stoessel, the agent I
had been talking to not a week before. He had a little guy with
him, around fifty, and they stood looking at me like I was some
ape in a cage, and then Stoessel nodded. "Mr. Ziskin, I believe
you're right. He's the type. He's the type you been looking for.
And he sings good as Eddy."

"I need a big man, Herman. A real Beery type."

"He's better looking than Beery. And younger. A hell of a
sight younger."

"But he's rugged. You know what I mean? Tough. But in
the picture, he's got a heart like all outdoors, and that's where
the singing comes in. A accent I don't mind, because why? He's
got a heart like all outdoors, and a accent helps it."

"I know exactly what you mean, Mr. Ziskin."

"O.K., then, Herman. You handle it. Three fifty while he's
learning English, and then after the script is ready and we start
to shoot, five. Six weeks' guarantee, at five hundred."

Stoessel turned to Hudson and Lahr. "I guess Mr. Ziskin
don't need any introduction around here. He's interested in this
man for a picture. Tell him that much, will you? Then we give
him the rest of it."

Lahr didn't act like he was any too fond of Mr. Ziskin, or
Stoessel either, for that matter. "Why don't you tell him yourself?"

"He speak English?"

"He did a minute ago."

"Sure, I speak English. Shoot."

"Well, say, that makes it easy. O.K., then, you heard what
Mr. Ziskin said. Get your make-up off, put on your clothes, and
we'll go out and talk."

"We can talk right now."

I was afraid to take my make-up off, for fear he would know me. They still thought I was Sabini, I could see that, because there hadn't been any announcement about me, and I was afraid if he placed me there wouldn't be any three fifty or even one fifty. I was down, that day, and he knew it. "All right, then, we'll talk right now. You heard Mr. Ziskin's proposition. What do you say?"

"I say go climb a tree."

"Say, that's no way to talk to Mr. Ziskin."

"What the hell do you think a singer works for? Fun?"

"I know what they work for. I handle singers."

"I don't know whether you handle singers. Maybe you handle bums. If Mr. Ziskin has got something to say, let him say it. But don't waste my time talking about three hundred and fifty dollars a week. If it was a day, that would be more like it."

"Don't be silly."

"I'm not being silly. I'm booked straight through to the first of the year, and if I'm going to get out of those contracts it's going to cost me dough. If you want to pay dough, talk. If not, just let's stop where we are."

"What's your idea of dough?"

"I've told you. But I've been wanting to break into pictures, and to get the chance, I'll split the difference with you. I'll do a little better than that. A thousand a week, and it's a deal. But that's rock bottom. I can't cut it, and I can't shade it."

We had it hot for a half hour, but I stuck and they came around. I wanted it in writing, so Stoessel took out a notebook and pen and wrote a memo of agreement, about five lines. I got a buck out of my pants and made him a receipt for that, first of all. That bound them. But when we got that far I had to tell my name. I hated to say John Howard Sharp, but I had to. He didn't say anything. He tore out the leaf, waved it in the air, handed it to Ziskin to sign. "John Howard Sharp—sure, I've heard of him. Somebody was telling about him just the other day."

■ ■

They went, and a boy came in for Sabini's trunk, and Lahr went out and came back with a bottle and glasses. "Guy has broke into pictures, we got to have a drink on that.... *Where* did you say you were booked?"

"With the Santa Fe, mashing down ballast."

"Happy days."

"Happy days."

"Happy days."

The crowd was gone and she was all alone when I ran down the hill, waving the cape at her. She turned her back on me, started to walk to the bus stop. I pulled out the wad of five Lahr had given me. "Look, look, look!" She wouldn't even turn her head. I took my coat off her, put it on, and dropped the cape over her shoulders. "... I wait very long time."

"Business! I been talking business."

"Yes. Smell very nice."

"Sure we had a drink. But listen: get what I'm telling you. I been talking business."

"I wait very long."

I let her get to the bus stop, but I didn't mean to ride on a bus. I began yelling for a taxi. There weren't any, but a car pulled up, a car from a limousine service. "Take you any place you want to go, sir. Rates exactly the same as the taxis—"

Did I care what his rates were? I shoved her in, and that did it. She tried to stay sore, but she felt the cushions, and when I took her in my arms she didn't pull away. There weren't any kisses yet, but the worst was over. I halfway liked it. It was our first row over a little thing. It made me feel she belonged to me.

We went to the Derby and had a real feed. It was the first time I had been in a decent place for a year. But I didn't break the big news until we were back at the hotel, undressing. Then I kind of just slid into it. "Oh, by the way. I got a little surprise for you."

"Surprise?"

"I got a job in pictures."

"Cinema?"

"That's right. A thousand a week."

"Oh."

"Hell, don't you get it? We're rich! A thousand a week—not pesos, dollars! Three thousand, six hundred pesos every week! Why don't you say something?"

"Yes, very nice."

I didn't mean a thing to her! But when I took the cape, and stood up there in my drawers, and sang the Toreador song at her, like I had at the Bowl, that talked. She clapped her hands, and sat on the bed, and I gave her the whole show. The phone rang. The desk calling, to ask me to shut up. I said O.K., but send up a boy. When he came I gave him a five and told him to get us some wine. He was back in a few minutes and we got a little tight, the way we had that night in the church. After a while we went to bed, and a long while after that she lay in my arms, running her fingers through my hair. "You like me?"

"Yes, much."

"Did I sing all right?"

"Very pretty."

"Were you proud of me?"

"... You very fonny fallow, you, Hoaney. Why I be proud? I no sing."

"But *I* sang."

"Yes. I like. Very much."

8

I didn't like Hollywood. I didn't like it partly because of the way they treated a singer, and partly because of the way they treated her. To them, singing is just something you buy, for whatever you have to pay, and so is acting, and so is writing, and so is music, and anything else they use. That it might be good for its own sake is something that hasn't occurred to them yet. The only thing they think is good for its own sake is a producer that couldn't tell Brahms from Irving Berlin on a bet, that wouldn't know a singer from a crooner until he heard twenty thousand people yelling for him one night, that can't read a book until the scenario department has had a synopsis made, that can't even speak English, but that is a self-elected expert on music, singing, literature, dialogue, and photography, and generally has a hit because somebody lent him Clark Gable to play in it. I did all right, you understand. After the first tangle with Ziskin I kind of got the hang of how you handle things out there to get along. But I never liked it, not even for a second.

It turned out he wasn't the main guy on his lot, or even a piece of the main guy. He was just one producer there, and when I showed up the next morning he seemed even to have forgot my name. I had his piece of paper, so they had to pay me, but I wandered around for a week not knowing what I was supposed to do or where I was supposed to do it. You see, he didn't have his script ready. But my piece of paper said six weeks, and I mean to collect on it. After four or five days they shoved me in what they call a B picture, a Western about a cowboy that hates sheep and the sheep man's daughter, but then he finds some sheep caught in a blizzard and brings them home safe, and that fixes it all up. I couldn't see where it fixed anything, but it wasn't my grief. They had bought some news-reel stuff on sheep caught in the snow, and that seemed to be the main reason for the picture. The director didn't know I could sing, but I got him to let me spot a couple of campfire songs, and on the blizzard stuff, Git Along, Little Dogies, Git Along.

They finished it toward the end of September, and gave it a sneak preview in Glendale. I thought it was so lousy I went just out of curiosity to see how bad they would razz it. They ate it up. On the snow stuff, every time I came around the bend with a lamb in my arms, breaking trail for the sheep, they'd clap and stamp and whistle. Out in the lobby, after it was over, I caught just a few words between the producer, the director, and one of the writers. "B picture hell—it's a feature!"

"Christ, would that help the schedule! We're three behind now, and if we can make an extra feature out of this, would that be a break! Would that be a break!"

"We got to do retakes."

"We got to do it bigger, but it'll get by."

"It'll cost dough, but it's worth it."

She hadn't come with me. We were living in an apartment on Sunset by that time, and she was going to night school, trying to learn how to read. I went home and she had just gone to bed with her reader, Wisdom of the Ages, a book of quota-tions from poetry, all in big type, that she practiced on. I got out the guitar and some blank music paper that I had, and I went to work. I split up that song, Git Along, Little Dogies, Git

Along, into five-part harmony, one part the straight melody, the other four a quartet obbligato in long four-beat and eight-beat notes, and maybe you think it wasn't work. That song is nothing extra to start with, and when you try to plaster polyphonic harmony on top of it, it's a job. But after a while I had it done, and went to bed with her to get a little sleep.

Next morning, before they could get together and really think up something dumb, I got the producer, the director, the writer and the sound man together in the producer's office, and I laid it down to them.

"All right, boys, I heard a little of what you said last night. You thought you had a B picture here, and now you find out if it's fixed up a little bit, you can get away with it for a feature. You want to do retakes, put some more money in it, do it bigger. Now listen to me. You don't have to put one extra dime in this if you do what I tell you, and you can make it a wow. The big hit is the snow stuff. You've got at least ten thousand feet of that that you didn't use. I know because I saw it run off one day in the projection room. The problem is, how to get more of that stuff in, and tie it up so it makes sense so they don't get tired of it before you've really made full use of it. All right, this is what we do. We rip out that sound track where I'm singing, and make another one. I do that song, but after the first verse I come in, singing over top of myself, see? My own voice, singing an obbligato to myself on the verse. Then when that's done, I come in and sing another one on top of that. Then I come in on top of that, so before the end of it, there's five voices there—all me—light falsetto for the tenor part, heavier for the middle point, and plenty of beef in the bass. Then we repeat it. At the repeat, we start a tympanum, a kettle drum, just light at first, but keeping time to the slug of his feet, and when he gets in sight of the ranch-house we bang hell out of it, and let the five-part harmony swell out so the thing really gets there. All during that, you keep cutting in the snowy stuff, but not straight cuts. Slow dissolves, so you get a kind of dream effect, to go with the cock-eyed harmony on that song. And it doesn't cost you a dime. Nothing but my pay, and you've got me anyhow, for another two weeks. How does it hit you?"

The producer shook his head. His name was Beal, and he and the director and the writer had been listening like it was merely painful, my whole idea. "It's impossible."

"Why is it impossible? You can put all those parts on your loops, I know you can. After you've checked your synchronization, you run them off and make your sound track. It's absolutely possible."

"Listen, we got to do it big, see? That means we got to do retakes, we got to put more production in, and if I got to spend money, I'd a hell of a sight rather spend it on that than on this. This way you say, I got to pay an arranger, I got to hire an orchestra—"

"Arranger, hell. It's already arranged. I've got the parts right here. And what orchestra?"

"For the kettle drum, and—"

"I play the kettle drum myself. On every repeat of the song, I tune it up. Just a little higher, to get a sense of climax, a little louder, a little faster. Don't you get it? They're getting near home. It'll build. It'll give you what you're looking for, it—"

"Nah, it's too tricky. Besides, how can a goddam cowboy be singing quartets with himself out there in the snow? They wouldn't never believe it. Besides, we got to pump up the rest of the picture, the beginning—"

"O.K., we'll do that, and then they'll believe everything. Look."

It had suddenly popped in my mind about my voice coming back at me, that night in the arroyo, and I knew I had something. "In that campfire song, the second one, Home On The Range, we do a little retake and show him singing it at the mountains. His voice comes back, in an echo. It surprises him. He likes it. He begins to fool around with it, and first thing you know, he's singing a duet with himself, and then maybe a trio. We don't do much with it. Just enough that they like it, and we establish it. Then in the snow scene it's not tricky at all. It's his own voice coming back at him from all over that range—out there all alone, bringing home those sheep. They can believe it then, can't they? What's tricky now?"

"It's not enough. We got to do retakes."

Up to then the sound man had sat like he was asleep. He sat up now and began to make marks on a piece of paper. "It can be done."

"Even if it can be done, it's no good."

"It can be done, and it's good."

"Oh, you're telling me what's good?"

"Yeah, I'm telling you."

The technical guys on a lot, they're not like the rest of them. They know their stuff, and they don't take much off a producer or anybody. "You went and bought ten thousand feet of the prettiest snow stuff I ever saw, and then what did you do? You threw out all but four hundred feet of it. It's a crime to waste that stuff, and the lousy way you fixed up the story, there's no way to get it in but the way this guy says. All right then, do like he says, and get it in. It'll build, just like he says it will. You'll get all those angle shots in, all those far shots of miles of sheep going down that mountain, all but the little bits that you never even tried to get in before, and then toward the end of it, the ranchhouse where they're getting near home. I'll give him a light mix on the first of it, and on all the far shots, and when we get near the end—we cut her loose. That kettle drum, that's O.K. It'll get that tramp-tramp feel to it, and go with the music. The echoes on Home On The Range I can work with no trouble at all. It's O.K. And it's O.K. all down the line. It's the only chance you got. Because listen: either this is a little epic all by itself, or it's a goddam cheapie not worth hell room. Take your pick."

"Epic! That's what I've been trying to get."

"Well then, this is how you get it."

"All right, then, fix it up like he says. Let me know when you've got something for me to look at."

So he, I, and the cutter went to work. When I say work I mean work. It was sing, rewrite the parts, test the mix, run it off, and do it all over again from morning to night, and from night to almost morning, but after a couple of weeks we had it done and they gave it another preview, downtown this time, with the newspapers notified. They clapped, cheered, and gave it a rising vote. The Times next morning said "Woolies" was "one of the most vital, honest, and moving things that had come out of Hollywood in a long time," and that "John Howard Sharp, a newcomer with only featured billing, easily stole the picture, and is star material, unless we miss our guess. He can act, he can sing, and he has that certain indefinable, je-ne-sais-quoi something. He's distinctly somebody to watch."

So the next day eight guys showed up to sell me a car, two to sell me annuities, one to get me to sing at a benefit, and one to interview me for a fan magazine. I was a Hollywood celebrity overnight. When I went on the lot in the afternoon I got a call to report to the office of Mr. Gold, president of the company. Ziskin was there, and another producer named London. You'd have thought I was the Duke of Windsor. It seemed I wasn't to wait till Ziskin got his script ready. I was to go into another one that was waiting to shoot. They had been dickering with John Charles Thomas for it, but he was tied up. They thought I would do just as well, because I was younger and bigger and looked the part better. It was about a singing lumberjack that winds up in grand opera.

I said I was glad they liked my work, and everything was fine if we could come to terms on money. They looked kind of funny, and wanted to know what I was talking about. We had our agreement, and I was pretty well paid for a man that started in pictures just a little while ago.

"We did have an agreement, Mr. Gold."

"And we still got it."

"It ran out today."

"Get his contract, Ziskin."

"He's sewed for five years, Mr. Gold, absolutely for five years from the date on the contract, with options every six months, same as all our talent, with a liberal increase, two fifty I think it was, every time we take up our option. A fine, generous contract, and frankly, Mr. Sharp, I am much amazed by the attitude you're taking. That won't get you nowheres in pictures."

"Get his contract."

So they sent down for my contract, and a secretary came up with it, and Gold took a look at it, put his thumb on the amounts and handed it over. "You see?"

"Yeah, I see everything but a signature."

"This is a file copy."

"Don't try to kid me. I haven't signed any contract. That may be the contract you were going to offer me, but the only thing that's been signed is this thing here, that ran out today."

I fished out the memo I had got off Ziskin that night in the dressing-room. Gold began to roar at Ziskin. Ziskin began to roar at the secretary. "Yes, Mr. Ziskin, the contract came though at least a month ago, but you gave me strict orders not to have any contracts signed until you gave your personal approval, and it's been on your desk all that time. I've called it to your attention."

"I been busy. I been cutting Love Is Love."

The secretary went. Ziskin went. London looked sore. Gold began drumming on his desk with his fingers. "O.K., then. If you want a little more dough, something like that, I guess we can boost you a little. Tell you what we do. We won't bother with any new contract. You can sign this one here, and we'll take up the first option right away, and that'll give you twelve fifty. No use quarreling about a few hundred bucks. Report on the set tomorrow morning to Mr. London here, and you better be going down and getting measured for your costumes so you can start."

"I'm afraid twelve fifty won't do, Mr. Gold."

"Why not?"

"I prefer to work by the picture."

"O.K., then. Let's see, this is on a six-week shooting schedule, that'll make seven and half for the picture. I'll have new contracts drawn up this afternoon with corresponding options."

"I'm afraid that won't do either."

"What the hell are you getting at?"

"I want fifty thousand for the picture, with no options. I want to work, but I want every picture a separate deal. For this one, fifty thousand. When we see how that goes, we'll talk again."

"Talk like you had good sense."

"Listen, I've been out here a little while now, I know what you pay, and fifty thousand is the price. Very low it is, too, but as you say, I'm new here, and I've got to be reasonable."

London left, talking over his shoulder as he went. "Stop work on the sets. I'll wait for Thomas. If I can't get him I'll take Tibbett, and if I can't get him I'll put an actor in and dub the sound. But I'll be goddamned if I'm paying fifty grand to this punk."

"Well, you heard him, Mr. Sharp. He's the producer. Fifty thousand is out of the question. We might up that seven and a half to ten, but that would be top. The picture can't stand it, Mr. Sharp. After all, we know what our productions cost."

"I heard him, and now in case you didn't hear me, I'll say it over again. The price is fifty thousand. Now beginning to-morrow I'm taking a little rest. I've been working hard, and I'm tired. But one week from today, if I don't hear from you, I'm taking the plane for New York. I've got plenty of work waiting for me there, and get this: I'm not just talking. I'm going."

"I hate to see you be so foolish."

"Fifty, or I go."

"Why—pictures could make you rich. And you can't get away with this. You're trying to put one over on us. You'll be blackballed all over Hollywood. No studio will have you."

"To hell with that. Fifty or I don't work."

"Oh, to hell with it, hey? I'll goddam well see that you *don't* work in Hollywood. We'll see if a lousy ham actor can put one like that over on Rex Gold."

"Sit down."

He sat, and he sat pretty quick. "Once more. Fifty or I'm going to New York. You got a week."

"Get out of my office."

"On my way."

I had bought a little car by then, and every day we would start out early for the beach or some place, and every day when we got back, around one o'clock, so she could take her siesta, there would be a memo to call Mr. Ziskin, or Mr. London, or somebody. I never called. Around five o'clock they would call again, and it would turn out that if I would go over and apologize to Mr. Gold, there might be an adjustment on the price, say up to fifteen thousand or something like that. I did like hell go over and apologize. I said I had done nothing to apologize for, and the price was still fifty thousand. Somewhere around the fifth day they got up to twenty-five. We were at the Burbank airport, going out to the plane, before they came around. A guy ran up, waving signed contracts. I looked them over. They said fifty thousand, but called for three pictures, one each at that price. I thought fast, and said if they'd pay for my tickets it was all right. He snatched them out of my hand before I even finished. Next day I went into Gold's office and said I heard he wanted to apologize. He took that for a gag and we shook hands.

All that time I was making "Woolies," I hardly saw her at all. By the time I got in from the lot, around seven or eight o'clock, she would be gone to night school. I'd eat dinner alone, then go and get her, and we'd have a little snack at the Derby or somewhere. Then it would be time to go home and go to sleep. Believe me, you work on a picture lot, and don't let anybody tell you different. She'd be still asleep when I left in the morning, and the next night it would be the same thing over again. But that week I took off, we did go out and buy her some clothes. We got four or five dresses, and a fur coat, and some more hats. She loved the fur coat. It was mink, and she would stroke it the way she stroked the bull's ears. And she looked swell in it. But the hats she couldn't get the hang of at all. Between me and the saleswoman, we managed to fix her up with a few that seemed to be all right, a kind of soft brown felt hat that would do for regular dresses and that went nice with the coat, and a big filmy one for night, and a little one for knocking around in the morning, or at night school, and two or three that went with what the saleswoman called sports dresses, the kind of thing they wear at the beach. But she never could get it through her head which hat went with which dress. We'd start out for the beach, and she'd come out of the bedroom with white dress, white shoes, white handbag, and the big floppy evening hat. Or she'd start out in the afternoon with a street dress on, and the fur coat, and one of the sports hats. And I'd have a hard time arguing her out of it, make her put on what she ought to have. "But the hat is very pretty. I like."

"It's pretty, but you can't wear evening hats to the beach. It looks funny. It's all wrong."

"But why?"

"I don't know why. You just can't do it."

"But *I* like."

"Well, can't you just take my word for it?"

"I no understand."

And then this thing happened that finished me with Hollywood, and everything about Hollywood, for good. Maybe you don't know what it's like to be a big Hollywood actor. Well, it's about like being the winning jockey in the Irish Sweepstakes, only worse. You can't turn around that somebody isn't asking you to some little party he's giving, or begging your autograph for some kid that is home sick in bed, or to take space in some trade paper, or to sing at some banquet for a studio executive. Some of that stuff I had to do, like the banquet, but the parties, I ducked by saying I had to work. But when "Paul Bunyan" was finished, and I was waiting around for retakes, I got this call from Elsa Chadwick, that played opposite me in it, asking me to a little party at her house the next night, just a few friends, and would I sing? She caught me with my mouth hanging open, and I couldn't think of anything to say. I mumbled something about having an engagement to take a lady to dinner, and she began to gurgle that I should bring her. Of course I should bring her. She would expect us both around nine.

I didn't know what Juana was going to say, but instead of balking, she wanted to go. "Oh yes. I like, very much. This Miss Chadwick, I have seen her, in the cinema. She is very nice."

Next day, early, I was called over to re-shoot a scene, and I forgot about the party till I got home. Juana was under the shower, getting ready to go. By that time I had a Hollywood suit of evening clothes, and I put them on, and went out in the living-room and waited. In about a half hour she came out, and I got this feeling in the pit of my stomach. She had gone out, all by herself, and bought a special dress for the party. Do you know what a Mexican girl's idea of a party dress is? It's white silk, with red flowers all over it, a red rose in her hair, and white shoes with rhinestone buckles. God knows where she found that outfit. It looked like Ramona on Sunday afternoon. I opened my mouth to tell her it was all wrong but took her in my arms and held her to me. You see, it was all for me. She wanted to wear a red *rebozo,* instead of a hat. It was evening, and didn't call for a hat, so I said all right. But when she put it on, that made it still worse. Those *rebozos* are hand-woven, but they're cotton, like everything else in Mexico. I'd hate to tell you what she looked like with that dress, and those shoes, and that cotton shawl over her head.

Chadwick went into a gag clinch with me when we came in, but when she saw Juana the grin froze on her face and her eyes looked like a snake's. There were twenty or thirty people there, and she took us in and introduced us, but she didn't take us around. She stood with us, near the door, rattled off the names in a hard voice. Then she sat Juana down, got her a drink, put some cigarettes beside her, and that was all. She didn't go near her again, and neither did any of the other women. I sat down on the other side of the room, and in a minute they were all around me, particularly the women, with a line of Hollywood chatter, all of it loud and most of it off color. They haven't got the Hollywood touch till they cuss like mule-skinners and peddle the latest dirty crack that was made on some lot. I fed it back like they gave it, but I was watching Juana. I thought of the soft way she talked, and how she never had said a dirty word in her life, and the dignified way she had stood there while she was being introduced, and the screechy way they had acted. And I felt something getting thick in my throat. Who were they to leave her there all alone with a drink and a pack of Camels?

George Schultz, that had done the orchestrations for "Bunyan," went over to the piano and started to play. "Feel like singing, boy?"

"Just crazy to sing."

"Little Traviata?"

"Sure."

"O.K., give."

He went into the introduction of *Di Provenza il Mar.* But this thing in my throat was choking me. I went over to Juana. "Come on. We're going home."

"You no sing?"

"No. Come on."

"Hey, where are you? That's your cue."

"Yeah?"

"You're supposed to come in."

"I'm not coming in."

"What the hell is this?"

We went out and put on our things and Chadwick followed us to the door. "Well, you don't seem to enjoy my little party?"

"Not much."

"It's mutual. And the next time you come don't show up with a cheap Mexican tart that—"

That's the only time a woman ever took a cuff in the puss from John Howard Sharp. She screamed and three or four guys came out there, screen he-men, all hot to defend the little woman and show how tough they were. I stepped back to let them out. I wanted them out. I was praying they'd come out. They didn't. I took Juana by the arm and started for the car. "There won't be any next time, baby."

■ ■

"They no like me, Hoaney?"

"They didn't act like it."

"But why?"

"I don't know why."

"I do something wrong?"

"Not a thing. You were the sweetest one there."

"I no understand."

"You needn't even bother to try to understand. But if they ever pull something like that on you, just let me know. That's all I've got to say. Just let me know."

We went to the Golondrina. It's a Mexican restaurant on Olvera Street, a kind of Little Mexico they've got in Los Angeles, with *mariachis,* pottery, jumping beans, bum silverware, and all the rest of it. If she had dressed for me, I was bound she was going to have a good time if I had to stand the whole city on its ear to give it to her. She had it. She had never been there before, but as soon as they spotted her they all came around, and talked, and laughed, and she was back home. The couple in the floor show made up a special verse of their song for her, and she took the flower out of her hair and threw it out there, and they did a dance with it, and gave her some comedy. Their comedy is a lot of bum *cucaracha* gags, with a lot of belly-scratching and eye-rolling and finger-snapping, but it was funny to her, so it was funny to me. It was the first time I had ever had a friendly feeling toward Mexico.

Then I sang. A big movie shot is an event in that place, but a Mexican would never pull anything, or let you know he was looking at you. I had to call for the guitar myself, but then I got a big hand. I sang to her, and to the girl in the floor show, and whanged out a number they danced to, and then we all sang the *Golondrina.* It was two o'clock before we left there. When we went to bed I held her in my arms, and long after she was asleep this fury would come over me, about how they had treated her. I knew then I hated Hollywood, and only waited for the day I could clear out of there for good.

■ ■

Under their contract, they had three months to call me for the next picture, and the way the time was counted, that meant any date up to April 1. It was just before Christmas that I got the wire from the New York agent that she had a tip the Met was interested in me, and would I please, *please*, let her go ahead on the deal? I began to rave like a crazy man. "Hoaney, why you talk so?"

"Read it! You've been going to school, there's something for you to practice on. Read it, and see what you've been missing all this time."

"What is 'Met'?"

"Just the best opera company in the world, that's all. The big one in New York, and they want me. They want me!—she'd never be sending that unless she knew something. A chance to get back to my trade at last, and here I am sewed up on a lousy contract to make two more pictures that I hate, that aren't worth making, that—"

"Why you make these pictures?"

"I'm under contract, I tell you. I've got to."

"But why?"

I tried to explain contract to her. It couldn't be done. An Indian has never heard of a contract. They didn't have them under Montezuma, and never bothered with them since. "The picture company, you make money for her, yes?"

"Plenty. I don't owe her a dime."

"Then it is right, you go?"

"Right? Did they ever give me anything I didn't take off them with a blackjack? Would they even give me a cup of coffee if I didn't pack them in at the box office? Would they even respect my trade? This isn't about right. It's about some ink on a dotted line."

"Then why you stay? Why you no sing at these Met?"

That was all. If it wasn't right, then to hell with it. A contract was just something that you probably couldn't read anyway. I looked at her, where she was lying on the bed with nothing on but a *rebozo* around her middle, and knew I was looking across ten thousand years, but it popped in my mind that maybe they weren't as dumb ten thousand years ago as I had always thought. Well, why not? I thought of Malinche, and how she put Cortés on top of the world, and how his star went out like a light when he thought he didn't need her any more. ". . . That's an idea."

"I think you sing at these Met."

"Not so loud."

"Yes."

"I think you're a pretty bright girl."

Next day I hopped over to the Taft Building and saw a lawyer. He begged me not to do anything foolish. "In the first place, if you run out on this contract, they can make your life so miserable that you hardly dare go out of doors without some rat shoving a summons at you with a dollar bill in it, and you'll have to appear in court. Do you know what that means? Do you know what those blue summonses did to Jack Dempsey? They cost him a title, that's all. They can sue you. They can sew you up with injunctions. They can just make you wish you never even heard of the law, or anything like it."

"That's what we got lawyers for, isn't it?"

"That's right. You can get a lawyer there in New York, and he can handle some of it. And he'll charge you plenty. But you can't hire as many lawyers as they've got."

"Listen, can they win, that's all I want to know. Can they bring me back? Can they keep me from working?"

"Maybe they can't. Who knows? But—"

"That's all I want to know. If I've got any kind of a fighting chance, I'm off."

"Not so fast. Maybe they don't even try. Maybe they think it's bad policy. But this is the main point: You run out on this contract, and your name is mud in Hollywood from now on—"

"I don't care about that."

"Oh yes you do. How do you know how well you do in grand opera?"

"I've been in it before."

"And out of it before, from all I hear."

"My voice cracked up."

"It may again. This is my point. The way Gold is building you up, Hollywood is sure for you, as sure as anything can be, for quite some time to come. It makes no different to him if your voice cracks up. He'll buy a voice. He'll dub your sound for you—"

"Not for me he won't."

"Will you for Christ sake stop talking about art? I'm talking about money. I'm telling you that if your pictures really go, he'll do anything. He'll play you straight. He'll fix it up any way that makes you look good. And most of all, he'll pay you! More than any opera company will ever pay you! It's a backlog for you to fall back on, *but*—"

"Yeah, but?"

"Only as long as you play ball. Once you start some funny business, not only he, but every other picture man in Hollywood turns thumbs down, and that's the end of you, in pictures. There's no black-list. Nobody calls anybody up. They just hear about it, and that's all. I can give you names, if you want them, of bright boys like you that thought they could jump a Hollywood contract, and tell you what happened to them. These picture guys hate each other, they cut each other's throats all the time, but when something like this happens, they act with a unanimity that's touching. Now, have you seen Gold?"

"I thought I'd see you first."

"That's all right. Then there's no harm done. Now before you do anything rash, I want you to see him. There may be no trouble at all. He may want you to sing at the Met, just for build-up. He may be back of it, for all you know. Get over and see him, see if you can fix it up. After lunch, come back and see me."

So I went over and saw Gold. He wanted to talk about the four goals he made in the polo game the day before. When we did get around to it he shook his head. "Jack, I know what's good for you, even if you don't. I read the signs all the time, it's my business to know, and they'll all tell you Rex Gold don't make many mistakes. Jack, grand opera's through."

"What?"

"It's through, finished. Sure, I dropped in at the Metropolitan when I was east last week, saw Tosca, the same opera that we do a piece of in Bunyan, and I'd hate to tell you what they soaked me for the rights on it, too. And what do I see? Well, boy, I'm telling you, we just made a bum out of them. That sequence in our picture is so much better than their job, note for note, production for production, that comparison is just ridiculous. Grand opera is through. Because why? Pictures have stepped in and done it so much better than they can do it that they can't get by any more, that's all. Opera is going the same way the theatre is going. Pictures have just rubbed them out."

"Well—before it dies, I'd like to have a final season in it. And I don't think the Metropolitan stamp would hurt me any, even in pictures."

"It would ruin you."

"How?"

"I've been telling you. Grand opera is through. Grand opera pictures are through. The public is sick of them. Because why? Because they got no more material. They've done Puccini over and over again, they've done La Bohème and Madame Butterfly so much we even had to fall back on La Tosca for you in Bunyan, and after you've done your Puccini, what you got left? Nothing. It's through, washed up. We just can't get the material."

"Well—there are a couple of other composers."

"Yeah, but who wants to listen to them?"

"Almost anybody, except a bunch of Kansas City yaps that think Puccini is classical, as they call it."

"Oh, so you don't like Puccini?"

"Not much."

"Listen, you want to find out who's the best painter in the world, what do you do? You try to buy one of his pictures. Then you find out what you got to pay. O.K., you want to find out who's the best composer in the world, you try to buy some of his music. Do you know what they charged me, just for license rights, on that scene you did from Tosca? You want to know? Wait, I'll get the canceled vouchers. I'll show you. You wouldn't believe it."

"Listen, Puccini has been the main asset of that publishing house for years, and everybody in grand opera knows it, and that's got nothing to do with how good he is. It's because he came in after we began to get copyright laws, and because he was handled from the beginning for every dime that could be got out of him from guys like you. If you're just finding that out, it may prove you don't know anything about opera, but it doesn't prove anything about Puccini."

"Why do you suppose guys like me pay for him?"

"Probably because you knew so little about opera you couldn't think of anything else. If you had let me help on that script, I'd have fixed you up with numbers that wouldn't have cost you a dime."

"A swell time to be saying that."

"To hell with it. You got Tosca, and it's all right. I'm talking about a release for the rest of the season to go on at the Met."

"And I'm talking about what's good for one of our stars. There's no use our arguing about composers, Jack. Maybe you know what's pretty but I know what sells. And I tell you grand opera is through. And I tell you that from now on you lay off it. The way I'm building you up, we're going to take that voice of yours, and what are we going to do with it? Use it on popular stuff. The stuff you sing better than anybody else in the business. The stuff that people want to hear. Lumberjack songs, cowboy songs, mountain music, *jazz*—you can't beat it! It's what they want! Not any of this tra-la-la-la-la-la! Christ, that's an ear-ache! It's a back number. Look, Jack: From now on, you forget you ever were in grand opera. You give it to them down-to-earth! Right down there where they want it! You get me, Jack? You get me?"

"I get you."

■ ■

"What did Gold say?"

"He said no."

"I had an idea that was how he felt. I had him on the phone just now, about something else, and I led around to you in a way that didn't tip it you had been in, but he was telling the world where he stood. Well, I'd play along with him. It's tough, but you can't buck him."

"If I do, what did you say my name would be?"

"Mud. M-U-D, mud."

"In Hollywood?"

"Yes, in Hollywood."

"That's all I wanted to know. What do I owe you?"

When I got home there were four more telegrams, saying the thing was hot, if I wanted it, and a memo New York had been calling. I looked at my watch. It was three o'clock. I called the airport. They had two seats on the four-thirty plane. She came in. "Well, Juana, there they are, read them. The *abogado* says no, a hundred times no. What do I do?"

"You sing Carmen at these Met?"

"I don't know. Probably."

"Yes, I like."

"O.K., then. Get packed."

9

I made my debut in Lucia right after New Year's, sang standard repertoire for a month, began to work in. It felt good to be back with the wops. Then I got my real chance when they popped me on three days' notice into Don Giovanni. I had a hell of a time getting them to let me do the serenade my way, with a real guitar, and play it myself, without the orchestra. The score calls for a prop mandolin, and that's the way the music is written, but I hate all prop instruments on the stage, and hate to play any scene where I have to use one. There's no way you can do it that it doesn't look phoney. I made a gain when I told them that the guitar was tradition, that Garcia used to do it that way, but I lost all that ground when somebody in the Taste Department decided that a real guitar would look too much like the Roxy, and for a day it was all off again. Then I got Wurlitzer's to help me out. They sent down an instrument that was a beauty. It was dark, dull spruce, without any pearl, nickel, or highlights on it of any kind, and it had a tone you could eat with a spoon. When I sounded off on that, that settled it.

I wanted to put it up a half tone, so I could get it in the key of three flats, but I didn't. It's in the key of two sharps, the worst key there is for a singer, especially the high F sharp at the end, that catches a baritone all wrong, and makes him sound coarse and ropy. The F sharp is not in the score, but it's tradition and you have to sing it. God knows why Mozart ever put it in that key, unless it's because two sharps is the best key there is for a mandolin, and he let his singer take the rap so he could bring the accompaniment to life.

But I tuned with the orchestra before the act started, and did it strictly in the original key. I made two moves while I was singing it. Between verses I took one step nearer the balcony. At the end, I turned my back on the audience, stepped under the balcony and played the finish, not to them, but to her. On the F sharp, instead of covering up and getting it over quick, I did a *messa di voce*, probably the toughest order a singer ever tries to deliver. You start it *p*, swell to *ff*, pull back to *p* again, and come off it. My tone wasn't round, but it was pure, and I got away with it all right. They broke into a roar, the *bravos* yipped out all over the house, and that was the beginning of this stuff that you read, that I was the greatest since Bispham, the peer of Scotti, and all the rest of it. Well, I was the peer of Scotti, or hope I was. They've forgotten by now how bad Scotti really was. He could sing, and he was the greatest actor I ever saw, but his voice was just merely painful. What they paid no attention to at all, mentioned like it was nothing but a little added feature, was the guitar. You can talk about your fiddle, your piano, and your orchestra, and I've got nothing to say against them. But a guitar has moonlight in it.

Don Giovanni, the Marriage of Figaro, Thaïs, Rigoletto, Carmen, and Traviata, going bigger all the time, getting toward the middle of February, and still nothing from Gold. No notification to report, no phone calls, nothing. It was Ziskin's picture I was supposed to do next. I saw by the papers he was in town and that night saw him in Lindy's, but I saw him first and we ducked out and went somewhere else. He looked just as foolish as ever, and I began to tell myself he still didn't have his script ready, and I might win by default.

The Hudson-to-Horn hook-up was something the radio people had been working on for a year, and God knows how many ministers, ambassadors, and contact men had to give them a hand, because most of those stations south of the Rio Grande are government-owned, and so are the Canadian. Then after they put it over, they had a hard job selling the time, because they were asking plenty for it, and every country had to get its cut. Finally they peddled it to Panamier. The car was being put out mainly for export, and the hook-up gave it what it needed. The next thing was: Who were they going to feature on the hour, now they had sold it? They had eight names on their list, the biggest in the business, starting with Grace Moore and ending with me. I moved up a couple of notches when I told them I could do spig songs in Spanish. I couldn't, but I figured I was in bed with the right person to learn. Then Paul Bunyan opened, and I went up to the top. I can't tell you what the picture had. Understand, for my money no picture is any good, really any good, but this one was gay and made you feel you wanted to see it over again. The story didn't make any sense at all, but maybe it was because it was so cock-eyed you got to laughing. One place in there they cut in the Macy parade, the one they hold about a month before Christmas, with a lot of balloons coming down Broadway in the shape of animals. One of the balloons was a cow, and when they cut them loose, with prizes offered to whoever finds them, this one floats clear out over Saskatchewan and comes down on the trees near the lumber camp. Then the lumberjack that I was supposed to be, the one that has told them all he's really Paul Bunyan, says it's Babe, the Big Blue Ox that's come down from heaven to pay him a Christmas visit. Then he climbs up in a tree and sings to it, and the lumberjacks sing to it, and believe it or not, it did things to you. Then when the sun comes up and they see what gender Babe really is, they go up the tree after the guy to lynch him, but somebody accidentally touches a cigar to the cow and she blows up with such a roar that all the trees they were supposed to cut down are lying flat on the ground, and they decide it was Mrs. Babe.

■ ■

That clinched me for the broadcast, and they ate it up when I told them how to put the show together so it would sell cars. "We open up with the biggest, loudest, five-tone, multiple-action horn you can find, and if you think that's not important, I tell you I've been down there, and I know what you've got to give them to sell cars. You've got to have a horn; first, last, and all the time you've got to have a horn. I take pitch from that and go into the *Golondrina,* for the spig trade, blended in with My Pal Babe, for the Canadian trade. I'll write that little medley myself, and that's our signature. Then we repeat it, you put your announcer in, and after he stops we go right on. We do light Mexican numbers, then we'll turn right around and do some little French-Canadian numbers, then one light American number, when it's time for the announcer again. Then we do a grand opera number and so on for as much time as we've got, and any comedy you want to put in, that's O.K., too, but watch they can understand it. On your car, plug the horn, the lock on the gas tank, the paint job, the speed and the low gas consumption. That's all. Leave out about the brakes, the knee-action, and all that. They never heard of it, and you're just wasting your time. Better let me write those plugs, and you let your announcers translate them. And first, last, and again: Sound that horn."

They struck together a program the way I said, and we made a record of it one morning with the studio orchestra, then went in an audition room and ran it off. It sounded like something. The advertising man liked it, and the Panamier man was tickled to death with it. "It's got speed to it, you know what I mean? 'Gangway for the Panamier Eight, she's coming down the road!'—that's what it says. And the theme song is a honey. Catches them north, south, and in the middle. Boys, we got something now. That's set. No more if, as, and but about it." I began to feel good. Why did I want that broadcast? Because it would pay me four thousand a week. Because they treated me good. Because I had had that flop, and I could get back at Mexico. Because it made me laugh. Because I could say hello to Captain Conners, wherever he was out there, listening to it. In other words, for no reason. I just wanted it.

That was around the first of March, and they would go on the air in three weeks, as soon as they could place ads in the newspapers all up and down the line, and get more cars freighted out, to make deliveries. By that time I had kidded myself that Ziskin would never have his script ready, and that I could forget about Hollywood the rest of my life. I woke up after I left them that day, and walked down to the opera house for the matinee Lucia. A messenger was there, with a registered letter from Gold, telling me to report March 10. I was a little off that day, and missed a cue.

What I did about it was nothing at all, except get the address of a lawyer in Radio City that made a specialty of big theatrical cases. Three days later I got a wire from the Screen Actors' Guild, telling me that as I had made no acknowledgment of Gold's notification to report, the case had been referred to them, that I was bound by a valid contract, and that unless I took steps to comply with it at once, they would be compelled to act under their by-laws, and their agreement with the producers. I paid no attention to that either.

Next morning while I was having a piano run-through of the Traviata duet with a new soprano they were bringing out, a secretary came up to the rehearsal room and told me to please go at once to a suite in the Empire State Building, that it was important. I asked the soprano if she minded doing the rest of it after lunch. When I got up to the Empire State Building, I was brought into a big office paneled in redwood, and marked "Mr. Luther, private." Mr. Luther was an old man with a gray cutaway suit, a cheek as pink as a young girl's, and an eye like blue agate. He got up, shook hands, told me how much he had enjoyed my singing, said my Marcello reminded him of Sammarco, and then got down to business. "Mr. Sharp, we have a communication here from a certain Mr. Gold, Rex Gold, informing us that he has a contract with you, and that any further employment of you on our part, after March 10, will be followed by legal action on his part. I don't know what legal action he has in mind, but I thought it would be well if you came in and, if you can, inform me what he means, if you know."

"You're the attorney for the opera house?"

"Not regularly, of course. But sometimes when somebody is in Europe, they refer things to me."

"Well—I have a contract with Gold."

"For motion pictures, I judge?"

"Yes."

I told him about it, and made it pretty plain I was through with pictures, contract or no contract. He listened and smiled, and seemed to get it all, why I wanted to sing in opera and all the rest of it. "Yes, I can understand that. I understand it very well. And of course, considering the success we're having with you here, I should certainly hesitate to take any step, or give any advice, that would lose you to us at the height of the season. Of course, a telegram unsupported by any other documents is hardly ground for us to make a decision, and in fact we are not bound to take cognizance of contracts made by our singers until a court passes on them, or in some way compels us to. Just the same—"

"Yes?"

"Have you had any communication from Mr. Gold, aside from his letter of notification?"

"Nothing at all. I did have a wire from the Screen Actors' Guild. But that's all."

"The—what was that again?"

I had the wire in my pocket, and showed it to him. He got up and began to walk around the office. "Ah—you're a member of this Guild?"

"Well—everybody is that works in pictures."

"It's an affiliate of Equity, isn't it?"

"I'm not sure. I think so."

"... I don't know what their procedure is. It's recently organized, and I haven't heard much about it. But I confess, Mr.

Sharp, this makes things very awkward. Contracts, court cases—these things I don't mind. After all, that's what I'm here for, isn't it? But I should be very loath to give any advice that would get the company into any mess with the Federation of Musicians. You realize what's involved here, don't you?"

"No, I don't."

"As I say, I don't know the procedure of your Screen Actors' Guild, but if they took the matter up with the musicians, and we had some kind of mess on our hands, over your singing here until you had adjudicated your troubles with your own union—Mr. Sharp, I simply have a horror of it. The musicians are one of the most intelligent, co-operative, and sensible unions we have, and yet, *any* dispute, coming at the height of the season—!"

"Meaning what?"

"I don't know. I want to think about it."

I went out, had a sandwich and some coffee, and went back to the rehearsal hall. We just about got started when the same secretary came up and said the radio people wanted me to come up right away, that it was terribly important, and would I please make it as soon as I could. The soprano went into an act that blistered the varnish off the piano. At plain and fancy cussing, the coloraturas, I think, are the best in the business. I got out on the street, tried to figure out which was uptown and which down. I thought about Jack Dempsey.

They were all up there, the advertising man, the Panamier man, the broadcasting men, all of them, and there was hell to pay. They had had a wire from Gold, forbidding them to use My Pal Babe, or any part of it, else be sued up to the hilt, and warning them not to use me. The Panamier man raved like an animal. I listened and began to get sore. "What the hell is he talking about? You can use that song. I don't know much about law, but I know that much—"

"We can't use it! We can't use a note of it! It's his! And those ads have gone out to two hundred key newspapers. We got to kill them by wire, we got to get up a whole new program—Christ, why didn't you tell us about this thing? Why did you let us start all this knowing you had that contract?"

"Will you just hold your horses till tonight?"

"For what? Will you tell me that, for what?"

"Till I can see a lawyer?"

"Don't you suppose I've seen a lawyer? Don't you suppose I've had Gold on the phone three times today while I was trying to find where the hell you were? And I've advertised it! I've advertised the goddam theme song! Golondrina, My Babe—don't that sound sick? And I've advertised you—John Howard Sharp, El Panamier Trovador—don't that sound sicker! Get out, for Christ sake—"

"Will you wait? Just till tonight?"

"Yeah, I'll wait. Why not?"

The lawyer was five floors down in the same building. He didn't have redwood paneling in his office. It was just an office, and he was a brisk little guy named Sholto. I laid it out for him. He leaned back, took a couple of calls, and started to talk. 'Sharp, you haven't got a leg to stand on. You made a contract, a contract that any jury would regard as perfectly fair, and the only thing you can do is go through with it. It may reflect credit on your aesthetic conscience that you prefer opera to pictures, but it doesn't reflect any credit on your moral conscience that you jump a contract just because you want to. As well as I can make out this picture company took you when you were a bum, put you on your feet, and now you want to hand them a cross. I don't say you couldn't lick them in court. Nobody can say what a jury is going to do. But you'll be a bum before you ever get to court. Show business is all one gigantic hook-up, Gold knows it frontwards, backwards, crosswise, and on the bias, and you haven't got a chance. You're sewed. You've got to go back and make that picture."

"Just give up everything, now it's breaking for me, go back and make a picture just because that cluck has an idea that opera is through?"

"What the hell are you trying to tell me? One more picture like this Bunyan and you can walk into any opera house in the world, and the place is yours. You're being built into a gallery draw that not one singer in a million can bring into the theatre with him. Haven't you got any brains? These musicals are quota pictures. They go all over the world. They make you famous from Peru to China and from Norway to Capetown, and from Panama to Suez and back again. Don't you suppose opera houses know that? Don't you think the Metropolitan knows it? Do you suppose all this commotion you've caused is just a tribute to your A flat in Pagliacci? It is like hell."

"I haven't sung Pagliacci."

"All right then, Trovatore."

"And that's all you've got to tell me?"

"Isn't it enough?"

I felt so sick I didn't even bother to go up to the broadcasting offices again. I went down, caught a cab, and went home. It was starting to snow. We had sublet a furnished apartment in a big apartment house on East Twenty-second Street, near Gramercy Park. She had liked it because there were Indian rugs around that looked a little like Mexico, and we had been happier there, for six weeks, than I had ever been in my life. She was in bed with a cold. She never could get it through her head what New York weather was like. I sat down and broke the news. "Well, it's all off. We go back to Hollywood."

"No, please. I like New York."

"Money, Juana. And everything. Back we go."

"But why? We have much money."

"And no place to sing. By tomorrow not even a night club will hire me. Unions. Injunctions. Contracts."

"No, we stay in New York. You take guitar, be a *mariachi*, just you, Hoaney. You sing for me."

"We got to go back."

I sat beside her, and she kept running her fingers through my hair. We didn't say anything for a long time. The phone rang. She motioned to let it alone. If I hadn't picked it up, our whole life would have been different.

Winston Hawes, the papers said, was one of the outstanding musicians of his time, the conductor that could really read a score, the man that had done more for modern music than anybody since Muck. He was all of that, but don't get the idea he was ever one of the boys. There was something wrong about the way he thought about music, something unhealthy, like the crowds you always saw at his concerts, and what it was I can only half tell you. In the first place I don't know enough about the kind of people he came from, and in the second place I don't know enough about music. He was rich, and there's something about rich people that's different from the rest of us. They come into the world with an inflated idea of their relation to it, and everything they find in it. I got a little flash into that side of him once, in Paris, when I strolled into an art store to look at some pictures that caught my eye. A guy came in, an American, and began a palaver about prices. And the way that guy talked gave me a whole new slant at his kind. He didn't care about art, the way you do or I do, as something to look at and feel. He wanted to *own* it. Winston was that way about music. He made a whore out of it. You went to his concerts, but you didn't sit out there at his rehearsals, and see him hold men for an hour overtime, at full pay, just because there was some French horn passage that he liked, and wanted it played over and over again—not to rehearse it, but because of what it did to *him*. And you didn't walk out with him afterwards, and see him all atremble, and hear him tell how he felt after playing it. He was like some woman that goes to concerts because they give her the right vibrations, or make her feel better, or have some other effect on her nitwit insides. All right, you may think it's cock-eyed to compare him with somebody like that, but I'm telling you that in spite of all his technical skill, he was a hell of a sight nearer to that fat poop than he ever was to Muck. That woman was in him, poodle dog, diamonds, limousine, conceit, cruelty and all, and don't let his public reputation fool you. She has a public reputation too, if she hands out enough money. The day the story broke, they compared him with Stanford White, but I'm telling you that to put Winston Hawes in the same class with Stanford White was a desecration.

You can't own music, the way you can own a picture, but you can own a big hunk of it. You can own a composer, that you put on a subsidy while he's writing a piece for you. You can own an audience that has to come to you to hear that piece if it's going to hear it at all. You can own the orchestra that plays it, and you can own the singer that sings it. I first met him in Paris. I hadn't known him in Chicago. He came from a packing family so rich I never even got within a mile of where they lived. And I didn't look him up, even in Paris. He showed up at my apartment one day, sat down at the piano, played off a couple of songs that were there, and said they were lousy, which they were. Then he got up and asked me how I'd like to sing with his band. I was pretty excited. He had started his Petite Orchestra about a year before, and I had gone to plenty of the concerts, and don't you think they weren't good. He started with thirty men, but by now he was up to forty. He raided everywhere, from the opera orchestras, from the chamber music outfits, and he took anybody he wanted, because he paid about twice what any other band paid. He footed the deficit himself, and he didn't have a man that couldn't have played quartets with Heifetz. What they could do to music, especially modern music, was just make it sound about twice as good as even the composer thought it was. He had some stuff with him he wanted me to do, all of it in manuscript. Part of it was old Italian songs he had dug up, where I would have to do baritone coloratura that had been out of date for a hundred years, and how he knew I could do it I don't know. Part of it was a suite by his first viola, that had never been performed yet. It was tough stuff, music that wouldn't come to life at all without the most exact tone shading. But he gave me six rehearsals—count them, six, something you couldn't believe. Cost didn't mean anything to him. When we went on with it I was with those woodwinds like I was one of the bassoons, and the response was terrific. I took out Picquot, the viola, before I took a call myself, and the whole thing was like something you read about.

That part of it, I wouldn't be telling the truth if I didn't admit it was an adventure in music I'll never forget. I sang for him four times, and each time it was something new, something fresh, and a performance better than you even knew you could give. He had a live stick all right. From some of them you get a beat as dead as an undertaker's handshake, but not from him. He threw it on you like a hypnotist, and you began to roll it out, and yet it was all under perfect control. That's the word to remember, perfect. Perfection is something no singer ever got yet, but under him you came as near to it as you're ever going to get.

That was the beginning of it, and it was quite a while before it dawned on me what he really wanted. As to what he wanted, and what he got, you'll find out soon enough, and I'm not going to tell any more than I have to. But I'd like to make this much clear now: that wasn't what I wanted. What I meant to him and what he meant to me were two different things, but once again, I wouldn't be telling the truth if I didn't admit that what he meant to me was plenty. He took to dropping into my dressing room at the Comique while I was washing up, and he'd tell me some little thing I had done, something he had liked, or some-times, something he hadn't liked. If he had been giving a con-cert, maybe he had heard only part of the last act, but there would always be something. You think that didn't mean any-thing to me? Singing is a funny job. You go out there and take those calls, and it's so exciting that when you get back to your dressing room you want to sing, to cut it loose till the windows rattle, just to let off the steam that excitement makes. You go back there and you'll hear them, especially the tenors, so you'd think they had gone crazy. But that excitement is all from out front, from a mob you only half see and never know, and you get so you'd give anything for somebody, for just one guy, that knew what you were trying to do, that spotted your idea without your telling him, that could appreciate you with his head and not with the palms of his hands. And mind you, it couldn't be just anybody. It has to be somebody you respect, somebody that knows.

I began to wait for that visit. Then pretty soon I was singing to him and to nobody else. We'd walk out, go to a café while I ate, then drop over to his apartment off the Place Vendóme, and have a post-mortem on my performance. Then, little by little, he began making suggestions. Then I began dropping in on him in the morning, and he'd take me through some things I had been doing wrong. He was the best coach in the world, bar none. Then he began to take my acting apart, and put it together again. It was he that cured me of all those operatic gestures I got in Italy. He showed me that good operatic acting consists in as few motions as possible, every one of them cal-culated for an effect, and every one made to count. He told me about Scotti and how he used to sing the Pagliacci Prologue before he got so bad they couldn't use him in Pagliacci. He made one gesture. At the end of the andante, he held out his hand, and then turned it over, palm up. That was all. It said it. He made me learn a whole new set of gestures, done naturally, and he made me practice for hours singing *sotto voce* without using any gestures at all. That's a tough order, just to stand up there, on a cold stage, and shoot it. But I got so I could do it.

And I got so I could take my time, give it to them when I was ready, not before. I began to do better in comedy roles, like Sharpless and Marcello. Taking out all that gingerbread, I could watch timing, and get laughs I never got before. I got so I was with him morning, noon and night, and depended on him like a hophead depends on dope.

Then came my crack-up, and when my money was all gone I had to leave Paris. He stormed about that, wanted to support me, showed me his books to prove that an allowance for me wouldn't even make a dent in his income. But it was that storming that showed me where things had got between him and me, and that I had to break away from him. I went to New York. I tried to find something to do, but there was nothing I could do except sing, and I couldn't sing. That was when this agent kidded me that no matter what shape I was in I was good enough for Mexico, and I went down there.

I had read in some paper that he had disbanded his orchestra in Paris, but I didn't know he was starting his Little Orchestra in New York until I got there. It made me nervous. I dropped in, alone, at his first concert, just so I could say I had, in case I ran into him somewhere. It was the same mob he had had in Paris, clothes more expensive than you would see even at a Hollywood opening, gray-haired women with straight haircuts and men's dinner jackets, young girls looking each other straight in the eye and not caring what you thought, boys following men around, loud, feverish talk out in the foyer, everybody coming out in the open with something they wouldn't dare show anywhere else. His first number was something for strings by Lalo I had heard him play before, and I left right after it. Next day, when I saw the review in the paper I turned the page quick. I didn't want to read it. I had a note from him after Don Giovanni, and shot it right back, and one word written on it, "Thanks," with my initials. I didn't want to write on my own stationery, or he'd know where I was living. I felt funny about asking for opera house stationery. I was afraid not to answer, for fear he'd be around to know why.

■ ■

So that's how things stood when I was sitting beside Juana and the phone rang. She motioned to let it ring, and I did for a while, but I still hadn't called Panamier, and I knew I had them to talk to, even if I had nothing to say. I answered. But it wasn't Panamier. It was Winston. "Jack! You old scalawag! Where have you been hiding?"

"Why—I've been busy."

"So have I, so busy I'm ashamed of it. I hate to be busy. I like time for my friends. But at the moment I'm free as a bird, I've got a fine fire burning, and you can hop in a cab, wherever you are—all I've got is your phone number, and I had a frightful time even getting that—and come up here. I just can't wait to see you."

"Well—that sounds swell, but I've got to go back to Hollywood, right away, probably tomorrow, and that means I'll be tied up every minute, trying to get out of town. I don't see how I could fit it in."

"What did you say? *Hollywood!*"

"Yeah, Hollywood."

"Jack, you're kidding."

"No, I'm a picture star now."

"I know you are. I saw your pictures, both of them. But you can't go back to Hollywood now. Why you're singing for *me*, one month from today. I've arranged your whole program. It's out of the question."

"No, I'll have to go."

"Jack, you don't sound like yourself. Don't tell me you've got so big you can't spare one night for a poor dilettante and his band—"

"For Christ sake, don't be silly."

"That sounds more like you. Now what is it?"

"Nothing but what I've told you. I've got to go back there. I don't want to. I hate to. I've tried to get out of it every way I knew, but I'm sewed and I've got no choice."

"That sounds still more like you. In other words, you're in trouble."

"That's it."

"Into the cab and up here. Tell it to Papa."

"No, I'm sorry. I can't. . . . Wait a minute."

She was grabbing for the receiver. I put my hand over it. "Yes, you go."

"I don't want to go."

"You go."

"He's just a guy—I don't want to see."

"You go, you feel better, Juana's nose, very snoddy."

"I'll wipe it, then it won't be snoddy."

"Hoaney, you go. Many people call today, all day long. You no here, you no have to talk, no feel bad. Now, you go. I say you gone out. I don't know where. You go, then tonight we talk, you and I. We figure out."

". . . All right, where are you? I'll be up."

He was at a hotel off Central Park, on the twenty-second floor of the tower. The desk told me to go up. I did, found his suite, rang the bell and got no answer. The door was open and I walked in. There was a big living room, with windows on two sides, so you could see all the way downtown and out over the East River, a grand piano at one end, a big phonograph across from that, scores stacked everywhere, and a big fire burning under a mantelpiece. I opened the door that led into the rest of the suite and called, but there wasn't any answer. And then in a second there he was, bouncing in from the hall, in the rough coat, flannel shirt, and battered trousers that he always wore. If you had met him in Central Park you would have given him a dime. "Jack! How are you! I went down to meet you, and they told me you had just gone up! Give me that coat! Give me a smile, for God's sake! That Mexican sunburn makes you look like Othello!"

"Oh, you knew I was in Mexico?"

"Know it! I went down there to bring you back, but you had gone. What's the idea, hiding out on me?"

"Oh, I've been working."

One minute later I was in a big chair in front of the fire,

with a bottle of the white port I had always liked beside me, a little pile of buttered English biscuits beside that, he was across from me with those long legs of his hooked over the chandelier or some place, and we were off. Or anyhow, he was. He always began in the middle, and he raced along about Don Giovanni, about an appoggiatura I was leaving out in Lucia, about the reason the old scores aren't sung the way they're written, about a new flutist he had pulled in from Detroit, about my cape routine in Carmen, all jumbled up together. But not for long. He got to the point pretty quick. "What's this about Hollywood?"

"Just what I told you. I'm sewed on a goddam contract and I've got to go."

I told him about it. I had told so many people about it by then I knew it by heart, and could get it over quick. "Then this man—Gold, did you say his name was?—is the key to the whole thing?"

"He's the one."

"All right then. You just sit here a while."

"No, if you're doing something I'll go!"

"I said sit there. Papa's going to get busy."

"At what?"

"There's your port, there's your biscuits, there's the fire, there's the most beautiful snow I've seen this year, and I've got the six big Rossini overtures on the machine—Semiramide, Tancred, the Barber, Tell, the Ladra, and the Italians, just in from London, beautifully played—and by the time they're finished I'll be back."

"I asked you, where are you going?"

"Goddam it, do you have to bust up my act? I'm being Papa. I'm going into action. And when Papa goes into action, it's the British Fleet. Sip your port. Listen to Rossini. Think of the boys that were gelded to sing the old bastard's masses. Be the Pope. I'm going to be Admiral Dewey."

"Beatty."

"No, I'm Gridley. I'm ready to fire."

He switched on the Rossini, poured the wine, and went. I

tried to listen, and couldn't. I got up and switched it off. It was the first time I ever walked out on Rossini. I went over to the windows and watched the snow. Something told me to get out of there, to go back to Hollywood, to do anything except get mixed up with him again. It wasn't over twenty minutes before he was back. I heard him coming, and ducked back to the chair. I didn't want him to see me worrying. "... I was astonished that you missed that grace note in Lucia. Didn't you *feel* it there? Didn't you know it *had* to be there?"

"To hell with Lucia. What news?"

"Oh. I had forgotten all about it. Why, you stay, of course. You go on with the opera, you do this foolish broadcast you've let yourself in for, you sing for me, you make your picture in the summer. That's all. It's all fixed up. Once more, Jack, on all those old recitatives—"

"Listen, this is business. I want to know—"

"Jack, you are so crass. Can't I wave my wand? Can't I do my bit of magic? If you have to know, I happen to control a bank, or my somewhat boorish family happen to control it. They embarrass me greatly, but sometimes they have a kind of low, swinish usefulness. And the bank controls, through certain stocks impounded to secure moneys, credit, and so on—oh the hell with it."

"Go on. The bank controls what?"

"The picture company, dolt."

"And?"

"Listen, I'm talking about Donizetti."

"And I'm talking about a son-of-a-bitch by the name of Rex Gold. What did you do?"

"I talked with him."

"And what did he say?"

"Why—I don't know. Nothing. I didn't wait to hear what he had to say. I told him what he was to do, that's all."

"Where's your phone?"

"Phone? What are you phoning about?"

"I've got to call the broadcasting company."

"Will you sit down and listen to what I'm trying to tell you about appoggiaturas, so you won't embarrass me every time you sing something written before 1905? Varlets in the bank are calling the broadcasting company. That's what we have them for. They're working overtime, calling other varlets in Radio City and making them work overtime, which I greatly enjoy, while you and I take our sinful ease here and watch the snow at twilight, and discuss the grace notes of Donizetti, which will be sung long after the picture company, the bank, and the varlets are dead in their graves and forgotten. Are you following me?"

His harangue on the appoggiaturas lasted fifteen minutes. It was something I was always forgetting about him, his connection with money. His family consisted of an old maid sister, a brother that was a colonel in the Illinois National Guard, another brother that lived in Italy, and some nephews and nieces, and they had about as much to do with that fortune as so many stuffed dummies. *He* ran it, *he* controlled the bank, *he* did plenty of other things that he pretended he was too artistic even to bother with. All of a sudden something shot through my mind. "Winston, I've been framed."

"Framed? What are you talking about? By whom?"

"By you."

"Jack, I give you my word, the way you sang that—"

"Cut out this goddam foolish act about Lucia, will you? Sure I sang it wrong. I learned that role before I knew anything about style, and I hadn't sung it for five years until I went on with it last month, and I neglected to re-learn it, and that's all that amounts to, and to hell with it. I'm talking about this other. You knew all about it when you called me."

". . . Why, of course I did."

"And I think you put me in that spot."

"I—? Don't be a fool."

"It always struck me pretty funny, that guy Gold's ideas about grand opera, and me, and all the rest of it. Anybody else would *want* me in grand opera, to build me up. What do you know about that?"

"Jack, that's Mexican melodrama."

"What about this trip of yours? To Mexico?"

"I went there. A frightful place."

"For me?"

"Of course."

"Why?"

"To take you by the scuff of your thick neck and drag you out of there. I—ran into a 'cellist that had seen you. I heard you were looking seedy. I don't like you seedy. Shaggy, but not with spots on your coat."

"What about Gold?"

". . . I put Gold in charge of that picture company because he was the worst ass I had ever met, and I thought he was the perfect man to make pictures. I was right. He's turned the whole investment into a gold mine. Soon I can have seventy-five men, and 'Little Orchestra' will be one of those affectations I so greatly enjoy. Jack, *do you* have to expose all my little shams? You know them all. Can't we just not look at them? After all they're nice shams."

"I want to know more about Gold."

He came over and sat on the arm of my chair. "Jack, why should I frame you?"

I couldn't answer him, and I couldn't look at him.

"Yes, I knew all about it. I didn't tell Gold to be an ass, if that's what you mean. I didn't have to. I knew about it, and I acted out one of my little shams. Can't I want my Jack to be happy? Wipe that sulky look off your face. Wasn't it good magic? Didn't Gridley level the fort?"

". . . Yes."

I got home around eight o'clock. I rushed in with a grin on my face, said it was all right, that Gold had changed his mind, that we were going to stay, and let's go out and celebrate. She got up, wiped her snoddy nose, dressed, and we went out, to a hot-spot uptown. It was murder to drag her out, on a night like that, the way she felt, but I was afraid if I didn't get to some place where there was music, and I could get some liquor in me, she'd see I was putting on an act, that I was as jittery inside as a man with a hangover.

I didn't see him for a week or ten days, and the first broadcast made me feel good. I said hello to Captain Conners, and there was a federal kick-back the next morning. Messages to private persons are strictly forbidden. I just laughed, and thought of Thomas. There was a federal kick-back on that "Good night, Mother," too, and they told him he couldn't do it. He just went ahead and did it. That afternoon there came a radiogram from the SS. *Port of Cobh:* TWAS A SOAP AGENTS PROGRAM BUT I ENJOYED IT HELLO YOURSELF AND HELLO TO THE LITTLE ONE CONNERS. So of course I had to come running home with that.

I made some records, went on three times a week at the opera, did another broadcast, and woke up to find I was a household institution, name, face, voice and all, from Hudson Bay to Cape Horn and back again. The spig papers, the Canadian papers, the Alaskan papers, and all the other papers began coming in by that time, and I was plastered all over them, with reviews of the broadcast, pictures of the car, and pictures of me. The plugs I wrote for the car worked, the horn worked, and all of it worked, so they had to put more ships under charter to make deliveries. Then I had to get Winston's program ready, and began seeing him every day.

I didn't have to see him every day to get the program up. But he dropped into my dressing room one night, the way he had done before, and it was just luck that it was raining, and she still had a hangover from the cold, and had decided to stay home. She was generally out there when I sang, and always came backstage to pick me up. There was a big mob of autograph hunters back there, and instead of locking them out while I dressed, the way I generally did, I let them in, and signed everything they shoved at me, and listened to women tell me how they had come all the way from Aurora to hear me, and let him wait. When we walked out I apologized for it and said there was nothing I could do. "Don't ever come around again. This isn't Paris. Let me drop up to your hotel the morning after, and we'll have the post-mortem then."

"I'd love it! It's a standing date."

From the quick way he said it, and the fact that he had never once asked me where I was living, or made any move to come and see me, it came to me that he knew all about Juana, just like he had known all about Gold. Then I began to have this nervous feeling, that never left me, wondering what he was going to pull next.

What I was going to do with her the night of his concert I didn't know. She had got so she could read the papers now, and had spotted the announcement, and asked me about it. I acted like it was just another job of singing, and she didn't pay much attention to it. Her cold was all right now, and there wasn't a chance she would stay home on that account. I thought of telling her it was a private concert, and that I couldn't get her in, but I knew that wouldn't work. Going up in the cab, I told her that as I wouldn't have to dress afterwards, it would be better if she didn't come backstage. We'd meet in the Russian place next door. Then I could duck out quick and we'd miss the mob of handshakers. I showed it to her and she said all right, then she went in the front way and I ducked up the alley.

When I got backstage I almost fainted when I found out what he was up to. I was singing two numbers, one the aria from the Siege of Corinth for the first part of the program, the other Walter Damrosch's Mandalay, for the second part. I had squawked on that Mandalay, because I thought it was all wrong for a symphony concert. But when he made me read it over I had to admit it was in a different class from the Speaks Mandalay, or the Prince Mandalay, or any of the other barroom Mandalays. It's a little tone poem all by itself, a piece of real music, with all the verses in it except the bad one, about the housemaids, and each verse a little different from the others.

One reason it's never done is that it takes a whole male chorus, but of course cost never bothered him any. He got a chorus together, and rehearsed them until they spit blood, getting a Volga-Boat-Song-dying-away effect he wanted at the end, and by the time I had gone over it with them two or three times, we had a real number out of it.

But what he was getting ready to do was have them march on in a body, before I came on, and I had to throw a fit of temperament to stop it. I raved and cursed, said it would kill my entrance, and refused to go on if he did it that way. I said they had to drift in with the orchestra after the intermission, and take their places without any march-on. But I wasn't thinking about my entrance. What I was afraid of was that those twenty-four chorus men, marching on at a Winston Hawes concert, would be such a murderous laugh that it would tip her off to what the whole thing was about.

I peeped out before we started, and spotted her. She was sitting between an old couple, on one side, and one of the critics, alone, on the other, so it didn't look like she would hear anything. In the intermission I peeped out again. She was still sitting there, and so was the old couple. She had sneaked a piece of chewing gum into her mouth, and was munching on that, so everything seemed to be all right, so far.

The chorus were in white ties, and they went on the way I said, and nothing happened. The orchestra played a number and Winston came off. He kidded me about my fit of temperament, and I kidded back. So long as everything was under control, I didn't care. Then I went on. Whether it was what Damrosch wrote, or the way Winston conducted, or the tone of those horns, I don't know, but before the opening chords had even finished, you were in India. I started, and did a good job of it. I clowned the second verse a little, but not too much. The other verses I did straight, and the temple-bell atmosphere kept getting better. When we got to the end, with the chorus dying away behind me, and me hanging above them on the high F, it was something to hear, believe me it was. They broke out into a roar. It had been a program of modern music, most of it pretty scrappy and this was the first thing they had heard that really stuck to their ribs. I took two calls, had the chorus stand, came off, and they called me out again. Then Winston did something that's not done, and that he wouldn't have done for anybody on earth but me. He decided to repeat it.

A repeat is something you do mechanically, God knows why. You've done it once, you've scored with it, and the second time out you do it with your mouth, but your head has already gone home. I went through with it, got every laugh I had got before, coasted along without a hitch. I hit the E flat, the chorus was right with me. I hit the F, and my heart stopped. Hanging up there, over that chorus, was the priest of Acapulco, the guy in the church, singing down the storm, croaking high mass to make the face on the cross stop looking at him.

"Who is these man?"

We were in the cab going down, and it was like the whisper you hear from a coiled rattlesnake.

"What man?"

"I think you know, yes."

"I don't even know what you're talking about."

"You have been with a man."

"I've been with plenty of men. I see men all day long. Do I have to stay with you all the time? What the hell are you talking about?"

"I no speak of man you see all day long. I speak of man you love. Who is these man?"

"Oh, I'm a fairy, is that it?"

"Yes."

"Well, thanks. I didn't know that."

It was a warm night, but on account of the white tie I had to wear a coat. I had been hot as hell going up, but I wasn't hot now. I felt cold and shriveled inside. I watched the El posts going by on Third Avenue, and I could feel her there looking at me, looking at me with those hard black eyes that seemed to bore through me. We got out of the cab, and went on up to the apartment. I put the silk hat in a closet, put the coat in with it, lit a cigarette, tried to shake it off, how I felt. She just sat there on the edge of the table. She had on an evening dress we had got from one of the best shops in town, and the bullfighter's cape. Except for the look on her face, she was something out of a book.

"Why you lie to me?"

"I'm not lying."

"You lie. I look at you, I know you lie."

"Did I ever lie to you?"

"Yes. Once at Acapulco. You know you run away, you tell me no. When you want, you lie."

"We went over that. I meant to run away, and you knew what I meant. Lying, that was just how we got over it easy. Then when I found out what you meant to me, I didn't lie. That's all ... what the hell squwk have you got? You were all ready to sleep with that son-of-a-bitch—"

"I no lie."

"What has this got to do with Acapulco?"

"Yes, it is the same. Now you love man, you lie."

"I don't—Christ, do I *look* like that?"

"No. You no look like that. We meet in Tupinamba, yes? And you no look like that I like, much, how you look. Then you make *lotería* for me, and lose *lotería*. And I think, how sweet. He have lose, but he like me so much he make *lotería*. Then I send *muchacha* with address, and we go home, go where I live. But then I know. You know how I know?"

"Don't know, don't care. It's not true."

"I know when you sing. Hoaney, I was street girl, love man, three pesos. Little dumb *muchacha*, no can read, no can write, understand nothing like that. But of man—*all*. . . . Hoaney, these man who love other man, they can do much, very clever. But no can sing. Have no *toro* in high voice, no *grrr* that frighten little *muchacha*, make heart beat fast. Sound like old woman, like cow, like priest."

She began to walk around. My hands were clammy and my

lips felt numb. "... Then the *político*, he say I should open house, and I think of you. I think maybe, with these man, no like *muchacha*, have no trouble. We got to Acapulco. Rain come, we go in church. You take me. I no want, I think of *sacrilegio*, but you take me. Oh, much *toro*. I like. I think maybe Juana make mistake. Then you sing, oh, my heart beat very fast."

"Just a question of toro, hey?"

"No. You ask me to come with you. I come. I love you much. I no think of *toro*. Just a little bit. Then in New York I feel, I feel something fonny. I think you think about *contrato*, all these thing. But is not the same. Tonight I know. I make no mistake. When you love Juana, you sing nice, much *toro*. When you love man—why you lie to me? You think I no *hear*? You think I no *know*?"

If she had taken a whip to me I couldn't have answered her. She began to cry, and fought it back. She went in the other room, and pretty soon she came out. She had changed her dress and put on a hat. She was carrying the valise in one hand and the fur coat in the other. "I no live with man who love other man. I no live with man who lie. I—"

The phone rang. "—Ah!"

She ran in and answered. "Yes, he is here."

She came out, her eyes blazing and her white teeth showing behind something that was between a laugh and a snarl. "Mr. Hawes."

I didn't say anything and I didn't move. "Yes, Mr. Hawes, the *director*." She gave a rasping laugh and put on the goddamdest imitation of Winston you ever saw, the walk, the stick, and all the rest of it so you almost thought he was in front of you. "Yes, your sweetie, he wait at telephone, talk to him please."

When I still sat there, she jumped at me like a tiger, shook me till I could feel my teeth rattling, and then ran in to the telephone. "What you want with Mr. Sharp, please? ... Yes, yes, he will come. ... Yes, thank you much. Goodbye."

She came out again. "Now, please you go. He have party, want you very much. Now, go to your sweetie. Go! Go! Go!"

She shook me again, jerked me out of the chair, tried to push me out the door. She grabbed up the valise and the fur coat again. I ran in the bedroom, flopped on the bed, pulled the pillow over my head. I wanted to shut it out, the whole horrible thing she had showed me, where she had ripped the cover off my whole life, dragged out what was down there all the time. I screwed my eyes shut, kept pulling the pillow around my ears. But one thing kept slicing up at me, no matter what I did. It was the fin of that shark.

I don't know how long I stayed there. I was on my back after a while, staring at nothing. It was dead quiet outside, and dead still, except for the searchlight from the building on Fourteenth Street, that kept going around and around. I kept telling myself she was crazy, that voice is a matter of palate, sinus, and throat, that Winston had no more to do with what happened to me in Paris than the scenery had. But here it was, starting on me again the same way it had before, and I knew she had called it on me the way it was written in the big score, and that no pillow or anything else could shut it out. I closed my eyes, and I was going down under the waves, with something coming up at me from below. Panic caught me then. I hadn't heard her go out, and I called her. I waited, and called again. There wasn't any answer. My head was under the pillow again pretty soon, and I must have slept because I woke up with the same horrible dream, that I was in the water, going down, and this thing was coming at me. I sat up, and there she was, on the edge of her bed, looking at me. It was gray outside. "Christ, you're there." But some kind of a sob jerked out as I said it, and I put out my hand and took hers.

"It's all true."

She came over, sat down beside me, stroked my hair, held my hand. "Tell me. You no lie, I no fight."

"There's nothing to tell. . . . Every man has got five per cent of that in him, if he meets the one person that'll bring it out, and I did, that's all."

"But you love other man. Before."

"No, the same one, here, in Paris, all over, the one son-of-a-bitch that's been the curse of my life."

"Sleep now. Tomorrow, you give me little bit money, I go back to Mexico—"

"No! Don't you know what I'm trying to tell you? That's out! I hate it! I've been ashamed of it, I've tried to shake it off, I hoped you would never find out, and now it's over!"

I was holding her to me. She began stroking my hair again, looking down in my eyes. "You love me, Hoaney?"

"Don't you know it? Yes. If I never said so, it was just because—did we have to say it? If we felt it, wasn't that a hell of a sight more?"

All of a sudden she broke from me, shoved the dress down from her shoulder, slipped the brassiere and shoved a nipple in my mouth. "Eat. Eat much. Make big *toro!*"

"I know now, my whole life comes from there."

"Yes, eat."

11

We didn't get up for two days, but it wasn't like the time we had in the church. We didn't get drunk and we didn't laugh. When we were hungry, we'd call up the French restaurant down the street and have them send something in. Then we'd lie there and talk, and I'd tell her more of it, until it was all off my chest and I had nothing more to say. Once I quit lying to her, she didn't seem surprised, or shocked, or anything like that. She would look at me, with her eyes big and black, and nod, and sometimes say something that made me think she understood a lot more about it than I did, or most doctors do. Then I'd take her in my arms, and afterward we'd sleep, and I felt a peace I hadn't felt for years. All those awful jitters of that last few weeks were gone, and sometimes when she was asleep and I wasn't, I'd think about the Church, and confession, and what it must mean to people that have something lying heavy on their soul. I had left the Church before I had anything on my soul, and the confession business, to me then, was just a pain in the neck. But I understood it now, understood a lot of things I had never understood before. And mostly I understood what a woman could mean to a man. Before, she had been a pair of eyes, and a shape, something to get excited about. Now, she seemed something to lean on, and draw something from, that nothing else could give me. I thought of books I had read, about worship of the earth, and how she was always called Mother, and none of it made much sense, but those big round breasts did, when I put my head on them, and they began to tremble, and I began to tremble.

The morning of the second day we heard the church bells ringing, and I remembered I was due to sing at the Sunday night concert. I got up, went to the piano, and tossed a few high ones around. I was just trying them out, but I didn't have to. They were like velvet. At six o'clock we dressed, had a little something to eat, and went down there. I was in a Rigoletto excerpt, from the second act, with a tenor, a bass, a soprano, and a mezzo that were all getting spring try-outs. I was all right. When we got home we changed to pajamas again, and I got out the guitar. I sang her the Evening Star song, *Träume, Schmerzen,* things like that. I never liked Wagner, and she couldn't understand a word of German. But it had earth, rain, and the night in it, and went with the humor we were in. She sat there with her eyes closed, and I sang it half voice. Then I took her hand and we sat there, not moving.

A week went by, and still I didn't see Winston. He must have called twenty times, but she took all calls, and when it was him she would just say I wasn't in, and hang up. I had nothing to say to him but goodbye, and I wasn't going to say that, because I didn't want to play the scene. Then one day, after we had been out for breakfast, we stepped out of the elevator, and there he was at the end of the hall, watching porters carrying furniture into an apartment. He looked at us and blinked, then dived at us with his hand out. "Jack! Is that you? Well, of all the idiotic coincidences!"

I felt my blood freeze for fear of what she was going to do, but she didn't do anything. When I happened not to see his hand, he began waving it around, and kept chattering about the coincidence, about how he had just signed a lease for an apartment in this very building, and here we were. She smiled. "Yes, very fonny."

There didn't seem to be anything to do but introduce him, so I did. She held out her hand. He took it and bowed. He said he was happy to know her. She said *gracias,* she had been at his concert, and she was honored to know him. Two beautiful sets of manners met in the hall that day, and it seemed queer, the venom that was back of them.

The door of the freight elevator opened, and more furniture started down the hall. "Oh, I'll have to show them where to put it. Come in, you two, and have a look at my humble abode."

"Some other time, Winston, we—"

"Yes, *gracias,* I like."

We went in there, and he had one of the apartments on the south tier, the biggest in the building, with a living room the size of a recital hall, four or five bedrooms and baths, servants' rooms, study, everything you could think of. The stuff I remembered from Paris was there, rugs, tapestries, furniture, all of it worth a fortune, and a lot of things I had never seen. Four or five guys in denim suits were standing around, waiting to be told where to put their loads. He paid no attention to them, except to direct them with one hand, like they were a bunch of bull fiddlers. He sat us down on a sofa, pulled up a chair for himself, and went on talking about how he was sick of hotel living, had about given up all hope of finding an apartment he liked, and then had found this place, and then of all the cock-eyed things, here we were.

Or were we? I said yes, we were at the other end of the hall. We all laughed: He started in on Juana, asked if she wasn't Mexican. She said yes, and he started off about his trip there, and what a wonderful country it was, and I had to hand it to him he had found out more about it in a week than I had in six months. You would have thought he might have conveniently left out what he went down there for. He didn't. He said he went down there to bring me back. She laughed, and said she saw me first. He laughed. That was the first time there was the least little glint in their eyes.

"Oh, I must show you my cricket!"

He jumped up, grabbed a hatchet, and began chopping a small crate apart. Then he lifted out a block of pink stone, a little bigger than a football and about the same shape, but carved and polished into the form of a cricket, with its legs drawn up under it and its head huddled between its front feet. She made a little noise and began to finger it.

"Look at that, Jack. Isn't it marvelous? Pure Aztec, at least five hundred years old. I brought it back from Mexico with me, and I'd hate to tell you what I had to do to get it out of the country. Look at that simplification of detail. If Manship had done it, they'd have thought it was a radical sample of his work. The line of that belly is pure Brancusi. It's as modern as a streamlined plane, and yet some Indian did it before he even saw a white man."

"Yes, yes. Make me feel very *nostálgica.*"

Then came the real Hawes touch. He picked it up, staggered with it over to the fireplace, and put it down. "For my hearth!"

She got up to go, and I did. "Well, children, you know now where I live, and I want to be seeing a lot of you."

"Yes, *gracias.*"

"And oh! As soon as I'm moved in, I'm giving a little house-warming, and you're surely coming to it—"

"Well, I don't know, Winston, I'm pretty busy—"

"Too busy for my housewarming? Jack, Jack, Jack!"

"*Gracias,* Señor Hawes. Perhaps we come."

"Perhaps? Certainly you'll come!"

I was plenty shaky when we got to our own apartment. "Listen, Juana, we're getting out of this dump, and we're getting out quick. I don't know what the hell his game is, but this is no coincidence. He's moved in on us, and we're going to beat it."

"We beat it, he come too."

"Then we'll beat it again. I don't want to see him."

"Why you run away?"

"I don't know. It—makes me nervous. I want to be somewhere where I don't have to see him, don't have to think of him, don't have to feel that he's around."

"I think we stay."

We saw him twice more that day. Once, around six o'clock, he rang the buzzer and asked us to dinner, but I was singing and said we would have to eat later. Then, some time after midnight, when we had got home, he dropped in with a kid named Pudinsky, a Russian pianist that was to play at his next concert. He said they were going to run over some stuff, and for us to come on down. We said we were tired. He didn't argue. He put his arm around Pudinsky, and they left. While we were undressing we could hear the piano going. The kid could play all right.

"I see his game now."

"Yes. Very fonny game."

"That boy. I'm supposed to get jealous."

"*Are* you jealous?"

"No. Jealous—what the hell are you talking about? What difference does it make to me what he does, once I'm out of it? But it makes me nervous. I—I wish he was somewhere else. I wish we were all somewhere else."

She lay there for a long time, up on one elbow, looking down at me. Then she kissed me and went over to her own bed. It was daylight before I got to sleep.

Next day he was in and out half a dozen times, and the day after that, and that day after that. I began missing cues, the first sign you get that you're not right. The voice was in shape, and I was getting across, but the prompter began throwing the finger at me. It was the first time in my life that that had ever happened.

In about a week came the invitation to the housewarming. I tried to beg out of it, said I had to sing that night, but she smiled and said *gracias,* we would go, and he put his arm around her and you would have thought they were pals, but I knew them both like a book, and could tell there was something back of it, on both sides. After he left I got peevish and wanted to know why the hell she was shoving me into it all the time. "Hoaney, with this man, it do you no good to run away. He see you no care, then maybe he estop. He know you have afraid, he never estop. We go. We laugh, have fine time, no care ... You care?"

"For God's sake, no."

"I think yes, little bit. I think we have—how you say—the goat."

"He's got my goat all right, but not for that reason. I just don't want any more to do with him."

"Then you care. Maybe not so, how he want. But you have afraid. When you no care at all, he estop. Now—we no run away. We go, you sing, be fine fallow, no give a damn. And you watch, will be all right."

"If I have to, I have to, but Christ, I hate it."

So we went. I was singing Faust, and I was so lousy I almost did get stuck in the duel scene. But I was washed up by ten thirty, and we came home and dressed. It wasn't any white dress with flowers on it this time. She put on a bottle-green evening dress, and over that the bullfighter's cape, and that embroidered crimson and yellow silk, sliding over the green taffeta, made a rustle you could hear coming, I'm here to tell you, and all those colors, over the light copper of her skin, was a picture you could look at. I put on a white tie, but no overcoat or anything, and about a quarter after eleven we stepped out and walked down the hall.

When we got in there, the worst drag was going on you ever saw in your life. A whole mob of them was in there, girls in men's evening clothes tailored for them, with shingle haircuts and blue make-up in their eyes, dancing with other girls dressed the same way, young guys with lipstick on, and mascara eyelashes, dancing with each other too, and at least three girls in full evening dress, that you had to look at twice to make sure they weren't girls at all. Pudinsky was at the piano, but he wasn't playing Brahms. He was playing jazz. The whole thing made me sick to my stomach as soon as I looked at it, but I swallowed hard and tried to act like I was glad to be there.

Winston had on a purple velvet dinner coat with a silk sash knotted around it, and he brought us in like it was all for us. He introduced us, and got us drinks, and Pudinsky slammed into the Pagliacci Prologue, and I stepped up and sang it, and clowned it with as good a grin as I could get on my face. While they were still clapping, Winston turned around and began to throw the show to Juana. She still hadn't taken off the cape, and he lifted it off her shoulders, and began going into a spasm about it. They all crowded up to look, and when he found out it was a real bullfighter's cape, nothing would suit him but that she had to tell them all about the fine points of bullfighting. I sat down, and got this feeling it wasn't on the up-and-up, that something was coming. I thought of Chadwick, and wondered if this was another play to show her up. But that wasn't it. Except that Winston would put his arm around Pudinsky every time he saw me looking at him, he didn't pull anything. He put her in the spot, and made her explain the whole routine of bullfighting, and she took the cape to show them, and she was pretty funny, and so was he. Nobody could make a woman look good better than Winston, when he wanted to. Pretty soon somebody yelled out: "How the hell does a man study to be a bullfighter, that's what I want to know."

Winston went down on his knees in front of Juana.

"Yes, will you tell us that? Just what are the practice exercises for a bullfighter?"

"Oh, I explain you."

They all sat down, and Winston squatted at her feet.

"First, the little boy, he wants to be a bullfighter, yes? All little boy want to be bullfighter."

"I always did. I do still."

"So, I tell you how you do. You find nice burro, you know what is burro?"

"A little jackass, something like that?"

"Yes. You get little jackass, you cut two big maguey leaf, you know maguey, yes? Have big leaf, much thick, much sharp—?"

"Century plant?"

"Yes. Tie leaf on head of little jackass, make big horn, like bull—"

"Wait a minute."

Some woman dug up a ribbon, and Winston broke off fronds from a fern, and with the ribbon and the fern leaves, he stuck the horns on his head. Then he got down on his hands and knees in front of Juana. "Go on."

"Yes, just so. You look much like little jackass."

That got a shout. Winston looked up, kicked his heels, and let out a jackass bellow. It was a little funnier than it sounds.

"Then you get little stick, for *espada*, and little red rag, for *muleta*, and practice with little jackass." Somebody dug up a silver-headed cane, and she took it, and the cape, and the two of them began doing a bullfight act in the middle of the floor. The rest of them were screeching and yelling by that time, and I was sitting there, wondering what the hell was up. The buzzer sounded. Somebody went to the door, came back, and touched me on the arm. "Telegram for you, Mr. Sharp."

I went out in the hall.

Harry, one of the bellboys, was out there, and shoved a telegram at me. I opened it. It was nothing but a blank form shoved in an envelope. "Is the messenger still there? He's given you nothing but a blank."

Harry closed the door to the apartment. You could still hear them in there, screeching over the bullfight. "Let me talk quick, Mr. Sharp, so you can get back in there before anybody thinks anything. I had to have a telegram in my hand, so it would look right. . . . There's a man down there, waiting for you. I told him you were out. He went up to your apartment, then he came down again, and he's down there now."

"In the lobby?"

"Yes sir."

"What does he want?"

"... Mr. Sharp, Tony put through three calls today for this new party, Mr. Hawes. They were all to the immigration service. Tony remembered the number from a year ago, when his brother came from Italy. Tony thinks this man is a federal, come to take Miss Montes away."

"Is Tony on?"

"We're both on. Get back in there, Mr. Sharp, before this Hawes gets tipped off. Get her out of there, and have her press the elevator button twice. Either me or Tony will get her out through the basement, and then you can stall this guy till she gets under cover. Tony thinks his people will take her in. They're fans of yours."

I had a wad of money in my pocket. I took it out and peeled off a ten. "Split that with Tony. There'll be more tomorrow. She'll be right down."

"Yes, sir."

"And thanks. More thanks than I know how to say."

I stepped back in. I took care to be stuffing the telegram in my pocket as I came. Winston jumped up from where he was still galumphing around the floor, and came over. "What is it, Jack?"

"Just some greetings from Hollywood."

"Bad?"

"Little bit."

"Well, what is it? By God, I'd love to wake the sons-of-bitches up and tell them where they get off."

"Wouldn't wake them up, that's the trouble. It's only ten o'clock there. To hell with it, I'll tell you later. And to hell with bullfighting. Let's dance."

"Dance we shall. Hey, professor—music!"

Pudinsky began to bat out more jazz, they grabbed each other, and I grabbed Juana. "Now get a grin on your face. I've got something to tell you."

"Yes, here is nice grin."

I laid it out for her fast. "This Pudinsky thing is nothing

but a smoke screen. He's turned in an anonymous tip against you, then you're to be taken to Ellis Island, then I'm to run to him for help, then he's to move heaven and earth—and fail. You're to be sent back to Mexico—"

"And then he gets you."

"So he thinks."

"So I think, too."

"Will you for God's sake stop that and—"

"Why you tremble?"

"I'm plenty scared of him, that's why. Now listen—"

"Yes, I listen."

"Get out of here, quick. Get out on some stall so he thinks you're coming back. Change your dress, pack, as fast as you can. If the buzzer rings, keep still and don't answer. Go to the elevator, ring twice, and the boys will take care of you. Don't call me. Tomorrow I'll reach you through Tony. Here's some money."

I had palmed the wad, and slipped it down the back of her dress. "And once more, step on it!"

"Yes, I step."

She went over to Winston. He was sitting with Pudinsky, the fern leaves still in his hair. "You want to play *real* bullfight, yes?"

"I just thirst for it."

"Wait. I get things. I come back."

He showed her out, then came over to me. "Lovely girl."

"Yeah, she's all of that."

"I've always said there were two nations under every flag, male and female. I wouldn't give a damn for all the Mexican men that ever lived, but the women are marvelous. What saps their painters are, with all that beauty around them, to spend their days on war, socialism, and politics. Mexican art is nothing but a collection of New Masses covers."

"Whatever it is, I don't like it."

"Who would? But if they could paint her face, that would have been different. Goya could have, but those worthy radicals, no. Well—they don't know what they miss."

I went over, sat down and watched them dance. They were getting lit by now, and it was pretty raw. I wished I had fixed up some signal from the boys, so I would know when she was out. I hadn't, so all I could do was sit there. I was going to wait till he missed her, then go down to the apartment to find her, then come back and say she didn't feel well, and had gone to bed. It would all take time, give her a start, but I had to take the play from him.

I had looked at my watch when she went. It was seven after one. After a hell of a time I slipped back to a bathroom and looked again. It was eleven after. She had been gone four minutes: I came back and sat down again. Pudinsky stopped and they all yelled for more. He said he was tired. The buzzer rang. Winston opened, and I began thinking of a stall in case it was the detective. Who stepped in was Juana. She hadn't changed her dress. Over her arm was the cape, in one hand was the *espada*, and in the other the ear.

They had got a little sick of bullfighting, but when they saw the ear they began to yell again. They passed it around, and felt it, and smelled it, and say "Peyooh!" Winston took it, held it up to his head and wobbled it, and they laughed and clapped. He got down on the floor again and bellowed. Juana laughed. "Yes, now you are no more jackass. Big bull."

He bellowed again. I was getting so nervous I was twitching. I went over to her. "Take that stuff back. I'm fed up on bull-fighting, and that ear stinks. Take it back where you got it, and—"

I grabbed for the ear. Winston dodged. She laughed and wouldn't look at me. Something hit me in the belly. When I looked around I saw that one of the fags in woman's clothes had poked me with a broomstick. "Out of my way! I'm a pic-ador! I'm a picador on his old white horse!"

Two or three more of them ran back and got broomsticks, or mops handles, or whatever was there, to be picadors, and began galloping around Winston, poking at him. Every time they touched him he'd bellow. Juana drew the *espada*, and spread the cape with it, like it was a *muleta*. Winston began charging it, on one hand and his knees, still holding the ear with his other hand and wobbling it. Pudinsky began to rip off the bullring music from Carmen. There was so much noise you couldn't even hear yourself think. I walked over and leaned on the piano, with my back to it, till she would get the clowning over and I would have another chance to get her out.

All of a sudden Pudinsky stopped, and this "Ooh!" went around the room. I turned around. She was standing there, like a statue, the way they do for the kill, with her left side to Winston, the sword in her right hand, up at the level of her eyes, and pointing right at him. In her left hand, down in front of him, she held the cape. He was down there looking at it, and wobbling the ear at it. Pudinsky began to play blue chords on the piano.

Winston snorted a couple of times, then looked up at her, like he wanted a cue on what to do next. Then he jumped up, and back, but a sofa caught him. A man yelled. I jumped for the sword arm, but I was too late. That *espada* thrust isn't something in slow motion, like you maybe have thought from reading the books. It goes like lightning, and next thing I knew the point of the steel was sticking out the back of the sofa, and blood was foaming out of Winston's mouth, and she was over him, talking to him, laughing at him, telling him the detective was waiting to take him down to hell.

It flashed over me, that mob at the novelladas, pouring down out of the *sol*, twisting the tail of the dying bull, yelling at him, kicking at him, spitting on him, and I tried to tell myself I had hooked up with a savage, that it was horrible. It was no use. I wanted to laugh, and cheer, and yell *Olé!* I knew I was looking at the most magnificent thing I had ever seen in my life.

12

She spit into the blood, stepped back, and picked up the cape. For a second all you could hear was Pudinsky, over at the piano, gasping and slobbering in an agony of fright. Then they made a rush for the door, to get out before the police came. They fought to get past each other, the women cursing like men, the fags screaming like women, and when they got to the hall they didn't wait for the elevator. They went piling down the stairway, and some of them fell, and you could hear more curses, and screams, and thuds, where they were kicking each other. She came over and knelt beside me, where I had folded into a chair. "Now, he no get. Goodbye, and remember Juana." She kissed me, jumped up, and rustled out. I sat there, still looking at that thing that was pinned to the sofa, with its head hanging over the back, and the blood drying on the shirt. Pudinsky lifted his head, where it was buried in his hands, saw it, let out a moan, and ran over to a corner, where he put his head down and broke out into more sobs. I picked up a rug to throw on it. Then something twisted in my stomach, and I stumbled back to a bathroom. I hadn't eaten since afternoon, but white stuff began coming up, and even after my stomach was empty it kept retching, and horrible sounds came out of me from the air it forced up. I saw my face in the mirror. It was green.

When I came out two cops were there, and four or five of the fags, and one of the girls in a dinner coat, and a guy in a derby hat. Whether he was the dick that had been waiting for Juana, and he grabbed some of them on the way out, I didn't know. When the cops saw me they motioned me to stand aside, and one of them went back to phone. Pretty soon two more cops came up, and a couple of detectives, and next thing, the place was full of cops. There was one guy that seemed to be a doctor, and another that seemed to be a police photographer. Anyway, he set up a tripod, and began setting off bulbs and throwing them in the fern pot. Pretty soon a cop went over, motioned to me, and he, a detective, and I went out. I didn't have any coat there, but I didn't say anything about it. I didn't know whether they had Juana, or even where she had gone, and I was afraid if I asked them to let me go to the apartment, they would come with me and find her. We went down in the elevator. Harry ran us down. When we got to the lobby, more cops were there, talking to Tony.

We got in a police car, drove down Second Avenue, then down Lafayette Street, and on downtown to a place that seemed to be police headquarters. We got out, went in, and the cops took me in a room and told me to sit down. One of them went out. The other stayed, and picked up an afternoon paper that was on the table. We must have sat an hour, he reading the paper and neither of us saying anything. After a while I asked him if he had a cigarette. He passed over a pack without looking up. I smoked and we sat for another hour. Outside it was beginning to get light.

About six o'clock a detective came in, sat down, and stared at me a while. Then he began to talk. "You was there tonight? At this here Hawes's place?"

"Yes, I was."

"You seen him killed?"

"I did."

"What she kill him for?"

"That I don't know."

"Come on, you know. What you trying to do, kid me?"

"I told you I don't know."

"You live with her?"

"Yes."

"Then what do you mean you don't know? What she kill him for."

"I've got no idea at all."

"Was she in this country illegal?"

I knew by that Tony had spilled what he knew. "That I can't tell you. She might have been."

"What the hell can you tell me?"

"Anything I know I'll tell you."

He roared for a minute about how he could make me tell him, but that was a mistake. It gave me time to think. That illegal entry was a way he could tie me in, and hold me if he wanted to, and I knew the only way I could be of any use to her was to get out of there. Whether they had got her or not I didn't know, but I couldn't be any good sitting behind bars. I kept looking at him, thinking over the entries on my passport, and by the time he began asking questions again I had it all in hand, and thought I could get away with a lie. "So you quit that goddam stalling. One more thing you can't tell me and I'll open you up. Come on. She was in illegal, wasn't she?"

"I told you I don't know."

"Did you bring her in?"

"I did not."

"What? Wasn't you in Mexico?"

"Yes, I was."

"Didn't you bring her in with you?"

"I did not. I met her in Los Angeles."

"How you come in?"

"I rode a bus up to Nogales, caught a ride to San Antonio, and from there took another bus to Los Angeles. I met her about a week after that, in the Mexican quarter. Then I began working for pictures, and we hooked up. Then she came with me to New York."

I saw I had led with my chin on that, on account of the white slave charge. He snapped it back at me before I even finished. "Oh, so you brought her to New York."

"I did not. She paid her own fare."

"What the hell are you trying to tell me? Didn't I say cut that stalling out?"

"All right, ask her."

Then came a flicker in his eye. I had a quick hunch they hadn't got her yet. "Ask her, that's all I've got to say. Don't be silly. I'm not paying any woman's fare from Los Angeles to New York. I heard of the Mann Act too."

"Who turned in the tip against her?"

"That I don't know."

"Come on—"

"I told you I don't know. Now if you'll cut out your goddam nonsense, I'll tell you what I do know, and maybe it'll help you out, I don't know. But you can just drop this third-degree stuff right now, or I'll be starting a little third-degree of my own before long that you may not like so well."

"What do you mean by that?"

"You know what I mean. You're not talking to some Hell's Kitchen gunman. I've got a few friends, see? I don't ask any favors. But I'm claiming my rights, and I'll get them."

"All right, Sharp. Shoot it."

"We went to the party, she and I."

"Yeah, that drag was a funny place for a guy like you."

"He was a pixie, but he was also a musician, and I had worked for him, and when he asked us to his housewarming—"

"Are you a pix?"

"Starting up again, are you?"

"Go on, Sharp. Just checking up."

"So we went. And pretty soon one of the boys came up, and—"

"One of them pixes?"

"One of the bellboys. And I found out there was a guy downstairs waiting to see me. And I found out Hawes had put in three calls that day to the Immigration Office—"

"Then he *did* turn her in?"

"I told you I don't know. I wasn't taking any chances. I told her what the boys had told me, and tried to get her out of there. I told her to leave, and she did, but then she came back with this sword, and they started up again this bullfight game they had been playing—"

"Yeah, we know all about that."

"And she let him have it. And goddam well he had it coming to him. What the hell business was it of his whether she—"

"What he turn her in for?"

"That I don't know either. He had tried to tell me once or twice that living with a girl the way we did wasn't doing me any good, that it was hurting my career—"

"Your singing career?"

"That's right."

"What he have to do with that?"

"He had plenty to do with it. I don't only sing here in New York. I'm under contract to a Hollywood picture company, and he controlled the picture company, or said he did, and he was afraid—"

"Hays office stuff?"

"That's it."

"Oh, I get it now. Go on."

"That's all. It wasn't just morals, take it from me it wasn't, or friendship, or anything like that. It was money, and fear that the Mann Act would ruin one of his big stars, and stuff like that. All right, he went up against the wrong person. She let him have it, and now let him count up his Class A preferred stock."

He asked me a few more questions and then went out. As near as I could tell I had done all right. I had fixed her up with a motive that anyway made sense, him trying to bust us up, and it would look a hell of a sight better after we were married, as I knew we would be before the case ever came to trial. I had kept out of it what was really between Winston and me. I would have even told him that if it would have done her any good, but I knew that one whisper of that would crack everything wide open, and ruin her. I had anyhow made some kind of a stall about the Mann Act and the illegal entry, and they couldn't disprove it unless she told them different, and I knew they'd never get anything out of her. Around seven o'clock they gave me something to eat, and I waited for their next move.

Around eight o'clock a cop came in with one of my traveling cases, with clothes in it. That meant they had been in the apartment. I was still in evening clothes, and began to change. "You got a washroom here?"

"O.K., we'll take you to it. You want a barber?"

All I had in my pocket, after giving her the money was silver, but I counted it. There were a couple of dollars of it. "Yeah, send him in."

He went out, and the cop that was guarding took me down to the washroom. There was a shower there, so I stripped, had a bath, and put on the other clothes. The barber came in and shaved me. I put the evening clothes in the traveling case. They had brought me a hat, and I put that on. Then we went back to the room we had left.

A little after nine I was still pounding on it in my mind, what I could do, and it came to me that one thing I could do was get a lawyer. I remembered Sholto. "I'd like to make a phone call. How about that?"

"You're allowed one call."

We went out in the hall, where there was a row of phones against the wall. I looked up Sholto's number, rang it, and got him on the line. "Oh hello, I was wondering if you'd call. I see you're in a little trouble."

"Yeah, and I want you."

"I'll be right down."

In about a half hour he showed up. He listened to me. About all I could tell him, with the cop sitting there, was that I wanted to get out, but that seemed to be all he wanted to know. "It's probably just a matter of bond."

"What am I held for? Do you know that?"

"Material witness."

"Oh, I see."

"As soon as I can see a bondsman—that is, unless you want to put up cash bond yourself."

"How much is it?"

"I don't know. At a guess, I'd say five thousand."

"Which way is quickest?"

"Oh, money talks."

He had a blank check, and I wrote out a check for ten thousand. "All right, that ought to cover it. I think we can get action in about an hour."

Around ten o'clock he was back, and he, and the cop, and I went over to court. It took about five minutes. An assistant district attorney was there, they set bail at twenty-five hundred, and after Sholto put it up, we went out and got in a cab. He passed over the rest of the cash, in hundred-dollar bills. I handed back ten of them. "Retainer."

"Very well, thanks."

The first thing I wanted to know was whether they had got her yet. When he said they hadn't, I grabbed an early afternoon paper a boy shoved in the window, and read it. It was smeared all over the front page, with my picture, and Winston's picture, but no picture of her. That was one break. As well as I could remember, she hadn't had any picture taken since she had been in the country. It was something we hadn't got around to. There was one story giving Winston's career, another telling about me, and a main story that told what had happened. Everything I had said to the detective was in there, and the big eight-column streamer called her the "Sword-Killer," and said she was "Sought." I was still reading when we pulled up at Radio City.

When we got up to his office I began going over what I had told the detective, the illegal entry stuff and all, and why I had said what I had, but pretty soon he stopped me. "Listen, get this straight. Your counsel is not your co-conspirator in deceiving the police. He's your representative at the bar, to see that you get every right that the law entitles you to, and that your case, or her case, or whatever case he takes, is presented as well as it can be. What you told the detective is none of my affair, and it's much better, at this time, that I know nothing of it. When the time comes, I'll ask for information, and you had better tell me the truth. But at the moment, I prefer not to know of any misrepresentation you've made. From now on, by the way, an excellent plan, in dealing with the police, would be to say nothing."

"I get it."

He kept walking around his office, then he picked up the paper and studied that a while, then walked around some more. "There's something I want to warn you about."

"Yeah. What?"

"It seemed to me I got you out very easily."

"I didn't do anything."

"If they had wanted to hold you, there were two or three charges, apparently, they could have brought against you. All bailable offenses, but they could have kept you there quite a while. They could have made trouble. Also, the bond was absurdly low."

"I don't quite follow you."

"They haven't got her. They may have her, tucked away in some station-house in the Bronx, they may be holding her there and saying nothing for fear of habeas corpus proceedings, but I don't think so. They haven't got her, and it's quite possible they've let you out so they can locate her through you."

"Oh, now I see what you mean."

"You going back to your apartment?"

"I don't know. I suppose so."

"... You'll be watched. There'll probably be a tail on you day and night. Your phone may be tapped."

"Can they do that?"

"They can, and they do. There may be a dictaphone in there by now, and they're pretty good at thinking of places to put it without your finding it, or suspecting it. It's a big apartment house, and that makes it all the easier for them. I don't know what her plans are, and apparently you don't. But it's a bad case. If they catch her, I'll do everything I can for her, but I warn you it's a bad case. It's much better than she not be located.... Be careful."

"I will."

"The big danger is that she phone you. Whatever you do, the second she rings up, warn her that she's being overheard."

"I'll remember that."

"You're being used as a decoy."

"I'll watch my step."

When I got up to Twenty-second Street a flock of reporters were there, and I stuck with them for about ten minutes. I thought it was better to answer their questions some kind of way, and get rid of them, than have them trying to get to me all day. When I got up to the apartment the phone was ringing, and a newspaper was on the line, offering me five thousand dollars for a signed story of what I knew about it, and about her, and I said no, and hung up. It started to ring again, and I flashed the board and told them not to put through any more incoming calls, or let anybody up. The door buzzer sounded. I answered, and it was Harry and Tony, on hand to tell me what they knew. I peeled off a hundred-dollar bill as they started to talk, handed it over, and then remembered about the dicta-phone. We went out in the hall, and they whispered it. She didn't leave right after it happened. She went to the apartment, packed, and changed her dress, and about five or ten minutes later buzzed twice, like I had told her to. Tony had the car up there all that time, waiting for her, and he opened, pulled her in, and dropped her down to the basement. They went out by the alley, and when they came out on Twenty-third Street he got her a cab, and she left. That was the last he saw of her, and he didn't tell it to the police. While he was doing that, Harry was on the board in the lobby, and didn't pay much attention when he saw the fags going out, and neither did the guy from the Immigration Service. How the cops found it out they didn't know, but they thought the fags must have bumped into one outside, or got scared and thought they better tell it anyway, or something. Tony said the cops were already in Winston's apartment before she left.

They went down and I went in the apartment again. With the phone cut off it was quiet enough now, but I began looking for the dictaphone. I couldn't find anything. I looked out the window to see if anybody was watching the building. There wasn't anybody out there. I began to think Sholto was imagining things.

Around two o'clock I got hungry and went out. The reporters were still down there, and almost mobbed me, but I jumped in a cab and told him to drive to Radio City. As soon as he got to Fourth Avenue I had him cut over to Second again, and come down, and got out at a restaurant around Twenty-third Street. I had something to eat and took down the number of the pay phone. When I got back to the apartment house, I whispered to the boy on the board if a Mr. Kugler called, to put him through. I went upstairs and called the restaurant phone. "Is Mr. Kugler there?"

"Hold the line, I'll see."

I held the line, and in a minute he was back. "No Mr. Kugler here now."

"When he comes in ask him to call Mr. Sharp. S-H-A-R-P."

"Yes sir, I'll tell him."

I hung up. In about twenty minutes the phone rang. "Mr. Sharp? This is Kugler."

"Oh, hello, Mr. Kugler. About those opera passes I promised

you, I'm afraid I'll have to disappoint you for the time being.
You may have read in the paper I'm having a little trouble
now. Can you let me put that off till next week."

"Oh, all right, Mr. Sharp. Any time you say."

"Terribly sorry, Mr. Kugler."

I hung up. I knew then that Sholto knew what he was talking
about. I didn't know any Mr. Kugler.

Harry kept bringing up new editions as they came out, and the
stuff that was coming in for me. They still hadn't got her. They
found the taxi driver that rode her from Twenty-third Street.
He said he took her down to Battery Park, she paid him with
a five-dollar bill, so he had to go in the subway to get change,
and then went off, carrying the valise. He told how Tony had
flagged him, and Tony took another trip down to headquarters. It said the cops were considering the possibility she had
jumped in the river, and that it might be dragged. The stuff
that was coming in was a flock of telegrams, letters, and cards
from every kind of nut you ever heard of, and opera fan, and
shyster lawyer. But a couple of those wires weren't from nuts.
One was from Panamier, saying the broadcast would temporarily be carried on by somebody else. And one was from Luther,
saying no doubt I preferred not to have any more opera ap-
pearances until I got my affairs straightened out. The last afternoon edition had a story about Pudinsky. I felt my mouth
go cold. He was the one person that might know about Winston
and me. If he did he didn't say anything. He said what a fine
guy Winston was, what a loyal friend, and defended him for
calling up the Immigration people. He said Winston only had
my best interests at heart.

I went out to eat around seven o'clock, dodged the reporters
again, and had a steak in a place off Broadway. My picture was
in every paper in town, but nobody seemed to notice me. One
reason was, most of those pictures had been taken while I was
in Hollywood, and I had put on a lot of weight since then. I
wasn't exactly fat when I arrived from Mexico. Then I had a

little trouble with my eyes, and had got glasses. I ate what I could, walked around a little, then around nine o'clock came back to the apartment: All the time I was walking I kept looking back, to see if I was followed. I tried not to, but I couldn't help it. In the cab, I kept twisting around, to see what was back of us.

There was another mountain of stuff when I came in, but I didn't bother to open it. I read back all the newspaper stuff again, and then there didn't seem to be anything to do but to go to bed. I lay there, first trying to think and then trying to sleep. I couldn't do either one. Then after a while I did drop off. I woke up in a cold sweat with moans coming out of my mouth. The whole day had been like some kind of a fever dream, chasing in and out of cabs, dodging reporters, trying to shake the police, if they were around, reading papers. Now for the first time I seemed to get it through my head the spot we were in. She was wanted for murder, and if they caught her they would burn her in the chair.

What waked me up the next morning was the phone. Harry was on the board. "I know you said not to call, Mr. Sharp, but there's a guy on the line, he kept calling all day yesterday, and now he's calling again, he says he's a friend of yours, and it's important, and he's got to talk to you, and I thought I better tell you."

"Who is he?"

"He won't say, but he said I should say the word Acapulco, something like that, to you, and you would know who it was."

"Put him through."

I hoped it might be Conners, and sure enough when I heard that "Is that you, lad?" I knew it was. He was pretty short. "I've been trying to reach you. I've called you, and wired you, and called again, and again—"

"I cut the phone calls off, and I haven't opened the last bunch of wires. You'd have been through in a second if they had told me. I want to see you, I've got to see you—"

"You have indeed. I have news."

"Stop! Don't say a word. I warn you that my phone is tapped, and everything you say is being heard."

"That occurred to me. That's why I refused to give my name. How can I get to you?"

"Wait a minute. Wait a minute.... Will you call me in five minutes? I'll have to figure a way—"

"In five minutes it is."

He hung up, and I tried to think of some way we could meet, and yet not tip off the cops over the phone where it would be. I couldn't think. He had said he had news, and my head was just spinning around. Before I even had half an idea the phone rang again. "Well, lad, what's the word?"

"I haven't any. They're following me too, that's the trouble. Wait a minute, wait a minute—"

"I have something that might work."

"What is it?"

"Do you remember the time signature of the serenade you first sang to me?"

"... Yes, of course."

"Write those figures down, the two of them, one beside the other. Now write them again, the same way. You should have a number of four figures."

I jumped up, and got a pen, and wrote the numbers on the memo pad. It was the Don Giovanni serenade, and time signature is 6/8. I wrote 6868.... "All right, I've got it."

"Now subtract from it this number." He gave me a number to subtract. I did it. "That is the number of the pay telephone I'm at. The exchange number is Circle 6. Go out to another pay telephone and call me there."

"In twenty minutes. As soon as I get dressed."

I jumped into my clothes, ran up to a drugstore, and called. Whether they were around the booth, listening to me, I didn't care. They couldn't hear what was coming in at the other end. "Is that you, lad?"

"Yes. What news?"

"I have her. She's going down the line with me. I'm at the

foot of Seventeenth Street, and I slip my hawsers at midnight
tonight. If you wish to see her before we leave, come aboard
some time after eleven, but take care you're not detected."

"How did you find her?"

"I didn't. She found me. She's been aboard since yesterday,
if you had answered your phone."

"I'll be there. I'll thank you then."

I went back to the apartment, cut out the fooling around, and
began to think. I checked over every last thing I had to do that
day, then made a little program in my mind of what I was to
do first, and what I was to do after that. I knew I would be
tailed, and I planned it all on that basis. The first thing I did
was to go up to Grand Central, and look up trains for Rye. I
found there was a local leaving around ten that night. I came
out of there, went in a store and bought some needles and
thread. Then I went down to the bank. I still had over six
thousand dollars in hundred-dollar bills, but I needed more than
that. I drew out ten thousand, half of it in thousand-dollar bills,
twenty-five hundred more in hundreds, and the rest in fives and
tens, with about fifty ones. I stuffed all that in my pockets, and
went home with it. I remembered about the two shirts I had
worn out of the hotel in Mexico, and pulled one just like it. I
took two pairs of drawers, put one pair inside the other, sewed
the bottoms of each leg together, then quilted that money in,
all except the ones, and some fives and tens, that I put in my
pockets. I put the drawers on. They felt a little heavy, but I
could get my trousers over them without anything showing.
Tony came up. They had got out of him how he had called the
taxi, and he was almost crying because he had squealed. I told
him it didn't make any difference.

When dinner time came, instead of going out I had something sent in. Then I packed. I shoved a stack of newspapers
and heavy stuff into a traveling case, and locked it. When I
dressed I put on a pair of gray flannel pants I had left over
from Hollywood, and over my shirt a dark red sweater. I put
on a coat, and over that a light topcoat. I picked out a gray

hat, shoved it on the side of my head. I looked at myself in the mirror and I looked like what I wanted to look like, a guy dressed up to take a trip. After drawing the money, I knew they would expect that. That was why I had planned it the way I had.

At nine thirty, I called Tony, had him take my bag down and call a cab, shook hands with him, and called out to the driver, "Grand Central." We turned into Second Avenue. Two cars started up, down near Twenty-first Street, and one left the curb just behind us as we turned west on Twenty-third. When we turned into Fourth, they turned too. When we got to Grand Central they were still with us, and five guys got out, none of them looking at me. I gave my bag to a redcap, went to the ticket office, bought a ticket for Rye, then went out to the newsstand and bought a paper. When I mixed with the crowd at the head of the ramp I started to read it. Three of the five were there too, all of them reading papers.

The redcap put me aboard, but I didn't let him pick the car. I did that myself. It was a local, all day-coaches, but I wanted one without vestibule. It happened to be the smoker, so that looked all right. I took a seat near the door and went on reading my paper. The three took seats further up, but one of them reversed his seat and sat so he could see me. I didn't even look up as we pulled out, didn't look up as we pulled into a Hundred and Twenty-fifth Street, didn't look up as we pulled out. But when the train had slid about twenty feet, I jumped up, left my bag where it was, walked three steps to the car platform, and skipped off. I never stopped. I zipped right out to a taxi, jumped in, told him to drive to Grand Central, and to step on it. He started up. I kept my eyes open. Nobody was behind us, that I could see.

When he turned into upper Park, I tapped on the glass and said I was too late for my train, that he should go to Eighth Avenue and Twenty-third Street. He nodded and kept on. I took off the hat, the topcoat, and the coat and laid them in a little pile on the seat. When we got to Eighth and Twenty-third I got out, took out a five-dollar bill. "I left some stuff in the car, two coats and a hat. Take them up to Grand Central and check them to leave them. Leave the three checks at the information desk, in my name, Mr. Henderson. There's no hurry. Any time tonight will do."

"Yes sir, yes sir."

He grabbed the five, touched his hat, and went off. I started down Eighth Avenue. Instead of a guy all dressed up to go away, I was just a guy without a hat, walking down for a stroll on a spring night. I looked at my watch. It was a quarter to eleven. I back-tracked up to Twenty-third Street and went into a movie.

At twenty after, I came out, started down Eighth Avenue again, and walked to Seventeenth Street. I took my time, looked in windows, keep peeping at my watch. When I cut over to the pier it was a quarter to twelve. I followed the signs to the *Port of Cobh*, strolled aboard. Nobody stopped me. Up at the winch I saw something that looked familiar. I went up and put my arm around him.

"She's back in your old cabin—and you're late."

I went back there, knocked, and stepped in. It was dark in there, but a pair of arms were around me before I even got the door shut, and a pair of lips were against mine, and I tried to say something, and couldn't and she tried to say something and couldn't and we just sat on one of the berths, and held on to each other.

In almost no time there was a knock on the door and he stepped in. "You'll be going ashore now. Why didn't you get here sooner?"

"What are you talking about?"

"I cast my hawsers in two minutes."

"Hawsers, hell. I'm going with her."

"No, Hoaney. Goodbye, goodbye, now you are free, remember, Juana, but come not. No, I have much money now, I be all right. Now, kiss, I love you much."

"I'm going with you."

"No, no!"

"Lad, you don't know what you're saying. Alone, she can vanish like the mist. With you, she's doomed."

"I'm going with her."

He went out. A bell sounded on the tugboat, and we began to move. We looked out. When we straightened out in the river we were looking at the Jersey side. We slipped past it, and pretty soon we stepped out and found him on the bridge. He was at the far end of it, looking out at the Long Island side. I said something, but he paid no attention, and pointed. A cluster of lights was bearing down on us. "It's a police boat, and she's headed right for us."

We stood watching it, hardly daring to breathe. It came on, then cut across our bows toward Staten Island. We picked up speed. The first swell lifted our nose. She put her hand in mine, and gave it a little squeeze.

CHAPTER

13

We were in Guatemala, though, before we really knew what we were up against, or I did. The trip down was just one nightmare of biting our fingernails and listening to every news broadcast we could pick up, to see if they were on our trail yet. In between, I stuffed myself with food and beer, to put on more weight, and let my moustache grow, and plucked my eyebrows to give my face a different expression, and stood around in the sun, to tan. All I thought about was that radio, and what it was going to tell us. Then at Havana I was running around like a wild man, still trying to beat them to the punch. I found a tailor shop, and put in a rush order for clothes, and then at a little bootleg printshop I got myself a lot of fake papers fixed up, all in the name of Guiseppe Di Nola and where she figured in them, Lola Deminguez Di Nola. I speak Italian like a Neapolitan, and changed myself into an Italian as fast as the tailor, the printer, the barber, and all the rest of them could work on me. As well as I could tell, I got by all right, and none of them had any idea who I was. But one thing kept gnawing at me, and that was the hello I had said to Conners on that first broadcast. Sooner or later, I knew, somebody was going to remember it and check back, and then we would be sunk. I wanted to get a thousand miles away from that ship, and any place she would touch on her way down to Rio.

I had to work fast, because all we had was a three-day lay-over. As soon as my first suit was ready, I put my fake papers in a briefcase and went over to Pan-American. I found all we would really need was a vaccination certificate for each of us. The rest was a matter of tourist papers that they furnished. I told them to make out the ticket and that I would have the certificates at the airport in the morning. I went over to American Express and bought travelers' checks, then went down to the boat and got her. I had her put on some New York clothes, and we went ashore. Then we went to a little hotel off the Prado. Conners wasn't there when we left, and I had to scribble a note to him, and call that a goodbye. It seemed a terrible thing to beat it without even shaking his hand, but I was afraid even to leave our hotel address with anyone on board, for fear some U.S. detective would show up and they would tip him off. So far, none of them on the ship knew us. He had run into a strike at Seattle in the winter, and cleared with an entirely new crew, even officers. He had carried us as Mr. and Mrs. Di Nola, and Mr. and Mrs. Di Nola just disappeared.

There was no hotel doctor, but they knew of one, and got him around, and he vaccinated us, and gave us our certificates. About six o'clock I went around to the tailor and got the rest of my suits. They were all right, and so were the shoes, shirts, and the rest of the stuff I had bought. The tropicals were double-breasted, with a kind of a Monte Carlo look, the pin-stripe had white piping on the vest and the gray had black velvet, the hats were fedoras, one green, the other black, with a Panama thrown in to go with the tropicals. The shoes were two-toned. On appearance, I was as Italian as Mussolini, and I was surprised to see I looked quite a lot like him. I got out my razor and gave the moustache an up-cut under each corner. That helped. It was two weeks out now, and plenty black, with some gray in it. Those gray hairs startled me. I hadn't known they were there.

■ ■

In the morning we went to the airport, showed the certificates, and were passed through. The way the trip broke, we could make better time by going through to Vera Cruz, and then turning south, than by making the change at Mérida. There had been some switch on planes, and that would save us a day. I didn't want to spend one more hour in Mexico than I had to, so I said that suited me. Where we were going I had no idea, except that we were going a long way from Havana, but where we were booked for was Guatemala. That seemed to be a kind of a terminus, and to go on from there we would have to have more papers than they could furnish us with at Havana. She got sick as a dog as soon as we took off, and I, and the steward, and the pilots thought it was airsickness. But when it still kept up, after we got to the hotel in Vera Cruz, I knew it was the vaccination. She was all right, though, the next day, and kept looking down at the country we were going over. We had the Gulf of Mexico under us for a little while after we hauled out of Vera Cruz, and then as we were working down toward Tapachula we were over the Pacific. She had to have all that explained to her. She had never got the oceans quite straight, and how we could leave one, and then pick up another almost before we had time to look at the pictures in the magazines, had to be blue-printed for her, with drawings. To her, I think all countries were square, like a bean patch with lines of maguey around it, and it was hard for her to get through her head how any country, and especially Mexico, could be wide at the top and narrow at the bottom.

At Guatemala, we marched from the plane into the pavilion with a loud speaker blaring the Merry Widow waltz, a barefoot Indian girl gave us coffee, and then after a while an American in a flyer's uniform came and explained to me, in some kind of broken Italian, what I would have to do to go on down the line, if that was what I expected to do. I thanked him, we got our luggage, and went to the Palace Hotel. Then I got to thinking:

■ ■

Why are we going down the line? Why is Chile any better than Guatemala? Our big danger comes every time we fool with papers, and if we're all right so far, why not let well enough alone, and dig in? We couldn't stay on at the hotel, because it was full of Americans, Germans, English and all kinds of people, and sooner or later one of them would know me. But we might rent a place. I sent her down to the desk to ask how we went about it, and when we found out we didn't have to sign any police forms, we went out and got a house. It was a furnished house, just around the block from the hotel, and the gloomiest dump I ever laid eyes on, with walnut chairs, and horse-hair sofas, and sea shells, and coconut shells carved into skulls, and everything else you could think of. But there was a bathroom in it, and it didn't look like we would find one any better. The lady that owned it was Mrs. Gonzalez, and she wanted it understood that she didn't really have to rent the house, that she came of an old coffee family, that she preferred to live out of town, at the lake, on account of her health. We said we understood that perfectly, and closed at a hundred and fifty quetzals a month. A quetzal exchanges even with a dollar.

So in a couple of days we moved in. I found a Japanese couple that didn't speak any English, Italian, or Spanish, and we had to wigwag, but there was no chance of their finding out too much. I was practicing Spanish morning, noon and night, so she and I would be able to talk in front of other people without using English, and I tried to speak it with an Italian accent, but I still wasn't sure I was getting away with it. With the Japs, though, it was safe around the house.

So then we breathed a little easier, and began to shake down into a routine. Daytime we'd lay around, mostly upstairs, in our bedroom. At night we'd walk down to the park and listen to the band. But we'd always sit well away from it, on a lonely bench. Then we'd come back, flit the mosquitoes, and go to bed. There was nothing else to do, even if we had thought it was safe to do it. Guatemala is the Japan of Central America. They've copied everything. They've got Mexican music, American movies, Scotch whisky, German delicatessens, Roman religion, and everything else imported you can think of. But they forgot to put anything of their own in, and what comes out is a place you could hardly tell from Glendale, California, on a bet. It's clean, modern, prosperous, and dull. And the weather gives you plenty of chance to find out how dull it really is. We hit there in June, at the height of the rainy season. It's not supposed to rain in Central America, by the books, but that's wrong. It rains plenty, a cold, gray rain that sometimes keeps up for two days at a time. Then when the sun comes out it's so sticky hot you can hardly breathe, and the mosquitoes start up. The air gets you down almost as bad as it does in Mexico. Guatemala City is nearly a mile up in the air, and at night that feeling of suffocation comes over you, so you think you'll die if you don't get something in your lungs you can breathe.

Little by little, a change came over her. Mind you, from the time we left New York we hadn't said one word about Winston, or what she did, or whether it was right or wrong, or anything about it. That was done, and we steered around it. We talked about the Japs, the mosquitoes, where Conners was by now, things like that, and so long as we jumped at every noise, we seemed to be nearer than we ever had been. But after that eased off, and we began to kid ourselves we were safe, she began moping to herself, and now and then I'd catch her looking at me. Then I noticed that another thing we never talked about was my singing. And then one night, just as we started downstairs to go out in the park, just mechanically I did a little turn, and in another second would have cut loose a high one. I saw this look of horror on her face, and choked it off. She listened, to see if the Japs had caught it. They seemed to be in the kitchen, so we went down. Then it came to me, the spot I was in. On the way down I hadn't even thought about singing. But here, and any other place south of the Rio Grande, for that matter, my voice was just as familiar as bananas. My picture, in the lumberjack suit, was still plastered all over the Panamier show windows, Pablo Buñan had played the town not a month before, even the kids were whistling My Pal Babe. Unless I was going to send her to the chair, I couldn't ever sing again.

I tried not to think about it, and so long as I could read, or do something to get my mind off it, I wouldn't. But you can't read all the time, and in the afternoon I'd get to wishing she'd wake up from her siesta, so we could talk, or practice Spanish, and I could shake it off. Then I began to get this ache across the bridge of my nose. You see, it wasn't that I was thinking about the fine music I couldn't sing any more, or the muted song that was lost to the world, or anything like that. It was simpler than that, and worse. A voice is a physical thing, and if you've got one, it's like any other physical thing. It's in you, and it's got to come out. The only thing I can compare it with is when you haven't been with a woman for a long time, and you get so you think if you don't find one soon, you'll go insane. The bridge of the nose is where your voice focuses, where you get that little pull when you cut loose, and that was where I began to feel it. I'd talk, and read, and eat, and try to forget it, and it would go away, but then it would come back.

Then I began to have these dreams. I'd be up there, and they'd be playing my cue, and it would be time for me to come in, and I'd open my mouth, and nothing would come out of it. I'd be dying to sing, and couldn't. A murmur would go over the house, he'd rap the orchestra to attention, look at me, and start the cue again. Then I'd wake up. Then one night, just after she had gone over to her bed, something happened so we did talk about it. In Central America, they've got radios all over the place, and there were three in the block back of us, and one of them had been setting me nuts all day. It was getting London, and they don't have any of that advertising hooey over there. The whole Barber of Seville had come over in the afternoon, with only a couple of small cuts, and at night they had played the Third, Fifth, and Seventh Beethoven symphonies. Then, around ten o'clock, a guy began to sing the serenade from Don Giovanni, the same thing I had sung for Conners at

Acapulco, the same thing I had sung the night I came in big
at the Metropolitan. He was pretty good. Then, at the end, he
did the same *messa di voce* that I had done. I kind of laughed,
in the dark. "... Well, he's heard me sing it."

She didn't say anything, and then I felt she was crying. I
went over there. "What's the matter?"

"Hoaney, Hoaney, you leave me now. You go. We say goodbye."

"Well—what's the big idea?"

"You no know who that was? Who sing? Just now?"

"No. Why?"

"That was you."

She turned away from me then, and began to shake from her
sobs, and I knew I had been listening to one of my own phonograph records, put on the air after the main program was
over. "... Well? What of it?"

But I must have sounded a little sick. She got up, snapped
on the light, and began walking around the room. She was stark
naked, the way she generally slept on hot nights, but she was
no sculptor's model now. She looked like an old woman, with
her shoulders slumped down, her feet sliding along in a flat-
footed Indian walk, her eyes set dead ahead, like two marbles,
and her hair hanging straight over her face. When the sobs
died off a little, she pulled out a bureau drawer, got out a
gray *rebozo,* and pulled that over her shoulders. Then she
started shuffling around again. If she had had a donkey beside
her, it would have been any hag, from Mexicali to Tapachula.
Then she began to talk "... So. Now you go? Now we say
adiós."

"What the hell are you talking about? You think I'm going
to walk out on you now?"

"I kill these man, yes. For what he do to you, for what he
do to me, I have to kill him. I know these thing at once, that
night, when I hear of the *inmigración,* that I have to kill him.
I ask you? No. Then what I do? Yes? What I do!"

"Listen, for Christ's sake—"

"What I do? You tell me, what I do?"

"Goddam if I know. Laughed at him, for one thing."

"I say goodbye. Yes, I come to you, say remember Juana, kiss you one time, *adiós*. Yes, I kill him, but then is goodbye. I know. I say so. You remember?"

"I don't know. Will you cut it out, and—"

"Then you come to boat. I am weak. I love you much. But what I do then? What I say?"

"Goodbye, I suppose. Is that all you know to say?"

"Yes. Once more I say goodbye. The *capitán*, he know too, he tell you go. You no go. You come. Once more, I love you much, I am glad. . . . Now, once more. Three times, I tell you go. It is the end. I tell you, *goodbye.*"

She didn't look at me. She was shooting it at me with her eyes staring straight again, and her feet carrying her back and forth with that sliding, shuffling walk. I opened my mouth two or three times to stall some more, but couldn't, looking at her. "Well, what are you going to do? Will you tell me that? Do you know?"

"Yes. You go. You give me money, not much, but little bit. Then I work, get little job, maybe kitchen *muchacha*, nobody know me, look like all other *muchacha*, I get job, easy. Then I go to priest, confess my *pecado*—"

"That's what I've been waiting for. I knew that was coming. Now let me tell you something. You confess that *pecado*, and right there is where you lose."

"I no lose. I give money to church, they no turn me in. Then I have peace. Then some time I go back to Mexico."

"And what about me?"

"You go. You sing. You sing for radio. I hear. I remember. You remember. Maybe. Remember little dumb *muchacha*—"

"Listen, little dumb *muchacha*, that's all swell, except for one thing. When we hooked up, we hooked up for good, and—"

"Why you talk so? It is the end! Can you no see these thing? It is the end! You no go, what then? They take me back. Me only, they never find. You, yes. They take me back, and what they do to me? In Mexico, maybe nothing, unless he was *político*. In New York, I know, you know. The *soldados* come, they put the *pañuelo* over the eyes, they take me to wall, they shoot. Why you do these things to me? You love me, yes. *But it is the end!*"

I tried to argue, got up and tried to catch her, to make her quit that walking around. She slipped away from me. Then she flung herself down on her bed and lay there staring up at the ceiling. When I came to her she waved me away. From that time on she slept in her bed and I slept in mine, and nothing I could do would break her down.

I didn't leave her, I couldn't leave her. It wasn't only that I was insane about her. What was between us had completely reversed since we started out. In the beginning, I thought of her like she had said, as a little dumb *muchacha* that I was nuts about, that I loved to touch and sleep with and play with. But now I had found out that in all the main things of my life she was stronger than I was, and I had got so I had to be with her. It wouldn't have done any good to leave her. I'd have been back as fast as a plane could carry me.

For a week after that, we'd lie there in the afternoon, saying nothing, and then she began putting on her clothes and going out. I'd lie there, trying not to think about singing, praying for strength not to suck in a bellyful and cut it loose. Then it popped in my mind about the priests, and I got in a cold sweat that that was where she was going. So one day I followed her. But she went past the Cathedral, and then I got ashamed of myself and turned around and came back.

I had to do something with myself, though, so when she went I began going to the baseball games. From that you can imagine how much there was to do in Guatemala, that I would go to the baseball game. They've got some kind of a league between Managua, Guatemala, San Salvador, and some other Central American towns, and they get as excited about it as they get in Chicago over a World Series, and yell at the ump, and all the rest of it. Buses run out there, but I walked. The fewer people that got a close look at me, the better I liked it. One day I found myself watching the pitcher on the San Salvador team. The papers gave his name as Barrios, but he must have been an American, or anyway have lived in the United States, from his motion. Most of those Indians handle a ball jerky, and fight it so they make more errors than you could believe. But this guy had the old Lefty Gomez motion, loose, easy, so his whole weight went in the pitch, and more smoke than all the rest of them had put together. I sat looking at him, taking in those motions, and then all of a sudden I felt my heart stop. Was it coming out in me again, this thing that had got me when I met Winston? Was that kid out there really doing things to me that had nothing to do with baseball? Was it having its effect, her putting me out of her bed?

I got up and left. I know now it was just nerves, that when Winston died that chapter ended. But I didn't then. I tried to put it out of my mind, and couldn't. I didn't go to the ball games any more, but then, after a couple of weeks, I got to thinking: Am I going to turn into the priest again? Am I going to give up everything else in this Christ-forsaken dump, and then lose my voice too? It began to be an obsession with me that I had to have a woman, that if I didn't have a woman I was sunk.

She didn't go with me to hear the band play any more. She stayed home and went to bed. One night, when I went out, instead of heading for the park, I flagged a taxi. "La Locha."

"Sí, Señor, La Locha."

I had heard guys at the ball game talking about La Locha's, but I didn't know where it was. It turned out to be on Tenth Avenue, but the district was on a different system from in Mexico. There were regular houses, with red lights over the door, all according to Hoyle. I rang, and an Indian let me in. A whore-house, I guess, is the same all over the world. There was a big room, with a phonograph on one side, a radio on the other, and an electric piano in the middle, with a stained-glass picture of Niagara Falls in the front, that lit up whenever somebody put in a nickel. The wallpaper had red roses all over it, and at one end was a bar. Back of the bar was an oil painting of a nude, and in the cabinet under it were stacks and stacks of long square cans. When a guy in Guatemala really wants to show the girls a good time, he blows them to canned asparagus.

The Indian looked at me pretty funny, and after he went back, so did the woman at the bar. I thought at first it was the Italian way I was speaking Spanish, but then it seemed to be something about my hat. An army officer was at a little table, reading a newspaper. He had his hat on, and then I remembered and put mine on. I ordered *cerveza*, and three girls came in. They stood on the rail and began loving me up. Two of them were Indian, but one of them was white, and she looked the cleanest. I put my arm around her, and after the other two got their drinks, they went over with the officer. One of them turned on the radio, and the other one and the officer began to dance. My girl and I danced. By rights I guess she was fairly pretty. She couldn't have been more than twenty-one or two, and even in the sweater and green dress she had on, you could see she had a pretty good shape. But she kept playing with my hand, and everything I'd say to her, she'd answer in a little high squeak of a voice that got on my nerves. I asked her what her name was. She said María.

We had another dance, but God knows there was no point in keeping that up. I asked her if she wanted to go upstairs, and she was leading me out the door even before the tune was over.

We went up, she took me in a room, and snapped on the light. It was just the same old whore's bedroom, except for one thing. On the bureau was a signed photograph of Enzo Luchetti, an old bass I had sung with years before, in Florence. My heart skipped a beat. If he was in town, that meant I had to get out, and get out fast. I picked it up and asked her who it was. She said she didn't know. Another girl had had the room before she came, a fine girl that had been in Europe, but she had got *enferma* and had to leave. I put it down and said it looked like an Italian. She asked if I wasn't Italian. I said yes.

There didn't seem to be much to do, then, but get at it. She began dropping off her clothes. I began dropping off mine. She snapped off the light and we lay down on the bed. I didn't want her, and yet I was excited, in some kind of a queer, unnatural way, because I knew I had to have her. It didn't seem possible that anything could be over so quick and amount to so little. We lay there, and I tried to talk to her, but there wasn't anything to talk to. Then we had another, and next thing I knew I was dressing. Ten quetzals. I gave her fifteen. She got awfully friendly then, but it was like having a poodle bitch trying to jump in your lap. It was only a little after ten when I got home, but Juana was asleep. I undressed in the dark, got into bed, and thought I would get some peace. Next thing, the conductor threw the stick on me, and I tried to sing, and the chorus stood around looking at me, and I began yelling, trying to tell them why I couldn't. When I woke up, those yells were still echoing in my ears, and she was standing over me, shaking me.

"Hoaney! What is it?"

"Just a dream."

"So."

She went back to bed. Not only the bridge of my nose, but the whole front of my face was aching so it was two hours before I dropped off again.

From then on I was like somebody threshing around in a fever, and the more I threshed the worse the fever got. I went around there every night, and when I was so sick of María I couldn't even look at her any more, I tried the Indian girls, and when I got sick of them I went in other places, and tried other Indian girls. Then I began picking girls off the street, and in cafés, and taking them in to cheap hotels off the park. They didn't ask me to register and I didn't volunteer. I paid the money, took them in, and around eleven o'clock left them there and went home. Then I went back to La Locha's and started up with María again. The more I had of them the worse I wanted to sing. And all that time there was only one woman in the world that I really wanted, and that was Juana. But Juana had turned to ice. After that one little flash, when I woke her up with my nightmare, she went back to treating me like she just barely knew me. We spoke, talked about whatever had to be talked about, but whenever I tried to push it further than that, she didn't even hear me.

One night the Pagliacci cue began to play, and I was just about to step through the curtain and face that conductor again. But I was almost used to it by now, and woke up. I was about to drop off again, when a horrible realization came to me. I wasn't home. I was in bed with María. I had been lying there listening to her squeak about how the rains would be over soon, and then the good weather would come, and must have gone to sleep. I was the star customer there by now, and she must have turned off the light and just let me alone. I jumped up, snapped on the light, and looked at my watch. It was two o'clock. I jumped into my clothes, left a twenty-quetzal note on the bureau, and ran downstairs. Things were just getting good down in the main room. The army, the judiciary, the coffee kingdom, and the banana empire were all on hand, the girls were stewed, the asparagus was going down in bunches, and the radio, the phonograph, and the electric piano were all going at once. I never stopped. A whole row of taxis were parked up and down the street outside. I jumped in one, went home. A light was on upstairs. I let myself in and started up there.

Halfway up, I felt something coming at me. I fell back a step and braced myself for her to hit me. She didn't. She shot by me on the stairs, and in the half light I saw she was dressed to go out. She had on red hat, red dress, and red shoes, with gold stockings, and rouge smeared all over her face, but I didn't catch all that until later. All I saw was that she was got up like some kind of hussy, and I took about six steps at one jump and caught her at the door. She didn't scream. She never screamed, or talked loud, or anything like that. She sank her teeth into my hand and grabbed for the door again. I caught her once more, and we fought like a couple of animals. Then I threw her against the door, got my arms around her from behind, and carried her upstairs, with her heels cutting dents in my shins.

When we got in the bedroom I turned her loose, and we faced each other panting, her eyes like two points of light, my hands slippery with blood. "What's the rush? Where you going?"

"Where you think? To the Locha, where you come from."

That was one between the eyes. I didn't know she had even heard of La Locha's. But I dead-panned as well as I could.

"What's the locha? I don't seem to place it."

"So, once more you lie."

"I don't even know what you're talking about. I went for a walk and got lost, that's all."

"You lie, now another time you lie. You think these girl no tell me about crazy Italian who come every night? You think they no tell me?"

"So that's where you spend your afternoons."

"Yes."

She stood smiling at me, letting it soak in. I kept thinking I ought to kill her, that if I was a man I'd take her by the throat and choke her till her face turned black. But I didn't want to kill her. I just felt shaky in the knees, and weak, and sick. "Yes, that is where I go, I find little *muchacha* for company, little *muchacha* like me, for nice little talk and cup of chocolate after siesta. And what these little *muchacha* talk? Only about crazy Italian, who come every night, give five-quetzal tip." She pitched her voice into Maria's squeak. "*Sí. Cinco quetzales.*"

I was licked. When I had run my tongue around my lips enough that they stopped fluttering, I backed down. "All right. Once more I'll cut out the lying. Yes, I was there. Now will you stop this show, so we can talk?"

She looked away, and I saw *her* lips begin to twitch. I went in the bathroom, and started to wash the blood off my hand. I wanted her to follow me in, and I knew if she did, she'd break. She didn't. "No! No more talk! You no go, then I go! *Adíos!*"

She was down, and out the front door, before I even got to the head of the stairs.

CHAPTER 14

I ran out on the street just as a taxi pulled away from the corner. I yelled, but it didn't stop. There was no other taxi in sight, and I didn't find one till I went clear around the block to the stand in front of the hotel. I had him take me back to La Locha's. By that time there were at least twenty cabs parked up and down the street, and things were going strong in all the houses. It kept riding me that even if she had gone in the place, they might lie to me about it, and I couldn't be sure unless I searched the joint, and that meant they would call the cops. I went to the first cab that was parked there and asked him if a girl in a red dress had gone in any of the houses. He said no. I gave him a quetzal and said if she showed, he was to come in La Locha's and let me know. I went to the next driver, and the next, and did the same. By the time I had handed out quetzals to half a dozen of them, I knew that ten seconds after she got out of her cab I would know it. I went back to La Locha's. No girl in a red dress had come, said the Indian. I set up drinks for all hands, sat down with one of the girls, and waited.

Around three o'clock the judiciary began to leave, and after them the army, and then all the others that weren't spending the night. At four o'clock they put me out. Two or three of my taxi drivers were still standing there, and they swore that no girl in a red dress, or any other kind of dress, had come to any house in the street all night. I passed out a couple more quetzals, had one of them drive me home. She wasn't there. I routed out the Japs. It was an hour's job of pidgin Spanish and wig-wagging to find out what they knew, but after a while I got it straight. Around nine o'clock she had started to pack. Then she got a cab, put her things in it, and went out. Then she came back, and when she found out I wasn't home, went out. When she came back the second time, around midnight, she had on the red dress, and kept walking around upstairs waiting for me. Then I came home, and there was the commotion, and she went out again, and hadn't been back since.

I shaved, cleaned the dried blood off my hand, changed my clothes. Around eight o'clock I tried to eat some breakfast and couldn't. Around nine o'clock the bell rang. A taxi driver was at the door. He said some of his friends had told him I was looking for a lady in a red dress. He said he had driven her, and could take me to where he left her. I took my hat, got in, and he drove me around to a cheap hotel, one of those I had been to myself. They said yes, a lady of that description had been there. She had come earlier in the evening, changed her clothes once and gone out, then came back late and left an early call. She hadn't registered. About seven thirty this morning she had gone out. I asked how she was dressed. They just shrugged. I asked if she had taken a cab. They said they didn't know. I rode back to the house, and tried to piece it together. One thing began to stick out of it now. My being out late, that wasn't why she had left. She was leaving anyway, and after she had moved out she had come back, probably to say goodbye. Then when she found I wasn't there she had got sore, gone to the hotel again, changed into the red dress, and come back to harpoon me with how she was going back to her old life. Whether she had gone back to it, or what she had done, I had no more idea than the man in the moon.

■ ■

I waited all that day, and the next. I was afraid to go to the police. I could have checked on the Tenth Avenue end of it in a minute. They keep a card for every girl on the street, with her record and picture, and if she had gone there, she would have had to report. But once I set them on her trail, that might be the beginning of the end. And I didn't even know what name she was using. So far, even with the drivers and at the hotel, I hadn't given her name or mine. I had spoken of her as the girl in the red dress, but even that wouldn't do any more. If they couldn't remember how she was dressed when she left the hotel, it was a cinch she wasn't wearing red. I lay around, and waited, and cursed myself for giving her five thousand quetzals cash, just in case. With that, she could hide out on me for a year. And then it dawned on me for the first time that with that she could go anywhere she pleased. She could have left town.

I went right over to one of the open-front drugstores, went in a booth, and called Pan-American. I spoke English. I said I was an American, that I had met a Mexican lady at the hotel and promised to give her some pictures I had taken of her, but I hadn't seen her for a couple of days and I was wondering if she had left town. They asked me her name. I said I didn't know her name, but they might identify her by a fur coat she was probably carrying. They asked me to hold the line. Then they said yes, the porter remembered a fur coat he had handled for a Mexican lady, that if I'd hold the line they'd see if they could get me her name and address. I held the line again. Then they said they were sorry, they didn't have her address, but her name was Mrs. Di Nola, and she had left on the early plane the day before for Mexico City.

Mexico looked exactly the same, the burros, the goats, the *pulquerías,* the markets, but I didn't have time for any of that. I went straight from the airport to the Majestic, a new hotel that had opened since I left there, registered as Di Nola, and started to look for her. I didn't go to the police, I didn't make any inquiries, and I didn't do any walking, for fear I'd be recognized. I just put a car under charter, had the driver go around and around, and took a chance that sooner or later I'd see her. I went up and down the Guauhtemolzin until the girls would jeer at us every time we showed up, and the driver had to wave and say *"postales,"* to shut them up. Buying postcards seemed to be the stock alibi if you were just rubbering around. I went up and down every avenue, where the crowds were thickest, and the more the traffic held us up, the better it suited me. I kept my eyes glued to the sidewalk. At night, we drove past every café, and around eleven o'clock, when the picture theatres closed, we drove past them, on the chance I'd see her coming out. I didn't tell him what I wanted, I just told him where to drive.

By the end of that day I hadn't even caught a glimpse of her. I told the driver to be on deck promptly at eleven the next morning, which was Sunday. We started out, and I had him drive me into Chapultepec Park, and I was sure I'd see her there. The whole city turns out there every Sunday morning to listen to the band, ride horses, wink at the girls, and just walk. We rode around for three hours, past the zoo, the bandstand, the boats in the lake, the chief of the mounted police and his daughter, so many times we got dizzy, and still no trace of her. In the afternoon we kept it up, driving all over the city going every place there might be a crowd. There was no bullfight. The season for them hadn't started, but we combed the boulevards, the suburbs, and every place else I could think of. He asked if I'd need him after supper. I said no, to report at ten in the morning. It wasn't getting me anywhere, and I wanted to think what I was going to do next. After dinner I took a walk, to try and figure out something, I passed two or three people I had known, but they never gave me a tumble. What left Mexico was a big, hard, and starved-looking American. What came back was a middle-aged wop, with a pot on him so big it hid his feet. When I got to the Palacio de Bellas Artes, it was all lit up. I crossed toward it, and thought I'd sit on a stone bench and keep an eye on the crowd that was coming in. But when I got near enough to read the signs I saw it was Rigoletto they were giving and this dizzy, drunken feeling swept over me, that I should go in there and sing it, and take the curse off the flop, and show them how I could do it. I cut back, and turned the corner into the town.

Next to the bullring box office is a café. I went in there, ordered an apricot brandy, and sat down. I told myself to forget about the singing, that what I was trying to do was find *her*. The place was pretty full, and three or four guys were standing in front of one of the booth tables against the wall. Through them I caught a flash of red, and my mouth went dry. They went back to their own table and I was looking right at her.

She was with Triesca, the bullfighter, and more guys kept coming up to him, shaking his hand, and going away again. She saw me, and looked away quick. Then he saw me. He kept looking at me, and then he placed me. He said something to her, and laughed. She nodded, kept looking off somewhere with a strained face, and then half laughed. Then he ogled at me. By the way both of them were acting I knew he didn't connect me with New York, and maybe he didn't know anything about the New York stuff at all. All he saw was a guy that had once taken his girl away from him, and had then turned out to be a fag. But that was enough for him. He began putting on an act that the whole room was roaring at in a minute. Her face got hard and set. I felt the blood begin to pound in my head.

A *mariachi* came in. He threw them a couple of pesos, and they screeched three or four times. Then he got a real idea. He called the leader, and whispered, and they started *Cielito Lindo*. But instead of them singing it, he got up and sang it. He sang right at me, in a high, simpering falsetto, with gestures. They laughed like hell. If she had dead-panned, I think I would have sat there and taken it. But she didn't. She laughed. I don't know why. Maybe she was just nervous. Maybe she played it the way the rest of them expected her to play it. Maybe she was still sore about Guatemala. Maybe she really thought it was funny, that I should be following her around like some puppy after she had hooked up with another man. I don't know, and I didn't think about any of that at the time. When I saw that laugh, I got a dizzy, wanton feeling in my head, and I knew that all hell couldn't stop me from what I was going to do.

He got to the end of the verse, and they gave him a laugh and a big hand. He struck a pose for the chorus, and then I laughed too, and stood up. That surprised him, and he hesitated. And then I shot it:

> *Ay, Ay, Ay, Ay!*
> *Canta y no llores*
> *Porque cantando se alegran*
> *Cielito lindo*
> *Los corazones!*

It was like gold, bigger than it had ever been, and when I finished I was panting from the excitement of it. He stood there, looking thick, and then came this roar of applause. The *mariachi* leader began jabbering at me, and they started it again. I sang it through, drunk from the way it felt, drunk from the look on her face. On the second chorus, I sang it right at her, soft and slow. But at the end I put in a high one, closed my eyes and swelled it, held it till the glasses rattled, and then came off it.

When I opened my eyes wide she wasn't looking at me. She was looking past the bar, behind me. The mob was cheering, people were crowding in from the street, and all over the place they were passing it around, *"El Panamier Trovador!"* But in a booth was an officer, yelling into a telephone. How long that kept up I don't know. They were all around me, jabbering things for me to sing. Next thing I knew, she was running for the door, Triesca after her. But I was ahead of him. I rammed through the crowd, and when I got to the street I could see the red of her dress, half a block away. I started to run. I hadn't gone two steps before some cops grabbed me. I wrestled with them. From up the street came shots, and people began to run and scream.

Then from somewhere came a rattle of Spanish, and I heard the word "gringo." They turned me loose, and I ran on. Ahead of me were more cops, and people standing around. I saw something red on the pavement. When I pushed through she was lying there, and beside her, this quivering smile on his face, was a short guy in uniform, with three stars on his shoulder. It seemed a long time before I knew it was the *político* from Acapulco. I got it, then, that order to lay off the gringo. He couldn't shoot me. I was too important. But he could shoot her, for trying to escape, or resisting arrest, or whatever it was. And he could stand there, and wait, and get his kick when I had to look at her.

I jumped for him, and he stepped back, but then I turned to water, and I sank down beside her, the cops, the lights, and the ambulance going around and around in a horrible spin. If he had done that to her, what had I done?

Once more I was in the vestry room of the little church near Acapulco, and I could even see the burned place on the bricks where we had made the fire. Indians were slipping in barefooted, the women with *rebozos* over their heads, the men in white suits, extra clean. Her father and mother were in the first pew, and some sisters and brothers I didn't even know she had. The casket was white, and the altar was banked with the flowers I had had sent down, flowers from Xochimilco, that she liked. The choir loft was full of boys and girls, all in white. The priest came in, started to put on his vestments, and I paid him. He caught my arm. "You sing, yes, Señor Sharp? An *Agnus Dei* perhaps?"

"No."

He shrugged, turned away, and pulled the surplice over his head. This horrible sense of guilt swept over me, like it had a hundred times in the last two days. "... Never.... Never again."

"Ah."

He just breathed it, and stood looking at me, then his hand

traced a blessing for me, and he whispered in Latin. I knew, then, I had made a confession, and received an absolution, and some kind of gray peace came over me. I went out, slipped in the pew with her family, and the music started. They carried her out to a grave on the hillside. As they lowered her down, an iguana jumped out of it and went running over the rocks.

LOVE'S LOVELY

COUNTERFEIT

Through the revolving door came a tall man with big shoulders, who crossed to the elevators, and after nodding to the starter, stood looking over the lobby. It was the standard lobby, for hotels of the first class in cities of the second class, to be found all over the United States: it had quiet, comfortable furniture; illuminated signs with green letters over the windows of grand functionaries; oil paintings of lakes, streams, and forests; and heavy urns, filled with sand, for cigarettes. Various desks, ta- bles, and booths, staffed with women in assorted uniforms, gave it a touch of high, wartime consecration. Yet, in spite of all this, it contrived to seem a bit disreputable. Possibly the clientele, now debouching from dining room, fountain room, and cocktail bar, grabbing its hats after lunch, and hastening away, had some- thing to do with this. It was made up of men distinctly political, together with the slightly too good-looking women one encoun- ters behind desks in city halls. Indeed, many of them, after leaving the hotel, streamed over to the City Hall across the street, a traffic cop blowing his whistle as each batch appeared, and making this rite seem portentous, as though the vehicles that he stopped had all the panting impatience of an Empire State Express.

The man at the elevators, however, noted little of this, and seemed so much a part of it that he may have been incapable of seeing it. He was at least six feet, and something about his carriage suggested that at some time in his life he had been a professional athlete. His face, however, was at variance with the rest of him. Although he was not far from thirty, it had a juvenile look, and the part that was face, as distinguished from the parts that were cheek, jowl, and chin, seemed curiously small. Allowing for that, he had a fair amount of masculine good looks. His hair was light, with the tawniness that touches such hair in the late twenties. His eyes were blue, his skin showed the sunburn of many seasons; his step, as he entered the car, was springy. He rode up to the seventh floor, got out, walked down a corridor, stopped before a door with no number on it, pressed a button. A slot opened, then the door opened, and he went in.

The room he entered was large, with the usual hotel furniture and a grand piano that was enameled in green and pointed in gold. He gave a wipe at this as he went by, so the keys made a startled clatter, and went on to an office that adjoined the big room. Seated at a desk here was the owner of the hotel, Mr. Sol Caspar, who had no share of masculine good looks or any other kind of good looks. He was a short, squatty man in his middle thirties, and although it was a warm day in May, and the people in the lobby had been wearing straw hats, he was dressed in a heavy brown suit, with handkerchief to match and custom-made shoes. There was a six-pointed star on his ring and a mazuza on the door-casing, but these were caprices, or possibly affectations for business reasons. Actually he had no Hebraic connections, for his real name was Salvatore Gasparro, and no doubt it was his origin that prompted him to name his hotel for Columbus, a popular hero with Italo-Americans. He was playing solitaire with his hat on the back of his head, and didn't look up when the other man came in and sat down. Nor did he look up a few minutes later, when a bellboy appeared, set a package on the desk, opened it, and tiptoed out. Soon, however, he put the cards away and gave his attention to the package. It was an album of records, and he put them on a phonograph that stood against the wall behind him. Then he snapped a button, sat at his desk, lit a cigar, and took off his hat. They were of the opera *Il Trovatore,* and evidently met with his approval. When the tenor sang an aria full of high notes he played it over, then played it over again. But when a minor tenor started a slow recitative he became bored, and stopped the machine.

Only then did he greet his visitor, who had sat staring straight in front of him, obviously not entertained by the music. In a rough, high voice, though without any trace of accent, he said: "H'y, Benny."

"Hello, Sol."

"How they treating you?"

"O.K. so far."

"They got you in the draft yet?"

"No, I still got my football hernia."

"Oh that's right. What you got on tonight?"

"I guess you forgot. This is my day off."

"I said what you got on?"

"... Nothing I can think of now. Why?"

"Little job."

"What kind of a job?"

"Don't take it like that, Benny. You ought to know by now I don't call on you for any rough stuff. This is nothing to be worried about. Political meeting."

"And what's that?"

"Where the voters get together and pick out who's not going to be elected. Or so I hear. I never been to one."

"And where do I come in?"

"You look it over."

"I still don't get it."

"They got a Swede that's running for mayor. A lug that says he's out to get me. It's about time I found out what he's up to."

"You mean this milkman, Jansen?"

"That's him."

"How would I know what he's up to?"

"Maybe you don't get all the fine points, but you can see who's there. That's the main idea."

"I don't know any of these birds."

Mr. Caspar's eyes were the most arresting part of his face. In color they were dark brown, but each of them was ever so slightly out of line, so that when they focused on an object they looked like a pair of glass eyes. They focused now on Ben Grace, and presently shifted with a decidedly maniacal flicker. When Mr. Caspar spoke he shouted, his voice trembling with rage: "Listen, Ben, quit cracking dumb. You go to that meeting, and see you get there on time. If it's just voters, nuts. But if this guy's got friends, I got to know it. I got tipped today there's wise money back of him, that's figuring to knock me off. You know who they are, don't you?"

"I guess so."

"And you can see if they're there, can't you? If you want to you can find out what's going on, can't you?"

"O.K., Sol, but make it plain."

"And let me know."

"When?"

"Tomorrow."

"Where's the meeting?"

"Dewey High."

"All right, I'll be there."

"And take the bookies today."

"How do you get that way? Isn't it enough that I work tonight? Have I got to work all day too? This is supposed to be my day off."

Caspar's eyes fastened on Grace again, and he opened his mouth to say something, but at that moment Mrs. Caspar came in. She was a small, fat, bright-eyed Italian woman, leading a four-year-old boy, Franklin, by the hand. Grace jumped up when he saw her, and she nodded at him pleasantly, then began a report to Caspar, of the dentist's examination of Frankie's tooth.

Ben, after giving Frankie a penny, started out. Caspar, however, hadn't forgotten him. "What do you say, Benny?"

"I say O.K."

In the big room, as Grace crossed it again, two men were sitting. One called himself Bugs Lenhardt, and sat reading a paper, near the door, where he could cover the slot with a minimum of effort. He was young, small, and vacant-eyed. The other, Lefty Gauss, had let Grace in, and now got up and walked out with him. He was of medium size and bandy-legged, with gray streaks in his hair and a frank, friendly air that suggested farms and other wholesome things. Actually he was a killer who had done considerable penal servitude, and the gray streaks in his hair came from operations in prisons, performed by doctors told off to get lead out of him, and not too particular how they did it. He and Grace stood silently in front of the elevators, then went down to the lobby, out to the street, and into a cocktail bar not far away with but a few glum words. It was only when they were settled in a dark corner that Ben began to talk and Gauss to listen.

Ben was full of grievances, some of them, such as his resentment that Caspar called him Benny, trivial, some of them, such as his dislike of gunfire, vital. This last he tried to place in an admirable light, as though it were a matter of citizenship, not fear. He insisted that he had never wanted his job in the first place, except temporarily when a serious injury ended his football career, and cited his refusal to wear a uniform as proof of his high-toned attitude. Yet a captious eavesdropper might have reflected that upright citizens do not as a rule become chauffeurs to notorious racketeers, whether they wear a uniform or not. Lefty listened sympathetically, shaking his beer to bring up the foam, nodding, and putting in understanding comment. Then presently he said, "Well, you got it tough, you sure have. But any time it gets too tough, just take a look at me."

"Anyway, he gives you a day off."

"Sometimes."

"And he don't stick you behind the wheel of a car that's

armored behind but wide open in front, and every street named Goon Street as soon as *he* climbs aboard.''

"Oh, no?"

"You too, hey?"

"Like today."

"Say, Lefty, what's going on today?"

"I got to split a heist, that's all."

"I didn't hear about it."

"They haven't got it yet. They're pulling it this afternoon—bank over in Castleton, right after closing time, the late depositor gag. *If* they pull it. If that depositor ever gets in, which isn't any more than a one to five bet."

"You'll know soon. It's three-thirty."

"Castleton's on mountain time."

"That's right. I forgot."

"You ever sat in on a divvy, Ben?"

"I don't know any yeggs."

"Four wild kids, anywhere from eighteen to twenty, scared so bad the slobber is running out of their mouths, couple of them coked to the ears, their suspenders stretched double from the gats they got in their pants. And Sol takes half, see? For protection, for giving them a place to lay up, he cuts off that much. O.K., he says part goes to the cops, but that don't help me any. There's the dough, all over the bed, in a room at the Globe Hotel. And there's the kids, kissing it and tasting it and smelling it. And there's me, that never seen one of them before, that hasn't got a pal in the bunch. I got to take half and get out. And maybe Sol crossed me. Maybe he *didn't* take care of the cops, and they come in on me, and it's ten years till the next beer. And for all that—now here's where it gets good—Solly, he slips me a hundred bucks."

"Why do we take it, what he dishes out?"

"Well, for one thing, bucking Sol is not healthy. And me, I *got* to take it. I'm not what I was. I don't get calls anymore. To help on a job, I mean. I got to play along. You, of course you're different."

"In what way?"

"I figure you for a chiseler."

"What do you mean by that, Lefty?"

"That's all."

"Sounds like there might be more."

"Not unless you ask for it."

"... O.K.—shoot."

"A chiseler, he's not crooked and he's not straight. He's just in between."

"Maybe he's just smart."

"I don't say he's not. I should say I don't. He takes it where he can get it, he's willing to live and let live, he don't want any trouble. If he can only hold it, what he's got, he'll die rich, and of a regular disease, with a doctor's certificate, 'stead of a coroner's. Still, he'll never be a big operator."

"Why not?"

"A big operator, he runs it, or he don't operate."

Lefty then gave a disquisition on the use of force: so long as Sol didn't mind trouble and Ben did, Sol would run it. It was diplomatically phrased, but Ben looked sulky, and Lefty added: "Listen, no hard feelings about it. Because maybe you're the one that *is* smart. You're putting it by all the time, or I *hope* you got that little savings account tucked away somewhere. You're young, and when Sol gets it you can always get a job."

"What do you mean, when Sol gets it?"

"Oh, he'll get it."

"You mean this Swede Jansen that's running for Mayor."

"He hasn't got a chance."

"He's got Sol worried."

"You mean Mayor Maddux has."

"I don't get it."

"Well, Sol's the main beneficiary of this, our present administration, isn't he? The boys had to figure some way to make him kick in. So Maddux told him who's back of the Swede."

"You mean Delany?"

"I mean our polo-playing, whiskey-drinking, white-tie-wearing, evil young man named Bill Delany, that gets by for a gentleman jockey but he's really a hoodlum bookie, and Sol has to cut him in whether he wants to or not, because he's got the Chicago connections. And for that reason, Solly hates him so hard that all Maddux has to do is wink him in and he's there, even if he's not. Delany, he's got no more to do with the Swede than you have, but he could have. It could be the Swede that's going to knock Solly off. It could be anybody. For big enough dough, plenty guys don't mind trouble. One of them sees his disconnect button and leans on it, that's all."

"And then?"

"You're sitting pretty and I'm not."

"But *till* then, I'm his English setter."

"His—what did you say, Ben?"

"It's a dog, Lefty, and you ought to get next to them. They're white, with gray spots. They don't bark, they don't chase, and they don't fight. And when they point a bird, you can be sure it's a bird and not a skunk. In other words—me. Up at that meeting tonight."

"I didn't say so, Ben."

"A fine pair, we are."

"Well, when you come right down to it, nobody isn't so hot. Not really they're not. But if they're buddies, they can generally figure an angle. Me, I got one right away. Say what you will, we're prettier than Solly is."

"That's not saying much."

"It's practically not saying nothing at all. Still and all, I get a satisfaction out of it that I don't look like Solly looks."

"If it helps, then O.K."

"Two beers, Ben, and they're on you."

The bookmaking establishments to which Ben was assigned ran wide open in downtown office buildings, but with a two-hour time differential on account of Western tracks, there was nothing he could do about them until seven o'clock. Leaving Lefty, he went to the Lake City RKO to kill time. The theatre was named for the city, which had 220,000 inhabitants, a Chamber of Commerce, an airport, a war boom, and a Middle Western accent. The feature was a pleasant little item with Ginger Rogers in it, but the picture at which Ben laughed loudest and applauded most included Abbott and Costello. When he came out it was nearly six, and he walked around to his hotel. It was called the Lucas, and had $1-$1.50-$2 on the marquee. His room, for which he paid $8 a week, was on the second floor, but he didn't bother with the elevator. He bounded up the stairs with absentminded ease, first stopping at the desk to see if there had been any calls. His room was small, and had a single bed in it, a night table, a reading lamp, two straight chairs, a small armchair, and two water colors of nasturtiums. He paid not the least attention to it. He pitched his hat on the bed, stripped off his coat and shirt, and entered the shower. There, at the hand basin, he washed his face, ears, and neck, great muscles leaping out of his arms as he did so. Then he dried himself with a face towel, putting it back on the rack in its original creases. Then he combed his hair, tucking his forelock into place lovingly, with little brush strokes of the comb, and taking more time about it than the rite seemed to warrant.

Then he stepped into the room and had a look at his shirt. He frowned when he saw the collar, and dropped it into a laundry basket that stood in a closet. Then he selected another one from a shelf at the top of the closet. He put it on, chose a necktie to go with it, and when both had been patted into place, shoved the tail of his shirt into his trousers, and tightened his belt. His motions were precise, his person clean. And yet there was something of small dimension about everything he did. In this tiny room, with his boyish face, his neat little piles of rather well-bought possessions, it was hard to realize that he weighed at least 200 pounds.

The freshening completed, he went outside, walked down the street to the Savoy Grill, went inside and had dinner. He then walked to the Columbus, got a small satchel from the cashier, and visited the first of the bookmaking establishments. It was on the first floor of the Coolidge Building, past the elevators, and was full of men. They were in jovial mood, for two favorites had won, and they were there to cash tickets. With the big blackboard on one side of the room, the permanent column captions lettered thereon, and the businesslike atmosphere, the place suggested a stockbroker's office in Wall Street. Ben didn't attempt a thorough audit. He accepted an adding machine tote, crammed money and stub-books into his satchel, and went on to the next place. By a quarter to eight he had completed his rounds and left the satchel at the Columbus, first pasting a sticker over the clasp to seal it. Then he walked back to his hotel, passed through the lobby to an areaway behind, and entered a shed where cars were stored. His was a small coupe, maroon in color, with white tires and a high polish. He got in, checked the gas against an entry in a little red book that he took from his pocket, and drove off.

Municipal campaigns, as a rule, are held in the spring, with the election falling in May and the winner taking office July 1. So it happened that at John Dewey High School Auditorium it was a warmish night, with the crowd attending in spring dresses and straw hats. It was not, however, a very big crowd. Possibly five hundred people were there, half filling the auditorium; Lefty, apparently, had judged correctly the strength of the Jansen following. They were quiet, folksy people, and although Ben looked a little out of place among them, they smiled at him in friendly fashion as he came up the steps to the hall, and made way to let him in. He took a seat near the door, and began a systematic scrutiny of every face he could see. When the candidates arrived he joined the applause, and when the speaking began he frowned hard, concentrating on what was being said.

What was being said, alas, was a little slack. The offenses of Mr. Caspar, abetted by the Maddux machine, were the general topic, but nobody seemed to know quite what they were, and everybody left the indictment to somebody else. When Mr. Jansen spoke he was a grievous disappointment. He was a stocky, pink-faced, good-looking man with a little red moustache, but he had a thick accent, and did little but tell how Caspar had moved in on his milk truck drivers, "und den I make oop my mindt I move in on Caspar." The meeting was a flop until the chairman introduced a girl, quite as an afterthought, while people were crowding to the doors, and she started to talk.

She was a very good-looking girl, in spite of the schoolteacherish way she spoke. She was perhaps twenty-five, with a trim little figure and solemn black eyes. She wore a dress of dark blue silk, which combined pleasantly with her wavy black hair, and she punctuated her remarks by tapping with a pencil on the table. Her point was that elections are not won with indignation, or talk, or registrations in the voters' books. They are won by ballots in the ballot box, and therefore she wanted everybody to stop at the table in the hallway, and fill out a slip with name, address, and phone number, and check what they would contribute on election day: time, car, or money, or all three. It was the first thing all night that had a resolute, professional sound to it, and once or twice it drew crackling applause. Ben got out his little red book, found the date, May 7, and wrote her name: June Lyons.

When Mr. Jansen came out of the school and entered his car, Ben was parked a few feet behind him, his lights out, his motor running. When Mr. Jansen started up, Ben started up, and seemed oddly expert at the job of following. On brightly lighted streets he cut his lights, and when he had to snap them on, fell back some distance, so the car ahead was not likely to notice him. Finally, when Mr. Jansen turned into the drive of a pretentious house in the swank Lakeside suburb, he parked nearby, and looked the place over, not missing the three Scandinavian birches growing in a cluster on the lawn. When another car drove up he watched Mr. Conley, the chairman; Mr. Bleeker, the candidate for city attorney; Mrs. Bleeker and Miss Lyons get out and enter the house, then got out his little red book, and under May 7 again, copied down the number of the car. He sat a long time, waiting for other cars to appear. When the four visitors came out, he followed their car again, noting the addresses as Mr. and Mrs. Bleeker dropped their passengers off. It was around two o'clock when he tucked his little red book away and drove to Ike's Place, a small honky-tonk about four miles from town.

The place was fairly full and fairly noisy, with the crash of pinball shattering the beat of juke music. In the murk at one end of the bar a couple was dancing. Waiters in gray jackets with brass buttons hurried about, serving drinks; they were addressed by name, mostly, and treated the customers as old friends. When Ben came in he waved at Caspar, who was sitting at a table with Lefty, Bugs Lenhardt, another guard named Goose Groner, and two girls. Then he sat down at the bar, ordered a drink, and scanned a paper devoting its front page to the Castleton robbery, which had gone even worse than Lefty had expected. The four wild kids had got $22,000 but killed a cashier doing it.

Presently Groner was beside Ben, mumbling that Caspar wanted to see him. The girls moved over so Ben could sit down, but Caspar didn't invite him. Instead he demanded savagely to know where he had been. Ben, evidently deciding that an offense was the only defense against a stupid inquiry, stuck out his chin and said: "Me? I been working. I been carrying out orders, some kind of hop dreams that were thought up by a jerk named Solly Caspar—no relation, I hope. I been tailing a Swede all over town, and copying down the car numbers of his friends, and making a sap out of myself—wasn't that a way to spend a spring night! And for what? Because they been taking this lug, this fathead named Caspar, for a ride the whole town is laughing at."

"Ride? What ride?"

"Come on, get wise to yourself. The ride Maddux is taking you for. Filling you up with that hooey about Delany—"

"Oh, so you think it's hooey?"

"Listen, I've seen this Swede's friends, and they wouldn't know Delany if they met him on the street. It's a gyp and you fell for it, that's all."

Ben got this off with quite a show of truculence, and it left Caspar blinking, and would probably have settled the argument if he hadn't slightly overplayed it. He took up the previous question, which was where he had been all night, reminding Caspar it had been clearly stipulated that he was not to report until tomorrow; and when Caspar weakly tapped his watch and said it *was* tomorrow, he said that as far as he was concerned it was not tomorrow until the sun came up. At this one of the girls, who had been eyeing Ben's curls with more than casual interest, let out an appreciative laugh. Caspar's eyes flickered. Lefty jumped up and began telling him a story, a meaningless thing about a couple of Irishmen that went into a hotel. Groner began whispering to him, patting his back and leaning close to his ear. The girl, frightened, poked him with her finger, and said hey, quit scaring her to death.

This went on for five minutes, and the place froze like a cinematic stop-camera shot. Ike, the proprietor, caught the eye of the bartender, who stood with a shaker in his hand, checking the position of the waiters. These came to a stop in the aisles, and stood staring at Caspar. He began to pant, and when Groner touched his arm, shook it as though something had stung him. Then, his seizure passing, he screamed: "O.K., you took the car number! Why don't you pass it over? What you waiting for?"

Ben, who had turned green, stared at him. He stared a long time, his eyes becoming small, cold, and hard. Then he took out his little red book, copied a number on the back of a beer mat, and rolled it to Caspar. Before returning the book to his pocket he creased the page with his thumbnail. But this page was not captioned May 7.

It was captioned April 29.

CHAPTER

2

Next afternoon, when Ben reported to work, Sol was in high good humor. He indulged in a little heavy-handed kidding, played a new swing record, and in other small ways tried to atone for his behavior of the previous night. Presently he said: "And was *you* fooled!"

"Yeah? How?"

"Them guys. That you seen with Jansen."

"Oh? You know who they were?"

"I had that license checked. The one you give me last night. I sent a special wire to Chicago, and I just now got a reply. You know who that car belonged to?"

"I got no idea."

"Frankie Horizon."

"Well, say—and he looked like another Swede."

"How many times I got to tell you, you can't go by their looks. Frankie Horizon—and him and Delany are just like that."

Sol held up two fingers to indicate a close degree of intimacy, as Ben stared incredulously. Compassionately, then, Sol shook his head. "I don't know what I'm going to do about you, Ben."

"How you mean, Sol?"

"Them Illinois plates. Didn't they mean nothing to you?"

"Well—plenty people live in Illinois."

"Wise money has generally got Illinois plates."

"I'll try to remember."

"It's O.K.—if you could remember something you wouldn't be driving a car, for me or anybody. And, you found out what I wanted, so take tomorrow off."

"Well, gee, thanks, Sol."

"That's a promise. Go on, make a date."

In the big room, however, Lefty seemed even more dejected, if that were possible, than he had been yesterday. He sat tipping one key of the piano, and when Ben presently asked him to cut it out, he announced: "He's going to die."

"*Who's* going to die?"

"That kid. That got it at Castleton yesterday."

"How you know he's going to die?"

"That doc, the look on his face."

"Where's the kid shot?"

"In the hip."

"Did the doc get the bullet out?"

"It came in and went out. The guard, before they got out of the bank, had time to grab his rifle, and it was with that that the kid got it, just a little hole that went right through. He's not in any pain. He thinks he's going to be moving soon. But the other three, they can see him behind, where he's turning black. They're getting jittery. They're getting worse than I am."

The shrug that Ben gave was perhaps more indifferent than one would expect, on a warm afternoon, at a piece of news of at least average quality, with nothing else to talk about. It was matched by the yawn he gave next morning, when Lefty arrived at the Lucas before he was up, and sat on the edge of the bed, and furnished a few more details. "His temperature's up, Ben. He's beginning to rave. And the other three, I don't know what they'll pull. They're liable to conk him to make him shut up or something. They're not old-timers. They're just kids. They don't know what to do when a guy gets it. And the hotel, they're turning on the heat."

"Can't you get him out of there?"

"Where to?"

It was at this point that Ben yawned, and Lefty went on: "What am I going to do, Ben? *He's going to die, and what am I going to do with him?* I can't serve no more time. I can't take it. I was already stir crazy, a little bit ..."

"Dogged if I know what to tell you."

When Lefty went, Ben got up, held the door on a crack, and peeped down the hall, to make sure he was really gone. Then, on his outside phone, he dialed a number and asked for Miss Lyons—Miss June Lyons.

A girl slowing down as a man held up a newspaper, the man climbing into the car she was driving, the two of them going on at the change of the light—it looked casual enough, yet it had been planned by Ben, and carried out by her, in such fashion as to make it impossible that they should be followed. She was driving Mr. Jansen's big green sedan, and for a few moments they studied each other. Then he laughed. "Hey, cut that out. Smile. Relax."

"You mean the frown?"

"It's just terrible."

"That's what my mother always says."

"You must have had it a long time if she's always saying."

"It comes from taking things seriously."

"What things?"

"Oh—this and that."

"Not Jansen?"

"Well, why not Jansen?"

"I wouldn't think he'd appeal to you. Fact of the matter, ever since I heard you make that speech the other night, I've been wondering why you're hooked up with him. You look serious enough, but you don't look dumb enough."

"Well, Jansen isn't really what I meant."

"And what did you mean?"

"Something personal."

"Romance?"

"I'd hardly take *that* seriously."

She was smiling now, and her face lighted up quite pleasantly, though there was still something solemn about it, as though back of any light idea that entered her mind there would always be some sobering consideration. He smiled a little too, and said: "If it's not love it's got to be money."

"It might be a little of both, but not the way you mean. Since my frown seems to interest you, and my connection with Mr. Jansen seems to interest you, they both have to do with my family, and it's a long story, and not at all exciting, and I'd rather not talk about it, if you don't mind."

"Your family live here?"

"Do *you* live here?"

"Looks like we got a little dead-end there."

"If, as you said over the phone, I'm not to ask questions about who you are, or anything about you, then don't ask questions about me, or my family, or where they live. What is this business you and I have, anyway? After that call, the very least I expected was a blue chin and a broken nose."

"You disappointed?"

"A little."

"I called about Jansen."

"Oh, the dumb candidate."

"He's dumb, but outside of Maddux he's the only candidate we've got, anyway, that's got his papers filed. So I've been looking him over. So I've been thinking it might be a good idea if he was elected, or perhaps I should say, if Maddux was defeated."

"And?"

"I'm kicking in with a little dirt."

"I'd rather have money, but—"

"You'll settle for dirt. You know the Castleton robbery?"

"The bank?"

"That's it. Suppose friend Jansen found out where that mob was hiding. Suppose he found out they were here, in Lake City, under protection of Caspar and the police department. Suppose he found out the exact hotel. Could he use it?"

Not waiting for a reply, Ben took out an envelope, tore off the back, and wrote down four names. "There they are. They're at the Globe Hotel, Room 38, a double room with two extra cots moved in. That last guy, Rossi, the one I checked, is shot. He's going to die, so if Jansen is going to use this he better do it quick. When he does die, the other three will certainly skip.''

Ben was obviously surprised at the hostile stare she turned on him. With an ironical laugh she said: "You must have gone to college, didn't you? To think up one like that?"

"Like what, for instance?"

"It's criminal libel, that's all—if Mr. Jansen mentions the name of the hotel, and not worth a plugged dime if he doesn't. And coming now, just a week before election, it's a trick, I would say, to send Mr. Jansen to the polls under indictment, and perhaps even under arrest. To say nothing of what could be done to his business and property in the civil action, later."

"You're a smart girl, aren't you?"

"Oh, I went to college too. And law school."

"You're about as dumb a girl as any candidate ever had back of him. Here I offer you dirt, and the first thing you tell me is that you'd rather have money. Well June, there comes a time when money's not enough. You've got to have dirt—not nice clean dirt, like calling names and all this stuff Jansen has been handing out. Dirty dirt. Dirt that stinks so bad something has to be done about it. And here I offer you some, with more to come, much as you want, enough to break Caspar and all the rest of them, and all you see in it is criminal libel. I guess you belong with Jansen, come to think of it. And now suppose we go back. Sitting this close to you makes me feel a little sick to my stomach."

She drove a little further, her face getting redder and redder. Then she turned around, and when they came to a car track he motioned her to stop. When he got out he didn't say goodbye.

After dinner, he walked slowly down Hobart Street, looking at movie notices, but none of them seemed to suit him. He went back to his hotel, entered his room, and lay down, first removing his coat and hanging it in the closet. In a moment or two his fingers found the radio, which was tucked on the second deck of the night table, and turned it on. For the better part of an hour he lay there, the light off, listening to dinner music from the Columbus. Then the Jansen meeting came in, and he scowled, starting to turn it off. Then he changed his mind and lay there listening, his face a sombre shadow in the half dark, while the same old speeches came in that he had listened to at the high school. When June was introduced he made a second motion to cut the radio off, and again changed his mind. Then suddenly he sat up in bed, and snapped on the light, and listened with rapt attention.

She was talking about the hook-up, the alliance between crime, the Mayor, and the police, and even the crowd sensed that she was leading up to something. Then with breath-taking suddenness it came: "You think there's no hook-up, do you? You think that's something *we* invented, to get Mr. Jansen elected? Then why are those four bandits, the ones that robbed the Security Bank at Castleton day before yesterday, the ones that took $22,000 from that bank and murdered Guy Horner, the cashier—why are they hiding in Lake City? Why are Buck Harper, Mort Dubois, Boogie-Woogie Lipsky, and Arch Rossi in the Globe Hotel right now, with nothing being done about them? You think Chief Dietz doesn't know about them? He does, because he told me so. I called him at four o'clock this afternoon, and told him I was the operator at the Globe Hotel, and asked him if there were any further instructions on the party of four in Room 38. He said: 'Not till Arch Rossi gets so he can travel, anyhow. But I'm not really handling it. You better talk to Solly Caspar.' "

The snarl from the crowd had an echo of the wolf pack in it, but June shouted over it: "Will somebody stop that officer? The one that's trying to get out, to telephone?"

Evidently the officer stopped, for there was a big laugh, and June said: "There's no use warning those boys, officer. You see, after I talked to Chief Dietz I called Castleton, and the Castleton detectives are at the hotel right now, and I think they'll move a little too fast for you to stop them—a little official kidnapping, so to speak. It's the only way, apparently, to bring murderers to trial under the conditions we have in Lake City."

An exultant light in his eye, Ben snapped off the radio. Then, moving with catlike silence, he went to the door, jerked it open. The hall was empty. Then he put on his coat, picked up his hat, and went out to the Tracy picture at the Rialto.

When he came in, Mr. Nerny, the elderly night clerk, was signaling with one hand. "Call for you, Mr. Grace. Party was just about to hang up when I told them I was quite sure I recognized your step. Take it down here if you like."

Into the house phone, Ben said: "Hello?"

"Mr. Grace?"

"Speaking."

"This is your friend that takes things seriously."

"*Who?*"

"The one you went riding with, today."

"Oh yes. I'll call you later. Goodbye."

Hanging up, he shot a glance at Mr. Nerny, but Mr. Nerny had put aside his earphones, and apparently had heard nothing. Upstairs, he paced about, and started to take off his clothes. But the knowledge that this girl knew who he was evidently threw him badly off step, and presently he clapped on his hat and went out.

"What was the idea, calling me?"

"Well, it was pretty successful, what I did. What you did. What—we did. I thought, after the way I acted today, the least I could do was call you and thank you."

"Over that hotel phone?"

"Oh, I was going to be careful."

"On a night like this, when we set off five tons of dynamite in this town, you were going to let a night clerk hear you being careful?"

"Is it as melodramatic as that?"

"Yeah."

He turned away from her, and became aware of the apartment she lived in. It was a bare little place, almost shabby, on the second floor of a small apartment house. To one side was a dining alcove, and a double door looked as though a bed might lurk behind it. He had not got up here without an argument through the door phone, for it was at least one o'clock in the morning, and when she finally let him up, she made him wait five minutes while she put on these lounging pajamas that she now wore. They were dark red, and certainly becoming, but he paid no attention to them. As she continued to smile, he seized her roughly by the arm and asked: "What's so funny about this melodrama thing? . . . O.K., they shoot off blanks, and I guess that's funny. But Caspar, he don't shoot off blanks. When he shoots, he throws lead. Is that funny? Go on, let's see you laugh."

She tried to pull her arm away, but he gave it another shake. "And how'd you find out who I am, by the way?"

"I don't see that that matters."

"Oh yes. It matters."

She turned to a table, opened a drawer, and took out a piece of paper. "When you tear up envelopes to write on, you might burn the part that has your name and address on it, or put it back in your pocket, or something. You were in such a hurry to jump out of the car today that you left this on the seat."

"And who did you show it to?"

"Nobody."

"And who did you tell about it?"

"Nobody."

"Come on! How about Jansen?"

"About you, I've told nothing, and I can prove it."

"O.K., prove."

"Were you there? At the meeting?"

"I heard it."

"You noticed I made that announcement myself?"

"Saving Jansen from criminal libel?"

"After I called Dietz and made sure that what you told me was true, I didn't have to worry about libel. No, I was thinking about myself. I was making sure that I, and nobody else, got the credit. I wanted to be certain that Mr. Jansen, if he gets elected, will have to do a lot more about me in the shape of a job than he would have to do if I was just a girl that handled secretaries, and had slips filled out. In that case I wouldn't be telling anybody the source of my information, would I? You see, I'm hoping for *more* tips."

He sat down and studied her intently. Relaxing, she sat down, not far away, on the same hard little sofa. Suddenly he asked: "Outside of my name, do you know who I am?"

"No."

"I'm Sol Caspar's driver."

"Then—you're Sol Caspar's driver."

"And that's O.K. with you?"

"It certainly gilt-edges your tips."

"And it don't bother you that I drive for him six days a week and then on my day off I call you up and give you tips?"

"I'm willing to believe you have your reasons."

"I got plenty of reasons."

"Then—I'm glad to know that."

"I'd rather fight him clean, right out in the open, the way you fight him. I'd be perfectly willing to quit my job, and tell him straight out what I'm up to, than knife him in the back this way. But if I could quit my job I wouldn't be fighting him at all. I'm not looking for trouble. He even laughs at me because I don't *like* trouble. But he won't let me quit. If I quit, it's curtains for me, and that's why I'm here with you. He asked for it. I didn't."

"I'm *very* glad to know that."

"O.K. Now who are you?"

"Nobody."

"Listen, I've got to know."

"I was born in Ohio, and raised there, just across the river from Kentucky. I went to school there, and high school, and college, and law school. Then I heard of a job in Lake City, and applied for it, and got it, and came here."

"What kind of a job?"

"With a law firm, Wiener, Jacks, and Myers. They pay me

a salary, about as good a salary as young lawyers get, more than you might think from this." She waved her hand at the apartment. "I only keep part of my salary for myself. And—I've got to have still more money. I simply *must* have it."

"Why you more than somebody else?"

"I told you it's a long story."

"More family history?"

"It's been going on a long time, and I'd rather not go into it. Anyway, Jansen came along. I'd done a little work for him, settling claims. And he was thinking about running for Mayor. And I was thinking about a job, one of those heavenly city hall jobs where you come down once a week to sign papers, and hold your regular job just the same. And—I guess I egged him on."

"For the dough?"

"Not entirely. I think he's a fine man, fit to be Mayor, a hundred times better than Maddux. Just the same—"

"The dough is the main thing?"

"Now I feel like a heel."

"No need to feel that way. Listen, if it was just idealism, I might give you tips, but I'd be plenty worried. I don't believe in that stuff, and I don't believe in people that do believe in it. Now I know it's the old do-re-mi, that's different. O.K., June. We can do business."

"I'm afraid it *is* idealism, just the same."

"You said it was dough."

"Yes, but not to have it, or spend it, or whatever people do with it. Money, just as money, doesn't mean much to me. But as a means to an end, as something that will permit me to deal with—a certain situation—"

"Back home?"

"It might be. Well, money for that purpose is important to me. Then it will mean something to me."

"Are you out to get it or not?"

"Indeed I am."

"That's all I want to know."

She got the solemn frown on her face again, as though she

wanted to make clear that it was no ordinary greed that prompted her present activities, but he ran his finger up the crease between her brows. She laughed. "I want to be an idealist."

"O.K., so I'm a chiseler."

"Oh, say *crook.*"

"A chiseler, he's not a crook."

"He certainly isn't honest."

"He's just in between."

Two days before, when Lefty had said it, Ben had obviously been annoyed. Now, just as obviously, he was beginning to be proud of it. She laughed. "Anyway, we're both walloping Caspar."

"I hope we are."

"But look *how* we're walloping him."

She got a paper from the alcove, and came back with it. It was a midnight edition, and all over the front page was the story of how the Castleton detectives had raided the Globe Hotel and grabbed three of the bandits without bothering to get in touch with the Lake City police. Ben seemed surprised that only three bandits were bagged, and she explained: "The other one, the one that was shot, had been taken away before the Castleton police got there."

"Alive?"

"We think so."

He was already reading the news story, but she pointed to the editorial, also on Page 1, and he read it with her, their heads nearly touching. It attacked Castleton savagely, but went on to say that the charges made by Miss June Lyons, a speaker at the Jansen meeting, were too serious to be ignored. An investigation of the Lake City police department should be made, and if Mayor Maddux wouldn't act, the Governor ought to. "It's the first time, Mr. Grace—"

"Call me Ben."

"It's the first time, Ben, that either of the big papers has taken us seriously. The little *News-Times* does what it can, but this is the *Post!* If I just had a little *more* dirt . . ."

"You *are* waking up, aren't you?"

"I'll say I am."

She was breathless, tense, eager. For a second their eyes met, and it seemed queer that he suddenly got up, instead of taking her in his arms, which he certainly could have done. He stood uncertainly for a moment, then picked up his hat. "One thing."

"Yes?"

"Tell Jansen to put a private guard on here. Outside, at least two men, day and night. I'd do it, but they'd know me. Ring him soon as I go, and have him attend to it tonight. *Tonight,* see? That's necessary, after what you did, and a Lake City police guard is the same as no guard at all. You hear me?"

"All right, I'll call him."

"I'll ring you tomorrow. With maybe more dirt."

"I'll see you soon, Ben."

"That's right. Soon."

Lefty sat down with Ben next morning as he was having breakfast in the Savoy Grill. A toothpick indicated he himself had
already eaten, and he began without preliminaries: "Well, it's
war."

"Blitz or sitz?"

"Blitz, I'd say. Sol and Delany."

"What's Delany done?"

"You heard what happened last night?"

"I'm reading about it."

"If it was just tipping that girl, O.K. It wasn't friendly, but
after them sharpshooters you seen with Jansen, Solly knew what
to expect. But about an hour before the Castleton bulls got
there, a Delany guy shows up, a guy that takes care of his
horses, over at the Jardine stables. And he takes Arch Rossi
out. He takes him out of the Globe and over to the Columbus.
Sol, he don't like that. If the kid has to die, he could die just
as good in Castleton, couldn't he? In a hospital, with good
doctors taking care of him? Dumping him in the Columbus,
right in Solly's own hotel, Solly takes that personal."

"So?"

"He's taking steps."

"Where *is* Delany?"

"He's in Chicago, but he'll come back."

"If coaxed?"

"On proper inducements, he'll come."

"Where's Rossi?"

"I don't exactly know."

Lefty stared vacantly at the hat stand across the room, laid the toothpick in an ashtray. "So it'll be an O.K. war, if that's getting us anywheres, and Solly, of course, he'll be nice and happy. Just the same, it's not Delany."

"Then who is it?"

"I figured it might be you."

As Lefty turned his cold, vacant stare full on Ben's face, Ben lit a cigarette. He let the match burn for a moment, and from the interested way he looked at it, one might wonder if he was testing, to know if his hand was trembling. When there was not the slightest flicker, he blew the match out, and asked languidly: "You tell Sol that?"

"Yeah."

"What'd he say?"

"He didn't believe it."

"But you, my old pal, you believe it, don't you?"

"Listen, Ben, I'm your pal, but this ain't the candy business. In this racket you can't take chances, and if you're crossing us, the pal stuff is out. Couple of things look pretty funny to me. If there was a couple of sharpshooters with Jansen the other night, both pals of Delany, why didn't you know it? Seemed a little off the groove that Solly had to find that out. And why would Delany start something? He's sitting pretty. On the bookies he gets his cut and it's not hay. He's got a nice daily double and he don't even have to stay here and watch it. Why would he bust it up?"

"And that leaves me, hey?"

"It could."

"Nuts."

"Oh, yeah?"

"Lefty, you're playing it safe, you got to do that. You got to feed me a lead and watch my face, just like I'd do for you, just like all pals got to do to each other in this swell business we're in. But you don't really think it's me. If you did you'd just rub me out and that would be that. Even if you halfway thought it was me, you'd have fed me a phoney just now, on where you're keeping Arch Rossi, and then if I ran to her with it you'd have me. When you didn't do at least that much I know you're not really bearing down."

"O.K., Ben. But it's *somebody,* and I'm worried."

"I'm a little worried myself."

"Then we're both worried."

"Pals?"

"Two beers, and they're on you."

Around nine, when Ben went back to his hotel, the day clerk said a lady had called, twice. He went to his room and dialed June, getting no answer. In five minutes his house phone rang, and when June spoke he gave her the number of his outside phone. Only when she had called him on this did he let her go ahead. "Something's happened, Ben."

"O.K., give."

"It's the boy that took Rossi out of the Globe."

"And what about him?"

"He showed up at Jansen's about an hour ago, and Jansen called me. I wouldn't let them come to my apartment, but I met them outside, and—I don't know what to do with him. He's been wandering around all night, and he's afraid to go home, for fear he'll be killed, and he can't go to the police, because they're hand-in-glove with Caspar, and—"

"Where are you now?"

"In a drug store, and he and Jansen are outside—"

"Don't say who I am, but get him to the phone."

In a few moments the boy was on the line, and Ben talked with the stern tone of a Governor, or at the very least of a prosecuting attorney. "What's your name?"

"Herndon, sir. Bob Herndon."

"And what's this about Arch Rossi?"

"Nothing, sir. I swear I never knew he was mixed up in the Castleton robbery. Me and Arch, we went to school together, and we was buddies. Then I didn't see him for a while, and then yesterday he called me, over at the Jardine stables, where I work for Mr. Delany."

"Bill Delany or Dick Delany?"

"Mr. Bill, sir."

"What do you do for him?"

"I take care of his horses, sir, all six of his polo ponies and his two thoroughbred mares. Of course I got to get help exercising them, but—"

"O.K., so Arch Rossi called you?"

"Yes sir, he said he'd been hurt in a car accident, and he was in Room 38 at the Globe, and would I call a taxi and come over and get him out of there. I thought it was kind of funny, and I couldn't do anything till six o'clock, when I was off, but then he called again, and when he said he had plenty of dough I called a cab and went over there. There were three other guys there, and they cussed Arch out and told him to get out and stay out. So I figured if it was a car accident, maybe the car was stolen. Then from the way Arch began talking in the cab I knew he was shot. Then when we got to the Columbus and I was helping him in through the service entrance I heard somebody say: 'Holy smoke, here comes one of those Castleton rats,' and I looked around and it was a guy that runs the Columbus for Caspar by the name of Henry Hardcastle."

"You know Henry Hardcastle?"

"I seen him at the track plenty of times."

"He know you?"

"I'll say he does."

"Herndon, what are you lying to me for?"

"Mister, I'm not lying."

"If Rossi was shot, why would he be leaving the Globe, unless he got orders? And if it was orders, why don't you say so? And if you're working for Caspar, what's the big idea, going to Mr. Jansen and handing him a lot of chatter about being afraid to go home?"

"I don't work for Caspar."

"Then it don't make sense."

"It makes sense if you heard what Arch was saying in the cab. He was shot, see? And he was laying up with three guys that he was afraid would knock him off just to get rid of him. And nothing was being done about him except a bum doctor would come in every day and tell him he was getting along swell. But from the way the other three were whispering he knew he wasn't getting along swell, and he figured his only chance was to get to Caspar, so—"

"O.K. Now it makes sense. Go on."

"That's all, except when I tumbled to what it was all about I beat it, and when I got home my sister was yelling out the window at me to go away, that they were after me, and I had to beat it again. And I been beating it ever since, and I don't know who you are, Mister, but if you got some place I can go, then—"

"Is the lady still there?"

"Yes, sir."

"Put her on and get back to the car."

When June answered again, Ben spoke rapidly and decisively. "O.K., the first thing you do, you shoot this bird over to Castleton. Have Jansen take him over in person, and start at once. As soon as they're gone, get over to Jansen headquarters, call the Castleton police and let them know what's coming. Then sit tight. Be at Jansen headquarters all day, just in case."

"Have Jansen take him in person?"

"That's it. We're playing in luck, terrific luck. This Herndon, he's just a lug that curries horses. But he curries them for Delany, and that's all we need. Solly fell for it last night, and he'll keep on falling for it if we just let him. We got him chasing his own tail and he don't know it."

"I'm terribly excited."

"Get going."

"I'm off."

Hanging up, Ben sat down on the unmade bed, his watch in his hand. At the end of fifteen minutes he dialed the *Pioneer*.

"City desk, please ... Hello, you want a tip on that bandit, Arch Rossi?"

"What do you think?"

"O.K., I can't tell you where he is, but I can tell you where his pal is, and if you hop on it, maybe you can get some dope from him."

"I'll bite, where is he?"

"Castleton."

"Why?"

"Caspar was after him, for dropping Rossi at the Columbus. He was afraid to go home, and he went to Jansen. So Jansen's taking him to the Castleton cops, for protection and maybe some evidence. They started ten or fifteen minutes ago, in Jansen's car."

"Who are you?"

"Little Jack Horner."

"O.K., Jack. Thanks."

When the first editions came out, it developed that the newspaper had done what Ben no doubt expected. It had chartered a special plane, and had reporters and photographers waiting when Jansen walked into Castleton police headquarters with Herndon. In the big room, Ben and Lefty read silently, studied the pictures of Jansen, of Herndon, even of Rossi, in a blown-up snapshot that somebody had dug up. The buzzer kept sounding, and Lefty kept jumping up to admit various personages: Jack Brady, secretary to the Mayor; Inspector Cantrell, of the Police Department; James Joseph Bresnahan, ace reporter for the *Pioneer;* photographers, bellboys, telegraph messengers. The Bresnahan interview broke for the financial edition, and Lefty began to curse when he read it. It was mainly Bresnahan, in an F. Scott Fitzgerald picture of Caspar, as though he were a great Gatsby of some credit to the town. But it was quite a little Caspar, too, in an interview that gave no names, but intimated all too plainly that if the citizenry wanted to know more about Rossi, or of the various scandals that had recently rocked the town, it might ask a certain society racketeer who knew much more than many might think.

In the five-star final, there was a picture of Dick Delany, standing beside his car, about to depart for Chicago, where, it was explained, he would interview his brother, as special correspondent for the paper, and find out what truth there might be in the Caspar charges, or in the various rumors that were flying around. When he saw this, Ben managed a fair imitation of a snicker. "Say, that's a laugh—they're hiring Dick Delany to drive over to Chicago and interview Bill on what Solly's saying about him."

"I see they are."

"I guess Sol's not in any real danger."

"How you figure that out?"

"If they really mean it, why don't they put a real reporter on it? What's the idea of sending Dick Delany, that stumble-bum that don't hardly know right from left? To me, that looks quite a lot like a coat of whitewash."

"To me it looks different."

"Yeah? How so?"

"What you say, that would be O.K. if Solly had it doped right. If Delany *was* back of this stuff that's being sprung by the Jansen people, and especially that girl, then sending Dick over would be about the dumbest play they could think up, because it would just be helping him cover up. But if Solly's got it wrong, and Delany's a little sore, and wants to shoot off his mouth, then Dick would just be the perfect guy for him to talk to, wouldn't it? To *me*—of course nobody pays any attention to what I say around here any more, and it's just one mug's opinion—but to me it looks like they straightened Solly up for the old one-two and no bell to save him. First they send Bresnahan over here and get him to shoot off his face, and you'll notice Dick's got that paper in his hand even while he's having his picture taken. If Bill needed anything more to open him up, that would do it."

Carefully, Lefty read the *Pioneer*'s write-up of Mr. Bill Delany; of his start as a hostler in the Jardine stables; of his rise to riding instructor, to exhibitor of mounts at local horse shows;

of his acquisition of various runners, particularly Golden Bough, a winner of purses some years before; of his reputed share in several tracks; of the rumors that connected him with organized gambling. As to this, however, the *Pioneer* was quite sketchy, and even jocular, as though nobody really believed the rumors, except perhaps Mr. Caspar. Then it went on to relate the strange relationship between Bill and his brother Dick; how the older brother self-effacingly kept behind the scenes, letting the younger brother do the family manners; how this last "tall, handsome, hard-riding man-about-town" had quite captured Lake City's imagination; how he entered horses at the leading tracks, played in local polo games, belonged to several clubs, including the Lakeside Country Club, and had been reported engaged to several of the younger members of the social set. As to his brains, or lack of them, the paper had nothing to say, unless something was to be inferred from the paragraph: "Yet it is an open secret that the man behind the silks is not Dick, but Bill. Not that Dick is merely a 'front' for his quite active brother. On the contrary, he leads a pretty full life on his own account. And yet it is Bill, not Dick, who captains the ship, buys the gee-gees, decides where they are to be entered."

Lefty shook his head. "You got it wrong, Ben. If the *Pioneer* was all, they mean it plenty."

"What do you mean, if the *Pioneer* was all?"

"I told you, we're taking steps."

"Oh, that's right, I forgot."

"Maybe one too many."

Pioneer Park, the local baseball grounds, was in striking contrast with John Dewey High School, just a few nights before. There the crowd had been small, quiet, and dispirited. Here, as a result of the sensational revelations of the last day or two, thousands of people were gathered, in a tense, excited mood. They overflowed from the space back of home plate, where seats had been placed, into the stand itself. On the speakers' stand that had been erected over the plate floodlights glared down, and as the loudspeakers carried every word that was said to the far corners of the grounds, loud cheers went up, with occasional calls for June, the mystery girl of the campaign.

Mr. Caspar arrived around eight, riding between Goose and Bugs on the back seat of the big armored sedan, with Ben at the wheel and Lefty beside Ben. Just what he was doing there, to judge from what was being said, was a puzzle to everybody in the car, and an unwelcome one, at that. His own explanation was: "It's time I had a look at that dame"; and this, coupled with his compulsion to show his power wherever he could, seemed to be about the only reason. His power was evident at once. The car no sooner arrived than a sergeant waved it past the turnstiles, where lesser folks entered to the vehicle gate, which he ordered open. There a motorcycle patrolman picked it up, and led it past the rear of the grandstand to a point where the bleachers ended, and from there to a dark spot just back of the coaching lines. Several other cars were parked on the infield. Bugs jumped out, to look them over, and keep an eye on things behind. But Sol paid no attention, and made remarks at the expense of the speakers. One of them, soliciting money, said that three $1,000 contributions had been received in the last twenty-four hours, and to this Sol said: "Three thousand bucks! Wha ya know about that! Gee, they don't look out they're gonna have enough to pay for a coupla funerals."

"Hey, Solly, cut it out."

"Three funerals, grand apiece."

"I said cut it out."

Lefty, as Sol made no effort to muffle his jibes, was growing increasingly nervous. Presently, after the crowd had been lashed to a frenzy by several speakers, by excerpts from the day's newspapers, by a brief speech from Jansen, June was introduced, and stepped into view, under the lights. The ensuing demonstration lasted five minutes, and Sol paid his respects to her clothes, her figure, and her general appearance, laughing loudly at his not very delicate sallies. But when she began to speak he fell as silent as he might have if he had been hit with an axe. "Mr. Chairman, honorable candidates, fellow citizens, Mr. Caspar."

"There it goes."

Lefty, perhaps with reason, obviously blamed the jocosity of the last half hour for June's knowledge of their presence. Sol froze into a small, compact ball as she lifted the mike, turned it around, and faced him, her back to the major portion of the crowd. "I'm glad you've seen fit to honor us with your presence, Mr. Caspar, because I've information that will interest you as a hotel owner. You were correctly quoted, I assume, in Mr. Bresnahan's article in today's *Pioneer,* in which you said that nobody by the name of Rossi, so far as you know, is staying at the Columbus Hotel. I must regretfully report that you don't know everything that goes on at the Columbus. Mr. Arch Rossi is at the Columbus, this very minute. He must be there, because I myself talked with him, less than an hour ago. Of course I had some difficulty getting him on the line. I had to put the call through Castleton police headquarters, and make it appear as though Bob Herndon was trying to talk to his old pal, and tell him things that might be of interest—"

There was a warning shout from Bugs, watching behind. Then lights flashed all around the car. The photographers, who were out in force, had probably started together, as soon as June started to speak. At any rate they had the car surrounded, and were snapping furiously to get pictures. Caspar began pounding Ben on the back, ordering him to get out of there. Ben spun his motor, fast. The outfield floodlights came on, as the crowd gave a roaring laugh. Ben, his head twisted backwards, caught the horn with his elbow, and it brayed grotesquely. The crowd gave a cheer. It seemed minutes before they cleared the bleachers, and were whirling away.

"Boy, you ought to hear them. I don't know where that dame came from, but she's going to cost Maddux the election if something's not done. Sol, he better look out."

Bugs, left in the ball park by the circumstance that cars have no running boards any more for lookout men to jump on, climbed in beside Ben, who was parked in the areaway back of the Columbus. "She's stirring 'em up, hey?"

"It's just murder. After you left she cut it loose and what she don't know about this outfit ain't hardly worth knowing. Where's Sol?"

"Inside."

"Goose and Lefty with him?"

"Yeah, but he said wait. We're going somewhere."

"Sure, with Arch Rossi."

"Oh, yeah?"

"He's got to get rid of the kid, hasn't he? Boy, after what that dame told them out there tonight he can't have him here any more. Not in the Columbus, he can't."

"What do you mean, get rid of him?"

"Ben, if I knew I wouldn't say."

When Sol came out of the hotel, however, he was alone. He climbed in the car and sat smoking, as though waiting for something. Presently, from the street, came the sound of police sirens. From where they were sitting they could see several cars pull up in front on the street, and spew officers all over the sidewalk. These disappeared, and Sol tiptoed to the rear of the hotel to listen. Bugs nodded at Ben, whispered that Solly was on the job, all right, and probably had the thing under control. This raid meant that Rossi was already out of the hotel, and the cops would find nothing. Even before the police cars had pulled away Sol was back in the car, and told Ben to drive to Memorial Boulevard. Bugs moved to the back seat with him, and they started out.

They drove out Memorial into a black, bleary waste of suburbs not yet become open country. Then Sol said to stop. When they were at a standstill, he told Ben to wink his lights. At once they got a wink in return from a side road, some distance ahead. Then Sol told Ben to keep the lights dark, and run to the other car. Cautiously Ben rolled ahead in the dark, but stopped at the sound of running footsteps. The footsteps drew nearer, while all three of them sat silent. Then Lefty was beside the car, his voice lifted in a quavering wail: "They've plugged him, Solly, they've plugged him—*they've plugged him!*"

Sol got out, followed by Bugs, and with apparent concern inquired: "Where they at?" But Lefty, as he turned to point, hit the ground in a sprawl, and the breath left his body in a grunting sob. Sol jumped on him, jammed his knee in his stomach, and slapped him eight, ten, or a dozen times. Then he told Bugs to give him a gun, and when Bugs drew one from an armpit holster, jammed it at Lefty's mouth. Lefty clenched his teeth, striking at Sol with his fists. Bugs seized his arms and held them against the ground. Sol pulled his cheek away from his teeth, and shoved the gun muzzle inside of it. Then he began to whisper, obscene, psychopathic threats as to what would happen if Lefty didn't "snap out of it." Presently he removed the gun and asked: "Wha ya say now, soldier?"

"O.K., Sol, O.K."

"Get up."

"O.K., now I'm O.K."

Sol, Bugs, and Lefty walked to the other car, leaving Ben alone. He sat there at the wheel of the car, his lights out, his motor always running, for perhaps ten minutes. Then Sol came back and told him to drive over to Rich Street. At Rich Street they headed out into another drab suburb, and at Reservoir Street Sol said stop. They sat in the dark car a long time now, Sol on the back seat smoking cigars, Ben up front, constantly checking that his motor was running. Some distance away, there was occasionally audible a low mutter, as well as a recurrent scraping noise. The only sign of the strain they were under came when Ben lit a cigarette. Sol savagely ordered him to put it out, not bothering to explain why he could smoke, Ben not. Presently Lefty appeared and got in, and Sol said drive to Ike's, and step on it.

At Ike's Lefty sat alone, in the shadows, drinking beer, and gave no sign that Ben should join him. Ben played pinball, having a small run of luck. Sol sat with Ike and two girls. He was very noisy, very gay.

■ ■

The sun was coming up as Ben got to his hotel room and dialed the outside phone. "O.K., June, get up. Sorry to rout you out this time of morning, but we got work to do."

"What is it?"

"They've knocked off Arch Rossi and we got to find him."

It was after seven, though, before she climbed into his car at Wilkins and Hillcrest; the guard that Ben had insisted on was proving more of a nuisance than a boon, and she had to telephone Jansen before she could shake clear without being followed. They drove first out Memorial, to the spot where Sol had disciplined Lefty, but the only thing in sight was a small toolshed, and it told them nothing. Next they cut over to Rich Street, and drove out to Reservoir, but by daylight, this was just as unpromising. However, across a car track a road construction gang was preparing for work, and she insisted that this must have something to do with their quest. "What makes you think so, June?"

"Why would they come way out here, Caspar and those gunmen of his? There's nothing else to account for it. Whatever they did with him, it had something to do with that road work."

"Such as?"

"Dumping him in that fill, maybe."

"Dumping him—*where?*"

"In that low place there, where they've been filling up to make the road level. They could have driven over there, dropped him off, and then pulled loose dirt over him, anyway enough to cover him up."

"That's no good."

"Why not?"

"It's just not hot, that's all."

"If we could only go over there and *look,* before that gasoline shovel starts piling *more* dirt on top of him."

The shovel was already warming up, giving a quite passable imitation of a battle tank. Ben pulled in his gear, but she touched his arm. "You stay here. *I'm* going over there to see what I can see."

"Look—be careful."

"Don't be so jumpy. Can't I be a naughty little thing? That was parked here last night with my boy friend? And lost my nice wrist watch? Can't I ask them to let me look before they—"

"O.K., but be careful."

She did look a bit like a naughty little thing as she went skipping across the track, in a black dress with a floppy straw hat, and one would have thought the foreman would bow her in with his hat off, wanting to know what he could do for her. He didn't, though. He seemed to be out of humor, and let her stand around while he roared at various workmen. In a few minutes she was back. "What's the matter with him, June?"

"Oh, somebody stole a barrel during the night, and half a sack of cement, and used one of his wheelbarrows for mixing, and—"

At the way his eyes were opening she stopped, stared, and then started to laugh. "Ben! You don't really mean they'd—put him *in* that barrel, and fill it up with concrete, and—"

"You think they got too much character?"

She got in, and they drove around, cudgeling their brains to think where the hypothetical barrel of concrete, with the just as hypothetical body in it, might have been hidden. She was inclined to minimize the necessity for finding it, but he quickly set her right. "Look, we got to find it, see?—that is, if we're going to lick Caspar. Because he's not licked yet, not the way things are now. You've done fine, you've stirred things up, but it's not enough. Specially since you've made such a play over this kid Rossi. And it won't do any good to say he's dead. They say they never heard of him, and how do you prove your end of it? That's how it is in a court of law, and that's how it is in a political campaign—no body, no murder. We got to find him, see? There's no other dirt that'll do it. Maybe there is, but I don't know any. This is it, or we lose."

They got nowhere that day, though. Around ten o'clock she dropped off, to report to campaign headquarters, and around two Ben reported at the Columbus, as usual. And as usual, these last few days anyway, he and Lefty sat around the big room, reading newspapers, while another procession of visitors went through to the office beyond.

At six Lefty had sandwiches sent up, and at eight Sol came out, while Lefty tuned in the big radio on the speech that Maddux was making in the Civic Auditorium. It was, said the Mayor, the only speech he was making during the campaign, and he would not even have thought it necessary to make that if charges had not been made recently, vicious charges, serious charges, leaving him with no choice but to defend himself. He then reviewed events since the first charges made by "a speaker campaigning for my opponent," with regard to the bandits in the Globe Hotel. But what, he wanted to know, could he have done about that? His opponent did not notify him. Instead, he had called the Castleton police, and these officers had staged one of the most high-handed acts that he, a man many years in public life, had ever heard of. They had come to Lake City, and without one word to Lake City police, or one jot of warrant from a Lake City court, had seized three of the bandits and carried them off.

The fourth, according to the latest charges, had been secreted in the Columbus Hotel. But here again, his opponent, instead of acting in a manner to get lawful results, had preferred making political capital to serving the ends of justice. Instead of offering this information to the Lake City police, he had, through his campaign speaker, screamed it from the rooftops, so that while Lake City police had acted the instant this information came through their radios, they were already too late, the quarry having fled. That is, if there *was* any quarry. Where, the Mayor demanded to know, was this Arch Rossi? On whose word did they have it that an Arch Rossi was mixed up in the Castleton robbery? So far as he was concerned, he was beginning to doubt whether there was such a boy ...

Nodding exultantly, Sol went back to his office. Lefty listened to the whole speech, then screwed up his face reflectively at the cheers which marked the end of it. "That does it, maybe."

"Does what, Lefty?"

"Settles Jansen's hash."

"Why?"

"When you come right down to it, Arch Rossi was all that really meant trouble. With him out of the way, they can't do much to Sol, or Maddux, or any of them. Well, he's out of the way, boy. A fat chance they'll find him now. And Maddux knows what that means, and so does Sol. He wrote that part of the speech, as a matter of fact. He copied it out this morning and phoned Maddux this afternoon. Oh, yeah—those three in Castleton can talk all they please, but the crime was committed in Castleton, you can't laugh that off. Rossi, of course, he would have been different."

"Looks like we're in."

"Looks like it. Four more years."

Again it was daybreak when Ben got home to his hotel, and he undressed slowly, with pauses while he scratched his head and frowned. Then, when the light was off, he lay there in the gray murk, staring at the ceiling, thinking, concentrating. Then his hand went up in the air, a thick middle finger met thick thumb and hesitated a fraction of a second. Then came the snap, like a pistol shot, and he reached for the phone.

"We're early birds this time, Mr. Grace."

"What time is it, by the way?"

"I have five-thirty."

"O.K., we got the road to ourselves."

"And what is the big idea?"

"*Why* would they put him in a barrel?"

"Now *that,* I can't even imagine."

"I couldn't either, till a half hour ago. I heard about this concrete overcoat, as they call it. But then, when I got to thinking about it, the more I thought the dumber it seemed. I mean, it looked like going out of your way to be crazy, putting yourself to a whole lot of trouble and not getting any advantage out of it. But that's one thing about friend Sol; he never does anything without a reason—unless he gets sore at you or something, and flies off the handle, but even then there's generally something in it for Solly. So I thought and I thought. And the only case I could remember, I don't know if I saw it in movies or read about it in the papers, was a bunch in New York that knocked off a guy and put him in concrete and dropped him in the East River. Does that mean something to you?"

"Not a thing."

"They put him in concrete *to sink him!*"

In the early morning light every grain of powder stood out on her face, and what seemed passably girlish at other times was now woman, squinting at him, trying to guess his meaning. Talking as he drove, he went on: "If it would stay down, there's no place for a body like deep water, is there? But it won't. Pretty soon it's coming up, and ain't that nice? But—imbedded in concrete it'll stay down. Then it's *really* out of sight, and I guess that's why Lefty was bragging to me, how fine this guy was put away."

". . . you mean the lake?"

"It's the only deep water around here."

He spoke with the exultant tone of one who has already solved his problem, but when they arrived at Lake Koquabit they both fell silent, their spirits somewhat dampened. It looked, indeed, quite big; certainly its five miles of length and two of width were sufficiently appalling if Ben had had some idea of dragging the bottom for one barrel of concrete. Slowly they began running past the cat tail marshes on the south shore. Then presently she asked, "How did they get it into the East River?"

"Boat, I think."

"That would be pretty hard here."

"Why?"

"Well—*what* boat?"

"Sol has a boat."

"Is it *big?* Concrete is heavy."

"Big enough. It's a cruiser."

"Where does he keep it?"

"In front of his shack. Moored to a buoy."

"Then they didn't use that.... To get it out to the cruiser they'd have had to put it in the rowboat, and that would have been impossible. Or else they would have had to run their car, with the barrel aboard, out on a dock, and run the cruiser around to meet it, and the only dock they could have used would have been the Lakeside Country Club dock, and they'd have run the risk of meeting late poker players, or the watchman, or yacht parties—they simply couldn't have risked it. And besides, they were caught by surprise, from the way you said Lefty acted the other night. They had to get rid of this body in a hurry, and they had no time for a complicated maneuver with a car, a cruiser, and wharf, and I don't know what all."

"So?"

"Maybe they rolled it into the lake direct."

"How?"

"Just push it to the top of a bank and let it go plopping down over the sand. Unless it hit rocks or something it would keep on rolling, even under water, for quite a way. Anyway, until it was out of sight."

"We'll look for marks."

They rode along more purposefully now, their eyes staring at the shore. Once or twice, where the road ran out of sight of the water, she got out and looked, from the top of the bank. But at the end of a mile they had seen nothing, and hadn't even come to a place where a barrel could have been rolled in, considering the problem of the marsh. Then they came to the bridge, and he instinctively pressed the brake, and they looked at each other.

"This is it, Ben. This is where they got rid of it. It was right on their way out from town, and there was no other place. Especially not at night."

To him at least, her confidence didn't seem at all farfetched. Koquabit, local philologists agreed, came from the Navajo "K'kabe-bik-eeshachi," meaning silver arrow, and this is a fair description of the lake's geography. The lake proper was shaped like an arrow's point, with barbs and all. Making into it was a small lagoon, known as the Inlet, and shaped like the wedge to which the shaft is attached. And Lowry Run, emptying into the inlet, would make a sort of shaft. Connecting inlet and lake was a deep narrows, perhaps two hundred yards across, and it was over this that the bridge ran that they had now come to. It was, as she said, about the only place where a barrel of concrete could be conveniently disposed of, at least by a panicky crew of thugs anxious only to do their work and run.

Ben started over the bridge in low gear, and they both saw the mark at the same time: a white, zig-zagging scratch that would be just about the trail left by a heavy barrel if it were rolled over the concrete parapet. They stopped, counted spans, and then he raced for the end of the bridge, and presently for a side road that forked off the main highway, and made off through the trees.

"You know where you are, June?"

"Haven't the slightest idea."

They had nosed up behind a pleasant shingled house, and stopped, and got out. "This is Solly's shack."

"Oh, my—are we safe?"

"I wouldn't bet on it."

"What are you doing?"

"Throwing off the burglar alarm. That'll help."

He peered under the eaves of a garage, found a switch, and threw it off. Then he led the way, by a narrow board walk, around front, and then down to a boathouse at the water's edge. "What in the world are you up to?"

"You'll see. We got to find that barrel."

Under the rubber mat he found a key, unlocked the little

building, and they went inside. At the warm, stuffy smell he started to raise a window, but she stopped him. "I can stand a little heat, even if it's not as fresh as it might be. This morning air has me shivering."

"O.K. Now if you'll turn your back . . ."

"I won't look, but I refuse to go out."

Apparently in completely familiar territory, he took a pair of shorts from a rack, pitched them on a camp chair. Then he began dropping off his clothes, folding them neatly on another chair. In a moment or two he stood stark naked. Then he was in the shorts, finding a pair of canvas shoes to slip on his feet. "You'd better take your coat, Ben."

"Guess that wouldn't hurt."

"While we're paddling over, anyway."

"You handle a canoe?"

"Oh, well enough."

The way she shipped the paddles, however, rolled back the front door, and helped carry the canoe down to the float, indicated she was more expert than she said. When the boat was in the water she had him hold it a moment, while she raced back for the bag of shot she had spied near the camp chairs. "If you're going to be overboard, it'll keep the bow down."

"You better take stern right now."

"All right, you sit forward."

He climbed in the bow, his light overcoat around him, she in the stern. It was less than half a mile, straight across the water, from the shack to the bridge, and it didn't take them long to get there. Presently he slipped his paddle under the strut, caught the abutment, dropped his coat, and stood up.

"You getting out, Ben?"

"Yes."

"Then move the shot bag."

Holding the gunwale, he reached for the bag of shot, caught it, and hefted it forward, clear into the bow. It brought the bow down, but when he stepped on the narrow ledge that ran around the abutment, the boat righted itself. He stood, looking first at the bridge above him, then at the water below, shivering only slightly, managing quite a businesslike air. She swung the boat under the bridge, out of his way and out of sight from above. Then, marking a spot with his eye, he went off.

He was up in a flash, his eyes rolling absurdly, his breath coming in the gasps that only extreme cold can induce. Then a low moan escaped him, and he struck out for the ledge. A stroke or two brought him to it, and he tried to climb out, but couldn't. There were no handholds by which he could pull himself up, and not enough space for his body while he drew up his legs. He gave one or two frantic kicks, as though he would throw himself out by main force. Then he turned and lunged for the boat. "Ben! Watch it!"

It wasn't the shriek of a girl afraid of a ducking. It was the low, vibrant command of a woman who remembered they were half a mile from car and clothes; that a canoe capsized with a bag of shot in the bow would certainly sink; that it would be no trouble for Mr. Caspar to guess what they were doing there; that life thereafter would take on a highly hazardous aspect. Her tone must have reached him, for the hand that was raised to grasp the gunwale didn't grasp it. It slapped back into the water, and he went under, gulping. He came up driving with arms and legs for the shore.

She shot the canoe onto the gravel just ahead of him, stepped to the bow, and jumped out. Seizing his hand, she ran him up and down the beach, until he was a little dry and a little pink, instead of blue. Then she whipped up his overcoat from the bow of the canoe, put it on him, and held it tight against him, her arms around his body. Only then did he begin to talk: a lame, chattering explanation of his sorry performance. It seemed that he had forgotten the peculiarity of the lake, that it remained at an icy temperature until Lowry Run dried up, in July, and the inflow of cold water stopped, giving the sun a chance. However, he said, just let him get his second wind and then he'd go down again.

She listened, and when his shivering stopped they climbed into the canoe and shoved off. They paddled back to the spot they had left and sat silent, he trying to screw up his courage to drop off his coat again and go off. The boat began to shake, shiver, and twist, but he didn't have the curiosity to look and see what she was doing back there. He stared vacantly, first at the sunlight that was now touching the hills back of the shore, then at the water. When the boat went down like an elevator, until the water was within a few inches of the gunwale, he gave a frightened yelp, and only then did he turn his head. The stern was sticking straight up in the air, and she was on the ledge, in pants and brassiere, smiling at him.

"Hadn't you better move aft?"

"Guess that would be a good idea."

She was but a few feet away, and certainly quite an eyeful, but there was no desire in the look he gave her, after he had crawled aft, and adjusted feet, paddle, and coat to the feminine clothes that were draped over the strut. There was only relief; somebody else had taken over his dreadful task. She continued to smile, but checked all details in the boat with her eye, particularly that the shot in the bow made it easily manageable. Only when he was safely settled did she catch the truss above her, chin herself, pull up her feet, and complete the first stage of her climb. Then she reached the top of the parapet and stood there, a pink figurine in the pink morning sunlight, scanning the road for cars. His voice rumbled up, a little peevish: "Look, I'm getting dizzy. If you don't turn around you'll be going over backwards."

"I *am* going over backwards."

"You're—*what?*"

"Well, what's the use of doing a front dive and winding up ten feet further out than I want to get? With a nice back dive I'll half circle around and come right down on the barrel. You haven't forgotten our darling little barrel, have you?"

"*If* you come down on it."

"Oh, I'll come down."

"Little cold down there, you'll notice."

"Oh, for a man, yes."

"Oh, a woman don't feel cold?"

"Not the way a man does, I've noticed it often. I don't care what the weather is, a man's got himself all bundled up in exactly twice as many clothes as a woman wears. Why, look in any street car, and—"

"You haven't forgotten our barrel, have you?"

"Oh, *that.*"

A shadow crossed his face, and he looked up to see her in the sky, her arms out, her head back, her back arched in a perfect back dive. Then she floated over, and struck the water with a quick, foamy splash that shot high in the air. She was down a long time; then she came up, with gasps like the gasps that had shaken him. With one hand she pitched a barrel hoop into the canoe, with the other a lump of wet concrete.

"Know what I'm thinking?"

"Look, June, *I'm* thinking. Cut the comedy."

"I'm thinking how funny you looked. When you came up. And you started to snort. And your eyes started to roll. You looked like a wet puppy."

"O.K., so I looked like a wet puppy."

"A *wet* puppy."

It had been Ben's turn to shoot the canoe up on the gravel, run the shivering swimmer up and down the shore, and wrap her in a coat. They had taken turns in the boathouse, to dress, and felt a little better when they were back in the car, their clothes on, the motor giving heat. But it wasn't until they got their breakfast that they felt like themselves again. They came to a bar-b-q place, and being afraid to go in together, for fear they might be recognized, they ran a little past it, and Ben went back for hot dogs and pasteboard containers full of scalding hot coffee. Then they ran into a woods, stopped the car, and sat there munching like a pair of wolves. Then she began to talk. He tolerated her kittenishness for a moment or two, but quickly returned to the business in hand.

"What day is today?"

"Saturday."

"You have another meeting tonight?"

"The last of the campaign."

"Where?"

"Municipal Stadium. We were going to have it at Civic Auditorium, but we've been drawing so much bigger crowds lately that we decided to make it a big outdoor rally."

"Then spill it."

"You're sure we found what we were looking for?"

"A barrel don't prove it yet. Maybe somebody else rolled a barrel down there, or one fell overboard while they were building the bridge. But it's as good as we can do, and sooner or later we got to take a chance."

"I was going to, anyway."

"Then I'll call the *Pioneer*."

"Beforehand?"

"Oh, I don't tell them all of it. I just say it's their pal Jack Horner again, and Rossi's body has been found, and you'll tell where at tonight's meeting. It'll build up the crowd."

"So I know what to tell the reporters."

"Let's go."

"*I* said you looked funny."

"Some people got a funny sense of humor."

She reached out with her finger and smoothed the crease between his brows, imitating what he had once or twice done to her. However, he caught her hand and put it aside. "You ought not to be laughing at people. You're an idealist, or supposed to be."

"Can't an idealist think a chiseler looks funny?"

"That don't work."

"It might."

"No."

CHAPTER

5

Lights were pleasantly soft in the big room at the Columbus, and humors were high, almost hectic. Sol had visitors: his wife, rather dressed up, and looking a little queer, with her old-world face under a stylish hat; Inspector Cantrell, of the city police, a dapper man in a double-breasted suit; a florid blonde named Irene, in a black satin dress, who had come with the Inspector; and Giulio, a barber. Giulio still wore his white coat, and had come, as a matter of fact, toward the end of the afternoon, to trim Sol's hair. But he had been prevailed upon to stay for dinner and a bellboy had been sent for his accordion; accompanying himself on this, he now gave a series of vocal selections, in a high tenor voice that kept breaking into grace notes. But he would get only two or three numbers sung when Sol would say: "Sing the Miserere," and he would have to launch into *Trovatore,* becoming chorus, soprano, tenor, and orchestra all rolled into one. It is only fair to say that this simplification of the number seemed to improve it.

Ben sat in the shadows, as did Lefty, Bugs, and Goose; they said little and laughed much, as befitted their rank. When eight o'clock came, Lefty tuned in the Municipal Stadium, and cheers came out of the radio, as well as hints by the speakers of disclosures to come. Sol began to clown the discovery of Rossi's body, under the piano, in the radio, behind Giulio's chair. Once, when he yanked open a closet door, Mr. Cantrell's eyes narrowed suddenly at the unmistakable sheen of rifle butts. At each antic the blonde would scream with laughter, say, "Ain't he the limit," and pick up her highball glass. It would be hard to say what lay back of these monkeyshines; whether the whole Rossi question was absurd, whether June was thus due to make a fool of herself, or whether they covered real nervousness. At any rate, Sol was loud, silly, and irritating, for the grins around him were masks. Underneath, these revelers were worried.

Presently, to a volley of comedy from Sol, June was introduced and came on. She took perhaps five minutes on the subject at large, on teamwork, organization, getting voters to the polls next Tuesday, the necessity for electing Mr. Jansen. Then quietly she said she would tell why it was necessary to elect Mr. Jansen, and began to talk about Arch Rossi. She told of her visit that day to Mrs. Rossi, the boy's mother, and to his sister and three little brothers. She told what a good boy he had been, on the testimony of all, until he fell in with the Caspar gang. She told about the Castleton robbery, and the part Arch had played in it, of the way he had been shot, and how he had been brought to the Globe Hotel. She told how he had called up Bob Herndon, and had himself brought to the Columbus, so he could see Caspar, and ask for some decent medical attention.

"Do you know how Caspar answered that plea? Do you know what he did for this poor kid, this nineteen-year-old boy who had helped him get rich, who had kicked in with his share of the $11,000 that Caspar took for so-called 'protection' in Lake City? He took Arch out of the Columbus, for a destination I don't know, because the boy never got there. On the way he was shot and killed. Do you want to know where you can find Arch Rossi now? He's in a barrel of concrete, at the bottom of Koquabit Narrows. I paid a visit to that barrel this morning. I swam down to it, and saw it with my own eyes, between a yellow rowboat that's lying on the bottom, and a white kitten, with a stone tied around its neck, that somebody dropped there to drown. Here's a hoop I took off that barrel, and here's a handful of the concrete!''

It would have been interesting to study a photograph of the scene in the room, as the crowd in the park began to roar, and roar still louder, so that it was several minutes before June could go on. Sol, who had been increasingly comic during the first part of the speech, abruptly fell silent at the words "Koquabit Narrows.'' Cantrell jumped up and stood listening. Then he looked at Sol, and Lefty looked at Sol, and Goose looked at Sol. In spite of the forecasts in the afternoon papers, something had been said which was wholly unexpected. But Bugs looked at Ben and Ben looked at Bugs; obviously these two didn't know what Sol knew and the other three knew. Giulio and the blonde looked blankly at Mrs. Caspar; just as obviously they were completely in the dark. And Mrs. Caspar looked wearily at the floor, with the ancient dead pan of a woman who knows nothing and can guess all that matters.

"That does it, Solly.''

It was Cantrell who spoke, and it was some seconds before Sol looked at him. Then, in a rasping hysterical whine, he said, "Well, come on, let's get out of here! *Le's go, le's go!*''

He grabbed his hat and went lurching out of the room. Mrs. Caspar, seeing cues that would have been invisible to anyone else, got up and followed. Cantrell motioned to the blonde, and they went out. Impatiently, Goose motioned to the barber, who went out like some sort of frightened rabbit, followed by Bugs, and in a moment by Goose and Lefty. Ben, for five minutes or so, was alone. Lighting a cigarette, he smoked reflectively, listening with half an ear to the rest of June's speech, and cutting off the radio when she finished. Once, hearing something, or thinking he heard something, he jumped and wheeled, but there was nothing behind him but the portable bar, with its dirty glasses. He sat down again with the air of a man who is trying to quiet down, to get a grip on himself. When Lefty came in he asked, "What's going on out there?''

"Are you deaf, Ben? Didn't you hear what she said?''

"It was in the papers."

"Not about the Narrows, it wasn't."

"If Sol put him there, why's he surprised?"

"Whatever it is, it's a break for you."

"How?"

"I didn't get no dinner. Let's eat."

Ben walked over, doubled up his fist, brushed Lefty's face with it. "You want that in the kisser?"

"Ben! Let me alone! I've—got the jitters."

"Then talk. How is it a break for me?"

"We been suspicioning you."

"You mean you have."

"O.K., then I have. You bet I have. It's somebody, and I don't know nobody I wouldn't suspicion. O.K., when she said the Narrows, that let you out. No way you could have known about that."

"And what's the idea of Solly's fainting fit?"

"He's not there."

"Who?"

"Rossi! In the Narrows!"

If Lefty noticed Ben's suddenly wide eyes, there was no sign. He sat down, then got up and repeated that he had had no dinner, and "Le's eat." When Ben reminded him they were on duty, he said vaguely that that was right, and then inanely repeated: "Le's eat."

"I don't know about you, but I'm hired to work."

"For who?"

"Caspar, last I heard of it."

"You lug, Caspar's gone."

". . . Where?"

"Where you think? China. Canada. Mexico, maybe. You want to see him, give a listen to the air and a look in the sky. He's on a plane, or will be, soon as him and Maria can wake up that kid, and get him dressed, and hustle him to the airport. I said I'm hungry. Le's eat."

"O.K., pal. Le's eat."

■　■

It would be risky, of course, to be too sure about the elements that go into the making of a great American folk drama, such as the arrival of Lindbergh in New York after his flight to Paris, the imprisonment of Floyd Collins in the cave that became his tomb, the celebrations by Brooklyn of the triumphs of its bums. However, sufficient build-up seems to help, as does an emotional premise that stirs great masses of people, and perfect weather. These things were all present that Sunday afternoon when Sheriff Orcutt, of Lake County, searched Koquabit Narrows for a body, imbedded in concrete. The build-up, to be sure, was rather brief, but of its kind, excellent. It should be remembered that the Narrows was in the county, which had a government all its own, located at Quartz, the county seat, and that as a county Official Sheriff Orcutt was wholly independent of the Caspar-Maddux-Dietz machine that functioned so fearsomely in the city. He was so independent that he had attended, as a matter of legitimate curiosity, the final Jansen rally of the campaign, and had acted on this occasion with true shrieval decision, as Ben would have learned if he had not snapped off the radio so soon.

When June finished speaking he strode majestically to the platform, accompanied by wild yells as the crowd recognized him, divined some exciting purpose, and cheered him. Then he faced Jansen and the crowd, and announced bluntly that if there was any body in Koquabit Narrows he was going to fish it out, and that if they didn't believe him they could all come out there tomorrow afternoon, when he would have divers up from St. Louis, if any were available, and a tow car with a crane, a block, and a falls on it, and a hundred feet of cable.

Thus the newspapers had the story, in ample time for all but their early editions, and that ingredient, the build-up, was taken care of. For the rest, it was Sunday, a circumstance probably not forgotten by the sheriff, who was a bit of a showman himself. And it was a beautiful balmy day, with bees buzzing in the trees, birds twittering in the marshes, and thousands of soldiers free on passes. And there was suspense and sub-suspense of a sort not commonly present on these occasions, created by these agonizing questions: Were divers available, and would they consent to board the sheriff's police plane, not celebrated, exactly, for perfect performance? And, assuming they appeared, would they get the barrel? Would the barrel have Arch Rossi in it? A somewhat ghoulish reek that hung over the project probably didn't diminish its interest; at any rate some 100,000 people gathered to see what could be seen. Their cars were parked along the road at least a mile from each end of the bridge, and their boats were anchored by the dozen, in both lake and inlet. The surrounding hills were black with spectators, as were the shores. Motorcycle police roared back and forth, keeping order and strict lines, and pennants on poles, every twenty or thirty yards, proclaimed ice cream, hot dogs, popcorn, and even lemonade. On the bridge, which was roped off, the sheriff himself was in dramatic command, riding the pinto horse that he used at such festivities, and wearing a ten-gallon hat.

Ben arrived around one-thirty, parked a long way from the bridge, then trudged toward it on foot, along with dozens of others. Profiting by his better knowledge of its topography he turned into a little path that made off from the road, skirted the knolls where most of the spectators were packed, and reached the main abutment at the point where it touched the shore proper. With a quick vault he was on top of it, and sat comfortably down not more than fifty feet from the main theatre of operations. He watched impassively as a plane flew overhead, and people began to call to each other excitedly; as a car arrived, and June, Jansen, and other reform dignitaries stepped out of it; as three other cars arrived, with reporters aboard, and photographers who at once began taking pictures. Once June came quite near, and stood with her back to him, leaning with both elbows against the parapet. He pitched a stone into the water directly beneath her. She didn't turn her head. By this he knew she had already spotted him.

At a roar of approaching motorcycles, he looked around quickly and two officers trotted out to let down the ropes. A truck came through, with two men in undershirts aboard it, and a lot of gear. It crossed the bridge, ran a short distance on the main road, then turned into the side road Ben had taken the preceding morning when he had gone to Caspar's shack. It was intermittently visible through the trees, then ran down on the Lakeshore Country Club dock, where a work boat was waiting. The gear was loaded aboard, and then, as the crowd set up another excited shout, the boat started for the bridge. In a few minutes it arrived, one of the men in undershirts caught an abutment, and a colloquy ensued, between him and June, on the bridge. She pointed directly under her, he nodded, and several police jumped down on the abutment and the one next to it to manage the boat's lines. One of the men in undershirts climbed into a diving suit, the other began to test pump, phones, and cables. A towcar, parked at one end of the bridge, ran out and took position near June, so that its crane, with dangling hook, was just above the spot she had indicated.

The man in the suit was now sitting with his helmet on his knees, his feet hanging over the water, almost ready to go off. There was a hitch, however, when the sheriff climbed down for more pictures, and invited June, Jansen, and the divers to pose with him. This involved persuading a boat to edge in and take the photographers aboard, but presently the thing was done. The subjects of the picture climbed back on the bridge, and the man at the pump put his partner's helmet on, slipped on his earphones. The partner slipped into the water.

In a surprisingly short time, the man with the phones motioned the man on the crane. "O.K., down with your hook." The hook was lowered to him, and he hung cable and clamps over it, and let it go. With a splash it went down in the water, and for perhaps five minutes there was silence, a strained, queer silence as thousands of people waited. Then the man with the phones motioned the man on the crane, and power hit the drum. Jerking a little, like a thin snake, the cable slipped upward. Then the barrel broke water, shedding a shower of drops. It shot upward, dangled for a moment above the parapet, then swung in over the bridge and dropped gently to the roadway.

Two policemen stepped forward, with wrenches and sledges. The photographers closed in, making a circle which completely obstructed vision.

There was a delay, as the cable was removed. Then one of the policemen raised his sledge. Ben stood up to see, then climbed to the parapet to see better. The sledge came down. Then it rose and came down again. The cameras began snapping. Then a photographer turned, put his camera under his arm, and came running to Ben's end of the bridge. He didn't jump into the car that had brought him. He ran past it, to a taxi parked in the road. Ducking under the rope and jumping in, he yelled: "The *Post,* and step on it—it's not Arch Rossi, *it's Dick Delany!*"

In utter astonishment Ben's hand went to his brow, and he lost his balance. He teetered perilously for a second or two before he could stoop, jump, and regain his place on the abutment.

"You love me, Ben?"

"I could try."

"Turn your mouth around, and try."

"Hey, I'm driving."

"Let me drive. I know a place we could go."

"Your place?"

"No, a real nice place."

"O.K., then, the wheel is yours."

It was around ten of the night after election, and they were driving back from Castleton, where they had gone to have dinner, and thus celebrate their victory at the polls. It was the first time they had seen each other since the cold morning at the Narrows, and her amusement at how funny he had looked seemed to have ripened in the interval; her laugh had a tear in its eye and a catch in its throat. A psychiatrist might have found her an interesting study, might have used her, indeed, as an argument against too much innocence in the feminine gender. For no wise lady would have let her affection run wild as June was doing, or at any rate, have let the man see it running wild. She had had a tremendous, grotesque, and dangerous adventure with him that couldn't be denied. Yet this didn't quite account for the way she acted. She gave the impression it was her first contact with such things; that she had never been around much, or if she had, it was by day, to work, and not by night, to play. Certainly she showed no familiarity with the ancient traditions of her sex; she was quite silly, and it was no argument for her performance that after a fashion she was getting away with it. Perhaps Ben too had been around very little. For although he was slightly uncomfortable, occasionally at a loss for an answer to her too-direct sallies, he seemed on the whole to be having a good time. He brought the car to a stop, and let her slide over him to take the wheel, and even pulled her down on his lap for a kiss. When she had the car going again he sat sidewise, to face her, and sometimes lifted her curls with his finger. Presently she said: "Well!"

"Yeah? What's on your mind now?"

"We've been talking all night about what *I* did on election day, and what Mr. Jansen did, and how he hired twenty cars to bring the voters in—let's talk about you. What did you do?"

"Nothing."

"Did you vote?"

"Nope."

"Why not?"

"No civic spirit."

"Why did you help *me?*"

"I told you. Get back at Caspar."

"What did Maddux do?"

"Tried to commit suicide."

"*What?*"

"They didn't put it in the papers, though I know a couple of those reporters had it. Maybe it wasn't really news. Maybe if he *hadn't* tried to knock himself off, that would have been news. Anyway, he had some kind of pills ready, and when the returns began to come in, he down the hatch with them, and the night gang at the Columbus had an awful time getting him pumped out in time to concede Jansen's election."

"How is the dear old Columbus, by the way?"

"Haven't you been around there?"

"Me? The girl that started it all?"

"You ought to drop in, have a look. Oh, it's perfectly safe. Caspar's gang, you couldn't find one of them with a search-warrant—except Lefty. Lefty, of course, he's a special case. But that hotel, it looks like a morgue. Saturday night, before you went on the air, it was like a bee-hive—politicians, newspaper men, racketeers, women, women, and still more women—everybody you could think of was there, and the orchestra was playing 'Oh Johnny.' Sunday night, after that body was found, it was all over. The night clerk, a cashier, a couple of porters, the bartender—sitting around the bar with me and Lefty, too sick even to have a drink. They knew. They didn't have to wait for any election day."

"Some day I hope to meet Lefty."

"He's scared bad."

"What about?"

"About whether he'll be indicted for the Delany thing. Or something else. About what he's going to do now. About anything else you can think of. Lefty, he's got so he can be scared and not be able to remember what he's scared about. If you ask me, the last two or three stretches did things to him. For that matter, he admits it."

"Caspar is going to be indicted."

"For Delany?"

"Yes. They can't indict him for Rossi. They haven't found any body yet. That's the funniest thing. Here less than a week ago all the town could think of was Rossi, and now everybody seems to have forgotten him."

"Delany's enough. After that, Sol dare not come back."

"What on *earth* did he kill him for?"

"Lefty cleared that up. Delany was an accident. The idea was, they were going to bring him back after he left in his car that day to see his brother in Chicago and write it all up in the *Pioneer*. They were going to bring him back, and hold him somewhere downtown, maybe at the Globe, and then Bill De-

lany would have to beat it back here, and make a deal, and that
would put an end to it, all the stuff that was being pulled. So
that's how they started it. Sol put three guys on it, to tail him
out of town, and they did it, and about thirty miles out, when
he stopped for a light, they closed in on him and one of them
took his car and the other two took him, and started back
to town with him. But out on Memorial, where they were supposed to switch cars, and Sol was to talk to him before they took
him to the hotel, he made a break to get away. And one of
Sol's punks let him have it. And that's what Lefty had just
found when he came running up to our car that time, and said
somebody'd been knocked off, and Sol had to put his knee in
his stomach to kick a little wind back in him. I thought it was
Rossi, and that was why you and me had the right barrel but
the wrong body."

"And they still haven't found Rossi?"

"That's right. He's the big where-is-it."

"What are *you* going to do now, Ben?"

"I hadn't thought."

"Are you in any danger? I mean, like Lefty? Can they indict
you? Or try you? For what Caspar was doing?"

"You didn't do anything, you needn't fear anything. As for
a job, I'll loaf a few days first."

"Ben, there's one thing."

"Yeah?"

"He's practically given me my pick. I mean, Mr. Jansen has.
Of what I want in the way of a city job. And if I were to make
a recommendation, he regards my ideas very highly. After what
I showed in the campaign. I might—"

"Oh, nuts."

"Why?"

"What would I be doing with a city job? He wouldn't give
it to me anyhow. Soon as he found out who I was he'd say he
was terribly sorry, he appreciated any help I gave him, but his
set-up wouldn't let him do anything for me like that. Then he'd
probably offer me a job in his dairy, milking cows. I'm not

interested. I don't like him. And I don't need it. I got a little dough saved up. I got *quite* a little."

"I'm kind of proud of you, Ben. It's quite true, what you say. About his probably not being able to do anything about you, even if he wanted to. And another thing, some of these people, these neighborhood people that supported him, might get to talking. They're not very bright at such things. And it might get around *why* you were being taken care of. And you might be on the spot. With some of Caspar's gang. And—there's other reasons."

"O.K.—forget it . . . *Hey!*"

"Look familiar?"

"I'll say."

Her idea of a place to go, it turned out, was Caspar's boathouse, headquarters of the mad quest they had pursued a few mornings before. When she stopped back of the garage, he sat staring at the dark place, then got out, whispering she shouldn't slam her door. They crept around by the board walk, lifted the rubber mat, got the key. Then he turned, stared at the shack itself, put the key back, and motioned to her. Excitedly she followed him. From the top of a shutter he took another key, softly opened the door. They stepped into the dark interior, closed the door behind them, and stood for a time within a few inches of each other. His breath came in tremulous inhalations, perhaps from the reflection that Sol might not have gone to Mexico; that he might have come right here, and laid low, and be holding a gun at this minute in some dark corner before he loosed its crashing, murderous fire.

She whispered: "You scared?"

"Yes."

"Isn't it delicious?"

He caught her in his arms, then felt his head pulled down, as a pair of lips were pressed against his.

He would probably have thought little of all these matters if she had not insisted, around one o'clock that she had to go home, as Mr. Jansen's guard was still on, and would unquestionably report the time of her arrival; and if, after he had dropped her near the apartment in which she lived, he had not passed a parked car of the identical make, year, and color as Mr. Jansen's. He drove by, headed for home. Then suddenly he stopped, got out, and walked back to the other car.

In his little red book he copied the license.

6

He saw her the next night, the night after that, and the night after that. She continued to act with that complete abandon of a novice having her first drink, and yet, when he suggested dinner at the Savoy Grill, she preferred Castleton; when he wanted to linger longer at the shack, she had to get home; when she dropped off at a corner, pleading an errand at a drug store, he found the green car, parked half a block away. His manner, these three evenings, changed just a little. He didn't exactly resist her; he would hardly have been human if he had, considering the inducements. But he was not quite so oafishly pleased, not so completely at a loss for replies. They were a little flat, perhaps, but they were articulate, and quite coolly considered. And constantly he studied her, as though he were trying to make up his mind about something, or to figure out something, into which she definitely fitted.

Sunday night her high spirits had vanished, and she was glum, sad-eyed, clingy. Some men would have been bored, but he studied her more narrowly than ever, and patted her with tender sympathy. In the shack she broke down completely. They didn't dare burn electricity here, but they had become sufficiently bold as to light a candle, and stick it to the floor, in front of the sofa in the living room. By this murky light her eyes glittered as she sobbed, and when he gathered her in his arms, and whispered in her ear, she quieted down, pulled herself together, and began to talk. "It's the same thing, Ben."

"Family?"

"Not my whole family. Just my—sister."

"She the one that causes that frown you got?"

"Ever since I can remember I've had to think about her, worry about her, get her out of messes. She's all right, Ben. She's the sweetest kid you ever saw, but—she's always in trouble. And it's always me that has to get her out."

"She younger than you?"

"Three years. She's twenty-two."

"What's she done this time?"

"Well, you see, she's in college, and—"

"You pay for her there?"

"Pretty near all."

"That's why you can't keep all you make?"

"Yes, of course."

"Go on."

"So, she has a room-mate—a girl I never did like—and this girl took some things. From other girls, in the dormitories. And Dorothy had no more sense than to let her store them in the room. In a trunk. And—then day before yesterday the room was searched. And the things were found. And—"

"The cops got her, hey?"

"No, it's not that bad, yet. Nobody wants to prosecute. But yesterday a lot of the things were traced, and this girl, Dorothy's room-mate, has to pay for them, or else."

"How much does it tote?"

"Over two hundred dollars."

"Quite a lot of dough."

"And I don't know what I'm going to do."

Ben got up, lit a cigarette, flicked the match into the fireplace, and stood facing her. For a time he smoked, eyeing her steadily. Then: "I don't see why you're taking it so hard. Two hundred bucks, sure that's a lot of money. But you can get it easy enough."

"Where?"

"Jansen."

"No, I couldn't do that."

"Why not?"

"Oh—I couldn't go to him, that's all. He—he's going to make me Chief of Social Service, and I can't ask for more than that. I could pay it out of my salary, if I only had time. But my first pay check will be in August, and if I don't make this thing good she'll be put in jail, and—"

"You sure that's why you can't go to Jansen?"

"Of course it is."

"You're not stuck on him, by any chance?"

"... You! Can ask that!"

"Sure. Why not?"

"I don't even know what you mean."

"No? That first night we were out together, you had to leave here because the guards were at your place, and they'd tell Jansen what time you came in. But Jansen's car was outside, and Jansen was downstairs waiting for you. He was there Thursday night, and Friday night, and last night. Each night he stayed over an hour. What are you trying to do, kid me? I say you're stuck on him."

He was cold, but not particularly indignant. From his manner, one might think he was playing a carefully rehearsed scene. She shook her head emphatically. "No, you're wrong, though I can see why you think what you do. I'm not stuck on him. And—he has no personal interest in me. It was business, things we had to talk over. He's married, and—"

"His wife's in a sanitorium."

"I wouldn't know. I—"

"No? I'd imagine he'd have quite a lot to say about that wife, how long she's been in the sanitorium, how sick she is all the time, how much he loves her, how much it means to him that he has somebody he can tell about her, and that understands how he feels. If you're not stuck on him, it certainly looks like he's stuck on you. It looks—"

"All right, then, but if somebody got stuck on me, I'd certainly not go and tell anybody. You, or anybody."

"Then O.K."

"And I'd never go and ask them for—"

"Then O.K. . . . There's other places to get dough."

"Where?"

She was eager, but he took his time about answering, lit another cigarette, flicked another match into the fireplace. "Well, me for instance."

"You? Would you let me have two hundred dollars?"

"I got two hundred. I got two thousand."

"Why couldn't you have made this offer without all these ugly insinuations about me and Mr. Jansen?"

"I got to know where I stand."

"Yes, of course he likes me. He—likes me a lot. He *ought* to, after all I've done for him. But—honestly, Ben, I just hate it that you stood out there and—"

"Can't a guy be jealous?"

He didn't look jealous. He looked like a man who had thought up something he was sure would score. It did. She drew breath to say something, then got up, put her arms around him, looked him in the eye, and kissed him exaltedly on the mouth. "I think that's one of the sweetest things I ever had said to me. I—just love you for that."

"What she do it for?"

"Who? That girl?"

"Yeah, Dorothy."

"It was the room-mate, Ben. She—"

"Hey, hey."

"All right, there isn't any room-mate. Are you really going to let me have the money?"

"Sure. How much is it?"

"Two twenty. And the wire charges."

"You'll have it. Tomorrow morning. By the way—"

"Yes?"

"Is Jansen going to be there tonight?"

"Not if you object."

"Oh, I don't object."

"That's right. There's nothing to be jealous of."

"You could ask him a favor, though."

"Anything you say."

"Ask him to appoint Cantrell Chief of Police."

"Appoint—whom did you say?"

"You heard me."

They had been standing in front of the fireplace, she snuggling against him, he patting her on the shoulders. Now he walked over and sat down near the candle, so its light shone upwards on his face as he looked at her. It gave him a curiously wolflike look. She stared, then came over and sat beside him. "Ben, what on earth are you talking about?"

"Cantrell."

"But he's a dirty crook. Why, he—was hand in glove with Caspar. Why, Ben, *how* could Jansen appoint him? It would make a laughing stock of the whole campaign."

"If Jansen really wants to appoint the best available man, and goes into the qualifications of them all, he'll find that Cantrell is the best officer on the force. It's not his fault if crooks get elected and he has to play along. Give Cantrell a break, and he's one of the best officers in the country. And a good officer Jansen will have to have, if he's going to put across what he's been promising the voters. He can't deliver with jerks and thugs."

"He can't appoint Cantrell."

"O.K."

He yawned, coldly and indifferently. "You mind if we blow along now? I been thinking about it, and I think I better be making an early start over to Castleton, start looking for a job."

"How early?"

"Ah, seven, eight o'clock probably."

"Before the bank opens?"

"Oh yeah, long before that."

She sat a long time looking at him, her face wearing a look

of pain. "I guess I see it now, Ben. What this is all about. Why you've been acting just a little peculiarly these last few days."

"Yeah? Why is that?"

"Once you found out that Jansen was insanely in love with me, you knew, or thought, you had him, didn't you? That through me you could make him do whatever you wanted him to do, even to appointing that filthy swine, Cantrell. And to-night, when you heard about Dorothy, you saw something that played right into your hand, didn't you?"

"I haven't asked for a thing in this campaign."

"That's right. You were satisfied just to get Caspar, and be a free man once more. But the Jansen angle—I don't have any idea how you found out about it. You seem to have a habit of finding out things, and thinking up schemes. But when you did find out about it, you decided to use it for your own ends, didn't you? Just as you used what you knew about Caspar—"

"So did you. Don't forget that."

"I wasn't working for him."

Ben got up, picked up the candle, blew it out. In the dark there was a long pause. Then he said, "Just one more thing about Cantrell—"

"No, not even one thing. I know what you can do it you can get Cantrell made Chief of Police. You can run this town exactly as Caspar did. Well, you won't, that's all. He'll not be appointed."

"O.K. Sorry about Dorothy."

". . . Never mind—about Dorothy."

Lefty materialized from a shadow when Ben headed into the parking shed, and walked with him into the hotel and up to his room. He wanted to borrow $5. Ben let him have it, and lay down on the bed. He lay there a long time, his eyes on the ceiling, listening to Lefty's downhearted view of the future. He was preoccupied, as though he were waiting for something. When the outside phone rang he stiffened a little, reached for it, then changed his mind. It rang a great many times, until Lefty became annoyed, and wanted to know why he didn't answer. When it stopped, Ben abruptly sat up. "Lefty, how much did Sol pay you?"

"Eighteen."

"What—a week?"

"O.K., then laugh, let's see you laugh. For all I did, taking a chance on my neck every other day—he paid me eighteen a week and I took it, that's the funny part. For something special he slipped me extra."

"You can start tomorrow at twenty-five."

"Who from?"

"From now on I'm running it."

"... Ah, so it *was* you!"

"So what?"

"Not a thing. I got not a word to say."

"Pals?"

"Two beers, Ben, and they're on you."

7

Inspector Cantrell raised his eyes as Ben came in, motioned vaguely to a chair, went on reading. In his manufacture, one would say that God had started with the feet, shaping them delicately; then proceeded to the body, making it strong and at the same time supple, not too large and not too small; then reached the head as the whistle blew for lunch. It was a round, bulletlike head, on the front of which a face had indeed been moulded, but a face hastily conceived, whose component parts didn't noticeably match; the heavy jaw was out of kilter with the narrow, low forehead; the right side was seamy, the left side not; it was even somewhat out of plumb, skewing off at an angle in a baffling way. Yet its dark mahogany color gave a startling, sharklike vividness to the light blue eyes, so that while one might instinctively avoid Mr. Cantrell, one would hardly trifle with him. He was, at this moment, taking his ease after lunch. His feet rested comfortably on the desk, his knee cradled a magazine. Under his chin, a light blue handkerchief protected a dark blue shirt, and behind him, a hanger spread his double-breasted coat. He wore no waistcoat. His belt, as it rose and fell with his regular breathing, was held by a monogrammed clasp.

Presently he yawned, pitched the magazine aside, clasped his hands behind his head. "Well, Ben, what do you know?"

"Not a thing, Joe."

"Me neither. Things awful slow. What you doing?"

"Nothing yet."

"You hear from Sol?"

"No, nobody does."

"Sol, when he skipped he skipped high."

"He going to be indicted?"

"You couldn't prove it by me. You wouldn't hardly expect him to be, many friends as he's got right now in the D.A.'s office. But when this new gang comes in, I don't know. I wouldn't put much past them."

"When's the new outfit come in?"

"Week from tomorrow."

"Gee, time sure does fly, don't it?"

"Sure does. Well, Ben, what's on your mind?"

"Who's the new chief?"

"Search me."

"O.K., stand up."

"... *What?*"

"I say come over here and back up. I might be able to find a card or a letter or something with the name of Cantrell on it."

Mr. Cantrell smiled the smile of one who wants to be polite in the presence of the feeble-minded. "No, Ben, sometime your number's up and sometime it's not. For the next four years I imagine I got outside position."

"Suppose they disqualified the winner, the place horse, the show horse, and the horse that was trailing them, and you saw your number going up to the top—what then?"

"They don't often do that."

"Not in a straight race."

"I figure this one's not fixed—for me, anyway."

"Suppose you're wrong."

"It's too hot for supposing. What you want, Ben?"

"Take your feet off that desk."

"... Says who?"

"You think I came in here to crack jokes?"

There was quite a change in Ben's manner since the last time Mr. Cantrell had seen him. Then he had been a face in the shadows of Sol's big room, grinning appreciation of barbers, blondes, and cops; now he was callous, calm, and cold. How much of this was real, how much was an imitation of Caspar, and how much was play-acting, to bring Cantrell to heel, it would be hard to say. Possibly it involved all three, and yet it wasn't all bluff. Ben evidently felt a great sense of power, an intoxicating sense of power. He lit a cigarette, walked over, dropped it into the constabular ashtray, and stood looking at Mr. Cantrell's feet, as though they were almost more than his patience could endure.

Mr. Cantrell stared for some time, then said: "If my feet bother you, Ben, I can take them down. I can treat you with courtesy, or hope I can. But I don't take them down, for you or anybody, or any such say-so as that."

"If you don't mind, Joe. I ought to have said that."

"That's a whole lot better."

"You ready to suppose?"

"That all depends, and I got to know a lot more about it first. But you can get this straight, right now: I don't take anything, off you or anybody. I didn't even take it off Caspar. You did, Ben, but I didn't."

At this reminder of the lowly role he had played, Ben's eyes flickered. Obviously he would have liked to let the thing rest there, to let Mr. Cantrell have his dignity, to get on with the deal. It would be less trouble that way, and he hated trouble. But something must have told him this was really a test of strength, that if he weakened now, he couldn't handle this man, even if he bagged him. He smiled pityingly. "So you never took it off Caspar, hey? It's a good thing he's not here to hear you say that. Now you know and I know and we all know that if you stuck around Caspar you took it or you didn't stick. I notice you were there, right up to the last whistle blow, and that means you took it. So that's what you're doing now."

His big halfback's paw hit Mr. Cantrell's feet, which were still on the desk, and Mr. Cantrell's feet hit the deck. Mr. Cantrell came up standing, then walked around the desk, and the two men faced each other malevolently. Then Mr. Cantrell's face wrinkled into a grin, and he nudged Ben in the ribs. "Hey, Ben, you forgot something."

"Yeah, and what's that?"

"It's not the heat makes me like this, it's—"

"The humidity?"

"Right!"

Both roared at this sally, in a room-shaking, tension-easing laugh, and Mr. Cantrell felt in Ben's pockets for a cigarette. "Were we supposing, Ben?"

"That's it, copper."

"Go on, tell me some more."

"If you want to be Chief, I might swing it."

"You in person?"

"Yeah, me."

"You and Jansen; I didn't know you were that thick."

"We're not."

"O.K., just getting it straight."

"Just the same, I can swing it."

"Keep right on."

"Of course, you got to sell him. You got to convince him that you, or any cop, can clean this town up in twenty-four hours, providing one thing."

"Which is?"

"You get a free hand."

"And then?"

"Surprise, copper, surprise! Then you clean it."

"A clean tooth don't grow much fat."

"You follow the chickens?"

"Yeah, a little."

"O.K., then you know how they cut off the spur, just a little way from the foot. And you know how they fit that gaff over the stump—that pretty-looking thing that's all hand-forged steel, with a point on it that would go through sheet-iron, and a nice

leather band to go around his leg, soft, so it don't hurt him
any, and he likes it ... So you clean up the town, you do it for
Jansen, just like you said you would. You cut off the spur, and
that cleans it. How can a chicken violate the law with no spur
to fight with? O.K., you just don't tell him about that gaff in
your pocket, that's all. You got it now?"

"No."

"Well, you will."

"Look, smart guy, what do I *do?*"

"Do? You do nothing, You get called in, that's all. You and
about twenty others, one at a time you get called in to say what
you got to say, if anything. And you, you got nothing to say.
Sure, you can clean the town up. Any cop can—providing you
get a free hand. You don't polish apples, you don't shake his
hand, you don't even care. But you mean business, if he does."

"Well, *does* he?"

"He appoints you acting chief."

"And?"

"Then you hit it. Then you're in."

"Boy, it's clear as mud."

"Oh, mud settles if you give it time."

A half hour later, in another place, where he could be friendly
and frank, Ben was more natural, seemed to be having a better
time. This was in the office of Bleeker & Yates, a firm of lawyers in the Coolidge Building, whereof the senior partner, Mr.
Oliver Hedge Bleeker, had just been elected District Attorney
by a majority as big as Mr. Jansen's. So it was with Mr. Yates,
the junior partner, that Ben had his little visit. He was a graying
man in his thirties, and kept his blue coat on, as befitted an
attorney with an air-conditioned office. Ben took him completely, or almost as completely, into his confidence, and made
no secret of his former connection with Caspar. But he hastened
to explain the circumstances: the abdominal injury, received in
professional football; the need of work, and the offer from Caspar; then the absurd situation that developed, wherein his dis-
taste for the job collided with the unpleasant probability that if

he quit it he would be killed, for what he knew, and to gratify Caspar's conceit. As Mr. Yates' eyes widened, Ben went on, telling of his activities for Jansen. He didn't say what they were, and insinuated they were pathetically slight. Yet he insisted he had been a Jansen man. "I just about got to the point where if I couldn't call my soul my own I was going to call my *carcass* my own. Yes, I worked for Jansen, and I'm proud of it. I want you to know it, because before we go any further you'd better know the kind of guy I am."

"Were you the—'leak spot,' as we called it?"

"The what?"

"Well—Miss Lyons, as I suppose you know, had a source of information about Caspar. In the Jansen organization, we never knew exactly who that source was, as she never told us. We always called it the 'leak-spot.'"

"I can't tell you the source of Miss Lyons' information. I played a small part in the campaign. It was small, and believe me it was unimportant. But I'd like you to know I was against Caspar, I was helping to break him, before now. During the campaign. While it was still a fight."

"And what do you want with me?"

"You know anything about pinball?"

"Why, I've played it, I guess."

"I mean the hook-up."

"Well, not exactly."

"You reform guys, you don't know much, do you?"

"Well, is it important?"

"Look, I can't tell you from way-back, but in my time there's been just two rackets. Two really good ones. Two rackets that made money, and kept on making it, and were safe—or safe as a racket ever gets. One was beer, until prohibition got repealed, and the other is pinball, and both for the same reason. You know what that reason is?"

"Human greed, I suppose."

"No—human decency."

"I don't quite follow you."

"Beer—I don't talk about hard liquor, because that was really intoxicating—but *beer,* that was against the law mainly because the great American public thought it was, well, you know, a little—"

"Scandalous?"

"That's it. But once they went on record about it, they didn't really care. It was just a little bit against the law, if you know what I mean. That meant it was just as illegal as some D.A., or enforcement officer, or maybe both of them working together, said it was. That meant you could make a deal. Not all over, maybe, but most places. You remember about that?"

"Oh yes, quite vividly."

"O.K., then beer went, didn't it?"

"You mean it became legal?"

"That's it—anybody could sell it, and the racket went. So the boys had to find something. So for a while they made a mess of it. They tried stick-ups, and kidnapping, and Murder, Inc., and a lot of stuff that didn't pay and that landed plenty of them in the big house and quite a few on the thirteen steps. And then they got wise to gambling. Of course, that wasn't exactly new."

"I wouldn't think so."

"No, that cigar-store front with a bookie behind, and that guy on the corner, selling tickets to a policy game, and the big bookie places downtown—most of that had been going on a long time. But beer, when it made its comeback in the drug stores and markets and groceries, that gave the boys an idea. Why not put gambling in the drug store too? Why not bring it right to the home, so Susie and Willie and Cousin Johnny can drop their nickel in the slot? And when they went into it a little they found out that pinball was like beer. The great American public frowned on it, but didn't really care. It was against the law, but not very much. So that meant they could make a deal. So they did. And all over the United States you'll find these machines, in drug stores, cafes, ice cream parlors, bowling alleys, and restaurants. They're outlawed in New York now, and Los Angeles, and a few other places, but everywhere else, they're wide open."

"Wait a minute, you're going too fast for me."

"Yeah? What's bothering you?"

"Who owns these machines, Mr. Grace?"

"O.K., now I'll give it all to you, quick. You understand, anybody can make amusement machines, and plenty of them are made locally—juke boxes, shovel games, pinball, whatever you want. They're made in those little tumbledown places over on the other side of the carline, where you wouldn't hardly believe there'd be a factory at all. But most of them, the good ones, with shiny gadgets on them and patent attachments, come from Chicago. That's the center, and two or three of the big houses there make ninety percent of the national product. Some of them are O.K. The juke boxes, for instance, they're not against the law anywhere, and they got good tone quality if you like tone. I don't."

"Me neither."

"But the rest, the pinball machines, no manufacturer in Chicago takes a chance on what some D.A. is going to do. They've got to be owned locally, and they've got to be paid for in cash. In Lake City, they're owned by about the sickest bunch of jerks you ever saw—stooges for Caspar, that could scrape together a few hundred dollars to buy some machines, and that had to scrape it together, for one reason or another. Then they were set. They had their machines, and they gave him his cut, and the machines paid, clear of the fifty percent to the drug store man, and Solly's cut, and one or two other little rake-offs we've had, three or four bucks a month to the owner. That meant that in a year he had his money back and the rest of it was gravy. The drug store man, he was sitting pretty. He had two or three machines in, and they paid seven-eight-nine bucks a month apiece, and that was a good slice of the rent. And it was cash. And—"

"It's *still* going on, isn't it?"

Ben, who had been striding around, giving Mr. Yates the benefit of his researches and reflections for the last few weeks, sat down now with a cryptic smile. "As to that, suppose *you* tell *me*."

"I—what would I know about it?"

"They're still going, of course, but whether they'll be going, or what the situation is going to be after the new administration goes in—that depends pretty much on your partner, Mr. Bleeker, the new D.A."

"I can't tell you what he's going to do."

Mr. Yates spoke quickly, sternly, conscientiously. Ben shrugged amiably. "Just gagging. None of my business what he's going to do, but—"

"Once more: What do you want with *me?*"

"Oh, I'm coming to that. Now, Mr. Yates, I'm going to surprise you. So far as Lake City is concerned, *I* believe pinball is doomed."

"Why?"

"Because it's wrong. To the extent that it's gambling, it's wrong, and that temptation ought to be taken away from our young people, and if I know your partner, Mr. Yates—of course I can only judge from the speeches he made in the campaign, but he made himself pretty clear—he's going to take that temptation away. I'm betting my money that that's the way the cat is going to jump, and that's why I've come in to see you."

"Yes, I'm listening, Mr. Grace."

"To the extent that it's a game of chance, it's wrong, and that part is against the law. But to the extent that it's a game of skill, it's good clean recreation, and that's *not* against the law."

"Just how do you separate these two aspects of pinball—or is that metaphysical operation supposed to be *my* useful function?"

Mr. Yates' tone was dry, his expression ironical, his eye cold and steely. Ben jumped up and gave him a little, just a little, of the manner he had turned on Mr. Cantrell.

"Listen, pal, I didn't come in to ask you to turn black into white, or whatever you mean by that crack about metaphysics. I've come in to offer you a perfectly legitimate and honest and decent job, so let me finish before you crack smart ... I separate them, by using different machines, a completely different class of amusement equipment. Those companies in Chicago, they haven't been asleep either, brother. They can read the writing on the wall just as well as I can. The law, it's pretty much the same in every city of the country, and it prohibits a game of chance. A game of chance, with a pay-off, is out, and they know it. Understand, this is local legislation all over the country, but one by one, communities are going to put that game of chance on the skids. But those kids, and those drug stores, between them, they've developed a demand for a decent, honest game of skill—baseball, football, softball, all sorts of table imitations of the big stuff outside, that kids can play with each other at night, have a good time, and not lose every dime they've got. There's no pay-off. Have you got that? *There's no pay-off.*"

"I think you make that clear."

"The most those kids get is a certificate, or engraved diploma, whatever it is, saying they made a home run, or hole-in-one, or dropkick from the fifty-yard line, just a souvenir, because experience shows you've got to give them *something*, or the game don't pay. But, experience also shows that this class of game is just as profitable, to the drug store owner, as gambling—"

"How can it be?"

"They enjoy it better. They play each other, not the machine, so it's all on the up-and-up. They get a break. That's what cuts the machine's take on gambling pinball: those kids wake up, sooner or later, that they're being cheated. This way they're not."

"Now I've got it. Go on."

"All right, so I've got a hook-up, I've got it arranged to bring in this new class of machine and install them in Lake City—if, as, and when the old ones are thrown out. I don't know what Mr. Bleeker is going to do, and I don't ask you even to ask him what he's going to do. But this much I've got to know: Is my class of machine legal? I can't take a chance on bringing in five thousand machines here—"

"Five *thousand?*"

"Look—there's five hundred drug stores around Lake City, two or three hundred cafes, I don't know how many ice cream parlors—I'm trying to get it through your head that this is *big business.* I can't take a chance on that much dough, and then have friend Bleeker decide that the felt on the table don't meet the requirements of Section 492 of the Sanitary Code, something like that. I've got to know where I stand, and I've got to know in black and white. That's the first thing. You know him, and you can certainly put a legal question to him that he's bound, as I see it, to answer. The next thing is, just to protect the interest of all the little guys that want to put machines in, I'm going to organize an association. I don't kid you about it. That association is going to know from the beginning that it's politically powerful. It's got two or three men in key spots of every precinct, and it can make any D.A., whether his name is Bleeker or whatever it is, treat it polite, with no kicking around. I want you to represent that association, as attorney. For that, you'll receive a pretty nice yearly retainer. Just how much I don't know today, but we can work it out. I don't ask you to do anything but represent us legally—but we want real representation, and you look to me like you've got some stuff. I don't mind saying I've had my eye on you since before the election. Well—now you know where *you* come in, at last."

Mr. Yates got up and took several turns about his office. Presently he sat down. "Well—there's a little question of ethics here."

"I don't quite know what you mean."

"You see, I'm Bleeker's partner."

"That's O.K. by me."

"I'm not sure it is by me. Or—by the bar association. Or—by Mr. Bleeker. I'd say it was one of those things—"

"Well, if the ethics bothers you I can go somewhere else and no hard feelings. I came in here, as I told you, because—"

"Hey, wait a minute."

"O.K. Sorry."

"I haven't turned your offer down. But I *would* like to think it over a bit. Perhaps talk to Mr. Bleeker about it. See what *he* thinks of the propriety of my accepting such a—"

"Now I get it."

"Shall we meet again—say next week?"

"Next week is fine."

So it happened, some days after Mr. Jansen's inauguration, that a throng of frightened druggists, cafe owners, and other such people, assembled in one of the convention rooms of the Hotel Fremont. It had been, indeed, a somewhat disturbing week. First of all, there was the alarming circumstance that Mr. Jansen, the afternoon he took office, appointed a police board of three of the leading reformers of the town. Two days later this board had named Joseph P. Cantrell as acting Chief, and for a brief time there was a false dawn, a hope that Mr. Jansen wasn't quite so stern as he had pretended. Then, in quick succession, came two occurrences that had nothing to do with Mr. Jansen, but which didn't harmonize, somehow, with an easy view of life. The Federal grand jury indicted Mr. Caspar for certain violations of the income tax law. Then the county grand jury indicted him for the murder of Richard Delany. Then, after these straws blowing down the wind, the tornado struck. A uniformed patrolman, one afternoon, entered every place in the city where pinball machines were in operation, and stood guard over them until a truck appeared outside, and expert workmen came in, took the machines apart, and stowed them in the truck. After the truck had departed, to the wail of sirens, the uniformed patrolman left a summons with the owner, notifying him to appear in police court next day and defend himself against preposterous charges: the maintenance of a nuisance, the maintenance of devices tending to the corruption of minors, the operation of common gambling machines.

Then next morning had come the postcard that might mean an answer to all these bewildering things: it was signed by Benjamin L. Grace, and simply informed the recipient that a meeting of the Lake City Amusement Device Operators' Association would be held that day at the Fremont, and that any operator of an amusement machine would be eligible to attend. The time of the meeting, 2 P.M., had been set, obviously, with an eye to the time of the hearings, which were to be in the Hall of Justice Building at four o'clock. By 1:30, worried little men in gray mohair coats began to appear at the Fremont, to be led by a bellboy to Ballroom A, where they sat down in groups to whisper, and wait for whatever was forthcoming. Ballroom A had been furnished by the hotel as an accommodation to Ben, who was living there now, in one of the Sky-Vista apartments, consisting of living room, bedroom, bath, and pantribar alcove. Of the better hotels in Lake City, the Fremont was the oldest, and the most serious rival of the Columbus.

By two o'clock, Ballroom A was a beehive, with every folding chair occupied, and people standing in the aisles. Ben entered with Mr. Yates, who sat down at the table which had been placed at one end of the room. Ben didn't sit. He faced the crowd, rapped them to order with a large glass ashtray, and asked somebody near the doors to close them. He had changed perceptibly, even since the interview with Mr. Yates, and enormously since that day when a sniveling chauffeur had told his woes to Lefty. Yet there was something of that chauffeur in him now, as he threw back his shoulders and began to talk in quick, jerky, confident sentences. Perhaps it was his inability, in spite of his effort to do so, to give more than the meanest of assurances to this crowd, who were nervous about today, and worried about tomorrow. He tried to be lofty, to appeal to their civic spirit, or pride in their establishments, or something of the sort, as he told them what he had told Mr. Yates about the association and the new class of machine which he would make available to members; and yet somehow he sounded like a professional football coach, haranguing his men before a game, and barking, rather than talking.

Fortunately, however, it was an occasion where sense counted more than manner. They listened to him intently. When, coming to the question of membership, he borrowed a device from June and broke open a package of slips, they sprang forward, those on the front row, to help him distribute them, and when they had been filled out, to collect them and pile them on the table. Practically everybody, it seemed, wanted to be a member, to be supplied with the new type of machine, to be represented in court by Mr. Yates, to pay a moderate assessment, which would be collected only from the earnings of the machines.

Ben spoke perhaps twenty minutes, the formalities with the slips took another twenty, and then there were quite a few questions.

Then Mr. Yates took the floor. "Before we leave here to appear in court, I'd like to make my position clear. I represent association members and association members only. But any others, and any members who want to appear individually, with different counsel or with no counsel, are welcome to do so, and will merely have to ask the court that their cases be disjoined, and they'll have separate trial. Now just to get straight whom I represent and whom I don't will those who want separate trials please raise their hands?"

There were no hands.

"Very well, then I take it I represent you all. Now this isn't binding on you, but my advice is that when your case is called—whichever one of you happens to be called first as a sort of test case—you plead guilty. I can then ask the court to let me put into evidence, before it imposes sentence, the circumstances that attended the installation of these machines, the pressure from the Caspar organization, the intimidation, the 'heat,' as they say, that was turned on, and that ought to have great weight with the court in fixing the degree of guilt. There may be a small fine. If so, it will be credited to you, against the dues of the association—in other words you will have to pay the fine today, in cash, but the association will reimburse you. Now are there any questions?"

There weren't any, and a half hour later the throng was in Magistrate Himmelhaber's courtroom, filling it to the last row of benches, and streaming out into the hall and down the marble staircase into the lobby of the Hall of Justice. The police sergeant's voice sounded small and queer as he read the charges, and started to read the names, but Mr. Himmelhaber stopped him.

"Call the first case."

"Roscoe Darnat."

"Here."

"Roscoe Darnat, you are charged with the maintenance of a nuisance, in violation of Section 448 of the—"

"Dismiss it."

Mr. Himmelhaber looked a little annoyed, motioned to the sergeant. "Dismiss all those funny ones, try him on gambling charges only."

"Yes, Judge. Roscoe Darnat, you are charged with the operation of games of chance, on or about your premises at 3321 West Distler Avenue, on July 7 and various dates previous thereto—are you guilty or not guilty?"

"Guilty."

Mr. Himmelhaber leaned forward with interest, looked at Mr. Yates. "Are they all taking a plea?"

"Yes, your honor. I would like the court to hear a little testimony on the pressure that was put on them to let the games come into their establishments, as establishing extenuating circumstances—"

"O.K."

Led by Mr. Yates, with occasional questions from the magistrate, Mr. Darnat told his harrowing tale, of how under pressure from Mr. Caspar's lieutenants he had installed one machine; of how, after downright intimidation, he had accepted another; of how, when he was afraid for the lives of his wife and children, he had accepted a third and a fourth; of how he asked only to be clear of gambling in any form; how he actually threw up his hat and cheered, if the Judge didn't believe it he could ask his wife, when the truck carried off the four machines—

"O.K., that's enough."

Mr. Himmelhaber looked at Mr. Bleeker, who was prosecuting the case in person, and who had said nothing so far. He looked over his glasses at the judge, said: "Your honor, I have no questions to ask the witness. In fact, I'm sure that every word he says is true. . . . I may say, to make the position of the prosecution clear, that I have no desire to harry these people, or inflict undue hardship. If they were actually the owners of the machines, that would be different. But since no owners have come forward to claim their property—quite naturally, I would say—what I am interested in is the destruction of the machines, so that the nuisance they represent can be abated, for good and all."

Mr. Himmelhaber looked at Mr. Yates. "That's all right with me, your honor. My clients, so far as I know, don't own a single machine."

"Then, sergeant, will you write the order?"

"I got it already wrote."

In the old Ninth Street station house, not used since the erection of the Belle Haven building further out, the machines had been stored pending court order for their disposal, and thither, around eight that night, flocked the photographers who had snapped the throng in the Hall of Justice. They were to take pictures of an ancient constabular rite: the destruction of equipment seized in a gambling raid. The attorneys were not there for the occasion, but Mr. Cantrell was, dressed in a neat pinstripe, with a white carnation in his buttonhole. His hair was rather specially combed, as was the hair of various officers, who opened the front door for the cameramen, and consulted with them as to the scene of the ceremony.

The big front room, with the old sergeant's desk in it, seemed the only likely place, as the rest of the building was jammed with equipment to be destroyed. So the pitch was made there, and the police, with unusual courtesy, helped adjust lights, set up cameras, and pick out the most colorful equipment. Then two of them stepped forward, armed with axes. Then Mr. Cantrell was posed, and warned not to smile, as it was a solemn occasion. Then various prominent detectives were posed, in the background, to be "looking on," in the picture caption, later.

Then the cameras began to shoot. Amid frantic cries of "Hold it," "One more," "Don't drop that axe yet," and so on, several more shots were made, and then abruptly, with scarcely a word of thanks, the photographers left, to rush their pictures into their papers.

Ben, who had sat to one side during this, now jumped forward, just in time to stop one of the axemen from crashing down on the machine, a beautiful thing that had been plugged into a socket and illuminated for the occasion. Mr. Cantrell looked at him questioningly, but he beckoned the new Chief back to one of the cells in the rear. "Joe, you ever been abroad?"

"No, Ben, I haven't."

"Neither have I, except once to Mexico."

"Mexico, south of the Rio Grande."

"Juarez, across the river from El Paso. Well, when I came back, I thought I'd bring in some perfume. Just a fool notion I had, but—"

"Well, we all get drunk."

"Just what I said to myself. Now get this: On some of that perfume, they got a rule that the customs officer has to destroy the label before it's brought in. You got that?"

"Gee, you sure can spread light, Ben."

"You know how he destroyed it?"

"No, but I'm dying to hear."

"He drew a blue pencil across it. He made one blue mark on it, and legally that destroyed it. Listen, Joe, if one blue mark will destroy a label, why won't it destroy a pinball machine?"

Mr. Cantrell jammed his hands into his trousers pockets and stared at Ben for a long time. "Say, you can think of things, can't you?"

"I do my best."

"You mean, destroy it *legally?*"

"Yeah, legally."

"If you got a blue pencil, I could try."

"I got one, right here."

"Then we'll see."

"And one other thing."

"Yeah, Ben?"

"You'll want those trucks again, hey? To haul the destroyed machines over to the Reservoir Street dump?"

"Why—they got to be put *some* place."

"O.K.—I'll have them here tonight. And if you don't mind, have a police photographer at that dump tomorrow, to take pictures of the destroyed machines. Of course they'll be nothing but junk, but it'll prove I hauled them—and that you destroyed them."

"Funny how a blue pencil ruins stuff, isn't it?"

"Oh, and another thing."

"Just one?"

"Sign these vouchers."

"What vouchers?"

"For the trucks! The trucks I furnished the city yesterday, to haul these gambling machines from various and sundry addresses, here to the Ninth Street station house. Three hundred bucks in all—"

"Hey, what is this?"

"You think trucks work for nothing?"

"No, but I got to check—"

"Costs money to clean a town up, you ought to know that. Now if you'll sign there, where I put the pencil check, I can get over to the hotel with them before they close the safe, and—"

"Won't they keep till tomorrow?"

"Joe, I need cash to pay workmen. I—"

"O.K., Ben, but don't run a good thing to death."

"Nuts, it's the people's will."

"What?"

"You forgot that mandate to cleanliness. Sign."

Around nine, however, Ben wasn't so cynically confident. He walked up and down the main room of a big warehouse with a neat little man in a blue gabardine suit and a soft straw hat. It was a shabby warehouse, and the only illumination was from a single poisonous light hanging very high. He kept looking at his watch, but presently a horn sounded outside, and he hurried to open the big trolley door at one end. Shaking the building, while the man in gabardine yelled to "cut those lights," a truck rolled in, and when it was squarely in the middle of the room, stopped. Cutting lights and motor, three men jumped down, peeled tarpaulins from the load, and proceeded to unload it. It was the same equipment as had been seized, condemned, and legally destroyed in the last twenty-four hours, but appeared to be in quite passable condition. Working rapidly, under the direction of the man in gabardine, the three from the truck stacked the machines against the wall and departed, saying the other crew would report at ten, and from then on they'd make time.

The man in gabardine looked over the machines with professional interest, testing springs here, counting bright steel balls there. Ben, however, seemed uneasy. Presently he said, "Listen, Mr. Roberts—of course I'm sure you know your business, but are you really sure these games can be transformed?"

"Of course I am."

"Yeah, but—look, this is what I mean. Like in golf, which is one of the games we're going to have, there's only so many things a player can do. He can get in the rough, he can shoot past the green, he can pitch *on* the green, he can sink a putt—I don't know *how* many, but it's just *so* many. Well, suppose that don't correspond to the number of holes on the table? Without we plug some holes up, or put new ones in, or redesign the whole thing, how do we—"

"O.K., now—pick out a table."

"Well, *that* one. What do we make out of it?"

"Baseball."

"How?"

"I'll show you."

Taking off his coat, Mr. Roberts went over to a chest that stood in one corner, opened it, and took out a hammer and screw driver, then selected a number of metal clips from little compartments inside that were arranged like printers' type cases. These he dropped into a paper bag. Then he took the table Ben had pointed out, upended it, and screwed legs into it. Then he stood it rightside up, and for a moment inspected its metal fittings, its gleaming pins, springs, and bells. Then he motioned at the legend LUCKY BALL WIN 5¢—10¢—25¢—$1, which rose over one end. "You understand, that comes off and the new one goes on: Baseball, the National Game, Play One Whole Inning for Five Cents—"

"Yeah, I understand about that part."

"O.K., then. Watch."

Deftly, Mr. Roberts began unscrewing tags that labeled each hole with numbers from 0 to 1,000. Soon Ben interrupted: "All right, I've doped this out. The batter can get a strike, or a ball, or he can single, double, triple, or pole one over the fence, or he can sacrifice, or maybe a couple of other things. Not over fifteen, though. That's top. Well there's exactly twenty holes on that table. What then?"

Without answering, Mr. Roberts began screwing new tags in front of the holes. They bore legends, in neat red letters, of "Strike," "Ball," "Out on Fly," etc., just as Ben had anticipated, but when all of them had been screwed into place there were still four unlabeled holes. Mr. Roberts smiled.

"Now, then, here's where we equalize."

So saying, he screwed on four tags. Ben, peering, saw that two of them read: "Out on foul," and two others, "Hit into Double." On the last two, Mr. Roberts dropped loose metal covers. "Those holes are dead till there's a man on base. Can't have a double play without anybody on. Same way with a sacrifice. But don't you get it? If there's too many holes we equalize by having a few of those holes read the same thing—that doubles the chances for foul balls, maybe, but who says this ain't fast pitching we got? If there's not enough holes, we knock out sacrifice bunt, advance on error, whatever we want. Look: they play the game you got, not the game you wish you had. You get it?"

"Well, gee, it's simple, isn't it?"

"O.K., you be the Gi'nts, I'll be the Dodgers."
"You mean that's all? We can play *now?*"
"I like pinball. Buck on the side?"
"McPhail, show what you got."
"I've singled, big boy."

The midsummer twilight was fading as Ben entered his living room and lit it, not with the wall brackets, which were harsh, but with the floor lamps, which were soft. He checked the contents of a tray which had arrived a few minutes before: shaker, evidently full; two glasses, bottoms up, in a bowl of ice; a saucer of cherries, with fork; a dish of tiny canapes, six anchovies, six eggs, six cheese; two napkins, folded. The buzzer sounded, and he hastened to the door with the springy stride that seemed never to desert him.

June came in, nodded, and sat down, pulling off her gloves. She too had changed since that night a few months ago when she had made the speech at the high school auditorium, and a man had made a note in a little red book. The neat, schoolteacherish blue silk had given way to a smart black polka-dot, with belt, bag, and shoes of coral alligator skin, hat of red straw, and stockings of powdery sheer that set off an exciting pair of legs. It all combined beautifully with her dark, creamy good looks, and it seemed that perhaps she knew it. She came in with languid hauteur, or at least the imitation of languid hauteur; it might be recent, but it was innocent.

Ben, however, seemed neither surprised nor unduly upset. He righted the glasses, flipped a cherry in each, and poured the Manhattans. Setting one beside her, he said, "Here's how," took a sip of his own, put it down. Then he took an envelope from the inner pocket of his coat and handed it to her. "Your share."

"... Of what?"
"Of what we're doing."
"Oh, thanks. I'd forgotten."
"You'd better count it."

She opened the envelope, started in spite of herself when she saw the thick mat of $20's, $10's, and $5's that it contained. Her voice shook a little as she said: "Well—that's very nice."

He suddenly remembered something he had meant to tell her: about a suite that would be vacant next week, at the hotel. It seemed she was living here now, in a suite on the third floor, but the one to be vacated would give her a better view, at the same price. She said something about her apartment, which she had under lease until January 1, and hadn't been able to rent. He made no comment, and she returned to the envelope, actually counting the money this time. Then she counted it again, and drew a trembling breath. Then she lapsed into a long, moody silence. He asked, "How's social service?"

"All right, thank you."

"Plenty of milk for the anemic kids?"

"Not as much as we want, but—"

"That can be fixed. Or helped, anyway."

"Any help will be welcome."

"I told you before, the main kick I get out of having a little dough is to be able to help on a few things where help counts. Tomorrow, I'll send a little check, and it's a promise."

"It'll be quite welcome."

"Speaking of milk, how's Jansen?"

"Very well, the last time I saw him."

"When was that?"

"Does it concern you?"

"Yeah, a little."

". . . It was last night."

"And he was very well, you say?"

"So far as I could see."

"Great work he's doing here. Cleaning the town up—"

"Suppose we leave Mayor Jansen out of this."

"Well—if so, why?"

"This talk about cleaning the town up makes me a little sick to the stomach, I find, especially in view of this dirty money you've handed me."

"What do you mean, dirty?"

"I mean it's gambling money, and from children's gambling, at that. Their nickels and dimes, that they got to buy ice cream with, or earned from their paper routes, or whatever way they got it—about the cleanest money there is, so long as *they* have it. But when we get it, it's dirty, just about the *dirtiest* money there is and I don't want any more talk about the town's being clean."

"Listen, we're operating legitimate enterprises, and—"

"Ben, I know exactly how legitimate our enterprises are, because I patronized one the other day, and stayed with it to the bitter end, to see how it worked. It was a golf game, and it took me an hour to make a hole in one, but finally I did, and received my certificate, with my name written on it in the druggist's flowing script. Then I took it to Room 518 of the Coolidge Building where I had heard that such a certificate can be redeemed for $1. I faced Lefty over a glass-top desk, and he knew who I was and I knew who he was, but we didn't speak. I took the silver dollar he gave me, and went out, and I knew that the legitimacy of our enterprises is so slight that it probably can't be found by any test known to science. It's dirty money. So let's say no more about it."

"I notice you take it."

"I take it because I happen to have a sister who makes me a great deal of trouble and costs me a great deal of money. I pretend to be romantically interested in a man that's finer, that's worth more, than you and I will ever be, taken together or separately. Because he happens to believe in me he does a great many things that I ask him to do, as Mayor of this city. Because of that, you're able to do things, to operate enterprises, that pay. I take my share, because I have to. I hate it. I hate myself. I hate you, if you must know the truth. And don't let's have any pretense that what we're doing is any different from what it really is."

"How is she, by the way?"

"Who?"

"Your sister. Dorothy."

"She's fine. She's working in a summer camp, it may interest you to know. That money you lent me, that money I had to send the college authorities to cover what she stole, I made up my mind she had to pay it back. I saw to it that she got a job in a summer camp waiting on tables. It's hard work, and she hasn't much time to get into mischief. And she's paying me back. She's paying me back at the rate of $5 a week."

"Aren't you the skinflint."

"There's a principle involved, and she can learn it."

"*Can* anybody learn how to be honest?"

"If not, she can wait on tables in a summer camp."

"That money, by the way, is deducted."

"You mean I get all this in addition to what—to that two hundred and some that you put up on account of Dorothy?"

"Everything in the envelope is clear."

"My, my."

"—And dirty."

"I—asked you not to talk about that."

"Now suppose you get out."

"... *What?*"

"We're not going to dinner. You and I are through."

"Oh. I see."

"So beat it."

"Very well, then ... May I ask *why?*"

"For *you* being dishonest. With *me.*"

"... I still don't—"

"Oh, that's all right. Just go."

She was standing by now, wholly bewildered, every inch the amateur at love who had wooed him so avidly before. He sat on the sofa coldly staring at her. He was suddenly the man who had faced Cantrell. But since then he had faced a great many people, had taken part in countless bullying scenes. It was impossible to tell where reality began in him, and where play-acting ended; everything, in a sense, had become a colossal bluff, and apparently something of the sort figured here. He watched her as she started for the door, made no sign as she stopped and came marching back, her bottom switching quickly, angrily, absurdly. "So you're throwing me out, is that it?"

"Yes."

"That's what you think. Mr. Benjamin Grace, you have just about three seconds to take back what you've said to me and apologize for it. If you don't, I'm going straight to Mr. Jansen, who, as you probably know, is Mayor of this town. I'm going to tell him everything you've done, everything you're doing, and there, I think, will go your perfectly legitimate enterprises, and the thousands you hope to make out of them, and—"

"Get out."

Her mouth twitched as her little flurry crumpled, and once more she started for the door. This time when she stopped and turned, tears were running down her cheeks, and she was cravenly contrite. "Ben, what have I done? Why are you doing this to me?"

"That's more like it. Keep on talking."

"I don't understand—"

"Keep talking!"

"What—do you want me to say?"

He got up, yanked off her hat, sent it skimming into a chair. He cuffed the back of her head so her hair went tumbling over her face. With a quick hip movement, reminiscent of football, he sent her spinning to the sofa. Then he stood over her. "Get this: you can go to Jansen any time you want. If you want to go now, you can go now, and I'll help you out that door with a kick."

"Ben, I don't understand you. I—"

"Then I'll make it plain. In the first place, don't try to tell me you're hooked up with me on account of that bum, Dorothy. She's all paid up, and you've got a grand in that envelope, and so far as she's concerned you got no obligation whatever. You know why you're doing it?"

"It's Dorothy! I've told you, she's been—"

"It's not Dorothy. You know who it is?"

". . . Yes."

"Then who is it?"

"You."

"That's right."

He stood away from her, lit a cigarette, while she broke down and cried, great tears squirting out of her eyes and streaming down her face. "That's right, it's me. And from now on suppose you don't forget it."

"I've heard of men like you."

"What do you mean, men like me?"

"Men that pretend to love a girl, and then make her go out and—love other men for the money they bring back, and—"

"Are you loving Jansen?"

"Almost."

"That word is important."

"I don't see that it is."

"It is to me."

"Ben, why do you treat me like this?"

"Didn't you hear me? If you want to go, you can."

"I don't want to. I can't."

"Now we got that straight at last."

He sat at the other end of the sofa, squashed his cigarette, looked at her with heavy-lidded eyes, said, "Now we can talk about love." She had doubled over into a tiny knot, her face on her knees, and there ensued an interval in which she sobbed, and twisted her handkerchief, and seemed to go through some sort of inner struggle. Then she threw herself on him, held her mouth against his, twisted his hair with her fingers, and gave way to tremulous, half-sobbing little laughs.

8

Lefty, dropping in at Ben's apartment, looked exactly as he had looked the day of the Castleton robbery; the elegant surroundings, indeed, only accentuated his ill-fitting suit, his bandy-legged walk, his air of bucolic simplicity. He came in with a friendly hello, marched vacantly around for a few moments, then stood at the window, taking in the view from the high tower of the hotel. The whole city was visible, and in the distance the lake looked blue under the haze of approaching autumn. Something caught his ear. He looked, and a smile spread over his face. "Did you hear it, Ben? There's nothing like it, I swear there isn't—that sound of a shoe on a football. I knew it, soon as I heard it, and sure enough, there they are down there, kicking it around. Don't you love it?"

"Not noticeably."

Surprised, Lefty turned around. Ben seemed dejected. He sat on the sofa, his elbows on his knees, and stared at his feet. They were turned inwards, with a juvenile, ineffectual, pigeon-toed effect that enhanced the suggestion of smallness that hung over everything that he did. Lefty blinked, then laughed. "Oh—I forgot."

"You expect me to love football you'll be disappointed."

"How long did you play, Ben?"

"I played grammar school, my last two years, then four years high school. I played three years college, then two more years college, under a phony name, until a place up the line found out who I was and I had to quit. Then I played two years pro. I played so many games I can't remember them all, and them that I can remember, I generally don't if I can help it."

"Thirteen years, altogether."

"Something like that."

"What position did you play?"

"I started in the line, because I was big. When I was sixteen I weighed one seventy. I played guard and tackle, and my last year high school I played center. Then my growth caught up and I began to get fast and they moved me out to end. Then they found out I could pass and for a season I played quarter, but I was no good at it."

"Why not?"

"Dumb on plays."

"Where next?"

"Two steps rear. Somewhere along the line I'd learned to kick, and I did all right at fullback. Then I began to show class at broken-field running, and they shifted me to half. That was what I was really good at, staying with an interference and holding my feet in a field. I was good for a couple of yards even after I was tackled—just stagger yardage, but it helped. Sometimes you could score with it. At that stuff I was O.K."

"Every position there was, hey?"

"Oh, and coach, I forgot. My last year at pro."

"And still you don't like it?"

"You ever play, Lefty?"

"Little bit in high school."

"I never saw a player that liked it. Maybe he tells the girls he likes it but he wouldn't try to tell another player and get away with it. There's nothing about it to like. First you got to train. You can't take punishment and smoke, booze, or do any of those things. Then it hurts. All of it hurts, from blocking an end to blocking a punt. Boy, is that one for the books, taking a football right in the puss and then grabbing it to score. And there's no soft spots, like in baseball where you play half the game on the bench. It's all right, I guess. You get some cheers and you get some dough. But the cheers, they're in the stand and the dough's in the dressing room. What goes on out there on the field is just nothing to write home about. I hear those kids down there, kicking it around, sure I hear them. But I'm not getting up to look. You don't mind, do you?"

"Say, that's a laugh."

"What's a laugh?"

"You, dumb on plays. You can call 'em now, hey?"

"They said I was dumb, and I let it go at that, but that wasn't really my trouble. When a guy was all in, when he was out on his feet and had no more to give, I hated to hit him with the whip. I kept trying to do it myself. Well, there's spots in a game where a quarterback run's not smart, that's all. I got the same trouble now. I call 'em, because I got to. But I don't like it any, and I'm always wishing I could do it myself. What's on your mind?"

"Cantrell."

"And what about him?"

"He wants to see you."

"I'm right here and I'm not made of glass."

"Ben, can I say something?"

"Sure, go ahead."

"Why can't you be like you used to be, a guy that was reasonable and that somebody could get along with? What are you trying to pull off, anyhow? A bum imitation of Solly Caspar? It's not you, Ben. For instance, there's no reason why you can't drop over to see Cantrell. And you ought to. Chief of Police is no office boy's job. And he's dangerous. He can do things to you."

"You really want to know?"

"I do, indeed. We're pals, aren't we?"

"I got to make him come here."

"Why?"

"Well, in the first place I tried being nice to Joe. I tried being reasonable and doing business the way I like to do it. And what happened? He began telling me where to get off. He began measuring it up, what he'd take and what he wouldn't take. And right there was when I remembered something I'd been trying to forget—something you said that day when we were fanning along waiting for the bank to be held up. You said: A big operator, he runs it or he don't operate. And what I was trying to be was a big operator. It was just a piece of luck that gave me the chance, but there it was, if I wanted it. You think I was letting Cantrell stand in my way? You think I was caring about his feelings? I let him have it. I *got* to make him come here. If I don't I got no team. Call him up now. Tell him to come over."

"Look, you call him. I—"

"Didn't you hear me? I said call him."

Mr. Cantrell, who always looked as though he had just emerged from a barber shop, arrived in a surprisingly short time. He said that by a singular coincidence he was on his way to this very hotel, on another matter, when Lefty caught him. He asked how do you explain that? He said his wife was a great believer in thought transference, but that he himself didn't pay much attention to it, except that when something like this happens it sure does look funny. He said Ben was gaining weight, the least little bit. He said: "What's bothering you, Ben?"

"Heard you wanted to see me."

"Yeah, there's a couple of things."

"Uncouple them, then."

"Like, for instance, the bookies."

"They giving trouble?"

"Well, have we got bookies, or not?"

"Well, they're there, aren't they?"

"Yeah, but are they *supposed* to be there?"

"Go on, Joe. What's the rest of it?"

"Well, look, this Jansen has tasted glory and he likes it, see? After I cleaned up pinball and he got all those editorials in the newspapers patting him on the back, why, he wants more, only a lot. Well, there they are, those bookies, and there's Jansen, coming in to my office every day, talking about them."

"Does Jansen really buy it, what we did on pinball?"

"He's fooled, right down the line."

"He thinks pinball is cleaned up?"

"Listen, on stuff like that, Jansen's not any too bright. You remember, even in the campaign he wasn't getting anywhere till that girl got in it—this Lyons that he's put in charge of the Social Service department. Maybe she could tell him about pinball, but she don't seem to be doing it, for some reason. Maybe the police department could tell him, but I don't regard that as advisable just now. Maybe the District Attorney could tell him, but his law firm is working for you, the last I heard of it. So nobody's telling him. So he thinks he's done a big job. Well, is he so dumb? Didn't every paper in town eat it up, us grabbing those machines, and destroying them? Has any one of them taken the trouble to investigate these new machines, and find out who owns them, or how they work?"

"And Jansen's hot after the bookies now?"

"I don't talk about the neighborhood places. He don't know so much about them. But these big dumps downtown, if he keeps on, I'll have to close them down. Well, what about it? You're supposed to know, and you're not telling me."

"You seen Delany?"

"... Haven't *you* seen him?"

"I've been letting those bookies alone."

"Ben, you don't mean you haven't *collected* off them?"

"What else you got?"

"The houses."

"What houses?"

"The ones with red lights in front."

"And what about them?"

"The same, only worse. In addition to Jansen, I got the men on the beat to worry about. I mean, they've begun taking it off those places direct, and that's bad. It leaves everything wide open for a stink any time the grand jury happens to stumble on it. The way Caspar did, he collected that dough and made the kick-back himself, so there was nobody that had anything on the cops direct. This way it's just a mess with anything likely to pop. I don't even dare bust a sergeant for fear he'll crack it open."

"What else?"

"Paroles."

"And what about *them?*"

"You know what about them. They bought their paroles, a whole slew of these mugs. They bought them off Caspar, and he made the kick-back, so the police would let them alone. Only a lot of them couldn't pay it all at once and they still owe the dough on the deals that were made before they got sprung. Well, now Caspar has skipped. Have you collected any of that money?"

"No."

"You going to?"

"I'll let you know."

"I want to know now."

They had been sitting, or at least Lefty and Mr. Cantrell had been sitting, near the low cocktail table that stood in front of Ben's fireplace, Lefty in a big armchair, Mr. Cantrell on the sofa. Ben, a little restless, had walked aimlessly about, smoking into two or three ashtrays, listening to Mr. Cantrell intently, if without any evidence of enjoyment. At the rasp in Mr. Cantrell's voice his head came slowly around and his big, lithe body stiffened. Mr. Cantrell met his gaze for a long second, then looked away. "... Or pretty soon, anyway."

"I thought that's what you meant."

"Well, look, Ben, there's no argument about it, we got a nice set-up if we can just hold our lead. But we can't sit around and let things slide. I got to know where I'm at, the bookies have got to know, my men have got to know. *I got to know who's running this.* If it's you—O.K., you know how to run it, or ought to, by now. But if you're not *going* to run it, why—"

"I'll let you know."

After Mr. Cantrell had gone, Ben resumed his restless walk, then went into the pantribar, poured two glasses of beer, came out, set one in front of Lefty. His own he sipped standing up, blotting the foam from his lips with his handkerchief. "You heard what he said, Lefty?"

"Well, somebody's got to collect that money."

"That's what *he* thinks."

"Well?"

"You think I can treat him decent?"

"You can be reasonable."

"Not with him I can't, or with you, or with any of you. He wants his dough, and that's all he wants. If he don't get it— say, is Goose Groner around?"

"I haven't seen him. Why?"

"I think I need a guard."

"Bugs Lenhardt's in town."

"I don't want Bugs. I could use Goose, though. . . . Do I look like a guy that would take it off women? Dumb girls that haven't any more sense, or that maybe ran into some tough luck and got started on something they couldn't stop? Or off parolees? Poor cons that are trying to get a fresh start, and only ask that the cops let them alone."

"I told you already. Someone's going to take it."

"Would *you* take it?"

"Nobody's asking me to."

"Being a big operator, it's not all gravy."

"Pretty near all."

"No, pal, no."

Ben looked a little surprised when the clerk asked him to have a seat, and said Mr. Delany would be right down. The main lobby of the Lakeside Country Club, with men, women, and children scampering about, did seem like an odd sort of place to discuss a confidential matter of bookmaking. However, if that was the way Mr. Delany chose to do business, there wasn't much help for it, so Ben sat down, lit a cigarette, and watched the animated scene at rear, where four pretty girls prepared to tee off the terrace that inaugurated the pleasant rolling golf course.

Before he could get up, a tall thin man dropped into the chair across the table from him, nodded briefly, and contemplated him with a hostile, lowering stare. It was not the first time Ben had seen Mr. Delany, but it was the first time he had met him, and he looked at him with considerable interest. He was, indeed, a curious type, as American in appearance as a streamlined hearse, as world-wide in distribution as the gambling on which he lived. He was an adventurer, and illustrated a frequently-forgotten principle: If a man but worship the great god horse, he may associate with whom he pleases, and few will inquire as to his morals, his honor, or his means of support. Mr. Delany chose to associate with the outdoor set of Lake City, where he was born, and since he was unmarried, to live at the Lakeside Club. He came of passable family, but gossip had it that his early life had been hard, and that he had improved his circumstances by paying attention to influential ladies, who had gained him entree into certain clubs. Then he had played polo. As he was even taller than Ben, who was over six feet, and thin, and a fine rider, he cut a figure at this, and acquired a rating. Then he bought horses and became a gentleman jockey. Then he began an association with bookmakers, though he promulgated the fiction that this was an amusing outgrowth of his equine activities, a matter of no importance. His associations developed into what are known as connections, particularly in Chicago, and eventually with Mr. Caspar. Now, at the age of forty, he was a lean, leathery man, who faced Ben in breeches, boots, and rough tweed coat, and spoke with a cavalryman's voice: curt, clipped, and harsh, but with a touch of the grand manner.

After the moment in which he eyed Ben as sharply as Ben eyed him, he began with no word of greeting: "All right, Grace, what did you come here about?"

"I thought I told you over the phone: Business."

"Then state it."

"Some bookies are operating downtown. You and Caspar ran those boys, I believe—you because you had a hook-up with Chicago, and he because he was Mr. Big around town here, and between the two of you it was a pretty good set-up. Well, Caspar's not here any more now, and to some extent I've taken things over. The matter I wanted to take up with you is whether you'd like to come in with me, running those bookies, and we'd do it on pretty much the same arrangement as you had with Caspar."

"No."

"It would be unfortunate if those bookies got closed."

"The answer is still no."

"May I ask why?"

"You killed my brother."

For the first time Ben realized that the eyes that glowered across the table at him held hate, not merely ill-humor. He licked his lips, blinked, heard himself say: "I—I didn't kill your brother."

"Not alone. Caspar instigated it, if that's what you mean. But you were in it. You were one of those rats and you helped dispose of his body."

"Wait a minute, Mr. Delany. I was not in on it. I drove Caspar the night it was done, and I knew something was afoot. But that often happened with Sol, as you may imagine, and I give you my word I knew nothing about your brother until two days later, when they lifted him out of Koquabit Narrows. I thought it was Arch Rossi they had got, if you have to know what I thought. And you may be interested to know that it was I, working with Miss Lyons, who made the discovery of that body. You didn't know that, did you?"

"Yes."

"Then—"

"I knew it, and I think you played it both ways. I think you helped kill my brother, and then I think you crossed Caspar, and showed June Lyons where the body was. Now get this, Grace. I didn't want to see you at all. But for the last week you've been calling me and sending me messages, and I thought it best to settle this with you, once and for all. In the first place if I see you again, I'm going to kill you, and I advise you to stay out of my way. In the second place, I decided to see you today in a public place, where there'd be twenty witnesses to what happened, if anything. I'm unarmed, and I have three men, within twenty feet of me as I sit here, who'll grab me if I start anything. But get this: if you don't keep out of my way you're playing with death, and nothing can save you. Now get out."

The muscles in Mr. Delany's brown, leathery cheeks began to work, and his hands gripped the arms of his chair. Ben, his eyes flickering, got up, turned, started for the door. He walked with unhurried calm, and yet his heels seemed to lift a little, just a little too quickly as he neared the door. A man, sitting near a pillar with a golf club in his hand, watched him with a fish-faced stare.

Once more the sirens were screeching in Lake City, and this time they led the trucks to the six bookmaking establishments that Ben had visited the day he first saw June. Once more equipment was carted off: blackboards, with certain electrical attachments, and many boxes of tickets, with stub-books. And once more there was a hearing in Mr. Himmelhaber's court, with heavy fines being levied this time, and once more there were photographers at the old Ninth Street station house, taking pictures of equipment being destroyed in accordance with court orders. But on this occasion Ben wasn't present, and the next day actual fires were visible on the Reservoir Street dump.

About a week later, on Market Street, near the center of town, a place opened for business. It was a regulation store front, but lettered on the window was the legend:

MERCURY MESSENGER SERVICE

Above was the trademark of the firm, a winged Mercury holding lightly to the tailskid of an airplane, and below was a group of horses, running under a blanket, their jockeys swinging whips. Quite a crowd gathered the day of the opening, and to these Ben made a little speech, or rather a series of speeches, for he kept saying the same thing over and over, in a sort of mechanical sing-song:

"This is a messenger service, not a bookmaking establishment. We don't post odds, and for information about horses, jockeys, or track conditions you will have to consult the daily papers which are posted on the board at right. If you wish us to do so, we shall transmit any money you give us to S. Cartogensis & Son at Castleton, in a sealed envelope, whose perforated stub you will retain. Any instructions for use of the money you can place inside the envelope using the printed cards on the table at my left if you like. Any remittances to you from Cartogensis we shall be glad to transmit, and the perforated stub which you retain will be sufficient evidence of identity. The charge will be two and one half percent—five cents for every two-dollar remittance which we accept. The plane will leave every hour on the hour—first at noon, in time for the placing of remittances on horses running on Eastern tracks, then every hour thereafter until four, when the final trip will be flown. This is a messenger service, not a bookmaking establishment . . ."

The sirens led the way to this place, too, and quickly, for they arrived the very afternoon it opened, and Ben was ceremoniously driven to headquarters in the newest and shiniest patrol truck. Mr. Cantrell was worried as they sat in the captain's office, just before they started for Magistrate Himmelhaber's court. "This is no way to do, Ben. If you had to do it, if there was no way to get out of the pinch, then O.K. But nobody but a cluck would go out of his way to get pulled on a thing like this."

"You ever been to Washington, Joe?"

"Once, when I was married."

"Did you hock something?"

"No, we bought round-trip tickets."

"I don't know how it is now, but hock shops used to be illegal in the District of Columbia. The government clerks, they were in hock so bad that something had to be done about it, so hock shops were made against the law. You know how they got around that?"

"Messenger service?"

"That's right. There was a place just off the avenue that had a motorcycle service. It ran over to Virginia, and you gave them your watch, and they ran it over there for you, and one hour later you came back and got your money."

"But that was—different."

"I don't see any difference."

Whether Mr. Cantrell's face was any redder than usual, whether his expression of embarrassment was real or feigned, it would be hard to say. At any rate, he received a stiff reprimand in court. Mr. Bleeker, the District Attorney, was no more unpleasant about it than he could help, but he made it plain that if the police, instead of taking things in their own hands, had consulted his office about it, the town would be spared an exhibition of over-zealousness that went beyond anything in his experience. The truth was, he went on without bothering to look at his former partner, Mr. Yates, who was defending Ben, that there was no law under which the case could be prosecuted. So long as no book was made in Lake City, so long as the Mercury Company acted solely to transmit moneys entrusted to their care, there was nothing that could be done about it and he would have to move to dismiss. Mr. Himmelhaber nodded. "Chief Cantrell, this doesn't happen to be your case."

"I acted as I thought best, your honor."

"As Castleton is across the state line, it's clearly a Federal matter, so I wholly agree with Mr. Bleeker: there's nothing for me to do but dismiss your prisoner."

"It's not up to me to decide it, your honor."

"This is a Federal matter."

Mr. Yates soliloquized a little, as soon as he and Ben were on the street again. "You'd think it was a Federal matter. It would certainly *seem* that they'd have a law covering it, so the F.B.I., or somebody, could take charge and rub you out. However, they haven't. I've been looking it up. It's perfectly legal."

■   ■

The five o'clock Mercury plane was just winging in as Ben poured June's cocktail, and he stepped to the window to admire it. "Look at that little green beauty—and think what she's bringing in with her. All but one favorite lost today, and that means there'll be four hundred we split on this one trip alone. Plenty of dough you're making for Dorothy. How is she, by the way?"

"She's all right, thank you."

"Summer camp closed?"

"Yes. I sent her back to college."

"Oh—I didn't know that."

"Not to the one she'd been attending, of course. I couldn't have got her back there, after the trouble over the—missing articles. But there's another little place where they accepted her, and she can complete her senior year."

"Near here?"

"Does it matter?"

"Just being sociable."

"I prefer not to say."

The plane was dipping down for the airport now and Ben watched it for a minute or two, taking sips out of his cocktail, always blotting his lips with his handkerchief.

Presently he said: "I love that little thing. And the beauty of it is, the whole thing's on the up-and-up. We're not putting anything over on Jansen this time. It's legal, the District Attorney says it's legal, the court says it's legal. And to think of what Delany would have cut in for, if he'd wanted to stick—just because he knows a lug in Chicago by the name of Frankie Horizon. The hook-up in Castleton was so easy it made me laugh. The cops fixed it up on account of the favor we did them after the bank stick-up. You and I, we just didn't realize that we'd made a few pretty good friends."

"Do you have to say 'we'?"

"Anything you like."

"I'd rather you left me out, if you don't mind."

Ben sighed, went around turning on the lights, took June's

coat from her, hung it in a closet. It was a mink coat, of smart length and cut, and he admired it before he slipped it on the hanger. At any rate he sank his nose into it, to feel its softness, and to smell it. He seemed to be in an amiable humor. He sat on the arm of her chair, touched her black curls.

"One thing I did I think you'll like."

"What's that?"

"I ended this parole racket."

"How do you mean?"

"Quite a few of them owed money for paroles they'd bought—to Caspar, I mean. I could have made them cough up, if I'd wanted to. In fact, Cantrell was after me to turn on the heat. Nice guy, Cantrell is. . . . I told him it was out. If those people got out of jail, it's O.K. by me and they got nothing to fear from me. From now on they can start their lives over again, and I wish them all the luck in the world. You got anything against it?"

"Why should I?"

Her tone, which was wholly indifferent, rebuffed him. In a moment he said, "One other thing I did I *know* you're going to like."

"Yes? What's that?"

"Those houses. The red light places. I'm closing them down. I told Cantrell there was a few things I'd stop at, and one of them was taking it off a lot of poor girls for leading a life of—"

He stopped at the sudden blaze in her eyes. "But you'd take it off me, wouldn't you?"

"What do you mean, take it off you?"

"For leading a life of shame with Jansen, for doing just what those girls do, for keeping him under my thumb, so you can fool him with airplanes flying around, and pinball games that pretend to be something that they're not—for these little services, you're perfectly willing that I lead a life of shame, aren't you?"

"Are you that close to Jansen?"

"No, but if I had to be, you'd be perfectly willing. If it was a choice between my honor and the money, you'd rather have the money, wouldn't you?''

His face darkened and he lit a cigarette. Then he began the restless marching around that seemed to be his main occupation these days. After a few minutes he stopped in front of her, gave her foot an affectionate little kick. "What's the use of having one of these every week, anyhow? You know I don't want you to do anything with Jansen. You know that, because I've told you so—''

"Ben, keep quiet or I'll scream!''

Ben filled both glasses, emptied ashtrays, did as many little things as he could think of, then at length sat down. She had been staring at the ceiling, and now began to talk in a dull, lifeless way. "His wife died today.''

"Whose?''

"Jansen's.''

"When?''

"Just now. Before I came over here.''

"I—haven't seen the papers.''

"He asked me to step down to his office, as he had something to tell me. I went down there, and this was it. He was terribly broken up about it. I did what I could to help him. Then—he asked me to marry him. He hadn't intended to, then. He was going to wait till after the funeral. But it was the first time I had kissed him, and he broke down, and said it. And I said I would. And that was what I came over to tell you—''

"Hey, wait, this affects me.''

"Oh, don't worry. That was optimism, over there in his office. I'll not marry him. How could I, after what I've done to him? After what you and I have done to him? After all that he'd find out about me, that a hundred people would tell him, if I were ever fool enough to do this to him?''

Apparently there was more, but she couldn't go on. She broke down into low, hopeless sobbing, which went on for some time. Then she jumped up and threw her glass at him.

CHAPTER

9

Emerging from the bathroom in white shorts, Ben started the immemorial rite of donning a white tie, while Lefty lounged in the bedroom armchair, a fascinated witness. It was not, on the whole, an uninteresting performance, as Ben went through with it. For one thing there was Ben himself, as he stooped over the bed, putting studs into the shirt, checking collar, tie, and socks. Great muscles rippled in his torso, in his arms, in his shoulders, then disappeared. There was that curious accuracy of movement that seemed to mark everything he did: the sure way his fingers managed tiny problems, like buttonholes; the instinctive order that he achieved, so that nothing seemed to get lost. And then there was the absurdly brief investiture itself, the actual putting of the garments on. This show seemed to be all preparation, for once the harness was ready, it went on in a few seconds, even to tying the tie. Lefty missed no single detail, and even admitted he would give anything to be able to wear such an outfit. When he looked at his watch he started. "You going to a show you better shake a foot. It's after nine o'clock already."

"Show? This is a party."

"Oh—must be some shindig."

"June's giving it."

"You still see her?"

"Now and then, mostly then. Her old lady crossed her up on Christmas. 'Stead of having her and her sister home, she decided she and the sister would visit June. So they came, and June had to throw them a party."

"You heard anything about her and Jansen?"

"No, I haven't."

"They say they're thick."

"Who says?"

"It's going around."

"You couldn't prove it by me."

For a moment Lefty had watched Ben narrowly, but if the inquiry meant anything to him, Ben gave no sign. He led the way into the living room, got out Scotch, ice, and soda, and turned on the radio. Dance music came in.

"You know one thing, Lefty? The best thing about the night after Christmas is you don't have to listen to those hymns any more."

"I don't know. I kind of like them."

"I don't mind them, except for one thing. There's not over five or six of them and they sing them over and over again. After 'Come All Ye Faithful' and 'Silent Night, Holy Night' and 'It Came Upon a Midnight Clear,' why then, what have you got?"

"Trouble with you is, you just don't like music."

"Come to think of it, maybe that's right."

"I know all them hymns."

"Words and all?"

"I ever tell you how I started, Ben?"

"In a reform school, wasn't it?"

"In a way it was. They put me in a reform school, and I wore a denim suit, and worked on the farm, setting out tomato plants, and hoeing onions, and thinning corn. Corn was the worst. It almost broke your back. Then I got reformed. I got religion, and when they let me out I went around preaching. And then one summer I hooked up with a big evangelist, him doing the big night meeting and me talking to the young people in the afternoon. And the night of the big thank offering, I got all the dough, at the point of a gun from the treasurer of the outfit with a handkerchief over my face. But he caught my walk, as I skipped around the corner. He knew me by that, and they got me. That's how I know all them hymns, Ben. I started out as a preacher."

Even Ben, a little too prone to accept everything in life as an everyday occurrence, blinked at this recital. Lefty got out his wallet and began thumbing through the wad of papers it contained. He found what he wanted, a tattered square which he handled carefully, so as not to tear it. Handing it to Ben, he said, "A regular preacher with a license." Ben read the printing, under the imprimatur of some obscure sect, glanced at the signature, which was written over the title, Bishop of Missoula, Montana, and stared at the name which had been typed into the body of the certificate: Richard Hosea Gauss. He handed it back. "Well, say, I never knew that. That's a funny one, isn't it? I bet you could make them holler amen, too."

"I still can."

". . . Little highball?"

"You notice I generally drink beer?"

"Hold everything."

Ben disappeared into the pantribar, came back with two tall glasses, collaring creamily within a perilously short distance of the tops. He set one in front of Lefty, apologizing for being forgetful. Lefty took a meditative sip, waiting for the little *hic* that would follow. When it came, he said, "I guess maybe it's a hangover from them revival days, but it always seemed to me that liquor was wrong. However—there can't be no harm in beer."

"Remember Pearl Harbor."

"Oh we wouldn't forget that."

The party that Ben descended to, in Drawing Room B, was typically citified. That is to say, the clothes, the food, and the service were streamlined, straight out of the Twenty-First Century; the manners, the flirtation, the wit, a little dull. June had

invited the whole Social Service Bureau, which was mainly feminine, and these ladies had brought husbands, lovers, and friends
who ran a little to spectacles; she had invited also the firm of
lawyers for whom she had worked before she entered politics,
and these gentlemen had brought their wives; she had invited
the city comptroller, the city assessor, the city engineer, and
various other officials with whom she came in daily contact, and
these gentlemen had not only brought their wives, but in some
cases their whole families, consisting of in-laws, daughters, and
sons. A few of the gentlemen wore white ties, but most of them
wore black, and one or two of them red; there were even a few
uniforms present; the party certainly didn't lack for variety. Nor
did it lack for spirit. The Looney Lolligaggers, a five-piece orchestra that the hotel recommended for small private parties,
was dispensing its tunes, and most of the guests were dancing.
The lunacy of the Lolligaggers, so far as one could see, consisted mainly of bouncing up and down as they blew into their
instruments; otherwise they seemed to be very usual boys in
white mess jackets.

June let Ben in with civility rather than hospitality. She wore
a bottle green dress, with bracelet, comb, and cigarette holder
of the coral that she seemed so fond of. Now that the school-
teacherishness had been somewhat dissolved in cocktails,
tears, and a conviction of sin, she was really a striking-looking
woman, and it didn't hurt the general effect that she was mainly
ankles and eyes. Uneasily she took a look at the dancers, said
she guessed he knew everyone there. By this he knew that she
didn't want to introduce him around. He nodded coolly, said
he certainly knew everyone he wanted to know. She said drinks
were being served in the alcove, that the waiters would take
care of him. He said thanks, and started to edge his way around
the floor.

His path was blocked, almost at once, by a dumpy little
woman in light blue, who looked first at him and then at June
in a timid, uncertain way. June hesitated, then said, "Oh, this
is my mother. Mamma, Mr. Grace."

"I'm very glad to know you, Mrs. Lyons."

"What was the name?"

"Grace, but just call me Ben."

"I don't hear very well. I thought at first she said Jansen. I'm just crazy to meet him. I hear he's such a wonderful man."

"Mamma, I told you he's not coming."

"I said, I didn't *rightfully hear.*"

"Mrs. Lyons, a drink?"

"Yes, thanks."

Again Ben started past the dancers, this time guiding Mrs. Lyons by the arm, and again his way was blocked, by a slender, willowy girl with light hair in a peach-colored evening dress. She glanced with a smile at Mrs. Lyons, stepped lightly aside. Mrs. Lyons said, "And this is my other daughter. Dorothy, I want you to meet Mr. Grace, Mr. Ben—"

But Dorothy was gone, slipping between dancers with quick, sure ease, never once getting bumped. Ben, the former broken-field runner, watched fascinated. However, his brow puckered with puzzlement as he turned back to the mother, for he was sure Dorothy had heard.

Mrs. Lyons, once he camped down with her near the potted plants that flanked the alcove, turned out to be more of a trial than he had bargained for. For one thing, she was slightly deaf. For another thing, she was a little tight. For still another thing, she seemed to be under the impression that she was attending a function of high society, and to be elaborately nervous as to the niceties of her conduct. He tried to get her talking about June, of whom she seemed very proud, but she kept returning to the subject, titivating her imagination by wondering if she was properly dressed, if she was downing her drink in an elegant manner, if she should find dancing partners for a stag line that seemed to be forming near the punch bowl. First by one trick, then another trick, he managed to keep her under control. June seemed appreciative, for her frostiness eased a little, and she came over now and then, stood beside him, caught his hand, and squeezed it.

It was when she was drifting away, after one of these visits, that she stopped stock still and stared. The buzzer had sounded, a waiter had opened the door, and Mayor Jansen was entering the room.

There was a murmur, then the Looney Lolligaggers broke off their tune and launched into "O Sapphire Gem of Glory," the Lake City municipal anthem. Mr. Jansen smiled, bowed, and allowed his hat and coat to be taken from him. He had not put on evening clothes, no doubt because his dark gray suit gave suitable emphasis to the mourning band that was sewed prominently on his sleeve. Otherwise he had changed, in ways too subtle for the naked eye, from the archetype of a Swedish dairy-man into the archetype of an American Mayor. He was handsome, oily, and absurd. He had a word, a bow, and a smirk for everybody. When the anthem finished, he shook hands with June, then with her at his elbow made the circuit of the room.

When he got to Ben, he said: "Hello, please to meet you, nice party June geev us, hey, yes?" But when he got to Mrs. Lyons, he bowed low, kissed her hand, and said: "Ah, Mamma, Mamma, I been looking forwert dees meeting so much."

He said quite a little more, and she interrupted with little answers, trying to get started, but before she could do so June had him by the elbow again, leading him away, introducing him to people on the other side of the palms. Mrs. Lyons watched hungrily, then caught the expression "Mr. Mayor," as somebody bellowed it from the alcove. Horror-stricken, she turned to Ben. "Is that what you call him? Oh, I called him Mayor. I—"

"It's O.K. Anything."

"But I've got to apologize—"

"He's getting paid for it! What difference does it make? It's a free country, go up and call him Olaf and he's got to take it."

"Call him Olaf—why?"

"It's his name."

She settled back, shedding boozy tears and watching while His Honor passed a group of men, then happily squared off to face six women, all of them young, all of them reasonably pretty.

Suddenly she wriggled in her chair, making ready to get up. "Hey, where you going?"

"There's something I completely forgot."

"Yeah, and what's that?"

"Mr. Grace, I have to congratulate him."

"Oh, he got elected six months ago."

"No, no, I mean on his engagement. To June."

"His—where did you hear that?"

"Oh, she didn't tell me. She wouldn't give me the satisfaction. She thinks I'm dumb, she always treats me as if I didn't have good sense. His secretary told me. She was over here, the day before Christmas, bringing the flowers he sent, and—she told me. Let go of me. I've got to congratulate him. I—"

Ben, however, didn't let go of her. He held her firmly by the wrist until she subsided into another trickle of tears. Then he wig-wagged June. Busy with her important guest, she looked away. The next time he caught her eye his face was a thundercloud and in a moment she came over. "June, which is her deaf ear?"

"She can't hear you now. What is it?"

"You better get her out of here."

"What's the trouble?"

"She wants to congratulate him. On the engagement."

"What are you doing, being funny?"

"If so, why?"

"How would she know about—the engagement?"

"His secretary, darling."

June's eyes dilated until they seemed like big black pools, then she took her mother by the arm. Mrs. Lyons was quite amiable about it, and permitted herself to be led, as long as she was under the impression that she was being taken over to Mr. Jansen. When she saw she was headed for the door, however, she began to balk, and June had a ticklish time. Guests turned their backs, so as not to see the pathetic figure in blue, gesticulating foolishly toward the Mayor, and the Looney Lolligaggers suddenly started the "Maine Stein Song." This was played through, however, before June got Mrs. Lyons through the door.

Ben lit a cigarette of relief, and smoked for a few moments alone. Then he became aware of the figure that was standing on the other side of the palms. Dorothy, in her peach-colored dress, stared out at the room. It was the first time he had really had a look at this girl who had started such a chain of circumstances in his life, and he looked with lively interest. It was all the more lively, since he was totally unable to connect this face with all he knew about its owner. It was, in anybody's contest, an extremely beautiful face. It was perfectly chiseled, in profile, at least, its slightly droopy lines reminding him of pictures he had seen of ancient sculpture. There was some exquisite invitation about the mouth: it pursed a little, with an expression of expectancy. The skin was soft, with just a brush of bloom on it. What he could see of the figure was lovely too, not too tall, but slender, soft, willowy. He had decided that there must be some mistake when their glances met, and he saw the kleptomaniac.

Her eye had a bright, dancing light in it.

He squashed his cigarette, looked at the palms of his hands. They had pips of moisture on them. He had the dizzy, half-nauseated feeling of a man who has been rocked to the depths by a woman, and knows it. He got up, crossed in front of her, went into the alcove for a drink. When he had downed a hooker of rye he looked and she was still there. He started to cross in front of her again, and instead stood looking at her. He was to one side of her, and a little behind, only a few inches away. Soon he knew that she knew he was there. After a bellowing silence he heard himself say: "You're bad."

"I didn't speak to you."

"I said you're bad."

"Leave me alone. You belong to her."

"Says who?"

"I hear her call up everybody, to invite them here. When she came to you, I knew you were hers. Why do you talk to me? I haven't said a thing to you."

She leaned against the wall. Her head tilted up and she closed her eyes. His heart was pounding now. He knew he was courting danger, knew he should drift away, and all he could do about it was begin to talk rapidly, so he could finish before June got back: "You can break away from this party. You can if you want to. I'm going to break away. And I'll be on the sixteenth floor, in Number sixteen twenty-eight. You go up in the elevator, that's all. You slip away from the party and go right up in the elevator. You don't even need a coat."

Her eyes opened. She stared straight ahead of her, and for a long time she said nothing. Then she licked her lips. "You're bad, too."

"We're both bad."

Through the stillness of early morning, so profound that even the faint whine of elevator cables was audible, came the sound of hammering fists: a woman in green, with a great coral comb in her hair, was beating on the door of 1628. She took off one slipper, beat with the heel of that. Across the hall, a door opened and a middle-aged man in pajamas asked whether she realized that he was trying to sleep. She began to cry, and as the man closed the door, staggered hippety-hop back to the elevator, where she put on her shoe. Then she pressed the button. In a moment or two the door opened; one would have said the car was there waiting for her. She stepped in, trying to control her sobs.

Inside 1628, a man and woman looked at each other by the eerie light of a radio dial. Superficially, they were handsome: he tall, fair, big-shouldered in his evening clothes; she young, slim, lovely with her trick of throwing back her head and staring at some shadowy beyond. And yet, at closer inspection, they weren't handsome at all, or big, or lovely. There was something ferretlike about them both, something small in their faces, something wild, something a little wanton. They seemed, in some vague way, to be aware of this, and to realize that it was the reason for the intense, almost exalted delight that they took in each other, so that they touched each other eagerly, and stood close, inhaling each other's breath. Presently she said: "She's gone."

"Sounds like it."

"I've got to go, Ben."

"Oh nuts, sit down, stay a while."

"I've got to go, so she won't know. I've go to get back into my room so I can pretend it was all some kind of a mistake. I—don't want her to suffer. She's suffered enough from me."

". . . I don't want her to know either."

"Then—good night, Ben."

"Listen, did you hear what I said? I don't want her to know either. She—she's important to me. That cluck, that Swede, is stuck on her, and through her I can make him do what I want done."

"I know, I guessed all that."

"Look, you got to get this straight. She does it because—"

"She's in love with you, of course."

"And what do you say now?"

"You know what I say."

She hid her face in his coat, clung to him, dug her fingers into his arm. Obviously, they had got to a point where the word love, if either of them had uttered it, would have been somewhat inadequate. Insanity would have been better, and there was some suggestion of it as she raised her face to his. "I know, it means money. And so long as you give her her share, I don't care. I don't see how any of it could be helped. Don't worry. She won't know."

"You sure? How you going to work it?"

"I don't know . . . That's the funny thing, about what makes you bad. You can go through walls, Ben. Through walls. Once I went through a whole locker room and took four handbags and got out and I wasn't even seen. You know how I did it?"

"No."

"You never will."

He caught her in his arms, and for a few moments they seemed to have melted together. Then he released her, and she floated toward the door. "Don't worry, Ben."

She was gone, and he put away the highball tray he had put out for Lefty, emptied the ashtrays, set the room to rights. In the bedroom the phone rang. "Ben?"

"Yes?"

"June."

"Oh, hello."

"I'm terribly sorry, Ben."

"About what?"

"Didn't you hear anything?"

"I've been asleep."

"Thank heaven ... I did something terribly silly. On account of Dorothy. I—thought she was with you."

"With—*me?*"

"You don't have to snap my head off. I *admitted* it was silly. You can imagine what a ninny I felt when she popped out of the door a few minutes ago in her pajamas and all, and it was perfectly obvious she'd been asleep for hours."

"Well, it's all news to me."

"You might tell me it was a nice party."

"One thing at a time. I'm still asleep."

"*Well?*"

"Sure, it was swell."

"Good night, Ben."

"Good night."

He really was asleep the next time the phone rang, and he answered in a tone that was to remind June that enough was enough. But it wasn't June. It was Lefty. "Well, what do you want?"

"They got Caspar."

"You mean they rubbed him out? Who did?"

"They got him. In Mexico. They're bringing him back."

"... Who's bringing him back?"

"The U.S. government. For income tax violation."

"How do you know? Say, what is this, anyway? What time is it? And what's the big idea calling me up at this time of morning anyhow?"

"It's five-thirty A.M., and I been passing the time with Joe Cantrell and he just had Mexico City on the long distance wire. They're flying him back today. They've left for the airport already, the planes take off at six-thirty, he'll be in Los Angeles tonight, and Lake City tomorrow. Here's where it gets good, Ben: for income tax violation, they may give him bail."

"O.K., so he gets bail."

"Just thought I'd let you know."

10

Ben saw quite a little of Dorothy the next two or three days. He gave her a key to his apartment, and would find her waiting when he came in. She was insistent, however, that they find some other place to meet. "She knows, Ben. I fooled her the other night, but now she knows. We'll have to go somewhere else. I can't bear the idea of hurting her."

But Ben's mind was on other things, particularly on the newspapers, which were reporting minutely the movements of Mr. Caspar. They carried his arrival at Mexicali, at Los Angeles, at St. Louis. At this point reporters from the Lake City papers met his plane, and rode with him on the Prairie Central to the local airport, interviewing him on the way, and giving copious space to his remarks. The general sense of them was that he had been crossed, but that he believed in being a good sport and taking it until his turn came again. At the big pictures of him, wearing the charro hat with bells on the brim that he had bought in Mexico City, Ben waxed thoughtful, and read the caption carefully, to make sure they had really been taken at the Post Office Building, in connection with the rites of booking, fingerprinting, and incarceration.

That night, with Mr. Cantrell, the new and highly praised

Chief of Police, he visited his attorney, Mr. Yates, the former partner of Mr. Bleeker, the city prosecutor. He and Mr. Cantrell arrived first, and tramped the halls of the Coolidge Building for some time before Mr. Yates pattered up, opened his office, and motioned to them. Inside, he turned on the desk light and began his report. "Well, I just left Ollie Bleeker, and we spent most of the afternoon on it, and I think now I can tell you how it's going to break. Hovey Dunne, the United States Attorney, wasn't there, but we had it out with him over the telephone and I'm sure we know what he's going to do."

Mr. Cantrell fidgeted. "O.K., get to it."

"Caspar hasn't got a chance. In the first place, they've got him on so many violations of the tax law that barring slip-ups he'll be ten years serving his time."

"It's slip-ups we're worrying about."

"Chief, there can't be any slip-ups, really. The only conceivable one is that they would make a deal. The Federal people, I mean. That some sort of deal would be made for payment of those taxes, whereby they'd agree not to prosecute. But where does that get him? Your warrant is on file over there, and before they release him they've got to turn him over to you. Then he goes on trial for murder. This was a simple case of who caught him first, the city police or the Feds. Well, they've got him, that's all."

"Why don't they turn him over to us?"

"With their own charges untried?"

"Our charge is a capital offense."

"What difference does it make?"

"Plenty of difference, Yates. O.K., he serves ten years. He goes to Alcatraz, and he serves ten years. What then?"

"Then the State tries him for murder."

"And convicts him, I suppose. A fat chance! After ten years, you couldn't convict *Hitler* of murder. The witnesses have skipped, or died, or been seen, and besides the jury thinks if he served ten years he's been punished enough. The way you fixed it, after ten years he's out and it's bad."

"*I* didn't fix it."

"I'll say you didn't."

"He could be acquitted of murder, even now."

"O.K., then I got another murder. I got a million of them, and if the jury still won't say murder, I got a little larceny and maybe a couple of mayhems and assaults with deadly weapons. *Then,* if he's still acquitted, we got the Federal stuff to fall back on. But—get this, Yates—on murder he could burn. I don't say would, I only say could. But he'd have a good outside chance, and if that crook ever squatted hot, that would be doing something for the country."

"And you, I imagine."

"That's right."

"Not, I'm happy to say, for me."

"Yeah, even you."

As Mr. Yates looked up in surprise, Mr. Cantrell gave a short, harsh laugh. "You're right on the payroll of Ben's little outfit, his cute association that stole its machines from Caspar, and if you think Solly's going to be careful about it, and check it all up, to make sure you were told and all, why, you're flattering him quite a lot. He's not that conscientious. You're on the spot, right now."

"You mean—they're the same old machines?"

"Sure, don't you recognize them?"

"Chief, I had no idea of this."

"Yates, you're a liar."

Mr. Cantrell, after vainly pressing Mr. Yates for some other arrangement, was quite gloomy as they went out on the street, but Ben on the whole seemed relieved. He followed with interest the announcement, made late one afternoon, that Caspar had left the Post Office Building in company with F.B.I. agents, to lead them to the place he had hidden his bonds, so that he could make some sort of payment on the taxes that he owed. It was while he was dialing Mr. Cantrell, after dinner that night, to find out how this monkeyshine had turned out, that the house phone rang in the bedroom, and he went in to answer. "Ben?"

"Speaking."

"Dorothy."

"Come on up."

"I'm not in the hotel. Ben, I have another place."

"Yeah? Where is it?"

"You've been to June's old apartment?"

"Sure, I was there once or twice."

"I got the key for it today."

"You there now?"

"No. The phone's disconnected. I'm at the drug store."

"I don't like it."

"Why not?"

"It's hers, for one thing."

"There's not one single thing of hers in it. She's taken everything out, and there's nothing in it but the regular furniture. Besides, she only has it until January 1, and that's only two or three days off, and so far as she's concerned she's forgotten about it. I mean, she's out."

"Oh, come on over."

"Ben, I hate it there. I hear her out there, pounding on the door and crying. Ben, come on over, so I can put my arms around you in peace."

"Say, you sound friendly."

"I'll be waiting."

"O.K."

Her arms indeed went around him when he came in, and they stood for some moments in the shabby little foyer, holding each other tight, before they moved over to the sofa, and she snuggled into his arms, and they relaxed. "How in the world, Dorothy, did you find out about this place, anyway?"

"Through a friend of mine."

"Who's that?"

"Hal. Don't you know him?"

"Not by that name."

"He's a bellboy over at the hotel. He's on the late shift, the one that runs the elevator and gets you ice and does whatever you want done."

"How did *he* know about it?"

"June sent him over here, to bring her things back. He made several trips at one time and another. He even had a key, that he forgot to give back to her. So—he lent it to me. For a consideration. For five dollars. Give me five dollars."

He fished out five dollars, folded it neatly, handed it over to her. She nodded, twisted her mouth kittenishly, dropped it into the neck of her dress. Then all the breath left her body, and a look of horror appeared on her face. For a second or two he talked to her, trying to find out what the trouble was. Then his blood turned to whey. The closet door was open, and Mr. Salvatore Gasparro, alias Solly Caspar, was standing there looking at them. "H'y, Benny."

"Hello, Sol."

Sol came over, sat down in the small battered arm chair, lit a cigar. "Sure, Hal's a friend of mine, too. Great kid. Don't you remember him, Ben?"

"Not right now I don't."

"He run a poolroom for me, quite a while back. That was the trouble with you, Ben. You thought you was too good for your work. You was always high-hatting my organization."

"I'm sorry, Sol."

"It's O.K."

Benignly Sol puffed out smoke before he went on: "It don't really make no difference any more, because I'm going to kill you, Ben. Fact of the matter that's what I want to talk about. I'm going to kill you, then I'm going to kind of amuse myself with her."

It was perhaps five feet from Ben's feet to Sol's feet, and mentally Ben measured the distance, so as to be accurate with the feint, the spring, and the blow. But Sol was telepathic in these matters. An automatic appeared in his hand, and he told Ben to keep his eyes front and his hands in sight. Then, laying the cigar in an ashtray, he said: "Sister, you move over here to one side, so I can keep an eye on you while I'm killing Ben." Dorothy, as if in a trance, moved as directed, and obeyed when he told her to sit down in the wooden chair that stood against the wall. Ben, at a command, stood up. "That's good, Ben, just like you are now. Now I want you to walk backwards, slow so you don't stumble over nothing, and when you get to the bathroom I'll tell you to stop and you stop. Then you feel around back of you for the knob and open the door. Then when I tell you to start moving again I want you to back in there and climb in the tub and lay down. I'm going to kill you in the tub, so I can close the door and not hear no blood dripping while I'm playing around with her. I don't like to hear blood. And besides, when I shoot in the bathroom they're not so liable to hear it outside. You ready?"

"... I guess so, Sol."

"Then get going!"

Slowly, on jerky, shaking legs Ben began backing toward the bathroom. Slowly, his eyes fixed in a marble stare, his lips parted in a dreadful grin, the gun held in one hand while the other steadied it, Sol followed. He followed with a sort of creep, and whispered as he came, filthy, obscene things about Dorothy. When Ben reached the door, Sol breathed the command to halt, and Ben fumbled for the knob. Presently he found it, opened the door, resumed his backward progress. Sol resumed his creep.

In the bathroom, Sol became less cautious with his voice, and screamed at Ben, with appropriate curses, to get in the tub and lie down, and be quick about it. Sol was framed in the doorway, and Ben, in the dark bathroom, moved to obey. Then the place filled with light, and with the crash of a gun. Ben staggered, whimpered, clutched his belly. Then, to his astonishment, Caspar curled up and rolled over on his side.

He stepped over Caspar into the living room. She was still there, a gun in her lap, staring at the body, her face lovely. When she looked up her eyes were dancing, as though the two bright points of light in them were controlled by an electric switch. "I've always carried it. I've carried it since I was fifteen years old. In my handbag. This is the first time I've used it."

"O.K."

"I didn't miss."

"We got work to do, but one thing first."

"Yes, Ben."

"I'm nuts about you. You're the first woman I ever cared about, and you'll be the last. I'm nuts about you, and I want to tell you so. Now. While he's still warm."

"I love you, Ben."

"O.K., that's what I mean."

"I meant to kill him, and I did. Who was he?"

"A gangster."

"He's dead."

"Yes."

Suddenly himself again, Ben stooped down and kissed her, and went into the bathroom to look. Caspar was lying as he had fallen, looking small and queer.

"You got a mirror?"

"Yes, right here."

He held the little mirror she gave him in front of Sol's mouth, then in front of his nostrils. Nodding grimly, he handed the mirror back. Striding again into the living room, he took a quick look around. Sol's hat and coat he found in the closet, and carefully laid them on a chair. The cigar, still burning in the ashtray, he got rid of in the bathroom. "The next question is, how did he get here?"

"How do you mean, Ben?"

"Did he come alone?"

"Oh my, is there somebody waiting for him?"

"I don't think so. I've known this bird from way back. This is the celebrated Mr. Caspar you've been reading about in the newspapers, *if* you've been reading them. How he made his break from the Feds I don't know, but he wouldn't be taking anybody along, on a job like this, not even that bellboy. If it was somebody he could trust, he'd have had them knock me off in the first place. So—"

"What do we do with him? I'm known to be here."

"You mind waiting here a few minutes?"

"I'm not afraid, if that's what you mean."

"O.K., I'll tap three times when I get back."

"How long will you be?"

"Not long. Better turn out the lights."

"All right."

They turned out all lights, and he studied every window that looked down on the rear areaway. Then he tiptoed to the door, peeped out. Then, running lightly down the stairs, he emerged on the street, turned, and walked briskly away. As he went his eyes kept shooting from right to left. He had gone but a few steps past his own car before he came to what he was half hoping to find. It was Sol's old familiar armored car, that he had driven a thousand times, parked just above the little apartment house. He didn't stop by it, however. He walked past, staring at every tree, every car.

Then he quickly crossed the street and came down, doing the same thing on the other side. He couldn't be sure whether Sol had slipped into the storage shed back of the Columbus and got the car himself, or had phoned somebody to bring it around. He was taking no chances that a pair of eyes were on him somewhere, watching what he did.

The street, however, was deserted. He crossed over to the car, found it locked. Taking his keys from his pocket, he fingered them, found the one he had used daily, before, when he was driving for Sol. He unlocked the car, got in, put the key in the ignition. Starting, he threw on the lights and rolled silently down to the corner. This was a little neighborhood boulevard, and he was cautious about turning into it. He drove the half block beside the apartment house, then turned into the alley behind it, cutting his lights as he did so. He drove to the entrance of the rear areaway, stopped within a few inches of it, set his brake, got out without slamming the door. Then he hurried around to the front of the apartment house again, ran up the stairs, tapped on the door. Dorothy let him in. "O.K., now we got a chance."

Rapidly, in whispers, he explained what they had to do. Soon, in the areaway below, a girl stood motionless, watching. There was a sound of something heavy, dropping. She scanned the windows. When no face appeared, she gave a little cough. From the shadows a man came staggering under a heavy load. When he reached the alley, and no face appeared at a window, the girl flitted after him. Reaching the car, she jumped in and helped him wrestle his burden to the floor space in front of the back seat. Then she got out and disappeared. The man got in, backed into the street, put on his lights, waited. Soon another car came around the corner, stopped, winked its lights. The man winked his lights. Then he started, and the other car started, and this tandem procession wound its way through the streets of the city until it came to a short street, quite deserted, in the downtown shopping center. Here the man pulled over and stopped. Then he snapped down all locks. Then he took his keys. Then he got out and slammed everything shut. Then he walked back to the other car, which was just now coming to a stop. Then he got in and the girl at the wheel drove off.

"What now, Ben?"

"Alibi. Where did you tell June you were going?"

"Picture show."

"Then you'd better go to one. Get a program. Talk to an usher, or the manager, or somebody, to establish the date—"

"I know."

"Here's a buck."

"I love this car."

"It's yours."

"You mean it?"

"Yes."

"... You're mine, too."

"O.K."

For two days Ben and Dorothy took turns walking past the car on the downtown street, at hourly, and even half-hourly intervals. It remained there exactly as they had left it, until they thought they would go insane.

The newspapers shrieked the story of Caspar's escape from the officers. They told how he had brought them to the Columbus, on the assurance that his wealth was stored in a vault there; how he had led them to a room, sat them down, and spun a knob in the wall; how a panel had then opened, and how he had stepped through it, while the officers watched; how the panel had rolled into place behind him, and they had sat there for a full minute before waking up to what had happened; how they had then spent the next ten minutes making their escape from a locked room, via the cornice that ran around the building; how Caspar had appeared in the lobby and calmly greeted his friends; how he had sauntered back to the storage garage, got into his armored car, lit a cigar, commented that it looked like snow, driven out to the street, and vanished.

Details of the man-hunt that had been organized to capture him were published in succeeding editions. It was, according to the *Pioneer,* at least, the first man-hunt ever undertaken on a hemispherical scale, since all plane lines that ran north to Canada, or south to Mexico and Latin America, had agreed to cooperate. And all the time Sol's metal coffin stood in view of thousands of people, looking like every other car on the street, smart, streamlined, shiny.

On New Year's Eve, June came up for an afternoon visit, and Ben talked pleasantly of her party, her mother, even of her sister, who he said was a very nice girl. But he was nervous, and toyed with his key holder, a neat leather contraption that kept each key in its place, on a little hook. He dropped it, and it popped open. He picked it up by one key that stuck out from the others, and jiggled it back and forth, so it clinked.

"You do have so many keys, don't you?"

The juggling missed a beat, but only one. Ben then yawned, asked her if she would have a drink. She declined, and he said he thought he would have one. He went whistling to the pantribar, reappeared at once with the announcement he would have to open another bottle. Nonchalantly, he went into the bedroom, took his hat and coat from the closet, opened the door to the hall, looked out. Then quietly he walked to the elevator, pressed the button, stood looking at the entrance door of 1628. When the car stopped he was yawning, and remarked to the operator that these holiday parties sure didn't give a guy much sleep. The operator said they sure didn't. He asked for Hal. The operator said Hal must be sick, he'd been off for a couple of days. He said yeah, he'd missed him.

"But, Ben, *how* could she know?"

"She could know from Hal. She could know by trailing you, after not believing you were going to a picture show. She could know by hearing it at the City Hall. She could know plenty different ways, but you know what I think?"

"What that?"

"I think they found Caspar. I think they found him pretty soon, maybe that night. I think they found him and took him out and put something else under that robe, hoping we'd come back for something we forgot."

"What did we forget?"

"Do you know?"

"Nothing."

"So *we* think."

"A remark about keys is not much to go on."

"With the look in her eye, it was plenty."

"Where do we go now?"

"Honduras, maybe."

They were driving through the afternoon twilight, she at the wheel. They had taken a street that didn't quite go through the center of town, but suddenly his ear caught something, and he had her drive over to one of the main intersections. There he bought a paper, and held it up to her so she could see the great black headline: CASPAR BODY FOUND. After reading a moment or two he gave an exclamation.

"There it is."

"What is it?"

" *'It is understood the police will arrest a big local racketeer, prominent since the Jansen administration took office, and probably a young college girl—'* "

"How *could* they?"

"Never mind. Drive."

After a few miles, however, he gave another exclamation, took out his wallet, counted the contents. "Dorothy, do you have any money?"

"Fifty cents."

"I've got nine dollars."

He stared like a sleepwalker at the road ahead. "I've got money in the bank, thousands in the bank, and I don't dare cash a check. I've got this car, and I don't dare sell it. I've been just sitting around letting the grass grow under my feet. I was so sure we'd done a bang-up job that I thought they'd never guess it. I never once remembered I'd be the first man they'd think of, whether we did a bang-up job or not. And as for you, I've been with you morning, noon, and night—"

"What are we going to do?"

"I don't know."

"We'll need gas pretty soon."

"We're O.K. on that. We got the credit card—"

"What's the matter?"

"We don't dare use it."

"It's all right. We have each other."

"We don't even dare get married."

They drove some miles through the gathering dusk, aimlessly, aware that they were going nowhere. He looked at her then, and she turned her head, and for a moment they were staring at each other.

"Dorothy, we got one chance."

"What is it, Ben?"

"One crazy chance."

"I don't care if it's crazy."

"I always carry a little notebook."

"Yes, I've noticed it."

"There's something in there I don't understand. It's a flock of numbers. I don't know how they got in there, I don't remember copying them down any time, I don't place what they are. Maybe I never knew what they are. I copy a lot of things down, just in case. But the other day, when I rented a bigger box at the bank, I tumbled to what they are. They're a safe combination."

"Yes? Go on, Ben. Hurry up."

"Caspar, he hid his dough somewhere."

"Ben, I don't think it's crazy!"

"As to where he hid it, I think I know. I kept noticing we were out Memorial Boulevard oftener than there seemed any reason for us to be. And there's that toolshed out there, right in the middle of a vacant lot, that just don't make sense. Are you game to go there with me tonight? Will you—"

"Ben, I'll simply love it."

"Got a cigarette?"

"No, I'm sorry."

It was dark when they got back to Lake City, after buying gasoline, for cash. She threaded her way through the traffic area, and he bought another paper. It was a green one, the day's final, and his picture was in it, as well as hers. He was bitter against Cantrell, for giving him no warning, and against June, who he was sure was the only one that could have furnished both pictures. She made no comment, except that June had always been good to her. They drove out Memorial, to the place where Lefty had appeared screaming the night Dick Delany had been murdered. Here they turned into the side road. Cautiously, they kept on until they came to the toolshed that he and June had noticed, the morning they started checking up. Here they stopped. He took the flashlight with which the car was provided, and they got out.

Approaching the toolshed they peeped into it, through one of its small windows. Visible were picks, shovels, a wheelbarrow a trough for mixing mortar. "Don't look very promising."

He sounded glum, but she was staring straight in front of her nose. "This window is barred on the inside. That doesn't look like an ordinary toolshed."

Leaving him to watch for cars, she took the flashlight and made the rounds of the little building, presently calling him. Shooting the light under the roof, she pointed to a metal contrivance and asked if he knew what it was. He whistled. "I'll say I do. It's the switch of a burglar alarm, and it's exactly like the one at his beach shack, over by the lake." Reaching up, he threw the switch off. "Now I know we're getting warm."

They went around to the door now, and shot the flash at it. It was of heavy planking, and fastened with a modern lock. She stood thinking, then ran over to the car. When she came back she had a tire iron and the tow line. With the tire iron she had him force up the cheap little window. The tow cable she fastened to the bars inside. "Now when I back up you hook this on the rear axle." In a moment she was in the car, backing it unlighted into the lot, up to the shack. When she stopped he looped the cable around the axle and made it fast with the hook. She started the car. The cable tightened, then began to deliver all the incredible power of a modern automobile. The shack shook and made creaking noises. Then, to Ben's astonishment but evidently not to hers, it teetered for a moment and came crashing over on its side. She jumped out, and then stood watching to see if the noise had attracted somebody's attention. Traffic went by on Memorial as indifferently as it had before. She looked at him, excited, exultant. "I told you. I can go though walls."

Freeing the cable and putting it back in the car, so they could leave in an instant if they had to, they next gave their attention to what the shack had covered. But they no sooner shot the flash into the pile of tools now exposed to the night than she gave a little scream. He patted her arm, said it was nothing but a rat, said *scat*. Then the hair rose on his neck at what the rat had been carrying. It was a hand. Then he knew that here, some place, was all that was left of Arch Rossi, the boy who simply disappeared. She recovered before he did, and pointed to a ring in the boards. He put his finger into it, lifted, and a trapdoor came up. Under it was a hole, with a ladder leading into it, and concrete on one side. Guiding himself with the torch, he crept down the ladder, looked around. On three sides of the hole was raw earth. But on the fourth side, built into the concrete, was a steel door, and in the middle of it the shiny knob of a safe dial. "O.K., come on down."

"Somebody ought to stand guard."

"I'll need you."

"All right."

She was beside him in a few seconds. He handed her his little red book, after finding a page and turning it down. "Read me those numbers, one at a time, then soon as you read one, shoot the light on the dial."

"R six."

"Right six it is."

"L twenty-two."

"Left twenty-two."

There were six numbers in all, and as she read them he manipulated the dial. After the last spin, there came a faint click and he pulled. The door swung open and he grabbed the flash, shooting it inside. Visible were several large canvas sacks.

"Ha, he had the right idea, but they were too fast for him, just like they were for me. O.K. Now I'm going to climb halfway up the ladder and you hand me the sacks. Set the light on the floor, up-ended."

She could drag the sacks out of the vault but she couldn't lift them, and he had to come clear down the ladder, shoulder one, creep up, and buck it out onto the grass. Even so, it was only a few minutes before they were all out of the hole and in the car. He piled them on the floor of the coupe, so there was hardly room for his legs, and she took the wheel, and they scooted. He slid the clasps, got a sack open. "What is it, Ben?"

"I don't know, looks like bonds."

"They can be sold, can't they?"

"I think so."

He got another sack open, gave a quick, startled cry. "Dorothy! It's money! It's dough! Fives! *Packs and packs and packs of them.*"

"Oh my, let me see."

"Look."

"And tens, Ben—and twenties!"

"Now, thank God, we got a chance."

"In twenty-four hours, by taking turns driving, we can be in Mexico. We won't get any sleep, but we can do it."

". . . Mexico's out."

"We can't stay here."

"We're going to Canada. We're going to Canada, and we're going to join up for the war. Maybe we got to use other names, but we're going to join up. Then, when it's over, we can settle there, or somewhere. We'll have all the dough we need. And if we do get caught and brought back, we still got a chance. If you went in the war, you always got a chance."

"Will they take you?"

"You mean this hernia? That can be fixed. It's a simple operation. It takes ten days."

"Why the war, Ben? The real why, I mean."

"I want to. I want to do something I'm not ashamed of."

"It's not to get rid of me?"

"Didn't you hear me? You're going to join up too. If we work it right, we can get into outfits that'll let us see a lot of each other. Then when we got it lined up, we can get married. Even if it's under phoney names, *we'll* know it's legal."

"Then I want to, too. Kiss me, Ben."

"... I got to have a smoke."

"Me too. Here's a store. You hop off and get some, three or four packs, and I'll drive around the block."

He went into the drug store, bought four packages of ciga-rettes, dropped three of them into his overcoat pocket. Then he went outside, clawing the fourth package open with trembling fingers. Then he looked up and saw it happen, a perfect slow movie: her approach to the curb, just a few feet from the drug store; her obvious failure to see the fireplug; the toot of the traffic officer's whistle, and his slow, angry cross to the car; his comments to Dorothy, heated, no doubt, by the peevishness that comes from directing New Year's Eve traffic. For some seconds Ben stood, so close he could hear what the officer said. Then, all of a sudden the officer stopped, stared hard at Dorothy. By that Ben knew he recognized her from the picture in the paper. He started over, with some idea of getting close, of using some football trick, of disabling the officer somehow, so they could make their getaway with all the money in the world.

When the officer looked up he recognized him, too, and drew his gun. Ben opened his mouth to tell him to go easy with it, but he probably didn't picture to himself the size of his shoul-ders, the ominous resolution of his approach. The officer fired, and he felt a terrifying impact.

12

For the second consecutive day, Ben stared at Mr. Cantrell with calm, baleful malevolence, and insulted him. Less bitterly, he insulted Mr. Bleeker, the prosecutor, who sat across from Dr. Ronde, the young intern, and Miss Houston, the rather pretty nurse. Mr. Bleeker let Mr. Cantrell do the talking this time, advisedly, perhaps, because he had let his temper run away with him yesterday, and made things difficult. Mr. Cantrell began with the statement that they had news today. The girl, Dorothy Lyons, had practically confessed, and her gun had been found. Also, evidence had been found in the bathroom of her sister's apartment, quite a few things of interest. Also, the sacks of money had furnished a motive. To all this, Ben replied that Mr. Cantrell was a dirty liar; that both he and Mr. Bleeker were a pair of heels to boot, as they had been on his payroll, and now they had turned on him. To this, Mr. Cantrell returned a grin and the assurance that Ben didn't mean it. And just as a friend, he added that he wished Ben would make a clean breast of the whole thing, agree to a plea, and then be left in peace to regain his strength. For his own part, he wouldn't be surprised if Ben would be let off with a suspended sentence, especially in view of what the girl had to say.

To this, Ben replied that he wouldn't be surprised that Mr. Cantrell had had something to do with the death of Arch Rossi, and that he had better look out, now that the body had been found. Dr. Ronde protested against the whole proceeding, saying that every minute it lasted was just that much more drain on the patient's vitality, and declining to be responsible for what might happen if it kept up.

When they were gone, Ben lay back wearily on the pillow and said to the uniformed patrolman who sat in the corner reading magazines: "Why can't they let you alone? When they see you're not going to talk, what's the idea of coming in here and just hammering at you."

"Oh, you'll talk."

"I don't think you know me."

"I don't think you know what you got."

"What did you say?"

"Peritonitis, Grace. Oh, they sewed up all those holes in your intestines, and it don't hurt any, we all know that. I got shot once, myself. But that's just the start of it. After that comes the peritonitis, and then your temp goes up. It's 101 now, see? It'll go to 104, and maybe 105. O.K., the higher it goes the more you can't keep your mouth shut. You get wacky enough, you'll spill it, and the police department stenographer, he's right outside."

"I get it now."

"She killed him, didn't she?"

"I got nothing to say."

"O.K."

The nurse brought an ice pack, and around noon Lefty came in. Ben motioned him over, and they went into a long, whispered consultation, while the officer read his magazine. Lefty departed, and the nurse brought more ice.

The long afternoon wore on, with Ben fighting his tongue, trying to make it shut up. Presently he asked: "What time is it?"

"Four-thirty-five."

"O.K., I'm ready to talk."

"*What?*"

"Didn't you hear me?"

"O.K. I'll get the stenographer."

"Hey, wait a minute, not so fast. The pothook guy, he's all right, but I'm not telling it here. I got my own ideas on it."

"What do you mean, you're not telling it here?"

"I'm telling it at Caspar's shack."

"What shack?"

"His shack by the lake, stupid."

"Why?"

"Because there's where it happened."

"Hey, what is this?"

"I tell you I'm ready to talk, and I demand to be taken out where the crime was committed so I can show you and not waste any more juice than I have to. You heard what the doctor said. If I keep this up I'm going to die. You got to take me out to that shack. You got to have this girl there, Dorothy Lyons, and I want her sister there, and my lawyer, Yates. And I want Lefty there. You don't have to do anything about him. He's coming here and riding out with me. He's bringing some stuff I'll want to show you."

This strange harangue brought Cantrell over a half hour later, more than skeptical. He was quite sure, he said, that the crime had been committed in the sister's apartment. Then why this nonsense about going to the shack? "It's O.K. by me if we don't go there, Joe. You want me to talk and I'm willing, on my own terms. Well, nuts, if you don't think we were there go have a look at the cigarettes we were smoking while we sat around waiting. And our candle, stuck to the floor."

At this allusion to the visits Ben and June had paid to the shack, away back in the spring, Mr. Cantrell's eyes narrowed, and for a moment Ben feared the police had already been there, and noted the cigarettes. However, Mr. Cantrell, if not convinced, at least was sure that something was brewing, probably worth the trip.

"O.K., Ben."

"They've got to be there. All of them."

"No trouble about it. Take it easy."

"Lefty's coming here."

"We'll take him."

It was thought advisable to wait until after dinner though, and it was nearly eight o'clock when a strange company began to gather at the snow-powdered beach shack of the late Mr. Caspar. First came Mr. Cantrell, who put the lights on, and with his uniformed department chauffeur, began poking around with some interest. Then came Mr. Bleeker, shivering and asking if they couldn't have a little heat. Mr. Cantrell shook his head. Heat would be pleasant, but some of the evidence promised by Grace had already been found in the fireplace, and as there was no way of knowing what was coming, the case could not be jeopardized by starting a fire that might burn important items up. So far, he said, blowing on his hands with his steaming breath, it looked as though there were angles no uncovered yet. Possibly, he conjectured there was some connection between what went on here at the shack and what went on in the vault.

Mrs. Caspar arrived, in deep mourning, with a woman companion. Mr. Cantrell received her courteously, apologized for the cold, but said it could not be helped. Dorothy and June arrived, with police matrons. There was a wait, while everybody shivered, and then the ambulance siren was heard outside. Ben, on a stretcher, was carried in by two orderlies, with Dr. Ronde and Mr. Yates, and Lefty following along behind. "Where you want him, Doc?"

"Right here on the sofa, I think."

"Easy with him."

"Lay the stretcher right on it. Keep him covered!"

During this operation Ben stared at the orderlies, nodded when Mr. Cantrell asked if he was comfortable. Mr. Cantrell then launched into a speech. He said that Ben had put everybody to a lot of trouble, and he hoped he would make it as short and simple as he could, as it was cold, and they were all anxious to get some place where it was more comfortable. Was he ready? Ben, speaking clearly, said he was, and Mr. Cantrell motioned the various police functionaries who were stationed near the door to step forward. The stenographers sat down, put their notebooks on their knees. The guards stood against the wall. "O.K.," said Mr. Cantrell.

Ben closed his eyes, and one finger appeared from under the covers. It almost looked like some sort of weak, delirious signal.

"Do you, Ben, take this woman, Dorothy, to be thy wedded wife, to love and cherish, for better or worse?"

There was a stir, and nobody looked into the shadows more astonished than Dorothy, as she tried to see where the voice was coming from. Yet as soon as Ben said "I do" it resumed:

"Do you Dorothy, take this man, Ben, to be thy wedded husband, to love and cherish, for better or for worse?"

Quick comprehension lighted her face, then, and she replied, "I do," quickly, breathlessly.

The voice went on: *"I pronounce you—"*

Mr. Cantrell leaped and caught Lefty behind the ear with a right hook that sent him to the floor. Lefty jumped up, and for one second was the killer who had served time in more prisons than he could quite remember. Then he backed away from Mr. Cantrell, who had already drawn a gun. "Oh, no, you don't, Joe. You don't shoot me, because I haven't signed that marriage certificate yet. And when I sign it, it's legal, boy. I got a preacher's license, and the marriage license was issued in the Quartz Courthouse at four-thirty this afternoon, one minute before they closed. It's a county license, and we're in the county. That's why we came out here.... *I pronounce them man and wife, Joe."*

Looking up at Mr. Cantrell, his cheeks red, his eyes bright, Ben said, "Now try to make me talk against her, you rat."

"And try to make *me* talk."

Dorothy went over, knelt down, and put her arms around Ben. Almost at once she looked at him sharply. "My, but your face is hot."

Dr. Ronde, who had been stalking disapprovingly in the

shadows, turned quickly, came over. He put his hand under the covers, felt Ben's abdomen. Then he barked a command at his orderlies.

An hour and half later, patrolmen with red flashlights stood in the bushes, waving at a coroner, who drove a sedan, and an undertaker, who drove a light truck. At one side stood two women. One of them, small and dark, sobbed jerkily. The other stared unhearing into the night. For once her eyes did not dance, and for once she attained a great sombre beauty.

THE
BUTTERFLY

This story goes back to 1922, when I was much under the spell of the Big Sandy country and anxious to make it the locale of a novel that would deal with its mine wars and utilize its "beautiful bleak ugliness," as I called it at the time, as setting. I went down there, worked in its mines, studied, trudged, and crammed, but when I came back was unequal to the novel; indeed, it was another ten years before it entered my mind again that I might be able to write a novel, for I had at least learned it is no easy trick, despite a large body of opinion to the contrary. But then I did write a novel, and the earlier idea began recurring to me—not the part about labor, for reflection had long since convinced me that this theme, though it constantly attracts a certain type of intellectual, is really dead seed for a novelist— but the rocky, wooded countryside itself, together with the clear, cool creeks that purl through it, and its gentle, charming inhabitants, whose little hamlets quite often look as they must have looked in the time of Daniel Boone. And then one day, in California, I encountered a family from Kentucky, running a roadside sandwich place. Certain reticences about a charming little boy they had led me to suspect he was the reason for the hegira from Harlan County, and the idea for a story began to take shape in my mind. The peculiarities of a birthmark possessed by one branch of my family helped quite a lot, and presently I had something fairly definite: a girl's disgrace, in a mountain village, which causes a family to make the grand trek to California, this trek being the main theme of the tale; the bitter, brooding unhappiness of all of them over California, with its bright, chirpy optimism, its sunshine, its up-to-date hustle; finally, a blazing afternoon, when the boy who started it all blows in, orders an egg malt, and finds himself staring into the murderous eyes of the girl's father.

Quite pleased with this fable, I drove to Huntington early in 1939, and cruised up and down both forks of the old familiar river, stopping at the old familiar places, picking up miners, visiting friends, noting changes, bringing myself down to date. Back in the West, I started to write, and the thing began to grow. And then Mr. Steinbeck published his *Grapes of Wrath.* Giving the project up was a wrench, but I had to, or thought I did, and presently was at work on something else. Bit by bit, traces of the abandoned book began appearing in other books: a beach restaurant in *Mildred Pierce,* divers recovering a body in *Love's Lovely Counterfeit,* a tortured soul, in *Past All Dishonor,* cornered and doomed, writing his apologia before his destiny catches up with him—though that had appeared in previous books, as it is occasionally forced on me by my first-personal method of narration.

But last summer, while *Past All Dishonor* was in the hands of the various experts who had to O.K. it before I could send it to the publisher, and I was having an interlude where all I could do was gnaw my fingernails, I happened to tell *The Butterfly* to a friend, who listened, reflected for a time, then looked at me peculiarly and said: "Now I understand the reason incest never gets written about, or almost never."

"Which is?"

"Because it's there, not in fact very often, but in spirit. Fathers are in love with their daughters. It's like what you said in *Serenade,* about there being five per cent of a homo in every man, no matter how masculine *he* imagines himself to be. But if a father happens to be also a writer and cooks up a story about incest, he's in mortal terror he'll be so convincing about it all his friends will tumble to the truth. You, though, you haven't any children, and I personally think you're a fool to give this book up."

"After the Joad family trip if I had a Tyler family trip I'd never live it down."

"Well, if you don't mind my saying so, I think that Tyler family trip is just dull, and all that California stuff so phony you'd throw it out yourself after you'd worked on it awhile—a wonderful, hot conflict between your description of the look in their eyes and your description of the scenery. That story is the story of a man's love for his own daughter, and the more it stays right up that mountain creek where it belongs and where you can believe it, the more it's going to be good. And look what you're throwing away for the damned California sunlight. That abandoned mine you told me about just makes my hair stand on end, and it's absolutely in harmony with that fellow's disintegration. What does California give you that compares with it? California's wholesome, and maybe it's O.K., but not for this. You go to it, and pretty soon you'll have a book."

So I started to work and it began to come, slowly at first, but presently at a better rate. I had to suspend for the *Past All Dishonor* changes, but soon was back on it, and at last, after the usual interminable rewrite, it was done. Re-reading it, now the final proofs are in, I like it better than I usually like my work, and yet I have an impulse to account for it; for most people associate me with the West, and forget, or possibly don't know, that I had a newspaper career of some length in the East before I came to California. Also, the many fictions published about me recently bring me to the realization I must relax the positivist attitude I carried over from newspaper work and be less reticent about myself. In an editorial room we like the positive article, not the negative; we hate rebuttals, and even when compelled to make corrections as to fact, commonly do so as briefly as possible. Thus, when false though possibly plausible assumptions began to be printed about me, I let them pass, for as a polemist I had acquired a fairly thick hide, and the capacity to let small things bounce off it without getting unduly concerned. But when these assumptions are repeated and I still don't deny them, I have only myself to blame if they become accepted as fact, and if elaborate deductions, some of them not so negligible, begin to be made from them. This may be an appropriate place, then, to discuss some of them, and perhaps get them discarded in favor of the truth.

I belong to no school, hard-boiled or otherwise, and I believe these so-called schools exist mainly in the imagination of critics, and have little correspondence in reality anywhere else. Young writers often imitate some older writer that they fancy, as for example I did when I used to exchange with my brother *You Know Me Al* letters, except that instead of baseball players we had the sergeants of 1918. We gave wonderful imitations of Lardner, and some traces of them, for any who care to look, can be seen in my book *Our Government,* the first sketch of which was written for the *American Mercury* in 1924. Yet if he can write a book at all, a writer cannot do it by peeping over his shoulder at somebody else, any more than a woman can have a baby by watching some other woman have one. It is a genital process, and all of its stages are intra-abdominal; it is sealed off in such fashion that outside "influences" are almost impossible. Schools don't help the novelist, but they do help the critic; using as mucilage the simplifications that the school hypothesis affords him, he can paste labels wherever convenience is served by pasting labels, and although I have read less than twenty pages of Mr. Dashiell Hammett in my whole life, Mr. Clifton Fadiman can refer to my hammett-and-tongs style and make things easy for himself. If then, I may make a plea on behalf of all writers of fiction, I say to these strange surrogates for God, with their illusion of "critical judgment" and their conviction of the definitive verity of their wackiest brainstorm: You're really being a little naïve, you know. We don't do it that way. We don't say to ourselves that some lucky fellow did it a certain way, so we'll do it that way too, and cut in on the sugar. We have to do it our own way, each for himself, or there isn't any sugar.

I owe no debt, beyond the pleasure his books have given me, to Mr. Ernest Hemingway, though if I did I think I should admit it, as I have admitted various other debts, mainly in the realm of theory, that were real and important, and still are. Just what it is I am supposed to have got from him I have never quite made out, though I am sure it can hardly be in the realm of content, for it would be hard to imagine two men, in this respect, more dissimilar. He writes of God's eternal mayhem against Man, a theme he works into great, classic cathedrals, but one I should be helpless to make use of. I, so far as I can sense the pattern of my mind, write of the wish that comes true, for some reason a terrifying concept, at least to my imagination. Of course, the wish must really have terror in it; just wanting a drink wouldn't quite be enough. I think my stories have some quality of the opening of a forbidden box, and that it is this, rather than violence, sex, or any of the things usually cited by way of explanation, that gives them the drive so often noted. Their appeal is first to the mind, and the reader is carried along as much by his own realization that the characters cannot have this particular wish and survive, and his curiosity to see what happens to them, as by the effect on him of incident, dialogue, or character. Thus, if I do any glancing, it is toward Pandora, the first woman, a conceit that pleases me, somehow, and often helps my thinking.

Nor do I see any similarity in manner, beyond the circumstance that each of us has an excellent ear, and each of us shudders at the least hint of the highfalutin, the pompous, or the literary. We have people talk as they do talk, and as some of them are of a low station in life, no doubt they often say things in a similar way. But here again the systems are different. He uses four-letter words (this is, those dealing with bodily function); I have never written one. We each pass up a great deal of what our ear brings us, particularly as to pronunciation, which I never indicate, unless the character is a foreigner and

I have to give his dialect, or a simplified version of it, else have him pale and colorless. We are quite exact about the conventions we offer the reader, and accept Mark Twain's dictum that it must be made clear, in first-personal narrative, whether the character is writing or talking, all small points being adjusted to conform. We each cut down points being adjusted to conform. We each cut down to a minimum the *he-saids* and *she-replied-laughinglys,* though I carry this somewhat further than he does, for I use the minimum number it is possible to use and be clear, as a rule permitting myself only a *he-said* to begin a patch of dialogue, with no others in between. For, when I started my *Postman Always Rings Twice, he says* and *she says* seemed to be Chambers's limit in this direction, which looked a bit monotonous. And then I thought: Well, why all this *saying?* With quotes around it, would they be gargling it? And so, if I may make a plea to my fellow fiction-writers, I should like to say: It is about time this convention, this dreary flub-dub that lies within the talent of any magazine secretary, was dropped overboard and forgotten. If Jake is to warn Harold, "an ominous glint appearing in his eye," it would be a great deal smoother and more entertaining to the reader, though I grant you nothing like so easy, to slip a little, not too much of course, but just the right subtle amount, of ominous glint in the speech.

I grant, of course, that even such resemblances between Mr. Hemingway and myself do make for a certain leanness in each of us, as a result of all this skinning out of literary blubber, and might be taken, by those accustomed to thinking in terms of schools, as evidence I had in some part walked in his footsteps. Unfortunately for this theory, however, although I didn't write my first novel until 1933, when he was ten years on his way as a novelist, I am actually six years and twenty-one days older than he is, and had done a mountain of writing, in newspapers and magazines, including dialogue sketches, short stories, and one performed play, before he appeared on the scene at all. My short story *Pastorale,* which you are probably encountering in current reprint, was written in 1927, though I first read him when *Men Without Women* appeared in 1928. Yet the style is pretty much my style today. Before leaving the subject, I may say that although for convenience of expression I have thrown what appears to be a very chummy "we" around his neck, I intend no familiarity and claim no equality. This, as I well know, is a Matterhorn of literature, while my small morality tale is at best a foothill. But small though it be, it is as good as I know how to make it, and I take some satisfaction in the fact that it is made well enough to reap some of the rewards mainly reserved for the small fable: It translates, so that it is known all over the world; its point is easily remembered, so that it passes easily from mouth to mouth and so lives on from year to year; I don't lack for at least as much recognition as I deserve, which is a fortunate situation to be in. But it does strike me as a very odd notion that in setting out to make it good I would do the one thing certain to make it bad.

Except personally, with many engaged in it, I am not particularly close to the picture business, and have not been particularly successful in it. True, several of my stories have made legendary successes when adapted for films, and when I choose I can usually obtain employment at reasonably good wages. I have learned a great deal from pictures, mainly technical things. Yet in the four years or more than I have actually spent on picture lots, I have accumulated but three fractional script credits. Picture people like to have me working for them, they find me useful in solving difficult problems in their stories, they usually feel I earned my pay. But they don't do my scripts. My novels, yes, after other writers have worked them over. But not the copy I turn out in their employ; apparently it hasn't the right flavor. Why, I don't know and they don't, for as I have indicated, many of them are friends, and we discuss the riddle freely. Moving pictures simply do not excite me intellectually, or aesthetically, or in whatever way one has to get excited to put exciting stuff on paper. I know their technique as exhaustively as anybody knows it, I study it, but I don't feel it. Nor have I ever, with one exception, written a novel with them in mind, or with any expectation of pleasing them. The exception was *Love's Lovely Counterfeit*, which I thought, and still think, is a slick plot for a movie, and I executed it well enough. It didn't sell and is still for sale, if you happen to want a good novel, only slightly marked down. All my other novels had censor trouble, and I knew they would have censor trouble while I was writing them, yet I never toned one of them down, or made the least change to court the studios' favor. In *Past All Dishonor,* for at least four versions, the girl was not of the oldest profession; she was the niece of the lady who ran the brothel, and for four versions the story laid an egg. I then had to admit to myself that it had point only when she was a straight piece of trade goods. Putting the red light over the door, I knew, would cost me a picture sale, and so far it has; it is in there just the same, and it made all the difference in the world with the book.

To have it asserted, then, by Eastern critics, that I had been "eaten alive by pictures," as one of them put it; that I had done all my research in projection rooms, and that this story was simply the preliminary design for a movie, was a most startling experience. It was said there were anachronisms in the speech, though none were specified, and that there were various other faults, due to the inadequacy of my researches. Well, I do my researches as other novelists do, so far as I know their habits: wherever I have to do them, in field or library or newspaper file, to get what I need for my story. In the case of *Past All Dishonor,* I did them in the Huntington, Los Angeles, Sacramento, Reno, and Virginia City libraries; in the *Official Record of the War of the Rebellion,* as published by the War Department, I having a set of my own, and in various directories, histories, newspapers, and diaries of the 1860's. For accuracy of speech I read hundreds of pages from the stenographic reports of witnesses before committees of Congress at the time, and as an additional check I re-read the writings of U.S. Grant, not the Memoirs, whose authenticity in spots is open to doubt, but his letters, and especially the long report in Part 1 of Vol. XXXIV of the *Official Record,* which was unquestionably written by him, in early middle age, less than two years after the time of my book. This is a sort of check, to make sure the terse, short-cadenced style I had in mind for Roger Duval had justification in the writings of the time. Grant, of course, seems as modern as Eisenhower; indeed, on the basis of all this reading, I concluded that any notion the 1860's were noted for peculiarities of speech, or that quaint dialogue, such as some of these critics seemed to think indicated, should be used, was simply silly. Those people talked as we talk now. Some words they used differently. They said *planished* where we would say *burnished;* they said *recruit* where we say *recuperate;* they *amused* the enemy, where we would *divert* him. In general, however, they spoke in a wholly modern way, and I thought it would be delightful for a modern reader to have the lights turned up on a world he possibly had no idea had ever existed. That my integrity would be doubted, that it would be assumed that I got all this from picture sets, I confess astonished me. The Western reviewers, some of them specialists in the Nevada of the silver boom, were most respectful to my labors, as well as enthusiastic about the results; they got the point of what I was trying to do, and several of them called special attention to the circumstances that here at last were miners who actually mined, instead of standing around as extras in a saloon scene, and not only mined, but had a grievous lot of trouble about it, and formed unions, and ate, drank, and slept as miners did eat, drink, and sleep at that time and in that place. I was completely bewildered, I must confess, at the pat statement of the New York critics, but I can't let them pass uncorrected, which is the reason I ask your indulgence for this visit to the words-of-one-syllable department.

To revert, then, to Jess Tyler, the Big Sandy, and the mine: The river empties into the Ohio not far from Huntington, W. Va., and a few miles from its mouth divides into two forks: the Levisa, which flows through eastern Kentucky, and the Tug, which, with the Big Sandy itself, forms the boundary between Kentucky and West Virginia. To the towns I have given fictitious names, but they are really fictitious, a blend of characteristics, in so far as their characteristics are deemed of interest, from both sides of the river. Yes, I have actually mined coal, and distilled liquor, as well as seen a girl in a pink dress, and seen her take it off. I am 54 years old, weight 220 pounds, and look like the chief dispatcher of a long-distance hauling concern. I am a registered Democrat. I drink.

JAMES M. CAIN

Los Angeles, Calif.
August 6, 1946

CHAPTER

1

She was sitting on the stoop when I came in from the fields, her suitcase beside her and one foot on the other knee, where she was shaking a shoe out that seemed to have sand in it. When she saw me she laughed, and I felt my face get hot, that she had caught me looking at her, and I hightailed it to the barn as fast as I could go. While I milked I watched, and saw her get up and walk all around, looking at my trees and my corn and my cabin, then go over to the creek and look at that and pitch a stone in. She was nineteen or twenty, kind of a medium size, with light hair, blue eyes, and a pretty shape. Her clothes were better than most mountain girls have, even if they were dusty, like she had walked up from the state road, where the bus ran. But if she was lost and asking her way, why didn't she say something and get it over with? And if she wasn't, why was she carrying a suitcase? When I was through milking, it was nearly dark, and I picked up my pails, came out of the barn, and walked over. "How do you do, miss?"

"Oh, hello."

"Is there something you want?"

"How can I tell till I know what you've got?"

She laughed, and I felt my face hot again, because from how

she sounded and how she looked, she could have meant a whole lot more than she said. "Miss, I think there's a mistake. I think you're looking for somebody else's place, not mine."

"I'm looking for you."

"You never seen me before, so how do you know?"

"Maybe I saw your picture."

"Maybe you know my name?"

"Sure I know it. You're Jess Tyler."

". . . I asked you once, what do you want?"

"I told you once, how can I tell? . . . If you invited me in now, and told me to look around a little bit, why then I might pick something out."

"I don't like people making fun."

"Maybe I'm not."

She went to the pump, picked up the cup, and came back to where I had set down the milk. "I see one thing I want, right away."

"That milk's fresh, it's not cold."

"I like it warm, with foam on it."

She dipped up a cup, tasted it, then opened her mouth and poured it in. She gulped fast, but not fast enough, and a little ran out. "If somebody stuck their tongue out, they could stop that trickle on my chin."

I wiped with the back of my hand, and her eyes got a funny look in them, like I was pretty slow.

"Will you kindly tell your business?"

"Can't you take a hint? For one thing, it's supper time, and I kind of feel like I could put away a little food."

"I never sent anybody away hungry."

"That's what I heard."

"Who from?"

"Don't you know?"

"No, I don't."

"Look who's raring up."

My cabin is log, but it's better than most, because it's always been in my family, and we're not trash like a lot of them around here. Some of the furniture goes back a hundred years, as you can tell from the dates carved on the chairs, but the plaster, whitewash, and underpinning I did myself, and some of the stuff I got when the coal camp broke up and people left things behind, specially the super, that give me four rag rugs. While I was cooking supper she went all over the front room and looked at everything in it, the pictures, settles by the fireplace, and-irons, chairs, and knitted table covers, then got on her knees and felt the floor, because it's pine and gets scoured with sand every week, so it's white as snow and soft as silk. Then she did the same for the back room. Coming into the lean-to, where I was at the stove, she stopped and sniffed what I was cooking, and from the way her nose turned up I had her figured out, or thought I had. "Anyway, you're a Morgan."

"What makes you think that?"

"You favor them. They all look alike."

"The way you say it, it's nothing to be proud of."

"I wasn't saying any special way."

"Still, I guess no man likes his wife's family."

"He might, if he liked his wife."

"Didn't you like Belle?"

"Once, I loved her."

"And what then?"

"She killed it."

"How did she do that?"

"I don't want to talk about it."

"Did other men have something to do with it?"

"I don't say they didn't."

"And you put her out?"

"I never put her out. She left me."

"That was after the mine closed down?"

"It was after the mine closed down, and after the camp broke up. The seam feathered out to nothing, from a seven-foot seam of the finest steam coal in all this section, to just a six-inch layer that couldn't be worked. And for a year twenty or thirty of us drove tunnels in the rock, where they were hoping it would thicken up again, and we even put down a shaft, so if there was a jag in the seam we'd know it. We never found anything, but all during that time people were moving out, and she said them empty shacks got on her nerves. Then they backed up the trucks and took the shacks away, down to their No. 5 mine near Carbon City. Then they took the church and the store and the tipple and the railroad and everything away, so there was nothing there to get on your nerves. And then she moved out."

"Maybe she liked people."

"Maybe she liked a lot of things."

"You sound awful bitter."

"I told you once I don't want to talk about it."

"You ever see her anymore?"

"No, never."

"Or the children?"

"Not since she took them away."

"You ever want to?"

"Sometimes I think of them. Specially little Kady. Jane, she took after my grandmother, and had the same stony disposition. But Kady was cute."

"You know where they are?"

"Yes, I know."

We had hominy and chicken, that I had killed the day before and put in the well for the preacher, and after we ate she helped me wash up and it only took a little while. Then she wanted to see where the mine had been and the camp, so we took a walk in the moonlight and I showed her how it was laid out. Then we came back to my place and I showed her my cornfields and hog pens and stable and barn, and explained to her how I had been just over the line from the company land, so I never had to pay them rent when I worked in the mine, and I could make a little extra selling pop and stuff to the men, because I did it cheaper than the company store.

"Did you buy their land when the camp was taken away?"

"No, I didn't."

"That your corn growing on it?"

"I don't say it's not."

"You rent that field?"

"It might be I just plant it."

"You mean they like you?"

"Once a year they come out here and warn me to get off and stay off. Something about the law, I forget what. They can't admit I got a right there, I guess that's it."

"And what do you do?"

"I get off and stay off. One hour."

"You mean they just let you use that land?"

"I accommodate them a little bit. When they were first moving out, and all that machinery was up there in the tipple, I watched it for them. Things were kind of lively around here in those days, what with the union moving in and all, and sometimes dynamite got left in dangerous places, with the caps and stuff all ready to go off. Then later, if a rock got washed down, so it might fall on somebody and they'd be sued, I moved it for them or let them know. They treat me all right."

"I should say they do."

Under my apple trees she hooked little fingers with me. "Miss, you can stop doing things like that."

"Mister, why?"

"How old do you think I am?"

"I know how old you are. You're forty-two."

"Well, to you forty-two may look old, but to me it don't feel old. You don't watch out, something might happen to you."

"Not unless I want it to."

"If your name is Morgan, you would want it to."

"Even with you?"

"If he's a relation, that just makes it better."

"And if your name is Tyler, you wait at the head of the hollow till he goes by and then you shoot him in the back."

"I never shot anybody."

"We were talking about names, weren't we? Some people have got a name for one thing, some for something else."

"All I'm saying is, some things run in the blood."

"And all I'm saying is, there's blood and blood."

"And if it's there, you better fight it."

"What good does that do you?"

"If you don't know, nobody can't teach you."

"Maybe I already did some fighting. Maybe it didn't get me anything. Maybe I'm tried of fighting. Maybe I feel like cutting loose. Maybe I just want to be bad."

"That's no way to talk."

"It's one way."

When we got back to the cabin I told her she had to go, to get her things and I'd run her down to wherever she wanted to go, in the little Ford truck I use for hauling stuff. She went in the back room where her suitcase was, and was gone quite a while. When she came back she had taken off her clothes and put on a nightgown, wrapper and slippers. I tried to tell her to get dressed again, but nothing would come out of my mouth. She sat down beside me and put her head on my shoulder.

"Don't make me go."

"You got to."

"I couldn't stand it."

All of a sudden she broke out crying, and hung on to me, and talked all kind of wild stuff about what she'd been through, and how I had to help her out. Then after she quieted down a little she said: "Don't you know who I am?"

"I told you three times, no."

"I'm Kady."

". . . Who?"

"Your little girl. The one you like."

If I could write it down in this old ledger I'm using that I took her in my arms and told her to stay because she was my child, and could have anything from me she needed, I would do it, because on what happened later it would look like I never meant anything like that at the start, and like I got into it without really knowing what I was doing. But it wouldn't be true. I took her in my arms, and told her to stay, and fixed the back room for her, and took my own blankets to the stable, where there's a bunk I can sleep in. But all the time my heart was pounding at the way she made me feel, and all the time I could see she knew how she made me feel, and didn't care.

2

"What was it that happened to you?"

"What is it ever?"

"You mean a man?"

"If you could call it a man."

"And what did he do to you?"

"He left me."

"And what else?"

"That's all."

It was Sunday morning, and she was lying on the stoop in the sun, still in the pink gingham dress she had put on to help me with the feeding. I mumbled how sorry I was, and switched off to Blount, where Belle was running a boarding house for miners in the Llewelyn No. 3. Then all of a sudden she changed her mind, and did want to talk. "That's not all. There's a lot more to it than that. I didn't have much to say when you were talking about Morgans, did I? I know about that. I was twelve I guess when I woke up to a few things that were going on. Jane, she knew about them before I did, and we talked about it a lot, and kept saying we would never be like that. And we decided the whole trouble, when you see something like that, is how ignorant people are, like Belle not even being able to read.

And then we made up our minds we were taking the bus every day and going to high school. And that was when Belle got sick."

"Her sickness all comes out of a bottle."

"This was lung trouble."

"You mean she's really got lung trouble?"

"The doctor said if she was careful she'd get along, but she couldn't work hard—so one of us had to run the place. So Jane said it would be her."

"She sounds nice."

"She's just wonderful."

"She still favor me?"

"Yes, and we talked about you a lot, and it was on account of you we wanted to go to school, because we knew you read and wrote and went to church. So she studied my books at home. Then when I graduated I led the class, and at Blount last year they gave me a job, teaching the second grade. I mean, little kids. It caused a lot of talk that a miner's girl should teach school, and there was a piece in the paper about it."

"Well, I'm proud of it."

"So was I."

She lay there looking at the creek for quite a while, and I said nothing, because if she didn't want to tell me about it I didn't want to make her. But she started up again. "And then he came along."

"Who was he?"

"Wash Blount."

"He belong to the coal family?"

"His father owns Llewelyn. And because he used to be a miner, he thinks a miner's girl isn't good enough for his boy, and wants Wash to marry in a rich family, like the girl did, that lives in Philadelphia. So he kept after Wash. And at Easter he left me."

I said she'd get over it, and a couple more things, but then her face began to twist, and tears ran down her face, and she almost screamed the next thing she said. "And that's not all.

In May they made me quit the school. Because they could see what I didn't know, what I wouldn't believe even when they told me, because I hadn't been a Morgan, only loving him in the most beautiful way. But it was true just the same. A month ago, in July, they took me to the hospital and I had a baby—a boy."

"Didn't that make you happy?"

"I hate it."

I asked her a few questions, and she told how Old Man Blount had paid the hospital bill, and was giving Belle an allowance, for the baby's board. Then she broke out: "To hell with it, and to hell with all this you've been telling me, about being good, and always doing the right thing. I was good, and look what it got me."

"No, you were bad."

"I wasn't. I loved him."

"If he loved you, he'd have married you."

"And who are you, to be having so much to say? You were good too, and it got you just what it got me. Didn't you know what Belle was doing to you? Didn't you know she was two-timing you with Moke?"

"He still around?"

"Him and his banjo."

Moke, I guess, had made me more trouble than anybody on earth, and even now I couldn't hear his name without a sick feeling in the stomach. He was a little man that lived in Tulip, which is not a town at all, but just some houses up the hollow from the church. His place was made of logs and mud, and he never did a day's work in his life that anybody hear tell of. But he had a banjo. Saturday afternoons, he played in at the company store and passed the hat around, and the rest of the time he hung around my place and played it. Belle said it was good for the pop drinking, but all I could see it might be good for was to hit him back of the ear with it, and then listen which made the hollower sound, it or his head. I got so I hated it and hated him. And then one day I knew what was going on. And then next day they were gone. Kady must have seen, from the look on my face, what I felt, because she said: "Nice, how they've treated you and me."

"That's in the past."

"I want to be bad."

"I'm taking you to church."

But all during the preaching she kept looking out the window at the mountainside, and I don't think she heard a word that was said. And later, when we shook hands with Mr. Rivers and those people from Tulip, she tried to be friendly, but she didn't know one from another even after I spoke their names. And some of them noticed it. I could see Ed Blue look at her with those little pig eyes he's got, and I didn't care for Ed Blue, and had even less use for him after what happened later, but I didn't want him talking around. Some of those people remembered her when she was a little thing, and wanted to like her, and giving him something to talk about wasn't helping any.

For apple-harvest, corn-husking, and hog-killing, I always got in two fellows from the head of the creek, and she fed us all three, and did a lot of things that had to be done, like running into Carbon City in the truck for something we needed, or staying up with me until almost daylight the night we boiled the scrapple. But when it got cold, and things slacked off a bit, and Jack and Mellie went home, she began sitting around all the time, looking at the floor and not saying anything. And then one night, after I'd been shelling corn all day, she asked what I did with it. "Feed it to the stock, mostly."

"Two mules, six hogs, two cows, and a few chickens eat up all that grain? My, they got big appetites. I never heard of animals as hungry as that."

"Some of it I sell."

"For how much?"

"Whatever they pay. This year, a dollar ten."

"That all you get?"

"It's according's according. Now you can sell it. But I've

seen the time, and not so long ago, when you couldn't even give it away, and a dollar ten was a fortune."

"Bushel of corn's worth more than that."

"Who'll pay you more?"

"Café, maybe."

"Kady, what are you getting at?"

"You meal it and mash and just run it off once. You can get five dollars a gallon for it while it's still warm. You take a little trouble with it, you can get more. Put it away in barrels a couple of months you can get ten."

"People quit that when Prohibition went out."

"But they're starting up again, now the places can't get liquor. The mountain stuff goes in city bottles, and money is paid for it."

"Where'd you learn so much about this?"

"In Carbon, maybe I've been doing more than bringing back boxes for those apples of yours. Maybe I've found friends. Maybe they've told me how to get plenty of money quick."

"Did they tell you it's against the law?"

"Lot of things are against the law."

"And I don't do them."

"I want money."

"What for?"

"Clothes."

"Aren't those clothes pretty?"

"They look all right in a church on a mountain, but in Carbon they're pretty sick. I told you, I've been a sucker too long, and I'm going to step out."

"A church is better for you than a town."

"But not so much fun."

I shelled corn, and did no mealing or mashing. And one day she went off after breakfast and didn't come home till ten o'clock at night.

"Where have you been?"

"Getting me a job."

"What kind of a job?"

"Serving drinks."

"Where?"

"In a café."

"That's no decent job for a girl. And specially it's no job for a girl that has an education and can teach school."

"It pays better. And it is better."

"How do you figure that out?"

"Because if I feel like having a baby or something, they'd let me stay and not kick me out and after I had the baby they'd let me come back and be nice to it and be nice to me."

"What do you mean, feel like having a baby?"

"With the right fellow, it might be nice."

"Quit talking like that!"

She pulled off her hat, threw her hair around, and went to bed. It went on like that for quite a while, maybe two or three months, she staying out till ten, eleven, or twelve o'clock, us having fights, and me going crazy, specially when she began bringing home clothes that she bought, the way she told it with the tip money. But they must have been awfully big tips. And then came the night that she didn't come home at all, and that I didn't go to bed at all. I went down to meet the last bus, and when she wasn't on it I drove to Carbon City and looked everywhere. She was nowhere that I went to. I came back, lay on the bed, did my morning work, and then I knew what I was going to do.

That afternoon I saddled a mule and rode up a trail that ran up the mountain to a shack that the super had built when he was young and used to shoot. It was all dust and there was no furniture in it and it hadn't been used for a long time, but out back was what I was looking for. It was the old hot-water heater, with a coil inside, and the hundred-gallon tank, on a platform outside, that he had put in so him and his friends could have a bath any time they wanted.

"God but I'm glad you're back."

"Well look who's excited."

"I was afraid you weren't coming."

"We had to open a lot of cases, and we didn't get done until late and I missed the last bus. I stayed with a girl that works there."

My arms wouldn't let go of her, and we held hands while she ate the supper I had saved for her, and I was so happy a lump kept coming in my throat. And then when we were sitting in front of the fire I said: "That idea you had, remember?"

"About the corn?"

"Suppose I said yes. Would you quit this work you're doing, and stay out here and help me with it?"

"What's changed you?"

"I can't stand it when you're gone."

"Is it fifty-fifty?"

"Anything."

"Shake."

CHAPTER

3

The mine, which was where I figured to set up our plant, scared me so bad I almost lost my nerve and quite before we began. Except maybe for rats and dust and spiders, I had thought it would be the same as when they took the machinery away, but when we got up there we found some changes had taken place. The top, where the weight of the mountain was on it, had bulged down in a bunch of blisters, about like the blisters on paint, except that they were the size of a wagon wheel instead of the size of a quarter, and as thick as a concrete road instead of as thick as a piece of paper. Each blister had split into pieces, and a lot of the pieces had fallen down, with the rest of them hanging there ready to kill you if you happened to be underneath when they dropped. And the floor had pumpkined up in wavy bumps that about closed the opening in a lot of places. So in the main drift, where I had thought we'd haul stuff in and out on a mine car, and pull it up and lower it down with a falls to the old roadbed below, there were three feet of jagged slabs with a trickle of water running over them, and the car track all buried. When she saw what it was like she begged me not to go inside, but I crawled in to have a look. After a hundred feet I had to stop. Because in the first swag was a pool of water at least six feet deep, and overflowing to make the trickle that was running out the drift mouth.

When I got out we talked it over, and I had cold feet. But she kept saying a coal mine wasn't the only place, and she was sulky and I could see she didn't mean to give up. And then I happened to remember one of those tunnels we had driven the year when they were trying to find out if there was any more thick seam. It wasn't like a mine tunnel, where they drive their drift into a layer of coal, and there's rock top and rock floor, with coal for the rib and no need of timber, except of course in the rooms where they rob the coal and have to put in posts as they go or the whole thing would cave in. This tunnel was through shale, with sandstone top, and we had timbered as we went with cribbing. It was a quarter mile around the mountainside, at the top of a straight cliff that dropped into the creek, and we went around there. Sure enough, there it was, all dirty and damp and dark, but with the timbers still holding and the track still in place. I lit up and crawled in, and saw a string of cars on the first siding, about two hundred feet in. They weren't the heavy steel cars they used on motor trains, but little ones, that we had pushed by hand. I kept on, and found all entries open, even the ones that connected with the worked-out part of the mine, though they were full of slabs, like the main drift. And then at last I came to what I'd been headed for since I first crawled in the old drift mouth, which was the shaft that was sunk for ventilation, and because it would crosscut everything, and they could see if they had anything or not, and when they found out they hadn't, they quit.

"It's all there, everything, just like we want it, and specially the shaft. It's light enough down there to see what we're doing, we can set up scaffolds for our tubs, tanks, and kegs, so all our stuff will run downwards, and we won't have to pump. We even got our water just like we want it, because that pool in the swag, it comes from a spring that runs down one side of the shaft, and it's good sweet water, because I tasted it to make sure. We can trap it halfway up, and run it wherever we want. And nobody will find the top of that shaft, or see it from down on the road, or smell anything. And there won't be any smoke, because we'll use charcoal, and it don't make any. But how do we get anything up there?"

"You said a block and falls?"

"From the old railroad bed, not from the creek."

"Could we—use a boat?"

"Yeah, and we could put an ad in the paper."

"I guess it would look pretty funny."

"We could figure it out, maybe, why we got the only boat on the creek, but everybody from the state road to Tulip would ask us about it, and when you start something like this you can't have any asking."

We were climbing down, through the dogwood that was just coming out, and when we got to the water we crossed over the footbridge that led to my land, and began walking upstream. Then I noticed that the road and the cliff, from the way the stream narrowed at that place, weren't really so far apart. There was kind of a sandbar that made out from the bank where the road was, but just the same, by using a long boom, anybody on the cliff could throw a light line to somebody parked on the road, and if the line was attached to the block, it could be pulled across as it went down, and then when whatever was going up was hooked on, the light line would steady it, so it wouldn't smash against the cliff. Then when the hoisting was finished, everything could be pulled up out of sight, and put away till next time. I explained it to her, and she got it, but began asking questions about it. "My goodness, Jess, talk about a boat, me parked in a truck across the road, blocking traffic, while you pull stuff up with two or three pulleys squeaking, that's not exactly secret."

"What traffic? We do it at night."

"That's right. Nobody's out at night."

"We don't make any new track or path to give us away. You handle the truck and I handle the falls. If we hear anything I pull up and you drive off, that's all."

"I love it."

"Now we're set, except for one thing."

"What's that?"

"The tank, from the shack. We can't haul that up. We got to pack it by muleback, if I can ever figure some kind of cradle to put it in. We take it to the shaft mouth, then lower it down."

"Well, I bet we can haul it up."

"How do we get it through the tunnel?"

"Oh. Now I see."

"It's just not big enough."

So we went to work, and it split up about even, the things I could do and she couldn't, and the things she could do and I couldn't have made myself do in a hundred years. I'm no mechanic, but I'm handy with tools, and all the stuff that had to be made and connected up, there was no trouble about it, except it took time and was a lot of work. Like I told her, the first thing was the hundred-gallon tank from the shack up the mountainside, but I got a light wagon up there, and when I started down with it there were a couple of places where I had to use planks, ropes, and chocks to work it along, but I had a lot less trouble with it than I expected, and got it to the shaft mouth in one day. Another day saw it lowered down inside, and I could go ahead with my scaffolds. For them I used lumber from the old loading platform of the railroad, and for pipe to connect everything up I used the water pipe of the old filling station. I kept steady at work, and it wasn't very long before I had one deck of tubs, covered over with lids, and one leading to the other, where I trapped the water from the spring, and connected it with my mash tubs, on the next deck, and my still, which was right on the ground. For my heating chamber I used the tank, and for the cooling system the old heater, with the coils reconnected so they ran down through cold water. I figured everything out pretty good, like the intake of cold water down at the bottom, the drain for hot water at the top, so once we got started it all worked almost automatic.

She attended to whatever had to be done in Carbon City, and that was plenty, but I couldn't have gone in there and had people look at me, and know from what I was buying what I was up to. She got the tubs we needed for the water, and for the mash, and the kegs for aging the liquor. Everything had to be small, on account of the tunnel, as I didn't want to drag any more stuff to the shaft mouth than I could help, but nothing gave us much trouble but the kegs. They were supposed to be charred, but I couldn't see that they were, so we had to char them. While I worked on my pipe, she'd fill them with chips and shavings, until they were almost full up to the one end I'd left open after slipping the hoops and taking out the head. When it was going good with the flame she'd roll it around with the hook end of the fire poker she'd brought up from the cabin, until all over the inside was what they call the "red layer." Then we'd souse water in it, and next day I'd put the head back in and tighten the hoops, and we had one more container ready. For all that stuff I gave her money, but it didn't cost as much 'as I had thought it would, because she got a lot of it second-hand, and beat them down when she could. But some things, I don't know where she could have bought them. For instance, the hydrometer she got, that you have to have to test the proof with, came in a long pasteboard box. And stamped on the box was "Property of Carbon City High School." I kept telling myself I had to ask her about it, but I never did.

After a long time, after staying up late mealing corn, making charcoal, and doing all kinds of things that had to be done, came the day when we warmed some water in the still and put down our first mash. And three days after that we made our first run. I felt nervous, because even if nobody could see us it was against the law and against all the principles I had. But it was pretty too, after you got going with it. On a little still you put in a toothpick, but on this one we used a skewer, a wooden pin that you dress meat with, that's sharp on one end and six or eight inches long. We stuck it in the end of the pipe, where the coil came out, and as the fire came up, there came this funny smell I had never smelled before but that I liked, and the pin began to get wet. Then on the sharp end, that was outside, came a drop, like the drop of a honeysuckle when you pull the cord through to taste yourself some honey. It fell in the fruit jar we had under it, and then pretty soon here came another drop. Then the drops were falling one after the other. Then they came together in a little stream, the color of water, but clearer than any water you ever saw. When the first jar was full, she poured it in the tall glass that the hydrometer worked in, dropped the gauge in, and took the proof.

"What does it say?"

"One seventy."

"Very good."

"My goodness, if it's that strong at the start we can run it clear down to thirty and it'll still be one hundred when we mix it for the keg."

"We'll run till it mixes one twenty-five."

"The more we get the more we've got."

"Maybe this is a case where the less you act like a hog, the more you put on some fat. We can run it till we got a lot and put it in the wood at a hundred. But then it dries out and gets weaker, and if it's weak it won't sell. And the weaker it is, the slower the charcoal works on it. If we put it in strong, we got color, flavor, and mellowness in a month, anyway enough to be a big help when it's mixed with regular liquor. But at a hundred we could be a year and we'd get nothing they'd pay us for. The longer we got to keep it, the more kegs we got to buy, the longer we wait for our money."

"That money's what I want."

"Then watch it, it don't get too weak."

"Then anyway we can have music."

She had a little radio up there by then, and turned it on, and I didn't mind, as it would be a long day, watching that stream off the end of the pin.

"And a drink."

"What?"

"What we making the stuff for?"

"You mean this?"

"Sure."

She climbed up, got a bottle of Coca-Cola out of the basin the spring ran into, and the tin cup we kept there. When she came down she poured from the jar to the cup, dumped some Coca-Cola in, and handed it to me.

"Taste it, it's good."

Now nobody could live their life in mountain country without learning plenty about whisky, but that was the first time I ever tasted it. It tasted like Coca-Cola at first, but then I began to feel good, and wanted another swallow. She had the cup by then, taking a swig, and then was when I knocked it out of her hand.

"There's to be no drinking in this."

"I'll have a drink if I want to."

"No, you won't."

"Will you kindly tell me why?"

"We got work to do for one thing. I get careless with this fire, so it's too hot, this whole thing could explode so easy you wouldn't believe it. And later, when it's dark, we've only just begun. We've got to lower this spent mash down, so we can feed it to the hogs and not have it all over the place, and we can't do that or anything if we're up here drunk. And we'll get drunk, if we take enough of it. They all do. I've seen them. And besides, it's wrong."

"You believe all you hear in church?"

"I believe what I feel."

"For God's sake."

Because by then I loved her so much I wanted to be weak, and do what she meant we should do, but my love made me strong too, so I knew I wouldn't do it. With liquor in me, though, I didn't know what I would do, or what she could make me do. "You heard me, Kady? That's one thing we don't do."

"I heard you."

4

And there came the night when we drove into Carbon City with our first hundred quarts, packed in every bag and sack and poke I could find, and yet all you could hear was glass, rattling louder even than the truck. I thought I would die, and when she left me, after I parked by the railroad, everything from the chirp of crickets to the clank of yard signals just gave me the shivers. After a long time she was back, with a café man, and he had a flashlight, so I wanted to holler at him, and tell him to put it out. But we had it set that she'd do the talking, so I sat there and wiped off sweat. They talked along, and he put the light on a bottle for color, then did some tasting and handed it back. "It might not be so bad, sister, except it's all full of caramel."

"O.K. I'll take it up the street."

"Can't you taste it?"

"What would I be tasting it for? I made it, dumbbell. That color's charcoal, that I burned in the keg myself, as anybody would know except maybe a jerk that hadn't seen good booze for so long he's forgot what it's like. But it's all right, and no hard feelings. I'll just take it where they know what it means to have some hundred ten proof in the house that makes blended stuff taste like something, and kick a little bit too."

"What do you mean, hundred ten proof?"

"Get your tester."

"Mine's broke."

"Then I brought one."

She got out the hydrometer and let him take a reading. "If you think that gauge is loaded, try a slug yourself."

He took a swig, while she stood there looking at him so sinful it made me sick to think she was any part of me. Then he took another, and you could see it take hold. "What are you asking for it?"

"Ten dollars a gallon."

"I'll give you four."

"Oh, I'm going up the street."

"No, wait a minute, let's talk."

They closed at six, and I ran them to the alley back of his place, where he went in and got the money and had the bottles carried in. Then she jumped in beside me.

"Come on, Jess, let's celebrate."

"What do you call celebrating?"

"Just going somewhere, having a good time."

"What was the idea, looking at him like that?"

"Well my goodness, I was selling him booze."

"What else were you selling him?"

"The way you talk."

We drove under a bridge, then came to a café called the White Horse and stopped. I had never been in a place like that, but I no sooner saw it than I knew it was the kind of place I'd been hearing about all my life, and that it was bad. The lights were low, and on one side was a bar, on the other side booths, and in the middle a place where couples were dancing to slow music that came out of a box at one end, with lights in it. The crowd no sooner saw Kady than they began to yell, and come to find out it was where she used to work. I didn't thank her when she said she'd brought her old man, and I didn't offer to shake anybody's hand. We sat down in a booth and I told the girl two Coca-Colas. "Make mine a rum coke."

"Two Coca-Colas."

"Listen, Jess, I want a drink."

"We're going home."

"If you don't like it here, you can go home, and I'll stay, and I'm quite sure somebody will take me in for the night."

So anything that meant she might leave me, that got me, and I shut up. But I was swelling up thick inside.

In the next booth was a girl and two men, that were mine guards from the way they talked, and when one of them and the girl left, the other one got up and asked Kady to dance. She went off with him, and they went to the music box, and their heads were together while they dropped in their nickel. Then they danced, and when the tune was almost over they danced by the box, stopped, and dropped more money in, at least a dozen nickels, one right after the other. Then when a tune stopped, it would be only a few seconds before another one started, but during that time they didn't stop dancing. They stood there, swinging to the music that wasn't playing any more, and then when it started again they'd go off. About the third tune, they made signs to the bartender, and he made them drinks that they picked up as they went around, and sipped, and left on the bar. About the tenth tune they were dancing with their faces up against each other, and had forgot their drink. Then they stopped and stood there whispering. Then she came over and picked up her handbag. "I won't be long, Jess."

"Where you going?"

"Just for a walk. Get a little air."

"You're coming home."

"Sure. Soon we'll go."

"We're going now."

The man walked over and stepped between us. "Listen, pop, take it easy why don't you?—so we don't have any trouble."

"Do you know who I am?"

"You're Kady's father, so she says."

"And I'm taking her home."

"Not unless she wants to go, pop. Now the way she tells me, she feels like taking a walk, and that's what we're going to do. So sit down. Don't get excited. Have yourself a drink, and when her and me get back you're taking her home. But not before."

He put on his hat, one of those black felts turned down on one side like a mountain gunman wears, and looked me in the eye. He was tall and thin, and I could have broke him in two, but that gun was what I kept thinking about. A mine guard is never without it, and he knows how to use it, and he will use it. I could feel the blood pounding in my neck, but I sat down. He turned to his booth and sat down.

While we were having that, she had said something to him about the ladies' room, and gone back there. I sat with my throat pounding heavier all the time, until a door back there opened, and she started walking up to his booth. I don't remember thinking anything about it. But when she was almost to him, I grabbed that booth partition, and pulled, and it crashed down, and there he was, sprawling at my feet. I was on him even before she screamed, and when that gun came out of his pocket, I had it. I brought it down on his head, he crumpled, I aimed, and pulled the trigger. But I had forgot the safety catch, and before I could snap it off, they grabbed me.

"This court, unless compelled, is not going to make a criminal out of a father defending the honor of a daughter. But is not going to overlook, either, a breach of the peace that could have had the most serious consequences. Tyler, do you realize that if these witnesses hadn't prevented it, you would have killed a man, that you would now stand before me accused of the crime of murder, that it would be my unescapable duty to hold you for the grand jury, and that almost certainly you would in due time be found guilty, sentenced, and hanged?"

"Yes sir."

"Do you think that's right?"

"I guess I don't."

"How much money is in your pocket?"

"Fourteen dollars, sir."

"Then just to impress it on your mind that this is more than a passing matter, you can pay the clerk here a fine of ten dollars and costs for disorderly conduct—or perhaps you'd rather spend the next ten days in jail?"

"I'd rather pay, sir."

"Young woman, how old are you?"

"Nineteen, sir."

"Have you been drinking?"

"I—don't know, sir."

"What do you mean you don't know?"

"Well, I was drinking Coca-Cola, but you know how it is. Sometimes they put a little something in it, just for fun, but tonight I don't know if they did or not."

"Lean over here, so I can smell your breath. . . . How can you have the cheek to tell me you don't know if you've been drinking or not, when you're half shot, right now? Aren't you?"

"Yes, sir."

"Do you realize that I can hold you with no more evidence than that as a wayward minor, and have you committed to a school?"

"I didn't know it, sir."

"There are a great many things you don't seem to know, and my advice to you is that you turn over a new leaf, and do it now. I'm remanding you into the custody of your father, and on the first complaint from him, you're up for commitment. Do you understand that, Tyler? If there's any more trouble like what went on in there tonight, you don't grab a gun and start shooting. You come to me, and the proper steps will be taken."

"Yes, sir, I understand it."

"Next case."

Going home she was laughing at how funny it was, that he hadn't asked her how much money *she* had, because she still had every cent of the hundred and fifty dollars we had got for the liquor, but after we got home and got a fire going and ate something and drunk some coffee, I shut her up. "You want to go to that reform school?"

"You mean you'd send me?"

"If you don't shut up, I might."

"Can't I even laugh?"

"He was right."

Then we began to talk, and I tried to tell her how it scared me, that I had almost killed a man. "And you, don't it shame you, you were making up to two men tonight, within ten minutes of each other?"

"What's to be ashamed of?"

"It's blood."

"Listen, if I hear any more of this Morgan stuff—"

"I tell you, it's in-breeding. It's what we both got to be afraid of. It's in us, and we ought to be fighting it. And stead of that—"

"Yeah, tell me."

"We're not."

"Well say, that's terrible."

" 'Shining, shooting, and shivareeing their kin, that's what they say of people that live too long on one creek. I thought I was too good for that. But today, right up in that mine, I ran off five gallons of liquor that's against the law. This evening I almost killed a man."

"And tonight you'd like to have me."

"Stop talking like that!"

"What were you shooting him for?"

"You ought to know."

"You must be loving me plenty."

"I told you, quit that!"

"Have a drink with me?"

"No!"

"How about *you* going to reform school?"

One night when I got through the run I took a walk up the creek, and when I came to the church I kept on up the hollow, and pretty soon sat down by a tree and tried to think. We had had some trouble that day. Now the money was coming in she kept buying clothes, blue and yellow and green dresses, and red coats, and hats with ribbons hanging down the side, and every night we'd drive in town to the White Horse, and they wouldn't serve her liquor any more but we'd have some Cokes, and then she'd dance and carry on with whoever was there, and then I'd take her home. But in the daytime she got sloppier and sloppier, and one day when it got hot she took off her shoes. And this day she said it was so hot by the still she couldn't stand it, and slipped off her dress so she was in nothing but underwear and hardly any of that, and began dancing to the radio, swaying with the music with one hand on her hip and looking me in the eye. Well, in the first place, in a coal mine it's the same temperature all the year round, and that little bit of fire I had in there, what with the ventilation we had, didn't make any difference at all. So we had an argument about it, and I made her put her clothes on and cut off the music. Then she said: "Jess, did it ever strike you funny, one thing about this place?"

"What's that?"

"If a woman was attacked in here, there's nothing at all she could do about it."

"Couldn't she bite? Or kick? Or scratch?"

"What good would it do her?"

"Might help quite a lot."

"Not if the man was at all strong. She could scream her head off, and not one person on earth would hear her. I've often thought about it."

I made her get out of there and go down to the cabin and catch up on some of the work. But I was hanging on by my teeth by that time, and I was a lot nearer giving up the fight, and going along with her on whatever she felt like doing, even getting drunk, than I wanted her to know. That was when I took this walk up the creek, and past the church, and through Tulip, trying to get control of myself, and maybe pray a little, for some more strength.

And then, from up among the trees, I heard something that sounded like a wail. Then here it came again, closer. Then I could make out it was a man, calling somebody named Danny. And then all of a sudden a prickle went up my back, because I knew that voice, from the million times I had heard it at the company store and around the camp and in my own home. It was Moke, but he wasn't singing comical stuff to a banjo now. He was scared to death, and slobbering at the mouth as he called, and in between moaning and whispering to himself. He went stumbling along to his cabin, and I followed along after him, and watched while he stood in the door, a candle in his hand, and called some more. Then when he went inside I crept up and peeped through a chink in the logs. He was a little man, but I never saw him look so little as he looked now. He was sitting on the clay floor, in one corner, the banjo leaning against the wall beside him, his head on his arms, and shaking with sobs so bad you thought they were going to tear him apart.

I was shook up plenty myself, because if there was one person in this world I hated it was him, and after all Kady had said, and all I knew from before, I couldn't help wondering what he was doing here, and I knew it had to be something that meant me. So I could feel some connection when I came to my cabin, and from the back room I could hear a baby crying. I went inside, and at the sound of the door, a woman called to know if it was Kady. I said it was Kady's father. She came out then, and from the tall, thin shape she had, and the look of her face and color of her eyes, I knew she was a Tyler. "I think you're my girl Jane."

"And you're my father."

We shook hands, and I patted her hand, and then we sat down, and both of us wanted to give each other a kiss but were too bashful. "Can I call you Father?"

"I don't mind."

"I used to call you Pappy."

"You remember that?"

"I remember a lot, and how sweet you was to me, and how much I loved you, and how tall you was."

"Why not call me Jess?"

"Isn't that fresh?"

"Kady does, but of course she *is* fresh."

"It's so wonderful about her."

". . . What about her?"

"Everything."

She looked down at the floor, and you could see she was awful happy about something, and then she said: "You know about Danny?"

"Who's Danny?"

"Didn't she tell you?"

"Is that Danny in there crying?"

"He won't cry after he's fed. Kady took the truck and ran into town for a lot of things he's got to have, because all you've got here, that he can have, is milk. But she'll be back soon. And as soon as he gets a little something in his stomach he'll be sweeter than sugar."

"What's Moke got to do with him?"

"Have you see Moke?"

I told her what had gone on in the hollow, and she doubled up her fists and said: "I hope I don't see him. I might kill him."

"Hey, hey, none of that kind of talk."

"Moke took Danny."

"First my wife, then my grandson."

"Say that again, Jess."

"He is, isn't he?"

"I wasn't sure you'd remember it."

"I don't forget much."

"What Moke did, and how today I caught up with him, that's part of what's so wonderful. Last week, on account of Kady being gone and my mother not much caring one way or the other, little Danny was mine, and it was heavenly, because maybe I'll never get married, but still I had one of my own. Then when I came home from the store one day he was gone, and Moke was gone, and I went almost crazy, but I knew it had to be Moke that took him, because he was so crazy about him."

"Moke loves somebody?"

"Oh, he gets lonely too. And there I was, fit to be tied. Because Kady, that was my whole life before, was gone I had no idea where, and now with Danny stolen it was more than I could stand. But my mother said if Moke took him, he had to have some place to bring him to, and he still had his shack up in the hollow, and maybe it was there. So she drew it out for me how to get there, and I took the bus over from Blount, and even before I got to it I could hear Danny laughing and Moke playing to him on the banjo. So I wasn't going to take any chance on a fight with Moke. Maybe he wouldn't let me have Danny, but then he'd know I was around, and might run off again, somewhere else. So he said something to Danny about a drink, but I noticed there was no well out back."

"He gets water from a neighbor."

"I thought he might, and right away he came out with a pail and started across the clearing. I went in and grabbed Danny and ran down the path, and when I got to the road I made a man with a wagon give me a ride, because he said he was going as far as the bus line. But then, as we passed this cabin, *who should I see but Kady out back, hanging out clothes!* Jess, I jumped down, and ran over to her, and I wasn't crazy any more, I was the happiest person on earth, because I had my two darlings back, my little baby, and my sister that I'd loved ever since I could remember."

"How does Kady feel about it?"

"She loves it."

I didn't love it, and if Kady did, that wasn't how she told it to me, the last time she had mentioned Danny. But when she came in with the stuff she'd bought, her eyes were like stars, and she went in the back room with Jane without even a hello to me. I sat there trying to tell myself it was all right, it was just what I'd been praying for. If she could love her child, and stop all this drinking and dancing and carrying on, it was the best thing all around, and I could get some peace from her, and not be teased into having thoughts about her that made me so ashamed I hated to own up to myself they were there. It didn't do me any good. If she'd had a child, and she hated it, that squared it up, and I didn't have to remember it. But if she didn't hate him, it was between me and her, and would be, always. I sat there, while out back Jane explained how to mix this and how to cook that, and pretty soon they began feeding the baby, and his crying stopped and Jane began talking to him and telling him how pretty he was, and all of a sudden Kady was sitting beside me and picking up my hand.

"Want to see my baby, Jess?"

"I guess not."

"He's a pretty baby."

"So I hear."

"And he's your grandson."

"I know."

"It would make me happy, Jess."

"It wouldn't me."

"Then if that's how you feel about it, I won't try to change you. I'll take him away. There's a reason I can't go back to Blount just yet, but he and Jane and I can stay in a hotel at Carbon and you won't be bothered."

"I didn't ask you to leave."

"If my baby's not welcome, I'm not."

"You've changed a lot, that's all I can say."

"Didn't Jane tell you why?"

"Not that I know of."

"Didn't she tell you why Moke took him?"

"She said he was lonesome."

"He loved Danny, and specially after the way Belle began fighting with him, just before I left. He was crazy about him, and then when he found out he was to be taken away, he went off with him."

"Who was going to take him away?"

"Jane ran into Wash."

"The father?"

"Yes."

"Or it might be shorter just to say rat."

"He's no rat."

"He skipped like a rat."

"His father made him. And then, a week ago, Jane ran into him on the street, in Blount. And he asked about me, and Danny, and was friendly, and pretty soon Jane came right out with it and asked why he didn't marry me, and give his little boy a name, and stop being—"

"A rat."

"Anyway, Jess, what he said was wonderful."

"What was it he said?"

"He said he was always going to, soon as he was twenty-one, whether his family liked it or not. He's only twenty, Jess, one year older than I am. But now, he said they would give their consent too, before he was twenty-one. Because an awful thing happened to them. His sister, the one that married into the coal family in Philadelphia, had to have an operation, and now she can't have any children any more. And now they know if they're to have grandchildren, it's got to be through Wash. And now they feel different about Danny. And—so do I. I'm so ashamed how I treated him before."

"Well, it's all fine."

"Are you glad at all, Jess?"

"To me, a rat's a rat."

"Not even for my sake you don't feel glad?"

"I rather not say."

Tears came in her eyes and she sat there making little creases in her dress. It wasn't one of those she'd been buying, but a quiet little blue one, that made her look smaller and younger and sweeter. I said she should stay on till it suited her to go and I'd go to Carbon, but she said she'd go, and I hated it, the way I was acting, and yet I couldn't help how I felt. And then Jane was there, putting something in my lap, and looking up at me was the cutest little child I ever saw, all pink and soft and warm, with nothing on him but a clean white diaper. Kady reached over to take him, but I grabbed him and went over to one of the settles by the fire and sat there and held him close. And for a long time something kept stabbing into my heart, and I'd look at him and feel so glad he was partly mine that I wanted to sing. His diaper slipped down a little and I almost died when I saw a brown bug on his stomach, or what I thought was a brown bug, just below the navel. I reached for it with my fingers, but Jane laughed.

"That's his birthmark."

"I thought it was some kind of a moth."

"It's his butterfly."

"It almost scared me to death."

They went in the back room with him again, but I called Kady out. "I take it back, everything I said. He's so sweet I could eat him."

"But if you'd rather I went—"

"I couldn't stand it if you did."

"I can understand how you feel."

"But I don't! Not any more. It's all gone, the devilment that's been in me, and the onriness, and all what I've been thinking about. I want you to be happy. And if the boy wants to marry you, he's not any rat, and I want you to have him."

"I'm so glad, Jess."

"Me too."

"I want to be your little girl."

"And I want to be your pappy."

"Kiss me."

I kissed her, and she kissed me back, and it wasn't like those hot kisses we'd been having, but cool and sweet like the kiss Danny gave me just before they took him away.

6

Why she couldn't go to Blount right away she didn't tell me till one day when all four of us were sitting out under the trees and I spotted a big car coming up the creek from the state road. Then she owned up she had wired the boy, and yet she wasn't going back till he came and got her. So she and Jane ran in the house with Danny to get slicked up and in another minute there he was, kind of a tall, dark boy in slacks and blue shirt. He didn't put on any airs with me at all, but shook hands quick, and went around the cabin looking at it, and said it was just like the one his uncle had on Paint Creek, where he used to spend part of every summer. So then it turned out his father had got himself a mine, but his family were mountain people, like us. So that went with his bony look, and made me feel still better about him. Then when Kady came out and he took her in his arms, I had to begin fooling around with my shoe for fear they'd see the tears in my eyes. Then when he saw Danny for the first time in his life, in Jane's arms laughing and trying to talk as she brought him out, he went over and bent over and looked and bent down and called him old-timer and shook hands just like it was somebody he was being introduced to and could say something. Then he tried to brush off the butterfly, just like I had, and we all laughed and had some Coca-Cola and were friendly. But when they went in to get supper he said he'd have to leave for a little while. "If you're going back to town, I'll ride along with you. There's some things I ought to get."

"I'm going up the creek."

"There's nothing up the creek."

"There's a heel named Moke Blue."

"You know Moke?"

"I've seen him and I guess I've spoken to him, but I've never shaken his hand and until I got Kady's wire I never even thought about him. I'm thinking about him now, though. And I'm putting him in jail for kidnapping my boy."

"You're taking him in, yourself?"

"That's it, Jess."

"I'll go with you."

"You mean we'll do it together?"

"Soon as I get my rifle."

"I won't need it."

"How you know?"

"He's got no gun, I'm sure of it."

"He could get one, and anyway, all he'd have to do is holler and about eighteen brothers and in-laws and cousins would be there, and at least half of them have guns."

"If we bring a gun, Jess, I'll kill him."

"Maybe we better not."

We got in his car and rode up as far as the church, then got out and walked up the hollow to the end of the path, then followed the gully up to Moke's shack. Nobody was in it, and except for some beans in one corner that didn't prove much, there was no way to tell if anybody had been there for the last two or three days, or had just stepped out and would be right back, or was up the hollow or down the creek. But while we were whispering about it he held up his hand and I looked. Through a cornfield, just below us, a boy was moving on tiptoe, toward the woods on the other side of the gully.

"You know him, Jess?"

"Birdie Blue. He's Moke's cousin."

"He's gone to tip him."

"Then he'll be back, to keep watch."

"If we time him, we'll know how far he went."

He took out his watch, and we waited and I kept an eye on him, and the more I saw of him the better I liked him. He didn't talk, but kept staring at the place the boy had to cross on his way back, and he had that mountain look in his eye that said if it took a week he'd still be staring, but he'd do what he came for. In a half hour the boy showed, and then all of a sudden Wash got up.

"We're a pair of boneheads, Jess."

"What we done now?"

"The banjo's gone!"

"Well?"

"If he was in hell waiting to be fried he'd still have to pick the damned thing. Come on."

There was no window in the back of the shack, but there was a loose log, and we pushed it out and crawled through. Then we crept up the gully, keeping the shack between us and the boy, where he was squatting in the bushes, keeping watch on my hat, that we left in the doorway to keep him interested. It was around sun-down, and the mosquitoes were beginning to get lively, but we kept from batting them somehow, and pretty soon we came to a place where Wash stopped and looked around, and whispered if there was any sounds in the neighborhood, we'd catch most of them here, because sound travels upward. And sure enough, there were all sorts of things you could hear, from the creek going over the stones near the church to people talking in cabins and birds warbling before going to sleep. And then he grabbed my arm, and we listened, and there was the sound of the banjo. He stood up, and turned first one way, then the other way, then covered one ear, then the other ear, and in a minute he knew where it was coming from, and we crept over there. And when we got there it was a little stone well, with a frame over it and an iron wheel, and Moke was sitting on the rim, his head lopped over on one side, the banjo across his belly, plunking out sad chords that weren't like the comical tunes he used to play, and looking so little he was more like some kind of a shriveled-up, gray-haired boy than what he was, a man. Wash crept around the well from behind him, grabbed him by the shirt collar, and jerked him over on the side, so he let out a little whimper. "What you doing to me? Wash, what are you doing here?"

"Didn't the boy tell you I was here?"

"How would he know? He said Jess and a man."

"I'm taking you to Carbon City."

"What for?"

"Put you in jail. For what you did."

I stepped out then and told him to shut up with his bawling and told Wash to cut it short with his talk. Because you pass three cabins on the way down, and four more up the mountainside that you can't see but they see you, and if we ever gave them a chance to wake up to what was going on we might see something cutting the leaves. We hustled him down to the car and Wash drove and I sat on the outside. So when we got to my cabin, the table was set out under the trees with some candles on it and both Kady and Jane were looking down the creek to see what had become of us. Wash began talking to Kady. "Don't wait for us. We'll be back soon as we can after we get this thing booked, but don't let the stuff get cold waiting for us."

"Booked? What are you talking about?"

"Didn't he kidnap our boy?"

"He didn't mean any harm."

"It could have cost Danny his life."

"Wash, Moke is a friend of my mother's, and she's not well, and maybe she needs him. He's not any more than half-witted anyhow, no matter what he did, so why can't we forget it and go about our business instead of putting him in jail for the next five or ten years, where's he's not any good to anybody?"

"Maybe I'm not so half-witted as you think."

"Maybe a skunk don't stink."

It was me that said that, and then I told her there were some things that can't be forgotten, and that Moke was lucky we didn't shoot him, as that's what he had coming to him. But while I was talking she kept looking at me, and then she said: "Jess, you've had plenty to say since I've been living here about things that had to be fought if they were wrong and they were in you, and all I've got to say is that remembering things long after they do you any harm is another thing that people might fight a little bit, specially if they live up the creeks in this part of the country, and got the habit of remembering things long after anybody could remember what they were trying to remember."

"Do we take him in, Jess?"

"Let's go."

He had cut his motor, but now he started it again, and she stood aside. "All right, Wash, but you're taking a lot of trouble for nothing."

"You think it's for nothing?"

"He's not yet your child."

"He will be tomorrow."

"I'm not talking about what he will be. I'm talking about what he is, and what he was when he was taken. If they ask me, I'll tell them I've got nothing to say, and if the mother won't sign the writ, that ends it, unless of course the child has a father."

"Kady, why are you standing up for Moke?"

"Jess, are you crazy? Who's standing up for Moke? I'm standing up for myself, and for my little boy that nobody else is thinking about that I can see. Do you think I want this in the papers, and then have it come out that Danny is what they call a love child, and God knows what else they would think up to put in?"

"It's not any piece for the papers."

"A *kidnapping?*"

She stepped up to the window and talked straight at Wash. "Haven't you done enough to me without this, and for no reason except to give a simple-looking imitation of a West Virginia bad man?"

"I'm turning him over to the law."

"You can't even do that, right."

"So you know a better way?"

"You're turning him over to Carbon County when the crime was committed in Blount? Gee, but you're smart, aren't you? Gee, but you're going to look wonderful when you get to Carbon City with him and they say, sorry, son, you're in the right church but the wrong pew. Gee—"

"Suppose you shut up."

For a minute, steel had been facing steel, but now they weren't anything but a pair of kids jawing at each other, and next thing they were laughing and he got out and she said he was so dumb it was pitiful but there was no steam in it and the fight was over. So I got out and told Moke to get out of there and get quick. So he got out and started up the creek. So Wash, he ran after him and gave him a kick that knocked him over on his face. So he got up and began to cuss out Wash, mean, whispering cusswords, all covered with spit. That was when Kady walked over and slapped his face, and told him he'd got off pretty lucky. He stood there panting, and once or twice he stared to say something, and didn't. But when Jane got his banjo, where it had been pitched in the car, he went.

But there was one thing that could make us all feel good, no matter what had been said, and that was Danny. When Jane brought him out for a little whiff of air before tucking him in for the night, we were laughing and talking to him and me and Wash were taking turns holding him. And then without anybody knowing he was going to do it, he turned to Wash and stead of the goo-goo stuff he'd been saying, he said "Wash," and laughed. It was the first word he ever said, and it made us all so happy we didn't look at each other at all, and Kady picked him up and held him close, and pretty soon he said it again, like he was pretty proud of himself. And then we heard a car, and down the road I see the white tow car from the filling station on the state road that the fellow uses now and then to haul passengers up the creek for fifty cents. And it stopped and somebody got out and it went away and we all stood there trying to see who was coming up the path, a little satchel in her hand. And then I could feel my heart sink, because that funny walk, go three steps fast and then shuffle one, couldn't be but one person. That was Belle.

"Jess, what *is* she doing here?"

"It's got me buffaloed."

When supper was over, Kady and Wash went for a ride, and when Belle went to bed, Jane and I took a walk down the creek. Once Belle got there the party was ruined, because the half dirty Morgan jokes started right away, and the way she dressed made you feel the place had turned into a joint. I don't know what she did to clothes, but soon as she got them on they weren't clean any more, and they let you see more than you wanted to see. All she would take for supper was milk, and she kept explaining she had had to see Danny before Wash and Kady went away, though when they were going away, if they were going away, was something that nobody but her seemed to know about. And how much attention she paid to Danny, now at last she could see him once more, was about one look and a wave of the hand. In between, she seemed to be thinking about something, and even the dirty jokes didn't get the pounding she generally gave them. Belle always told a joke three times, once to tell it, once to tell it over again because maybe you didn't understand it, and once to holler and whoop at how funny it was. So when Jane fixed her a place to sleep in the front room, and she said she wanted to turn in, nobody put up any argument. Wash was staying at the Black Diamond Hotel in Carbon City, but he and Kady wanted to talk how they would get married, so they went off in his car, and Jane and I took our walk, trying to figure out Belle. "She's quite a lot thinner, Jane, and don't look like a fat little wood pigeon any more, but at that she don't look so bad, considering it's eighteen years since she went away."

"At night she don't."

"Of course candle light is not like sun."

"It's not the light, it's the fever. In the evening, when she's running over two degrees, her eyes are bright and her cheeks are red and she really looks pretty. But in the morning, when she's running below normal, she looks awful. Her face is gray, she coughs all the time, and her eyes have that look they get, like they see something far off."

"All this is the consumption?"

"She's got it, bad."

"I'm sorry."

"But what's she doing here?"

"If you ask me, it's got nothing to do with us, and nothing to do with Danny. Any time you try to figure Belle out, you can begin with Moke and go on from there."

"I don't think so."

"She's changed, then."

"She and Moke haven't got along since Danny came. Until then she didn't pay any attention to what Kady and I thought about him, and they got along all right. But soon as Danny came they started to fight, and there's more to it than they ever let on to anybody but themselves."

"Like what?"

"I don't know."

How long it had gone on I don't know, but it seemed that all my life I had heard it, this voice out there in the night, calling my name and beating on the door of the cabin. I wasn't in the cabin. I was in the stable, asleep in the bunk I used there, so by the time I got outside, Kady was already coming around from the back door. She lit the carbide lamp we had used in the mine, and when the light cut the darkness, there was Moke, whimpering and wailing and slobbering at the mouth. "Kady, I swear to God I never knew she was nowhere near here. I never even knew it was her till I threw her off me, where she was trying to kill me, and lit a match and seen the blood."

"What blood?"

"From her mouth! It's pouring out."

"You know what to do with her when she gets taken like that. Did you do it, or are you scared so bad you forgot everything?"

"I left her lay, right on the floor of my shack, just like I'm supposed to do, and come on down here for help. I run all the way. But she's never had nothing like this before."

"It's her lung, Jess."

"I know. I'll get a doctor."

"No, the first thing is to run me up there to his shack or as close as we can get to it. Then you run into Carbon City for a doctor, and the best way is to wake up Wash and have him bring the hotel doctor. But leave that part to him. You get back here right away with the main thing, which is ice, to pack her side in, so it chills the blood, and makes a clot inside, to stop that bleeding. Lots of it. Cracked ice if you can get it, but any kind of ice right away is better than waiting around for them to crack it up for you."

We got moving fast, then. She went inside, put on a coat, and went through Belle's bag for all the medicine that was in it. I went back to where Jane had been listening at the window, and told her she was to stay there with Danny no matter how long we were gone. Then I had her help me move Kady's bed on the truck, with sheets and all like it was, because in that shack was nothing but a dirt floor, and even if we weren't allowed to move her she had to have something to lay on. By then Kady was ready and got in and Moke got in. But all that time I had been thinking about what he had said, and the more I thought about it the more it didn't make any sense. "What's that you said about her trying to kill you?"

"You deef and can't hear me?"

"I asked you something."

"She crept in there while I was asleep. I don't know where she came from. First thing I knew somebody was slashing at me with a knife."

"I don't see any cuts on you."

"You will on the dog."

"What dog?"

"Birdie Blue's puppydog, that was out when I got home, and that I brung in for company. He was laying close to me, where I was sleeping on the gunny sacks, and he took the first stab and maybe some more. She stabbed like a wild woman, and when she felt the knife go in she thought she had me till I wrestled her off and the blood begun coming out of her mouth."

"Why did she do this?"

"I don't know."

"Come on, don't lie to me."

"Suppose you ask her."

There was no asking her anything, though, by the time we got there. By putting one side of the truck on the path and letting the other side bump, I got pretty close to the shack, and she was still laying on the floor, but two or three people from the hollow were there by that time with lanterns, and they were trying to get her up and move her. So the way Kady explained it to me, that was the worst thing in the world, so we stopped it and had those people carry the bed up, and the door was too small for it, but they began putting it up outside, and used the loose log, the one Wash and I had pushed out of the way, to wedge it up level. Then Kady rolled up a sheet to the middle, and laid it down beside Belle, and shoved the rolled part under her, then unrolled it, and we all helped lift and at last she was off the floor and on a bed. But the blood that was in a puddle on the other side of her, and the dead dog that was laying in the middle of it, you could see all that, and the blood began to run in a stream toward the door, and stunk, and it was a mess. So I told one of those people to take the dog out and bury it, and get started washing out the blood, but Kady said quit worrying about that, and get started after the ice. So I burned the road to the hotel, and called Wash, and told him to get a doctor out there, and told the man on the desk I wanted some ice, and be quick about it, so he hopped pretty lively. Because the last thing I did when I left the cabin on the way to the hollow was to strap on my .45 that hung across from my rifle, and there's nothing like having a six-shooter on you to get action when you want it.

The rest of the night was like a whirl-around dream you have when you're sick, with the doctor giving her some kind of stuff to inhale, and Kady tearing up sheets to make bags for the ice, and more and more people from the hollow standing around, watching what was going on and giving help whenever it was wanted. What they had heard when Belle and Moke were having it there in the dark, before he came to my place, if they heard anything at all, I don't know, but by the time Wash got there with the doctor the dog was gone and the knife was gone and nothing was said about anybody trying some killing. All the doctor saw was a woman bleeding from lung trouble, and so far as what was said to him went, that's all there was. Around daylight he got the bleeding stopped, and went home, but before he went he called Kady off to one side, and Wash and I drifted over to hear what he said to her.

"You're Mrs. Tyler's daughter, miss?"

"Yes, I am."

"You know what this means?"

"You think she's pretty sick?"

"If I had her in the hospital, where I could force-feed her with what she needs, sock a couple of quarts of blood into her, and then when she's in shape, collapse that lung for her, I might pull her through for a few more months, or even years. But I can't do it here, and by the time I got her to town she'd be dead. She's on the end of the plank. It could come any time now, but she'll probably last until tonight. Her mouth temperature is down to 97, and I can't get it up on account of the ice that has to stay there. It'll slip to 96, and then it'll take a sudden drop. With that she'll go in the coma, and then it's just a matter of when."

"We've more or less expected it."

"Call me, and I'll sign the papers."

"I'll do it from the filling station on the state road."

She was looking up at the trees, and was waxy color from losing the blood, but Kady had combed her hair out nice and put a ribbon in it, and just for a minute, with the sun coming up and the birds starting to sing, she looked like she had when I first saw her, in church one night, just after her father moved to town to work in the mine. She was looking up then too, and singing *Stand Up, Stand Up for Jesus,* and I kept looking at her, and next thing I knew she was looking at me, and winking. We got married the next month, she fourteen, I four years older, just the regular age for a coal camp. It seemed funny, after all that had happened, she was still only thirty-nine years old. After a while she put out her hand and took mine, where I was sitting near by. "Jess, I'm going to die."

"We're doing all we can."

"I know, but I'm going to die."

"I'm awful sorry, Belle."

"I'm not. I made a mess of my life, Jess."

"You lived it like you wanted it."

"I lived it like I liked it, but not like I wanted it. We could have been happy, you and me, because we loved each other, and that's enough. But I was born to mess things up, and I began to hold things against you. That you went to church, and believed what you heard there, and took things serious, and never took a drink. I thought that was all a pack of foolishness, and after I got the taste for liquor I couldn't hardly stand you at all. And I began doing things. I did a lot more than I ever told you, Jess. And then I started up with Moke. Ten of him wasn't worth what you was, and I knew it, but I couldn't help how I was going. He sung comical songs at me, and we'd meet by the creek and drink applejack, and when I'd come home I'd be so I could hardly stand up, and have to pretend I was sick after I chewed sassafras root so you wouldn't smell my breath. And then I went off with him."

"If he made you happy, I'm glad."

"He didn't."

"More than you think, maybe."

"Maybe worse than I could have imagined."

She closed her eyes, and I thought there would be more, and at last I would know what she had come up here for, and why she had tried to kill Moke, and why he had stolen Danny, and all the rest of what had been going on the last few days that I didn't understand. But she just asked if she could see Danny and I ran down in the truck to the cabin, and as soon as Jane could get him ready we brought him up. She looked at him a long time, and talked to him, and took his hand and played with it. All that time I was holding him. I liked that better than anything I had ever had in my life, and she must have seen it because she said: "You love him, don't you, Jess?"

"Love's no word for it."

"I want you to."

She began to cough then, and sank back on the pillow, and Kady came up in case there was trouble. But what I noticed was Moke, sitting there in the door of the shack, looking at me with such hate in his eyes I don't think I ever saw in a man before.

She called for the girls and said good-by to them, and when she talked to Kady she ran her fingers over her face, and looked up at her with an expression that hit me in the throat somewhere, because it was beautiful, and I was glad, because maybe you could understand why things had come between, but they were her daughters, and now she was going, both sides should feel some love.

And then she called for Moke, and he never even raised his head. "Moke, I want to talk to you."

"I got nothing to say to you."

"Moke, I'm dying."

"Then die."

"Moke, I've loved you, and there's something I've got to ask of you, and it's my right to do it, and you've got to listen to me."

"I won't."

"Then, Moke, will you sing to me once?"

To that he didn't say anything for a minute, then he came over to her and put his head on her shoulder and let her pat him and whisper in her ear. And if he sang to her I don't know. The last I saw of them, they were together up there, and I ran down to the cabin and watched Danny with Jane while he had his nap. Then Birdie Blue rode up on a mule, and told us Kady sent word to phone the doctor.

8

It was late afternoon when I got to Tulip with the doctor, and Kady was there at the church, and she and I waited while he went up to certify the death or whatever it is they do. In a minute a wagon came up the creek with two men in it, and they had a tool chest from the old drift mouth of the mine. They went on up to a cabin, and pretty soon here came the sound of hammering. "You hear that, Jess?"

"What are they up to?"

"They're making a casket."

"Who asked them to?"

"Moke I guess."

"What's he got to do with it?"

"He's burying her."

"Him and who else?"

"These women here, these relations of his, they've already got her washed, and soon as the doctor gets through they're going to lay her out."

"Funny they didn't speak to me about it."

"Is there any reason they should?"

"Before the law, she was my wife."

"Before God, she was his."

"He certainly didn't act much like it."

"They made up their quarrel, whatever it was about. He loved her, even if he is such a poor excuse for a man, and it seems to me you don't have to get up on your ear and be onry just because you don't like him."

"I loved her once."

"This is now."

Three boys came down the hill with bunches of laurel, for the funeral, and Kady took them inside the church and showed them where to put it. I knew them all, Lew Cass, Bobby Hunter, and Luke Blue, but I didn't pay any attention to it till later that not one of them spoke to me.

In the morning Mr. Rivers, that was doing the preaching, stopped by in his car to take us up to the church. Kady got in, and Jane got in with Danny, and I started to get in. "Hold on, Jess. Nothing was said about you."

"Does there have to be?"

"Well now I don't know."

"I don't need any special invitation."

I got in, and he sat there holding the wheel a minute or two, like he was thinking, then he drove on. In the clearing by the church were some cars and that's where he parked. The girls got out with the baby and we all started for the church. "Hold on, not so fast."

Ed Blue came out with three or four others, and they had rifles. "It's all right for Kady and Jane and the baby. But Jess, he stays out."

"Who says so?"

"Moke."

Kady and Jane looked at each other, and after a while Kady said: "Jess, I think it's awful of him, and if I could I'd leave with you, right now. But it's my mother. I can't just turn my back on her."

"That how you feel, Jane?"

"Yes, Jess."

"Then there's nothing I can do but go, but you're not taking

Danny in there. That runt stole him once, and maybe he takes some other fool notion now. I'm taking him home."

"Maybe you better."

When I got back to the house with him, walking, Wash was there, in his car, reading the morning paper.

"Funeral too much for him hey?"

"It wasn't him, it was me."

When he heard what had happened, he cussed and raved and said we should each take a gun and go up there and clean the place out.

"We can't do it, Wash."

"Why not?"

"In the first place, it's a funeral, and it's entitled not to be busted up by any shooting. And in the second place, if I start anything like that, I got to leave Danny, and they'll find some way to get back at me by getting back on him."

"I'd forgot about that."

He marched up and down by the creek, snapping his fingers, and then pretty soon he went in the cabin and came out with my rifle.

"Don't worry, I won't do any more than I have to. But we still got that little lookout back of his cabin, that I can get to up through the woods without being seen, and when he gets back from the church we're going to start right where we left off. I'm going to throw down on him, and he's coming with me, and he's going right off to jail, where he was headed before. What he's forgot is that he's still the kidnapper of my boy, and if Blount's where I've got to take him, I got all day, and not any stuff about Danny not having a name is going to stop me this time. He'll have a name in plenty time for the grand jury to do their stuff."

And he went up the path through the woods. But when he came back he was alone.

"Jess, you remember why we picked that spot?"

"So we could hear."

"And I heard everything. I could hear every word the preacher said, and the hymns they sung, and somebody crying.

And then, when I crept out to the bank of the gully and looked down, I could see them all. They came out of the church, six men, carrying a little gray casket."

"Made from a tool chest they stole."

'That's just about it. They had taken two pieces of rope, and stapled them along each side, so they had handholds. They carried it to the graveyard back of the church, and there they had some more preaching. Then they lowered it with two other pieces of rope into the grave. Then it broke up. And then I got my gun ready, because here came Moke, up the gully to his shack, alone. But Kady called him, and came running up to say good-by. He didn't pay much attention to her, and said he had heard she was going to get married, and he'd see her at the wedding. And she said she had decided to get married in town, in Carbon City, the first I had heard of it."

"First I heard of it too."

"She had wanted it in that little church."

"Until they kicked me out."

"That's probably it. So he said all right, he'd come to the cabin, and ride in to the church with her. She said there might not be room. He said he'd go in on the bus. And then, Jess, do you know what she said?"

"I'm listening."

"She said, 'Moke, at my wedding I only want friends, though I've tried to treat you as decent as I know how on account of my mother. And if you show up, I'm going to ask Jess to do to you exactly what you did to him. Keep you out, if he's got to take a rifle to do it. Good-by and good luck, but from now on, you keep out of my life.' "

"What did he say to that?"

"What could he say?"

"He took it?"

"He turned around and went in his shack. And Jess, maybe you think I'm a yellow quitting dog, but that satisfies me if it does you."

"It satisfies me."

"Then to hell with him."

"Like she said, let's kick him out of our life."

We shook hands, and he ran in to hang up the rifle again, before the girls got back and Kady found out what he'd been up to.

"Jess, are you happy?"

"For the first time in my life."

"Me too, I just can't believe it. Is it wrong to feel like that, the very same night you buried your mother?"

"Why would it be?"

"Maybe this is how it should be, Jess. That one part of my life should begin just when the other part ends. Because if there's one part of me I've got to fight, like you always told me, it's no trouble to figure out where it came from. And that part we just buried. And tomorrow, I start a new life. With the other part of me. And it's no trouble to figure out where that came from, either. You gave in a little bit, Jess. But no more than you had to, to keep me home, and out of the devilment I was sliding into. On the big things, you fought it out, and made me fight it out. If I'm beholden to anybody for anything, it's to you for that, Jess. I'll always be."

She put her hand in mine, with the moon hanging over the woods and making the creek look like silver. "I love you, Kady."

"And I love you, Jess. And I'm so proud of you."

"I hate it that you're going, but I'm glad."

"I've cost you money, Jess."

"No, you haven't."

"That still and all."

"That still, so far as I'm concerned, it's not even up there. We took in some money, a lot more than we spent. I blew out a lot of stumps, to put more corn in, and they were on my own land, and now I've got the new clearing, and I can grow more on it. I can put in more stock any time I want, and I got the cash to buy it. So stop talking about costing me money, or saying any more about it. We broke the law, but nobody's the worse off, and it all worked in together to bring us both a whole lot more happiness than we were ever going to have if we'd never met up and did like we did."

"You like Wash?"

"He's a fine boy."

"You coming to see us?"

"Any time I'm asked."

"You will be, because he loves you."

"I want Jane with us."

"Me too."

We went to the window and called, and Jane slipped on a dress and came out, and that was the first it came to us there was no more home in Blount, now that Belle had died and Moke had left it. And then we decided that Jane should move in and live with me, and that made it wonderful. "And specially with me here, because you can have Kady lend us Danny now and then, when she's going up to Philadelphia to visit her rich friends, and I can take care of him and you can teach him how to ride."

She was laughing at me, but I wouldn't have it that way. "It's not on account of Danny at all. It's on account of you, Jane. On account of both of us. We'll be happy."

"But we'll have Danny, sometimes."

"Then all right."

Kady got to laughing by then, and we all started laughing, and then we all got some Coca-Cola and drank it, and held hands.

"And I'm glad of one thing."

"What's that, Kady?"

"That I'm not going to be married in that church up there, where we held the funeral today. That's what I'm trying to get away from. The one I picked out, the Methodist Church in Carbon, is pretty. It's gray stone, with a square tower in front, and it's what I'm going to."

"That's right."

"And I've ordered flowers."

"What kind?"

Jane was so excited we were going to have regular flowers from a florist she had a flutter in her eyes. And when Kady told us how they were going to put lilies and things all around inside, I was glad too, and it seemed to me that was really the right place for her to go, and it was all going to turn out wonderful.

9

I was up before dawn, and got all my feeding and milking and cleaning done, and put on my best suit, and we had our breakfast. Then I took a rest while they worked, because they had to get Danny ready and get dressed themselves. Then women began dropping by from all up and down the creek, and they had to have it explained to them all over again, how Wash would come out around noon and take the girls and Danny in, while I would follow along in the truck, so I could take Jane back, while Kady and Wash would go over to the hotel with Danny and change into other clothes, so they could drive off some place. So then there was a lot of talk about the flowers Wash was going to bring, and I had never worn one in my life, but I thought for Kady's wedding I would put one in my buttonhole. So I knew where some wild roses were, down the creek a way, at the edge of a piece of woods, and started down there. But I didn't more than get started when up on the mountainside I saw something move. Now so far as I was concerned, that still up there I knew nothing about, had never seen, and never heard of. But that was so far as I was concerned. So far as an officer was concerned maybe I was the fellow that lived closest to it. Or maybe I had left something up there and forgotten about it.

Or maybe when I talked to him I'd have got a funny look on my face. I had to know who it was, because there was no regular business anybody could have up there, fifteen feet from the shaft mouth, but nowhere near anything else.

I crossed the creek on some stones, kept under the cliff so I couldn't be seen, and hit the path that led up to the timbered drift, the one we had used to roll our stuff into after we hauled it up on a block and falls from the road. About a hundred feet inside was a tool chest where I kept extra lamps, water, carbide, canned beans, and some dynamite, in case I had to shoot the tunnel down and get out quick through the shaft. It was the first I had been there since Jane came with Danny, and already I hated it that I had ever had anything to do with the liquor. Because the mash I had left fermenting was so high it turned your stomach to smell it, and the rats that had come in for our grain almost knocked me down jumping off the bins to get out of my way. You don't kill rats in a mine, because if something's going to happen they know it before God knows it, and the way they run out with men right on their tail, they're called the miner's best friend. Just the same, they turned my stomach worse than the smell.

I watched for a minute, but I didn't see anything so I started up the ladder, first putting out the light. Then I came down and took off my shoes. Then I went up again, and when I got to the top I raised my head easy, because if a deputy marshal would have me covered, or what would be there, I didn't exactly know. But it was no officer. It was Moke, and across his knees was the same Winchester Ed Blue had thrown on me the day before, when he wouldn't let me in the church. And where he was sitting was the one spot on the mountainside where he could cover a sharp bend in the road, where I'd have to come almost to a stop, on my way in to the wedding. I held my breath, because if he ever saw me I'd never make it down the ladder before he stepped over and plugged me. And then my heart stopped beating, and I almost fell down the shaft. Because it was hot, and he had taken off the jumper of his denims, so he was bare from the waist up. And I could see why Belle had fought with him over Danny, why he had kidnapped the boy, why he hated Wash, and all the rest of it, or thought I could.

By his navel was the butterfly.

When I got back to the cabin both girls were up the road with Danny, saying good-by to a woman that lived up the creek. Jane had on a dress, but Kady had on nothing but shoes and stockings and pants, with nothing over them but a blue checked apron she had slipped on to go out in. I waited while the woman, that was named Liza Minden, told it how she had known all the Blounts before Wash's father had owned a mine or anything, and how they were wonderful people, and Kady was going to like them fine. And the more she went on, the crazier I got. I took down my rifle and loaded it, and waited some more. Then I went to the window—and leveled it, and drew a bead on her. I meant to shoot her through the heart for what she was, a rotten little slut that would even go to bed with her own father if he would let her, and that had already gone to bed with her mother's lover, and was getting ready to marry a boy that was no more relation to the child she said was his than a possum was. But when I sighted the gun I couldn't pull the trigger. I went outside, so I wouldn't see her any more, and my feet lifted high off the ground when I walked, like I had just been hung and was dancing on air.

"Jess, you're crazy."

"No, I'm not."

"Everybody's got birthmarks."

"Wash, if the birthmark was all, I might not pay any attention to it either. But it's not. Ever since Jane got here and found the boy in his shack, I've been trying to figure out why he kidnapped him, and so have you and so has everybody. Ever since Belle came in that night, I've been trying to figure out what she was doing there, and since she tried to kill Moke, I've been trying to figure out why. So have you, so has Jane, so has everybody. All right, now we know. He kidnapped Danny because Danny's his child, and he knew it from the birthmark and so did Belle, and so did Kady. But Jane got him back, and then Kady had the chance to marry you, if she could ever keep it dark about this other thing. But Belle knew Moke better than anybody else knew him. She knew if it was the last chance he had, Moke would spill it. And she didn't have much longer to live anyhow, so she came up here to stop him, the only way she knew. And what the hell do you mean, everybody has birthmarks? How could a baby and a man have a birthmark like that and it not mean anything?"

He was sitting on the edge of the bed in his hotel room, all dressed for the wedding except for his coat, that was on the back of a chair with a carnation in the buttonhole, and two boxes of flowers in the same chair. He lit a cigarette and smoked a long time. Then he said: "Listen, Jess, it just can't be true. In the first place she's not that kind of a girl. And if she was that kind of a girl, she couldn't be that kind of a girl with Moke. And he's old enough to be her father. He's almost as old as you are, Jess."

"He's thirty-nine."

"Then she couldn't fool around with him."

"Yes, she could."

"Jess, I say she couldn't."

He snapped that at me with a killer light in his eye, and I don't know what kind of a look I had in my eye when I slung it back at him, but it must have said something, because he staggered back against the wall and said, "Jesus Christ."

"You think I'm just fooling?"

He lit another cigarette and thought a while, and said: "Then I've got to kill him, Jess."

"That I won't let you do."

"I wasn't asking you."

"You don't know where he is and I won't tell you and even if you did know you couldn't get to him without a guide. And by the time you find one, if you can find one, he'll be dead, because I'm going to kill him on my way back."

"She's the mother of my—"

He broke off and looked at me, and I think it was the first

time he got it through his head, the meaning of what I had told him.

"I really got nothing to do with it, have I?"

"Not a thing in this world."

"Unless—"

"You killed *her,* is that it?"

He didn't answer me. He just went and looked out the window, but that was what he had started to say. "Well, Wash, I tried it, but I couldn't."

"I could."

"Him, that'll be different."

There came a ring on his buzzer and he opened the door. It was his father and mother. His father was tall, like he was, with gray hair and a brown, sunburned face. But his mother was pink and pretty and sweet, and went over to him and kissed him and asked if the bride was here, and where was the baby, and lots more stuff like that. He said who I was, and both of them shook hands, and said they had hoped I'd be able to get to the wedding.

"There won't be any wedding, Mom."

"*What?*"

"Sorry you took the trip for nothing. Now we're going home."

10

When I got near the bend I stopped, hid the truck back of the old filling station, got the rifle out, and crossed the creek on the pillars of the old bridge. I kept on up on the other side, keeping under the cliff and out of sight from above till I came to the path. Then I crept up the mountainside without making any noise at all. When I came to the drift I went in, opened the tool chest, refilled the lamp, lit it, and set it down. I cut off about six feet of fuse, rolled it up, and stuck it in my pocket. I put a box of caps in there with it. I stuck a couple of sticks of dynamite in my pocket on the other side. Then I went on in. When I came to the shaft I laid out powder, fuse, and caps on a scaffold, and put my shoes beside them, tied to a scantling against rats. Then I picked up the rifle and started up the ladder. When I lifted my head out he had moved, with the sun, about six feet away from where he had been before, but that put him facing me more, and made it better. He was eating beans out of a can with his knife, and I let him finish them up before I raised my gun. I drew my bead right on the butterfly. He doubled up when I pulled the trigger, and held on to his stomach, and kicked like a cat trying to shake papers off its feet, and drew his breath in and out fast like a dog in the summer time, except instead of heat that made him do that, it was pain. That suited me fine. I stepped out, picked up his rifle from where he had set it down to eat, and sat down to watch him twitch.

"You dirty son of a bitch."

"Hello, Moke."

"God, that would be like you, Jess, to shoot me in the belly and then go on and leave me here to die."

"Oh, I wouldn't go off and leave you, if that's all that's worrying you. There's buzzards up there, and I couldn't have them flying around to tip anybody off."

"Couldn't you shoot me through the heart?"

"I shoot you where you got it coming."

"What the hell are you talking about?"

"I let you off once, because I thought neither you nor the woman was worth it. But now you went too far, and I got to tach you to lay off my daughter."

"Your *what?*"

"You heard me."

"Say, that's a joke."

"I shot you in the butterfly. That's what little Danny's got, isn't it? Isn't that what you did for your country? Leave a poor little kid that's birthmarked like you? Well, you don't do it with my daughter and live to tell about it."

"Kady never done nothing with me."

"I'll attend to her, later."

"You going to attend to Danny?"

"I'll take care of him, anyway."

"You like Danny, don't you?"

"That's none of your damned business."

"The hell it's not. Yeah, you'll attend to Kady. You'll hit her with a harness trace, and put her out, and act just like you always acted, with that religion-crazy disposition you got. But you won't put Danny out, oh no. You'll keep him, and let Jane take care of him, because you're crazy about him. No matter what she done, he's yours. Kady's nothing but a woman, and you never knew how to treat one. But Danny, oh yes, I seen you with him up there yesterday, when Belle was dying. You never seen nothing as pretty as he is, did you? He's yours, no matter what Kady done. He's your grandchild, ain't he? Well now you get it, you rotten, belly-shooting, dumb son of a bitch. He's not yours. He's mine."

"What did you say?"

"That butterfly, yeah, we got a butterfly in my family. But only the men got it, see? If the child's a girl, it skips. It skips to the next boy. He's not your grandchild, Jess, *he's mine!*"

He raised up on one elbow to shove his face closer to mine, then fell back from the pain and held both hands over his stomach and drew his legs up tight over his hands. "Jesus Christ, stuff is coming out of me!"

"What's that you said?"

"Get a doctor, stuff is coming out with the blood!"

"Never mind the stuff! Talk!"

I got up and hauled off my foot and kicked him where he was holding his hands, but he began to scream and said he'd talk but to get him some water or he can't stand it any more. I climbed down the ladder, dipped up some cold spring water in the bucket, put on my shoes and came on back up. Sweat was on his face when I filled the cup and give it to him to drink. He took it in one hand, then began to puke.

"The stuff that's all over my hand, it stinks!"

"Here."

I held the cup and let him wash out his mouth and drink three or four cupfuls. Then I poured water over his belly to wash off the stuff and the blood and the bugs that had got in it. "Now spit it out, what I asked you, and spit quick."

"I told you all I'm telling you."

"That Danny's your grandson?"

"You're goddam right. We never knew it, Belle and I, for twenty years, that Kady was ours, until Danny came, and we seen the butterfly. Then we knew."

"So Belle two-timed me even before she left."

"The way you treated her why not?"

"I loved her. What more did she want?"

"Yeah, you loved her. If she'd go to church three times on Sunday and pray every night and look at your sour face all the rest of the time, you loved her. Well who she loved was me. Because she liked a good time. And me, I had a banjo."

"That was something, wasn't it?"

"To Belle it was. You bet she two-timed you."

He called for more water, and I gave him some, and he cussed me out, and began calling Kady every dirty name he could think of. "She hated Danny. She hated him because his father walked out on her, and she's been so proud and stuck-up she couldn't stand it she was just a girl like anybody else. But I loved him." And then, after a while: "Belle was going crazy from fear I would spill it to Kady whose child she really was, and if I did, she would hate Belle. So that was late afternoon, and Belle caught the bus, to come up here and kill me. If it had been morning she wouldn't have done it. The fever, it came on as the day wore on. It made her crazy. After she come in my shack that night, and I knew she was going to die, I thought I'd wait till that was over, and then come out with it. It was all I had to live for. Why should I keep my mouth shut? Why should I give a hoot how Kady felt? She never cared how *I* felt. But Belle knew what she could do with me. She got me to come over there, just before she died, after you left and Kady left and they took Danny away, and promise I'd never say anything to Kady about it. So that's what I done. I give up the one thing I wanted in life, to please a woman that was dying, and that I loved. But I made up my mind, if I had to give it up, you'd give it up too. You weren't going to be happy with something that was mine. So I got Ed Blue's gun, and I'd have killed you, Jess. That's the only thing I'm sorry for, that you got me first. But by Jesus Christ, I'm going to take it away from you, that one thing that you want. I never promised not to tell you, and now I'm letting you have it. There's not one drop of Tyler blood in Danny, and you've just been making a fool out of yourself to think there is. Come here, you samsinging bastard, and let me spit on you."

I put his jumper over his chest, crossed the arms over his back, and tied them up tight. Then I used them for a handle and began dragging him.

"Stop it! That hurts!"

"It won't, much longer."

"Where you taking me?"

"You'll see."

I drug him to the shaft, and when he saw what I was going to do he began to scream. I slung him in, and he screamed clear to the bottom, but stopped when he hit. I slung Mort's rifle in after him, and stepped back in case it would go off. When it didn't I picked up my own gun and climbed down. He was at the bottom, all crumpled up, beside the bricked-in fireplace of the still. I tied the jumper on him better, lit the lamp, and began dragging him along the tunnel. But when I came to the first of the old entries I turned off, and began dragging him over the jagged rock that had fallen down, and it was the hardest work I ever did in my life. But it felt good, too, to know he was dead, and I had killed him, and I was going to put him where he never would be found, and nobody would ever remember he had been on this earth. I drug him at least two hundred feet. Then there was a swag, and I threw him in. Then I climbed back to the timbered tunnel, went on back to the shaft, took a bucket, scraped up some dirt and put it in, poured in some water, and mixed up some mud. Then I took my fuse, caps, and dynamite, stuck them in my pocket, and went back to the swag with them. The first blister that was hanging down on the other side, between the swag and the worked-out part of the mine, I cut off half a stick of dynamite, made a mudcap against one of the hanging pieces, stuck the dynamite in with a cap in it and six inches of fuse. The blister between the swag and the timbered drift, I made another mudcap, with a foot of fuse. Then I went in, lit the short fuse, scrambled to the next one and lit it, and stepped around to the angle of the timbered tunnel to wait. Why I had done that, I wanted those shots not to fire at once, and then I could check that they both went off. Sure enough, here came the first one. Then I almost dropped dead, because I had forgot the rifle.

I ran to the shaft mouth, got it, and coming back I ran sidewise like a crab, the way you have to do in a low tunnel. Smoke was pouring out of the tunnel, but I crawled in there and gave the rifle a pitch. Before I got to the timbered drift the second shot went off, and blew me right up against the rib. Then I was glad I had had to make the second trip in, for the rifle. Because by going in there I had seen what I'd always have been worried about. That powder had blown down the top until the tunnel was blocked up solid with rock, both sides of Moke, so it would take a hundred men a month to get in there, even if they could ever guess what they were digging for. Mr. Moke Blue could just as well have been at the bottom of the sea, so far as anybody in this world could ever find him.

When I got to the creek I took the empty shell out of my gun, threw it in the water, and put a fresh one in the chamber. Then I cut a switch and peeled it, and rammed a piece of my handkerchief through the bore, to clean it, so it hadn't been fired since it was loaded. Then I went down and pitched it on the truck and started over to Blount, to tell Wash what Moke had told me. I was already halfway over there, before it came to me what it meant, if what he said was true.

She wasn't my daughter any more!

CHAPTER

11

I cut my lights, ran in behind the old filling station again, and hid the truck like I had before. I crept on up the road without making any noise, and the first thing I did was look in the barn and the stable, and all the stock was inside, but they weren't bellowing or anything, and that meant they'd all been fed and the cows milked. I crept on up to the house and peeped in the front room. I peeped in the back room and Jane was there, with Danny in her lap, but no sign of Kady. Pretty soon Danny began to cry, and when Jane bent over him and began to rock him I saw she was crying too. "Little baby, that's always been treated so bad! Ever since his first day on earth he's been put on and stolen and left all alone and kicked around. Don't cry, little boy. Don't you mind a bit, my little Danny. I'm here. I'll always be here, and I'll always love you no matter what your mother does or your father does or anybody does."

It made a lump come in my throat, but I went down to the truck and got in and drove to town. When I got near the White Horse I parked, and went to a window and looked in. She was there, like I knew she would be, dancing with a man I had never seen, and plenty drunk, by her looks. I rubbed my hands on my coat, to wipe off the sweat, and went inside. I didn't pay any attention to her. I went to a booth and sat down. When a waiter came I ordered a drink and when he brought it I took a sip. Pretty soon I could feel her standing beside me. "Well this is quite a surprise."

"Oh. Hello, Kady."

"What are you doing here, Jess?"

"Just having me a corn and Coca-Cola."

"Since when did you take a drink?"

"Sometimes you need it."

"When, for instance?"

"Like when you expect to give a girl away, at her wedding, and she runs out on you and leaves you holding the bag there at the church and don't even come around to tell you why, then you feel like you could drink quite a little."

"You were at the church?"

"If you were eloping, why couldn't you tell me?"

"I didn't elope."

"All right then, get married somewhere else."

"Does it look like I got married?"

I cut out the thick talk then and really looked at her, and made her sit down across the table from me, and ordered her a drink.

"Kady, we got our lines crossed somehow. I been sick all afternoon, that you would just go off and leave me after all we'd been to each other, but if you didn't get married, it don't square up with what I thought. What happened?"

"We'll begin with what happened to you."

"Nothing happened to me."

"You were to follow us in to town in the truck, and instead of that you just disappeared and I can't get it out of my head that you doing that has some connection with what happened to me."

"Didn't you see me wigwag?"

"I didn't see anything."

"I went down to get myself a flower to put in my buttonhole from the woods across the creek, and I slipped on a stone and got mud on my shoe. If it was some other time I'd have given

it a brush and a grease, but for your wedding I wanted a shine.
But when I got back to the house Liza Minden was there, and
I knew if she ever saw me I'd be an hour getting her to go, so
I went inside and went to the window, where I was behind her
and you could see me, and wigwagged at you I was going to
town now, instead of later."

"If you did, I didn't notice it."

"You were looking right at me, and nodded."

"Why did you take the gun?"

"Just in case."

"Case of what?"

"After what they did yesterday at the funeral how did I know
what they might try? It didn't cost anything to pitch the gun
on the truck, so I did. It's still there."

"... Did you see Wash?"

"It's like I told you. I went in to get a shine, and where I
got it was a barber shop. I had me a haircut too, and by then
it was getting on to one o'clock. I supposed he had started by
then, so I went on around to the church to wait for you and
him and Jane, when you got there. Nobody was there, but I
didn't think anything of it, and sat down. I waited quite a while
before I began to get worried. Then I went around to his hotel
and asked for him."

"When was that?"

"About two o'clock."

"What did they tell you?"

"That he'd left, with a lady and gentleman."

By her face, I knew that stead of not believing what I was
saying, she was believing it. I shut up then, and talked when
she talked to me, for fear I'd overplay it.

"You thought that was me?"

"I thought I wasn't good enough for you."

"It was his mother and father."

"I still don't know what happened."

"He just didn't come."

"Why not?"

"Do I know?"

427 ■

"He just walked out on you?"

"I know what happened. Of course I do. They talked it over one last time, his father and that awful mother he's got, and changed their minds once more."

"Hasn't he got a mind of his own?"

"He thinks she's wonderful."

We each drank our drink, and had a couple more, and she sat there with a sour little smile on her face, looking into her glass. "Funny life, isn't it, Jess?"

"Treats you funny all right."

"Who gives a damn?"

"I don't like to hear you cuss."

"Come on, let's dance."

"I never danced."

"I'll teach you."

But I didn't need much teaching, because all we did was stand in the middle of the floor in each other's arms and swing in time to the music and touch our faces together and sometimes walk around a little bit. She had a hot place around her mouth that crept out until her whole cheek felt like she had fever. I inched her along till we were next to the side door and then I lifted her so we were dancing on the parking lot outside and then instead of our cheeks rubbing it was our mouths.

"Jess, let's go to a hotel."

"I'd be afraid."

"What of?"

"We'd have to say we're man and wife."

"Well? You ashamed of me?"

"I hear if they suspicion you at all, like if the man's a lot older than the girl, they ask you for your certificate. And we haven't one."

"You're a funny guy, Jess."

"What's so funny about me?"

"You're the same old Sunday-go-to-meeting, that thinks we

all the time got to be fighting something, and yet you've got to pretend it's something else."

"No, I've changed."

"Your kisses have."

"And I have. Honest."

"And it's only that you're scared?"

"We don't have to be, though."

"How do we fix it that we're not?"

"We could get married."

She gave a whoop, and laughed so hard I thought she'd fall down and I'd have to carry her to the truck. "Jess, you ought to get drunk oftener, so it wouldn't do such funny things to you. They won't let us, don't you know that?"

"Why not? We could say, 'no relation.'"

"Not here, we couldn't. Everybody knows me, from the drinks I've served in this honky tonk. And they know you, from that trial we had, with a big bunch looking at you, and specially all the newspaper and courthouse people looking at you."

"All right, then, we'll go to Gilroy."

"Don't they make you tell a whole lot of stuff about who your father and mother were and where you were born and all that? Who would I say?"

"... Well, how about saying Moke?"

"*What?*"

For just that long she sobered up, while she looked at me with the kind of fire in her eye a cat gets in front of a light.

"Listen, Jess, I don't say I wouldn't do some crazy things to get you in my arms, because to me you look awful pretty. But don't ever ask me to say that, and don't you even think it. Do you hear me? It was bad enough, having him around my own mother, but having to say I was any part of him would be more than I could stand. I asked you, do you hear me?"

"I hear you."

"What you sulking about?"

"Nothing."

"Do you want me?"

"I'm crazy for you."

"Do you want me bad enough, that if I went down there and held your hand in front of some preacher, you would take me, and not have any more foolish talk about fighting things and hollering hallelujah for fear the devil's going to get you for it?"

"Yes, I do."

"Then couldn't I make up some names?"

Our mouths came together hot this time, and I thought my heart would pump out of my chest from knowing I wouldn't have to give her up any more and at last she was mine.

12

We stayed for two days in a little Gilroy hotel, and all that time I kept wondering what we were going to say when we got home. She must have been doing some thinking too, because on the way back she said:

"Jess, we're keeping this quiet."

"You mean that we're married?"

"All right, we got drunk and meant it for a joke and didn't know what we were doing anyway. At least, we can tell that to a judge if we ever have to, and maybe he'll believe us. But I don't know any way to tell it to Jane, and I love her."

"We going to see each other?"

"I'll have to think about that."

"I can't do without you."

"We'll see."

When we got home I acted like I'd been away looking for her all that time, and Jane was so glad to see her she didn't even think whether it sounded fishy or not. She kissed me, and was glad to see me all right, but all she thought about was Kady, and how good Kady was going to feel at the nice way she'd kept Danny, and she took Danny in her arms, and talked to him, and listened to him now he practiced up some more words he had learned, or thought he had learned, though what they were was more than I could figure out myself. But that night, after I'd finished up all the work Jane had been doing the two days I'd left everything to her, and had gone to bed in my bunk down in the stable, the door opened and there was Kady, in her nightgown.

"Jess?"

"Come in, Kady."

"I made out I couldn't sleep."

I flipped back the blanket for her to come in with me, but she shook her head and sat on the edge of the bunk looking out the window over my head. After a while she said:

"Jess, what am I going to do about Danny?"

"You could eat him. He's sweet enough."

"I don't want to be around him."

"You ought to make up your mind."

"It's not like it was before. I hated him then. Now I see how cute he is, and understand why you're so crazy about him, and Jane is, and—why I was, for a little while. But I can't help it. I've got something in me. Every time I look at him I see Wash, and I can't forget what Wash did to me. I don't want to be around him."

"He's not Wash."

"I know it. I'm so ashamed."

"He's just a sweet, friendly little boy that's laughing at you all the time and sticking out his hand to touch your face and showing you how good he can kick and you ought to be thankful all day long that you've got him."

"I ought to, but I'm not."

What she did about him was try to swallow down how she felt, and play with him, and help Jane take care of him, and drink. She told Jane it was Coca-Cola, but all the time she was spiking it with the stuff we had made, that was hidden all over the place, and when she had a load of it she'd get a look in her eye, and I would almost explode from wanting her. Every night she'd slip down to me, and bring me some stuff, and we'd drink it together, and there was no end to how much we wanted each other. But Jane would get worried, and go out looking for her, and once she almost caught us, and that meant we had to do something. "Jess, we've got to have a hide-out."

"Yeah, but where?"

"Have you forgotten our mine?"

Now the mine, after what I'd done with Moke, was about the last place on earth I wanted to be. "I thought we were done with all that stuff."

"What stuff? We don't have to run the still."

"It'll be there just the same."

"It doesn't have to be. I can take it down and put it away if that's all that's bothering you. But it's secret. It's like we used to say. Anything in the world could be happening up there and nobody would ever know."

"You used to say it."

"And you used to think it."

She would borrow the truck after that and pretend she was going to Carbon City for stuff that we needed, and maybe she did go, I don't know. But one of those times I had a look around, and found it parked in a place that could only mean she had gone up the mountain. And then one day she came out to where Jane and I were giving Danny his lunch with a basket on her arm. "Want to carry this for me, Jess, while I get some of those grapes up there in the woods, so we can have us some jelly?"

"You lost an arm or something?"

"It takes two hands for grapes."

"I never noticed it."

"First you got to find them, then you got to lift the vine up, where it hangs down over them, and then you got to cut the bunches off with a knife, so you don't mash them up trying to break them. And I want company. Wild grapes take a long time."

"Go along with her, Jess."

So we went, up the same old path, her a little ahead, humming a little, in between catching her breath. When we got to the timbered drift she went past it, then stopped.

"Would you like to see the little nook I've made in there?"

"Some other time, maybe."

"Not now? You sure?"

She half closed her eyes, and I don't know which was worse, the way my stomach was fluttering over Moke, or the way my heart was pounding over her.

"It'll only take a minute. Come on."

We went in, and got lamps out of the tool chest, and got as far as the entry where I'd buried Moke. "This old tunnel caved in since we were here, but that blocked the draft that used to blow through it, so of course that makes it a nice place to sit and pass the time."

In the tunnel mouth she had hung some candlewick quilts like they sell on the way to town, and had fixed a seat. "But of course we can't have carbide, not romantic people like us."

Near the seat was a galvanized iron can we had used for water, with holes knocked in the bottom, and she held her lamp to one of them. It began to burn inside, and I saw it was half full of charcoal. "And with that good old Tyler corn and Coca-Cola, I thought we might cook ourselves something to eat."

She lifted the cover of the basket, and inside was a picked chicken. By then I wouldn't have left there if Moke had come right through the rock at me, so while she chased outside to grab some grapes quick, I went to the shaft mouth to grab some Coca-Cola we always kept in the spring water, and some corn. I was trembling so bad I never noticed that all the smell was gone, where she had emptied all that mash out, and put things in apple-pie order. I came back with the bottles, then went to the tool chest for a miner's needle, that I cleaned in the fire and ran through the chicken. I was almost done broiling it, trying not to think of her, when I jumped at the sound of music.

It was the radio, and she came in swinging her hips, and red fire shining up in her face, and looking right straight at me. That was one dance she never finished.

13

One morning, couple of months after that, there came a rap on the door and when I went out there it was Ed Blue. He wanted to know if I had seen anything of his rifle. I had my own rifle in reach, and after all that had happened I wouldn't have asked much to tell him to get the hell out and stay out or I'd plug him where he stood. But I thought I better see what he was up to. Because I knew where his rifle was all right. But at the same time I knew why he didn't have it. The way things were between him and Moke, Moke wouldn't have taken his rifle without him knowing it. And the way things were between me and Moke, Ed couldn't have helped knowing what Moke figured to do with it, even if Moke had said nothing about it, which wouldn't be like Moke. So when he began talking, I thought he was pretending rifle, but he really meant Moke. But after a while I saw that it was really his rifle he was after, and as well as I could tell, he had thought about it since Moke left him, and put it together something like this: Moke hadn't killed me, so something must have gone wrong with it. I hadn't killed Moke, or so far as he knew I hadn't, so what had happened? He probably said to himself, I'd run into Moke and maybe run him off the creek. But if I had I certainly wasn't letting Moke keep the gun. So why not come around, ask me about it, and watch my eyes?

I told him nothing, and he went off with a lot of talk about how he's a peaceable man, and sure would hate it if somebody got hurt by a gun that belonged to him, and by ganny he hopes he don't get sued. What anybody would get out of it if he did get sued he didn't say. But a couple of nights later, when the girls had gone to a picture show and taken Danny with them, and I had taken a walk by the creek to think things over and figure out where I was at with my life if I was anywhere at all, I started back to the cabin, and from down the road a ways I saw a light inside. I crept up on it, and there in the front room, shooting the light all around, was Ed. After he finished looking there he went on back and shot the light at the girls' clothes and under the bed. I waited till he was doing the same in the lean-to before I tiptoed inside, took my six-shooter down, and threw on him from the doorway of the front room.

"Put 'em up, Ed."

He had no gun, and he was reaching before he even turned around. I went over and took the light from him so it wouldn't burn down the house. "Now you goddam lop-eared cross-eyed good-for-nothing rat, for the last time what are you doing in my place and what do you want?"

"Jess, I'm only looking for my gun."

"You think I steal guns?"

"No—no, Jess, it ain't that. It's just that after what happened that day, when I done what Moke made me do at the funeral, I thought maybe you'd come up there and tooken it, just to be safe. That's all, I hope Christ may kill me."

"I didn't. You got that?"

"I got it, Jess."

"If I shot, you know, if I said a man was back there in my house and I shot him because I was afraid he would kill me, the law would uphold me. You know that?"

"I sure do know it, Jess."

"Suppose I let you go?"

"Anything you say, Jess."

"Cut out your snooping around."

I never said anything to her about it. I never said anything to her or anybody that would lead around to Moke. But it made me nervous. So of course she thought I was nervous on account of her, and that was how she liked it so she could laugh at me and sit in my lap and tickle my chin and say stop being so solemn. And then one day we were up there, behind the quilt that kind of cut us off from the timbered tunnel, and had had some drinks and stuff she had brought to eat, and the music was turned down soft, and she was dancing in front of me with not a stitch on. And then, from the other side of the quilt, I heard something no miner could ever mistake. It was the whisper that comes out of a carbide lamp when the flame has been cut but the water is still making gas.

I motioned her to keep on like she was, and hit the quilt with everything I had. Something went down, but so did the quilt, and it fell over the brazier, so the place went so black you couldn't see your hand. I hit, and landed. I hit again, and got one back in the jaw. I hit again, and just touched a shirt going away. Then there were steps, shuffling down the track. Then she screamed, and all of a sudden the place was full of light, where she had tried to get the quilt off the brazier, and red coals were all over, and the quilt was burning, and so were her clothes, where she had dropped them on the seat. When we put out the fire with water the place was full of steam. "Jess, who was it?"

"I don't know."

"What did they want?"

"I don't know."

"You think they saw anything?"

"I don't know that either."

But in my heart I knew it was Ed Blue, still snooping around after his rifle. And sure enough, next morning, when I was out back chopping apples for the cider press, Jane came out of the house and went running to a big tree on the other side of the barn, grabbed a boy that was hiding there, and slapped his face. When she came back she was white, the only time I ever saw her get mad. "The idea, talking like that!"

"What did he say to you?"

"It was to Kady. Calling her pappy-lover."

Kady came out, and listened, and didn't look at her or me. All morning I could hear Jane going on about it, but if Kady said anything I didn't hear it. Then in the afternoon she came to me, where I was up on the press turning it down, and said: "Jess, I'm going away."

"You're—what?"

"Going away. To Washington maybe. Some place."

"You mean you're leaving me?"

"I'm leaving you, and I'm taking Jane and Danny."

"But why?"

"You heard what happened this morning, and you saw how Jane carried on about it. I can't have any more of that. Maybe I've gone to hell, Jess, but I won't have her finding it out, and if she stays one more day on this creek she will. Somebody saw us, and somebody's spreading it."

"Maybe I won't let you go."

"I wasn't asking you."

"Maybe you forgot you're my wife."

"For God's sake, be your age."

I climbed down there to tell her the truth, but her eyes were just two slits in her face, and she looked cold. It came to me it wouldn't do any good to tell her. She wouldn't believe me, and there was no way in the world I could prove it.

"We're leaving today."

"You're in quite a hurry."

"I'm taking them away on the six o'clock bus out of Carbon City, and I'll thank you to drive us in there."

"Then all right."

■ ■

Jane came to me just before we started, and she didn't have any idea what was going on, but she was unhappy about leaving me and tried to tell how much she thought of me. I felt that way too, and tried to figure some way I could keep on with Kady and square it up somehow with Jane. So I said maybe if I could sell the place I would go east myself, and she put her arms around me and said that would be wonderful. And whether I meant to take them to town I don't know, but I think I was going to have a breakdown on the state road, to stall it for one night, and in that time I might be able to think of something. But while we were still on the dirt road that runs beside the creek, we met a car coming up. It had two men in it, and when they saw us one of them raised his hand for me to stop.

"Are you Jess Tyler?"

"Who wants to know?"

"Sheriff's deputy."

He showed a badge and I said I wasn't saying who I was and if he wanted to know he had to find out some other way. "Well, there's a simple way to find out, Mr. Tyler. I just look at you and then I remember you from the time I made out papers on you once before. When you pretty near killed a man. Remember?"

"What do you want?"

"Serve a warrant for your arrest."

"What for?"

"Incest, this says."

"That's a lie."

"If it's a lie, then all you got to do is prove it to the court. My job is to serve papers. Is this your daughter Kady?"

"I told you, find out for yourself."

"Miss Tyler, I remember you too, and I have a court order here for your detention as a material witness. Now then, how shall we do about the truck? Mr. Tyler, do you want me to drive in to Carbon with you, or would you and your daughters prefer to ride with the other deputy while I take your truck wherever you want it or have you got some idea of your own?"

"My other daughter will drive it."

"Then we're set."

Kady and I got out and got in the other car and neither of us said anything to Jane at all. But out of the corner of my eye I could see her sitting there in the sun, the baby on her lap, staring at us.

14

When the deputy brought me to court, Jane was waiting, with Danny on her shoulder, trying to keep him quiet where he was crying because it was away past his bedtime. A whole bunch of people were there, because the Carbon City radio had put out about the arrest on the seven o'clock broadcast, and half the people in town came running over to the courthouse for the hearing. My case hadn't been called yet, and while I was standing in the hall with the deputy, Jane came running over. "How could you do this to her, Jess?"

The deputy cut in to remind her that anything that was said could be used against me, but she didn't pay any attention to him.

"You knew all along what it had done to her, Wash walking out like he did. You knew she was drinking. You knew she wasn't herself, that she'd do almost anything that anybody told her to. And yet you would take advantage of her in the way you did."

"You sure I did?"

"If you didn't, wouldn't she tell me? She don't lie to me. If she won't look at me and won't say anything to me, that means you did just what they say you did."

"There might be more to it than that."

The jail warden's wife came in about that time with Kady, and Jane left me and went over to her. A minute or two later Ed Blue came in, with every man, woman, and child from Tulip, and I knew what I was in for.

It was the same old judge and he watched us line up and asked the deputies a few things, like did I have a lawyer, and kept looking at me like I was some kind of a toad frog he was afraid would give him warts if he wasn't careful. Then he began talking to me: "Jess Tyler, you stand before me accused of the crime of incest, consisting of sexual misconduct with your daughter, Kady Tyler, and of corrupting the morals of a minor, Kady Tyler. How do you plead?"

"What's plead?"

"You plead when you enter a plea, declaring yourself guilty or not guilty. If you plead guilty, it will be my duty to set bail, and pending its deposit, to hold you for sentence by the circuit court. If you plead not guilty, or elect not to plead at this hearing, as you have the right to do, it will be my duty to hear the evidence against you, and if in my judgment, it is competent, material, and substantial, to hold you for action by the grand jury, set bail, and pending its deposit, to turn you over to the custody of the sheriff."

"And what do you do to her?"

"Your daughter is not under charges."

"She's arrested just the same."

"As a material witness, entitled to bail."

"What I'm getting at, it looks to me like if I plead guilty and you hold me, then you wouldn't need a witness any more and she could go home. But I'm not doing it without I make sure."

"Mr. Prosecutor?"

A young fellow standing with Ed Blue spoke up and said: "Your honor, the only charge made against this girl was a complaint sworn out by the sheriff's office which charges her with indecent exposure, but as it describes an act not committed in a public place it sets up no violation of the statute and I am accordingly quashing it. Otherwise, unless evidence not now known to me comes to light, if this man chooses to save the state the expense of a trial and avoid further scandal, he's quite right. On his plea of guilty I won't need the witness, and while the higher court may want to question her before passing sentence, I wouldn't ask this court to require bail. To clear up our general attitude in cases of this kind, though not in any way binding myself or entering into a bargain of any kind, we rarely ask commitment to reform school, or penological steps of any kind, for a girl who is at the same time the mother of a young child, unless circumstances exist which compel us to. Does that answer you, Tyler?"

"I please guilty."

"Then I set bail at five thousand dollars pending sentence. Are you prepared to furnish it tonight?"

"No sir, I'm not."

"Take him to jail. Next case."

The next case was a colored fellow that had been arrested for stealing a tire, and he was on the front bench of the courtroom, and stood up with a deputy. My deputy started off with me, but I heard the judge tell somebody to stand aside, and when I looked around Kady was still standing there. And then all of a sudden she looked up, stared the judge straight in the eye, and said: "He's not guilty of anything."

"Your father has already pleaded."

"My husband, you mean."

"*What?*"

"We got married."

"Officer, bring that man back."

The prosecutor, that had seemed like a nice young fellow, turned into a wolf, and he took at least an hour, snapping question after question at her, until he had it all, how we had gone to Gilroy that day and said in the marriage license bureau we had the same name but were no relation, that her father's name was Hiram Tyler and he was dead, and that she was twenty-two years old. The judge cut in with a lot of stuff he wanted to know about, and after a while the prosecutor said: "Your honor, this is as shocking a thing as I've encountered in all my experience at the bar. Occasional morals cases come up, but this is the first time I ever heard of where two people went before an officer of this state and deliberately made a mockery of it and its laws. I don't know where it leads to, but the very least I can ask of this court is to hold the girl for the action of the grand jury."

"So ordered."

She had plenty of back talk, and said I had done what I had done because I loved her, and things were due to happen between us anyway, and I wanted it in wedlock, like it should be, and didn't know it was against the law. Where she got was nowhere. The judge tore into her and the prosecutor did, but all the time I was thinking of what they would do to her for perjury, and how at last I had to tell the truth, even if she hated me for it and I never saw her again. "I'm changing that plea."

"And how about your new plea?"

"What new plea, your honor?"

"To the new charge, perjury."

"My plea to that charge and both the other charges is not guilty. This girl is not my daughter, but she is my wife, and what law we've been violating I'd like somebody to explain me."

"What do you mean she's not your daughter?"

"I mean what I say."

"Whose daughter is she then?"

"Man by the name of Moke Blue."

"That's a lie!"

It snapped out of her before she even knew she was going to say it, and right away she apologized for it.

"I'm sorry, Jess, to use that word. I take it back, but you'll have to take back what you said too. Even if it's to save me I can't bear to hear that."

"It's not a lie and I don't take it back."

"Who's Moke Blue?"

I told them who Moke was, how he had broken up my home, how he and Belle had gone off together, how it had all started about a year before Kady was born. I didn't have any of it learned by heart or anything. I didn't even know what I was going to say next. "And you knew Moke Blue was her father?"

"I knew I wasn't."

"But you raised her just the same?"

"I never saw her from the day my wife took her away with her till a year ago when she came with me to live."

"And you started sleeping with her?"

"I did not."

"When did you start?"

"After we were married."

"You lived with her all that time in the same house and did nothing to her at all and then all of a sudden you decided it was time to marry her. Why didn't you marry her before?"

"I was already married."

"So we've got a little bigamy here too?"

"My wife, my first wife, this wife's mother, died. The day after that I asked Kady to marry me. She said all right and we went to Gilroy."

"You had her misrepresent her age?"

"I'd forgotten her age."

"And misrepresent the name of her father?"

"After we were married, when she told me she had put down her father's name as Hiram Tyler, was the first I knew she really thought I was her father. I thought she knew about Moke."

"Didn't you tell her?"

"Then? I tried to, but I couldn't."

"Why not?"

"You heard her just now. Moke was a shiftless, no-account nothing, and if I told her the truth about him I thought she'd hate me for it and I loved her and didn't want her to."

"Where is this Moke Blue?"

"I don't know."

The judge and the prosecutor looked at each other, and then

the judge said to Kady: "Young woman, do you believe any of this?"

She didn't answer, and he asked who Jane was and asked the same thing of her. She didn't answer, either. "Is there any neighbor of this man, who knew him and his wife at the time they were living together, who will testify he believes it, or had any knowledge of it at the time?"

Nobody said anything. I said Moke had the same butterfly on his stomach that Danny had, that only the men in his family were born with it, and that Kady didn't have it but the boy did, and they didn't even bother to wake Danny up to look, where he was stretched out on the desk, with Jane's hat over his eyes to keep the light out. I was sunk, and I knew it, and Kady was sunk, and I knew that too. Until, all of a sudden, I happened to look at Ed Blue, and the look on his face told me I wasn't sunk, that I was going to win, that I'd rip it right out of him, what I had to have to be turned loose. The judge got ready to wind up the case. "Well, Tyler, until you get Moke Blue in court and produce some sort of direct substantiation of what you say, I'm afraid I'll have to regard it as a farfetched invention to escape the consequences of several serious crimes, so—"

"I can't get him up here."

"Why not?"

"He's afraid to come."

"What's he afraid of?"

"That I'll kill him."

"Why would he be afraid of that?"

He was looking at me like I was making a fool of myself and didn't know it but he would give me all the chance I wanted, and that was just how I wanted him to feel. "Because I ordered him off the creek when he tried to kill me, with a rifle that was lent him to do it with by this lying rat that's come in here to testify against me, that's his half brother *and that has the same butterfly on his stomach this child has and that he's not saying anything about because he wants me sent up for something I didn't do!*"

If you think that don't set off a bombshell in that courtroom,

you don't know what a judge feels like when he thinks somebody has been trying to put something over on him. He was so
sore I thought he'd hit Ed. He had him take off his shirt, and
unbuttoned Danny's little suit himself, so gentle it was like he
was his own son. And on Ed, sure enough, was the butterfly, all
fixed up with curlicue feelers and red border, from the time he
fired on the railroad and a tattoo man in Norfolk had fixed him
up, or so he told the court.

"And this half brother of yours, this Moke Blue, has this
butterfly too?"

"I don't know, sir."

"Do you want to be charged with perjury too?"

"Yes sir, he has it."

"And only the men in your family have it?"

"I heard so."

The judge drummed on the desk with his fingers, then leaned
over and whispered with the prosecutor. Then: "Tyler, in the
light of this piece of evidence, I'm not at all sure that I'm
convinced of your innocence. Morally, it seems to me there was
something queer about your failure to tell this girl of her par-
entage, and let her go on thinking she was guilty of something
that must have struck her as utterly loathsome. But I am convinced that if these birthmarks are shown to a jury, whether
Moke Blue can be located or not, it is going to be impossible
to get them to convict you. So I'm dismissing the charge. But
God help you if you're in trouble, on the basis of new evidence,
in connection with this case again."

"I won't be. I'm not guilty."

"That reminds me: Why did you enter your plea of guilty in
the first place? That still seems a queer thing to do."

"I told you, I didn't want her to know."

"About Moke Blue being her father?"

"That's it."

"You must indeed be in love with her."

"I might be."

15

For the next week she hardly looked at me, and stayed on in the back room, while I stayed on at the stable. But she kept studying Danny and the butterfly, and you could tell she was trying to get used to it, what it meant. And then one day before the fire, while Jane was out back cooking supper, she picked him up in her arms, and said: "My little boy." She said it over and over, with tears shining in her eyes and running down her face. After that she began taking care of him, and wouldn't let Jane do anything at all. Then was when she began to notice me again, and watch me, like she was studying about something. And then one morning, just before daylight, she came down to the stable with a lantern, and I had a wild idea she had come to make up and be my wife. But she wasn't thinking of that, even a little bit. She hadn't undressed from the night before, and set the lantern down, and sat on my bunk with it shining up on her face, so I could see it but couldn't see her eyes. "Jess, ever since that night in the courtroom, I've been thinking back, trying to remember how it all was, and specially that's what I've been doing tonight. And there's one thing I've got to know."

"I'll tell you anything I can."

"When did you first know Moke was my father?"

"Before you were born, even."

"And how did you know?"

"I knew I wasn't."

"You mean there had been nothing between you and Belle for some time and that meant somebody else had to be my father and you figured it had to be Moke?"

"That's it."

"Why didn't he tell me?"

"Maybe Belle wouldn't let him."

"What reason could she have for not letting him?"

"Ashamed, maybe."

"Or maybe she didn't know it."

"If I knew it, she had to."

"Not if only the men in that family had the butterfly. I haven't got it. Maybe neither of them knew it until Danny came and they saw the birthmark. Maybe that's why they began to fight. Maybe that's why Moke took Danny. Maybe that's why Bell tried to kill him, to keep him from saying anything to me about it."

"I tell you, if I knew it—"

"Jess, there's a simple answer to that."

"What is it?"

"You might be lying to me. Right now. About knowing it before I was born, about how it was between you and Belle then, and all the rest of it."

"I might be an Indian, but I'm not."

She stretched out on top of the blankets and stared up at the harness that was hanging on pegs over our heads, and it was quite a while before she said anything. "Jess, you *are* lying."

"If you think so, all right."

"You didn't know it when we were up there in the mine every day, running liquor, and in town every night, selling it."

"What makes you think I didn't?"

"The passes I was making."

"I fought you off."

"But why?"

"Didn't you hear me in court? I was married."

"Jess, don't make me laugh."

"That's funny to you, being married?"

"Jess, the way you wanted me, being married wouldn't have meant any more to you than nothing. And what are you trying to tell me? You hadn't seen Belle for eighteen years, and just because you hadn't taken the trouble to get a divorce, and she hadn't, you think I'm going to believe it you were still worrying about being married? But laying up with your own daughter, that would be something else. That would be something you would think you had to fight. That would mean plenty to you on Sunday, when you were going to church and singing the hymns and worrying about hell-fire after you die. Jess, why don't you own up to it? At that time you thought I was your daughter."

"I own up to nothing."

It began to get light, and still she lay there, and after a while she said: "And you didn't know I wasn't your daughter that day Belle was dying."

"You seem to have it all figured out."

"That detective work you were doing, about why she tried to do something to Moke. If you knew about this, why couldn't you figure that out? But you never once thought of it."

"I told you, I thought you already knew it, only you hadn't said anything to me about it. Later, when I found out you didn't know it, then I began to get it, why she went out of her head so, on that trip up here."

"And you didn't know it my wedding day!"

"Our wedding day."

"Our wedding day, my eye. I've only had one wedding day, and it wasn't ours. But you, you're lying to me if you say you knew it that morning. You weren't married any more, and yet you were willing I should marry Wash, and glad of it. For your daughter, that makes sense. But for Moke's daughter? A girl that was no relation to you at all, and that you wanted so bad you couldn't sleep nights? Oh no, Jess. That day was the day you found it out. I thought then there was some connection between the way you disappeared and Wash not showing up, and now God help me I have the same feeling."

"No connection I know of."

"And Moke hasn't been seen since that day. Maybe there's some connection there too. If you saw him, why didn't you tell me?"

"I wanted to forget Moke."

"Why didn't you tell Ed Blue?"

"I still wanted to forget him."

"Seems funny you didn't snap it into Ed Blue's face about the rifle and how you warned Moke off the creek, like you told the judge."

"Let him look for his rifle."

"Where is the rifle?"

"I threw it in the creek."

"Where's Moke?"

"How should I know?"

"Jess, you killed Moke, didn't you?"

The prickle up my back had told me what she was going to say, but for once my mouth went off and left me. I said something. I hollered no, but it was after at least three seconds of trying to act surprised, like I didn't know what she was talking about. She was already laughing at me not being able to make up my mind when this croak came out of my throat, a cold, hard laugh that had my number, and knew it.

When I went in for breakfast, it was she that gave it to me. When Jane came in she was dressed to go out, with her hat on, and a coat.

"Well, Jess, I'll say good-by."

"Where you going?"

"Blount, I guess."

"You mean you're leaving me?"

"I'm not really needed any more, now that Kady takes care

of Danny so well, and there's a fellow over there that's offered me a job in his café, helping him run it. It's time I took him up."

"Kind of sudden, isn't it?"

"Oh I've been thinking about it."

But she said it all in a queer way, fooling with her bag while she talked, and it seemed to me she was going for some special reason she wasn't telling me. "Then I'll run you over there."

"I'm taking the bus."

"I'll run you to the state road."

"I can walk."

"You need any money?"

"I've got some."

On account of waking up early I felt tired that afternoon, and how long I slept I don't know, but Kady was standing there when I woke up, all dressed up, looking at me. "Good-by, Jess."

"And where are *you* going?"

"To be married."

"When?"

"Next week some time."

"You *are* married. Did you forget that?"

"No, I didn't."

"Then how can you get married?"

"Next week I'll be able to."

"That I don't understand."

"You will."

"And who's the lucky man?"

"Wash."

"Changed his mind again, hey?"

"He found out the truth, at last. Jane called him when she got to Blount. In fact, that might be partly why she went over there."

"I knew she wasn't telling me the reason."

"She called him and he came in and was crazy to know what had happened up here, because it was on the radio when you were arrested but not in the papers when they turned you loose, because if nobody gets convicted they're afraid. So she told him what you told the judge, and he ran her back over here again. Jess, you told him Moke was Danny's father. You told me he was *my* father. And both were lies. You're my father. But you don't tell any third lie. You got that, Jess? You understand why next week I can get married?"

"You'll get into plenty trouble that way."

"We don't think so."

"I tell you, the deputies will find out, sure."

"We're going to tell them."

It seemed funny, she was never going to believe the truth, and I had killed the one man that could prove it. And when they heard what she thought was the truth, no jury would hold her for what she meant to do to me.

Outside it had started to rain, and when I peeped through a crack she was running down the road to his car, that had the top up, and inside I could see Jane and the baby. She got in and the car drove off. I went to the cabin for my rifle. It wasn't there, and neither was the .45. I put on my hat and coat and started down to the barn, to get out the truck and run into Carbon to get sheriff's protection. But when I got to the door a shot cut the air, and splinters ripped off the wood. I started back to the house, and another shot clipped my hat. I slammed down on my face, and when it got darker I crawled. Out in the stable I could hear the stock bellowing, and down the creek the cows were hooking it up, but I was afraid to go outside. Later on, after I had made myself something to eat without stirring up the fire, for fear they were looking through the cracks and could see, I got all my money together and put on my raincoat and started creeping down the road. All over, you could hear bellowing from pigs and mules and chickens and cows that hadn't been fed or milked or attended to. I got about two hundred yards when something hit my leg and I heard a shot. I crawled back, doused it with liniment, and got the blood stopped.

■ ■

It's been raining for a week, they've been out there for a week, and I've been writing for a week. Maybe they've got to kill me to wipe it all out, what happened, so they can have each other again, or think they have, and maybe they're going to tell it, so they get off. But I've got to tell it too, because I didn't do anything but what I thought was right. What I told him I thought was true, and if he didn't think enough of her to go see her about it, to give her her chance to say what she had to say, then that was his lookout. After I found out how it really was, she was anybody's woman, and all I've got to say is, I love her as much as he does. So I'm putting it down. It's finished now, and tonight I'm taking it with me when I leave, and maybe there won't have to be any telling, and they'll decide they can have each other without any killing. Because my leg's better now, and there's one thing they've forgotten. And that's the mine.

I slipped out the back way when it got dark, crossed the creek above the cabin, and got up the path without their seeing me. I got to the timbered drift, went inside, and soon as I was well inside so no light could be seen from the road I got out the carbide lamp I had brought with me. All I had to do now was slip through to the bottom of the shaft, go up the ladder to the top, kill the light, and then slide down the mountainside and come out on the road about a mile below where they're laying for me. From there on to the bus stop is a short walk, and I'd be away. But when I hit the lamp to strike the flint, I dropped it, and I heard the top pop open and the carbide go all over the track. And while I was feeling around for a couple of crumbs I could put in there with a little spit, I heard something that almost made me drop dead. It was Moke, in there under the tunnel, prizing around with the gun barrel, trying to get out. He would hit a rock three or four times, then get the steel in a crack, twist it around, move a chunk, then start all over again. I gave a yell and started to run out of the place, but I fell and hit my head and that was the last I knew for a while. When I came to he was nearer, and I could hear his chinking plainer. I got out of there somehow. When I got back it was day.

It's still raining out, but it's daylight now, and I've been listening to the water run off the roof and I've figured out what that was in the mine. It wasn't Moke. It was water dripping. Now I know what it is, I won't mind it any more, and tonight I'll get out of here.

I'm cut off. Ed Blue is out there and

ABOUT THE AUTHOR

JAMES M. CAIN (1892–1977) is recognized today as one of the masters of the hard-boiled school of American novels. Born in Baltimore, the son of the president of Washington College, he began his career as reporter on the Baltimore papers, served in the American Expeditionary Force in World War I and wrote the material for *The Cross of Lorraine*, the newpaper of the 79th Division. He returned to become professor of journalism at St. John's College in Annapolis and then worked for H. L. Mencken on *The American Mercury*. He later wrote editorials for Walter Lippmann on the *New York World* and was for a short period managing editor of *The New Yorker*, before he went to Hollywood as a script writer. His first novel, *The Postman Always Rings Twice*, was published when he was forty-two and at once became a sensation. It was tried for obscenity in Boston, was said by Albert Camus to have inspired his own book, *The Stranger*, and is now a classic. Cain followed it the next year with *Double Indemnity*, leading Ross Macdonald to write years later, "Cain has won unfading laurels with a pair of native American masterpieces, *Postman* and *Double Indemnity*, back to back." Cain published eighteen books in all and was working on his autobiography at the time of his death.